BUT I DON'T KNOW YOU

But I Don't Know You

Stefan Kiesbye

Saddle Road Press

Saddle Road Press
Ithaca, NY
saddleroadpress.com

This is a work of fiction. Names, characters, places, and incidents either are the product of the author's imagination or are used fictitiously, and any resemblance to actual persons, living or dead, business establishments, events, or locales is coincidental.

Design by Don Mitchell
Author photo by Sanaz Kiesbye

ISBN: 978-1736525852
Library of Congress Control Number: 2021942960

v.1.03

Contents

To Parker and Sanaz

Chapter 1

After five months, the line where he ended and she began had softened. Shorat reached into him to retrieve crude lust, large lumps of patience, and pinches of anger, after the sun had moved to the front of the house and allowed them to sit in their plastic Adirondack chairs on the back patio. In early spring, after an exceptionally dry Northern California winter, they had shoveled sand and gravel and carried paver stones to extend that patio past the concrete slab poured by one subcontractor and irreparably dirt-stained by another. Shorat helped herself to what he felt were his last reserves of what might be called sanity, if sanity was the power to distinguish between what seemed real and what couldn't be. Isolated at home, quarantined from friends and the few relatives they were still talking to, sanity became ever more abstract, the border with madness a line shakily drawn into the darkening sky.

Cal helped himself to Shorat's stubbornness, soaked up the devotion she so easily spent without doubts or suspicion. Twenty years prior, she'd made the decision to love him and stay at his side and she never appeared to question her choice. When he felt his mind dissolving around the edges, she was there to firm its contours again. Their ups and downs complemented each other's. Rarely were they miserable together, happy together only in the brief moments when the sinking sun set the yard and everything else aglow, the drinks in their hands diminished to the point that he started thinking about the second refill. They managed to sustain this fragile equilibrium after long years of observing and mimicking each other's patterns and growing together.

One Thursday in August, he received word that his father had been diagnosed with stomach cancer. Cal hadn't visited the small northern German town in years, hadn't spoken to his parents since that last time and refused to answer emails and letters. It was his sister who kept him in the loop when things took a turn for the worse. She wrote in German, still called him by the name their parents had given him, feigning familiarity. Their father, she wrote, would start treatment soon.

Cal was alone in the house and free to stare at the few sentences on the screen, lightheaded and intensely focused, as though he had just swallowed a new illicit drug and were afraid and ashamed of the effect it might have on him. Shorat had left minutes earlier to buy spices, vegetables, yogurt, garlic, Ruffles. Only once every two weeks did they stock up on the essentials, trips in masks and with hand sanitizer to Costco, the only store whose aisles were wide enough to stay out of people's way, unless they sought to buy meats and cheeses. The refrigerated section was crowded even after seven in the evening. There had been reports about meat shortages; people were hoarding. Costco, however, didn't carry the finer things, the Persian foods Shorat craved, and so she left the house once or twice a week to afford Cal some unobserved time, to be among people and do something that had been routine just a few months ago, and to satisfy her own desire for dishes from her childhood.

A weight he didn't quite know he carried had lifted after Shorat pulled out of the garage and the engine sound evaporated. The dogs, Yuuki and Vanya, were dozing in his office; it was too hot to stir, too early for their late afternoon meal. The email from his sister didn't give any details about his father's situation. It was pitifully brief, failed to address how his mother was coping and what the next steps might be. Cal would have loved to tell Shorat the news right away, because without telling her, events refused to become real. Only by telling his wife about the small and even smaller occurrences of his day were they relegated to memory. Whatever he forgot to tell her would be lost.

Cal finally walked away from his computer to stand in the living room and feel himself breathe. What would he do with this new hour? He poured himself a drink, a crude approximation of a Manhattan, and sank into one of two identical sofas. He'd managed to finish a novel draft earlier in the week. Another day or two, and he'd be irritable, nervous to get back to work on the book, sand it down, polish it, shape it to the point of helplessness. In the meantime, straddling the fence between contentment and gloom as he so often did, the crude Manhattan pushed him toward safety and provided a soft landing. His worries about work and isolation appeared more orderly, ready to be stashed away until tomorrow. They fit handily into a single drawer, with room to spare, and he pushed that drawer shut and stared toward the ceiling, at the fan that reminded him of the propeller of an early plane. He would tell Shorat the news about his father's cancer as soon as she got home. Until then, he was free to put it out of sight.

Three years prior, their old house, standing on the same lot the new one was now occupying, had burned to the ground. Most of their neighborhood, fourteen-hundred homes, had been erased in that year's wildfire, the cheap wooden structures gone within minutes. The ensuing rebuild had been panicked and painful, and after false starts and plenty of delays, their contractor from the Central Valley had gone bankrupt and left the house half-finished. The previous year, Cal had spent all summer at the building site, haggling with the tile guys, the concrete guys, the plumbers, the gutter and fence companies, to get the work done and the final inspection approved. At times he'd felt his mind bend and twist sharply. Fissures had appeared, tears had grown deeper and wider. He remembered a moment, a month away from completion, standing in the office of the company they'd hired to provide the kitchen counters. The stone was delayed again, back-ordered indefinitely, and the clerk had looked at him with basset hound eyes, sympathetic but unconcerned. Cal had kept his voice in check — if he didn't get the stone on the agreed-upon date, the fabricators wouldn't get the kitchen done, the plumber would not be able to complete his work. Gas range, microwave, dishwasher and refrigerator wouldn't be installed on time. Final inspection and move-in date would again be postponed. The house was eight months overdue by then. Cal and Shorat had been paying both rent and mortgage for months, ravaging their accounts. Cal gripped the desk in front of him and told the clerk to look for some stone, any stone, right now, it didn't matter what color, what stone, what quality, he just had to order it, and he watched the clerk, Jimmy, make phone calls, and he could feel with immense clarity and precision that something in his brain was going to give and he would never be able to fix the damage. That night, he heated a knife over one of the gas burners in their rental and pressed it into his shoulder. The line still showed red, whereas the older burn marks had grown thick and white.

The new house was a quiet space, the colors muted, friendly without being chatty, without the need to be adored or even talked about. To Shorat's and Cal's surprise, the anguish had lifted and left the place; it had easily become theirs. Even so, after almost a year, Cal still felt tired by the effort the house had cost him. His back ached in new and complex ways. Stiffness had befallen his limbs. Getting up from the couch or his office chair required a moment of standing and readjusting awkwardly, as though he were thawing meat. Yes, he froze whenever he sat for too long. His neck hurt — and Cal blamed his phone for this — and his hips and ankles grew increasingly angry with him. It was so easy to blame age, yes, but had he aged twenty years in three years' time?

Cal opened the sliding glass doors and Vanya joined him on the patio, barking at two blackbirds — hundreds of them had moved into the neighborhood after the fires — before settling onto one of the dog beds. Cal petted his fur, feeling for the spot on Vanya's back that kept oozing a gooey mass. Every week, Cal removed the clot, and every week it grew back but without ever increasing in size. He couldn't imagine what this was, but failed to consult with the vet, who, in true Northern Californian fashion, would first suggest it was cancer, then order blood tests and x-rays, and, after those had come back negative, suggest a diet of freeze-dried meats. It was always the same.

Vanya was his sentinel, his devil dog, his monster. He'd joined them in New Mexico, where Cal had taught at a regional college. Vanya, emaciated and full of worms, had snuck into their yard, joining Yuuki and Starbuck, their first dog. They'd intended to find him a home, but no

one had wanted the shepherd mix, and maybe Cal was to
blame for posting a picture of Vanya with his usually floppy
ears tightly pulled backwards, his eyes showing too much
white. He'd wished to keep this dog with his loud, labored
breathing, his right side smashed in from an accident, his
right front leg a painful mess. He'd wished to keep the dog
who, despite badly healed legs and hip, was unstoppable,
running with Shorat and Cal every morning once they had
fed him back to life. For weeks he smelled bad, no matter
how many times they washed his fur. He peed in the house
and challenged Starbuck's status as the alpha dog, which
led to ugly fights over food or a certain spot on the leather
sofa, a certain squeaky toy. On walks he jumped from right
to left and back, marked car tires, barked at every pick-
up that came rattling down the street. He behaved how
Cal felt. That's what he told Shorat, who hated Vanya for
the first year he lived with them, then learned to tolerate
him, and, after Starbuck's death, embraced the dog with
a tenderness that surprised Cal. He was suspicious of her
shows of affection, though there had never been any reason
to distrust his wife. She didn't ever pretend, as though she
were naturally unable to express anything she didn't feel.
He envied her that obstinacy. In the company of friends
and colleagues, his own emotions were choreographed out
of fear that what he felt was inadequate, wrong, or ugly.
Cal doubted he'd ever felt anything beyond need, greed,
lust, and fear. When those subsided, there wasn't much
left of him.

Yuuki, too, came out onto the porch, offering Cal her
head for a pet, then sniffing the bushes they had planted in
the otherwise weed-infested yard, eating one of Vanya's tiny
turds that the sun had baked to a crunch before Cal's voice
had a chance to reach her. This was summer, as good as

any he'd ever known. He'd been successful enough to land a job at a decent college in the North Bay five years prior — though in darker hours he realized just how corrupt and incompetent its administration was, how ambition-free the enterprise of education had become — and while the pandemic isolated him from friends and acquaintances, he and Shorat were comfortable enough. When they had met each other, he hadn't expected such a comfortable life to be in store for them. Yes, he would have preferred more glamor, more fanfare, more of everything to keep himself from feeling too comfortable, but he'd negotiated a ceasefire with his existence as a largely unknown writer in a sea of largely unknown writers. There was more to life than book contracts and reading fees and international travel, though whenever he uttered this sentence in his mind, he failed to be convinced. What was that 'more' exactly? Still, the pandemic, Cal found, made the ceasefire with his unfulfilled ambitions easier to sustain. International travel? It would be months before anybody could think of traveling safely again.

After what he thought must have been an hour — he'd forgotten to check either watch he was wearing after Shorat had kissed him goodbye — he felt the joy of being alone with his dogs ebbing. A text beeped at him, and Cal answered a friend's question about whether a new pair of glasses bought online for fear of being exposed to the virus looked dorky; the friend had included a mug shot. Yes, the glasses did look dorky. Too large, the wrong color for his friend's skin tone. But the money was spent, local stores charged twice the price; he was stuck with beige oversized frames.

At 5:35, Cal texted Shorat. If she was in the car, she wouldn't answer. He searched for the sound of the garage door, which was only slightly quieter than the one in the old house. His ears were full of static, had been for six years now. His hearing aids kept the tinnitus in check, but for how long? On the patio, he might miss the sounds announcing his wife's return, but the dogs wouldn't miss her entrance and run to greet her by the door to the laundry room.

Ten minutes later he called, didn't leave a message after her voice had asked him to. She'd see the notification. She'd call back. Slightly annoyed, Cal stared at his bare feet — long, even feet that no one had touched in months. It was one of his stark regrets that the woman he had married couldn't understand his special fondness for feet. Although he had told her many times, she seemed to forget how sensitive his toes were, how they needed to be touched and prodded. Feet were disgusting to many. Not Shorat, whose own feet were delicate, white and unblemished. Yet she wore them the way Cal wore shoes, not giving them any thought unless they hurt. Feet were made for work, not pleasure, and not even after twenty years of marriage could she bring herself to remember Cal's yearning. This made him feel inadequate at times, unseen, as though his desires were too ungainly to be recognized. In all his years of dating, he'd never met his equal, and he expected to die without having been fully seen. Such a small thing, he chided himself, and still, still.

The next hour and a half he spent in one of the strange transition states he entered more and more frequently. Unable to focus on anything for longer than ten minutes, he made himself some coffee, picked up the dog poop in the yard, watered the plants in the front yard, all the while carrying around his phone, pulling it out every few minutes to see if his locked screen showed a message from Shorat.

Sometimes for his sake and other times for her own, she'd leave the house for several hours to drive to the beach or a county park. Yuuki accompanied her more often than not, and on their return, both Shorat and Cal acknowledged that the brief separation had been helpful. But today's excursion was strictly devoted to groceries, and the market Shorat preferred — seventy percent local offerings, most of them organic — was only three or four miles south, just before you hit the 12 toward Sebastopol.

At 7:30, he called the police. Had there been an accident on Marlow? Had somebody reported a crash? Public service announcements played during the time the voice on the other end of the line searched the computer. Maybe the voice wasn't searching at all. Maybe the voice was now shouting at someone else for information, or quietly drinking coffee — Cal remembered that he had brewed himself a cup but forgotten that cup altogether; it would stand, untouched, below the spout of the espresso machine, placidly waiting for milk — and then a crunchy sound made him jump, and the voice had returned and assured him that no such accident had been reported, nothing that had involved a female that fit the description he'd given of Shorat. As soon as he had ended the call, he thought of the darker possibilities. Accidents were brutal, violently meaningless. They disrupted and altered your life, could lift it off its tracks, and yet, in their utter simplicity they felt almost benign. More complex were robberies, muggings, arguments that became altercations, fights. He hadn't asked the police if there had been any robberies, any thefts involving a forty-five year old woman with very pale skin, glasses, and longish blond hair. Very blond, nearly white in places. The glasses were small and thick, and over her blond hair she was wearing a MATH hat — had anyone who fit that description been involved in something the police cared about?

He didn't call a second time. He decided he was overreacting, then, after five minutes, decided he was not reacting forcefully enough. Leaving the dogs in the house, he got into his own car and drove toward that local market Shorat preferred. On his way down Coffey Lane, he wondered if his alcohol intake was impairing his driving. What if the police stopped him? What if they smelled whiskey on his breath? Cal made sure to observe the speed limit, ignored the honking behind him at the Piner intersection and refused to turn right on red. All the while, he kept an eye on the oncoming traffic. Camrys were a dime a dozen, but he would spot Shorat's space-gray car, which wasn't gray at all but of such a dark metallic blue, it looked black. He considered the irony of maybe getting into an accident while Shorat was probably already at home, safe and sound, wondering where her husband had gone.

The light turned green, but before his foot hit the pedal, a shock passed through him and the vehicle, and he knew immediately what had happened. He would have whiplash again, his mind told him without raising its voice. Cal undid his seatbelt, opened his door. The driver of the old CRX behind him had already exited his car and now approached him with obvious exasperation. "What's wrong with you?" he shouted, while behind him the honking started up again.

"You rear-ended me." Cal's voice was steady enough. If he had learned anything from negotiating with contractors, it was that rage and attitude never led to anything constructive.

"It was green," the man said. "Were you asleep or texting or jacking off?" He was wearing shorts and a Warriors jersey.

He was a head shorter than Cal but sturdy, had muscle in places where Cal carried comfort.

"I'm sure the police will be interested in what you have to say," Cal said before remembering again his crude Manhattan. Still, he pulled his phone from his pocket and unlocked the screen. Cars were now driving around the two vehicles to turn right; someone shouted an obscenity through a half-open window.

"Fuck you," the man said, but his voice had grown more timid. "I barely hit you."

Cal looked at him for two seconds, said, "Let's see," and walked toward the rear of his SUV. The other driver backed away, no longer challenging Cal.

"Uh oh." Cal shook his head. "That's ugly."

"C'mon, man, it's just a tiny dent. It's not like your truck is brand new."

"But it's expensive to repair. I think I'll call the cops."

"I'm sorry man, I really am. But look, my ride took the brunt of it." It was true — the CRX, low enough to slide under Cal's bumper after leaving the factory, had been lowered after-market by a few inches. Now the hood showed an ugly dent and no longer aligned properly.

"You don't have insurance?" Cal asked.

"They'll jack it up again. Just got a speeding ticket. Costs me several hundred a year. I'm sorry. Look, it's really not that bad, hardly a scratch."

"Okay," Cal relented. "Let's forget about it. But I'll take a picture of your license. Just in case the damage is worse than it looks."

To his astonishment, the man pulled out his license and let Cal take the picture. They raised their chins in a brief acknowledgment of the other and got back behind the wheel. The light had turned red again, but this time

Cal took the turn anyway. I am smart, not strong, Cal told himself. I am a coward, but I do make enough money to make up for it. Too shaken still to look at the oncoming cars and check if he could spy his wife's Toyota, he felt deep shame and disappointment diminishing his wish to spot Shorat. What would he tell her about the obvious damage to his rear bumper? Why had he gotten into the car, after drinking his Manhattan, to go on such a silly drive? What did he expect? What do I expect? To find her in the grocery store's parking lot, bleeding from a vicious attack by an armed man on a bicycle who was after her purse, her yogurt and garlic? He was talking aloud now, embarrassed and ashamed. And yet, once he'd arrived at the market, he dutifully drove up and down the many lanes, checking on the cars. Then he did the same thing once more since his mind was so occupied with defending himself from all the possible arguments against undertaking this drive in the first place that he could hardly focus on makes and models and colors. No matter, Shorat's car was not among the vehicles parked in front of the market. She wasn't here. He took out his phone after pulling into an empty spot and tapped her picture, the only entry under 'favorites.' Her voice came on after four rings — 'Hi, this is Shorat, please leave me a message.' It was 8:14 on this Thursday night.

Her car was not parked in front of the house when he returned, nor inside the garage. The dogs greeted him with enthusiasm — their final meal was half an hour overdue. Cal filled their dishes with dry kibble while planning what to do next. No, the police had no information regarding his wife, and no, it was too early to file a missing person report. The nearby Kaiser hospital had no patient under Shorat's name, nor did they have any Jane Doe cases.

The Sutter and Santa Rosa Memorial hospitals checked dutifully but hadn't admitted anyone by that name.

From his chair at the kitchen table facing the open sliding glass doors, Cal watched the light in his backyard turn from orange to nearly magical to terribly sober to the imperfect darkness of a city suburb, city suburb being that awkward oxymoron time created if you let enough time pass without hindering the city from spreading. Santa Rosa, up until the '90s, had still been a backwater town. Its soul hadn't changed, however its dimensions had swallowed up vineyards, suburbs, and pastures alike. Remnants appeared incongruously on runs or drives around town — herds of cows surrounded by developments from the early 2000s, ranches and farms along a stretch of road connecting apartment communities with subdivisions.

The country started half a mile north of Cal's and Shorat's house, and while the neighborhood sank into something approaching darkness, which blotted out skies and stars, he wondered if Shorat's parents were still awake. In Western New York it was past midnight, and if their nightly action movie hadn't been one of the bloated mega-productions, they'd be in bed by now. In any case, he didn't feel comfortable calling them. What would he say? What would he ask of them? How would he explain his current situation? And while he was thinking about how to address her parents, Cal came to understand that he was afraid of calling them because they would confirm in no uncertain terms, friendly but firm, that Shorat had left him. The parents, while practical and accepting, had never truly taken to him. Shorat's father still regarded his son-in-law, after twenty years of marriage, as not-family. You had to have the same blood to be called family, that was what it took, and Cal's couldn't be helped. He'd always be a stranger, he would remain a stranger until the last day on earth had ended. Shorat's mother was less dogmatic — maybe because she, too, didn't share the clan's blood — but if Shorat had told her that she was going to leave Cal to marry a Peter, Doug, or Joe, she would have supported her without a word. She had supported Shorat at twenty-five, after her daughter had called to say she was leaving her boyfriend of four years and was going to marry a foreign student instead, right away. Shorat had not endured questions, doubts, or any attempts at making her reconsider. Francine knew there was no reasoning with her daughter, so she had accepted the news and started the wedding preparations.

Cal had been touched by this utterly resigned, understanding gesture, and yet, still sitting at the kitchen table with a mug of cold coffee in front of him, still that same cup he had brewed before getting into his car, he feared the moment in which Francine's practicality would cut him out entirely, irrevocably. He would be forgotten in a matter of days. Francine would never utter his name again.

Chapter 2

Sleepless nights differ greatly from one another, no two are ever the same. Technically, this one could not even be called sleepless, but Cal woke six times to check his phone, which lay charging by the side of the bed, and each time he closed his eyes again, dreams kept him awake. In one, Shorat had ordered an immense amount of shoes, boxes and boxes full of them, and they all looked the same. Was that a wise decision? he wanted to ask, but couldn't. What right did he have to scold her for something that she felt she needed to buy? Boxes of clothes arrived as well, and he stood stunned and slightly confused while Shorat unpacked and modeled for him.

Yuuki lay next to him when Cal awoke from this dream. The odd thing was that the Shorat of his dream had nothing in common with the Shorat he knew. She didn't spend much money on herself, never had, and he needed to encourage her to buy dresses, jewelry, books — all the things she didn't 'need.' Most of the times, he ordered these things for her. Shorat loved when he chose sweaters, bras, skirts and shoes for her. Decisions didn't come easy to her, and in any case, she trusted his taste. Cal petted Yuuki, who sat up, turned, and lay down again, closer now to him, soon offering him her belly for a rub. He got up to pee, called Shorat's number, listened to her message, and fell asleep once more, only to be greeted by his parents in their old house in the North of Germany, the one they'd lived in while he was a teenager hating every second of his life he couldn't spend away from his parents. It was past Christmas, his name was still Karl (the name his sister so stubbornly insisted on using even now), and he was going to hitchhike back to Berlin. That part — standing near the on-ramp of the highway — filled him with such dread that he awoke with a start and dry mouth. Had he screamed? Yuuki still lay next to him, and he could hear Vanya snoring beyond the open door to the living room. He checked his watch — he'd slept for only half an hour.

By the time light trickled past the curtains and dripped onto the floor, he was dead tired. Too tired to fully grasp that Shorat had not returned to him. How could he have slept at all? What kind of husband lay in bed instead of driving to all the hospitals, all the emergency clinics? What kind of man was he? A thought struck him and finally made him throw off the covers and walk on stiff and still-asleep legs into Shorat's studio. This room lay opposite of his own and had once been called an office as well. But ever since quitting her job as an event coordinator she had tried to dispel the odd flavor of the office word. She was working as an artist again, fashioning Islamic patterns, and artists didn't work in offices, they lived and breathed in studios.

Shorat's room couldn't be called cozy. His own office was cozy, dipped in continuous dusk the way he preferred it, and even Shorat preferred his room to hers. Instead, the studio was an exact interior architectural representation of Shorat's aura. Functional, with a certain flair for spirited practicality, sober and distant. He admired it more than he loved it and never stayed more than a minute or two.

Entering the studio with its two desks, orange swivel chair, record player and retro-styled boombox, her precise and oddly-colored work on the walls, he was reminded of how little he knew his wife. It wasn't an entirely disconcerting thought — he still woke up next to her after twenty years wondering who she was and why she hadn't left him a long time ago. Why she had stayed even though she often seemed strangely detached from her life with him. More than once had he credited that distance between them for their marriage's longevity — things he understood he grew bored with. He'd never grown bored of Shorat, though. Her beauty had stunned him the first time he spied her at the Delavan subway station in Buffalo, New York, on his way to work in the admissions office during his last summer in the city before entering grad school in Michigan. Hers was no easy beauty, nothing you could contain in a few well-worn words. He still couldn't explain her beauty, and who she truly was and what she wanted — from life, from herself, from him — he couldn't say. Friends asked him from time to time, How is Shorat? And Cal, who never failed to give as serious and honest an answer as he could, taking his time mulling over such a question, could not manage to get beyond mere descriptions of activities. This satisfied most questioners, yet these instances left Cal bereft. Who was the woman living with him, and how was she really doing?

That question stood with him in Shorat's studio while his eyes searched for a note, a few lines explaining where she had gone or why. Then he opened desk drawers and closet doors, yet without touching things, without making a mess. If Shorat had wanted to leave him a message, he'd find it without a problem. But no, her markers still lay scattered over the larger of the two desks. Her computer was still covered by the donut-shaped spread her mother had quilted. None of her things, as far as he knew them, was amiss. It was all still here, right here, with him. They were all waiting for Shorat's return.

Cal searched the refrigerator next. Magnets from Berlin — the Ampelmann in green and red — and from their vet, from Iowa, from terrible souvenir shops where people who were too cheap to buy a real gift had purchased these items with photos of places they had visited, or with sayings that attempted to be funny. The refrigerator in their old house had been full of these, but this new house was mercifully short on such trinkets, on trinkets of any kind. Unlike many of their neighbors, Shorat and Cal had not restocked cabinets, closets, and garage. They had what they needed, but little beyond daily use. Souvenirs and trinkets felt like false friends — they could so easily burn. Clothes and shoes could burn too, of course — Cal and Shorat had lost all the ones they hadn't worn on the night of the fire — and those had also lost their sheen of acquired personality and no longer represented who Shorat and Cal were, merely protected them from being arrested for public indecency.

No, Shorat had not left any message in her room or on the refrigerator, nor had she left a note on the white quartz countertops or on the dining room table. And — he checked — not on the toilet lid in the hall bathroom either. Whatever faint hope had driven him from his bed turned to a feeling that wasn't unlike finding a rejection email from your agent saying your manuscript was "too bleak and sinister" to be sold. A short burst of activity and anticipation would be followed by fruitless introspection.

Cal made himself some coffee, fed the dogs, opened the patio door for them without doing poop patrol first and sat down at the dining table. Had Shorat's behavior been peculiar the previous afternoon? He reflected on that, but no, she'd been wearing pig tails, the way she had when first they met, and she'd been in better than average spirits. She'd given him a kiss, inquired about anything he might want or need, and then opened the door to the garage. Nothing out of the ordinary had happened in the morning. They'd gone on their three-mile run, had made breakfast burritos together, and once he'd entered his office, Shorat had made him a third cup of coffee. Days felt all alike ever since the start of the pandemic, but the previous day had been, if anything, more harmonious than the many others he could no longer recall in any detail.

The older he became, the harder it was for Cal to distinguish seasons and months and days. Once you made a certain amount of money and lived in some comfort, days and weeks began to blur. He'd once said, only half-jokingly, that all the bad days he remembered he'd grown fond of, while all his good ones left a bad taste in his mouth. Good days, days with food they cooked for themselves, work they enjoyed, walks with their dogs and drinks on the patio became indistinguishable. By the time they went to bed there was nothing more to them. They wore well, like a pair of good underwear that didn't chafe or make your skin itch, like a pair of shoes that didn't give you blisters. What Cal missed while watching his dogs take shits in the backyard, were blisters, the moments of pain that in hindsight appeared benign. The marathon he and Shorat had run in Oakland the previous year, with its horrible stretch on the San Francisco - Oakland Bay Bridge, thousands of cars passing next to them at high speed, and, later, through half-deserted regions of the harbor; this marathon stood out as a marvelous adventure, even despite the fact that he'd walked most of the last four miles. The following day he'd hardly been able to step off the curb, but he'd been alive. And what had happened to the evenings, cocktail in hand, he had lived at his wife's side talking about work, politics, meals, possible trips? The effect that pouring chicken broth into Yuuki's dish had on the kibble was similar to that of comfort guiding your days. Kibble and days became easily digestible.

"Oh hello!" Francine's voice sounded pleasantly surprised, maybe more surprised than pleasant. He couldn't recall ever calling his parents-in-law before. It had never been necessary.

"Hello," Cal said, and then paused, because Francine hadn't been done yet with saying hello. "What a surprise."

"Yes, it's about a surprise I want to talk to you."

"Huh? Oh? It's who? Oh, Cal, hello. How is everything?" This was Dariush, Shorat's father. Cal's in-laws were in the habit of switching to speaker phone if a family member called. But Dariush was hard of hearing and too thrifty to buy himself hearing aids. His wife had to repeat what others had said. Hers was the only voice that seemed to reach him without fail.

"He wants to talk about a surprise," Francine explained.

"Are you guys coming to visit?" Dariush asked.

Cal felt an immediate relief; sweat was building on his forehead and under his arms in response to that question. Shorat had not spoken to them, was not on her way to Western New York to live with her parents. "Not yet," Cal said. Should he tell them that their daughter was missing?

"Let him talk," Francine said. "What's the surprise about?"

"Do you remember where we stayed for our honeymoon?" he asked. "That bed and breakfast near Ithaca?" Cal remembered it well, remembered even the name. It had been a very expensive, very exclusive bed and breakfast, one they couldn't afford. He'd been a grad student in Michigan, and Shorat had still been finishing her computer science degree in Buffalo. The drive from the wedding reception to the Rose Inn had taken only forty minutes. It had been raining so hard, water had entered the interior of Cal's rusty Ford Escort through the windshield seal and dripped onto his pants. Shorat had moved her fingers through his hair and he'd been relieved to have her to himself again. Inside his old car, they were alone in this world. Inside his car, he couldn't imagine ever being without her again.

"Oh, the Rose Inn, yes. I never visited, but Shorat said it was such a neat place."

"I want to take her in the fall, for our 21st anniversary, but I couldn't remember the name for the life of me."

"Oh, that's such a romantic idea. Of course, you would have to stay a night or two with us as well. Our place is very neat too."

"Will you give us warm cookies every night?" That's what they had received on their wedding night. Only the owner had still been awake in the kitchen, which doubled as a reception after hours.

"Well, we might be able to manage that."

"Cookies?" Dariush asked. "I like cookies."

"Of course, dear." Francine said. "He has such a sweet tooth," she spoke into the phone as though her husband wasn't sitting next to her.

"I'm glad you remembered the name."

"Of course I do."

"If the infections haven't gotten worse, we might even be able to fly to Buffalo or Rochester. We'll have to see."

"That's such a neat idea. Is my daughter around?"

"She's buying groceries," Cal lied. "She can't know what I'm planning."

"We won't say a word. I promise."

Their wedding night had not been their first night together, and yet, the weight of having taken responsibility for another life had made his hands clumsy. Shorat had changed out of her wedding dress before getting into his car, but she was still wearing the lacy white bra, her garter belt and stockings, anachronistic accoutrements that emphasized that this time, making love sealed their deal — they had bought each other, and no returns or refunds were possible. Cal wanted to prolong this night, wanted it to end only after the sun had swept up all darkness and the aroma of bacon would send them downstairs into the breakfast area of the inn, but after a short first time, just after midnight, Shorat became too tired and nauseous to make love again. She fell asleep quickly; that morning she had vomited after the rehearsal, so hungover she'd been from the night before drinking screwdrivers with Cal, her bridesmaids, and Cal's best man Olaf, who had flown in from Germany with his wife. Anxious, Cal was lying wide awake next to her. This felt unplanned, undreamed, and how could he adjust to the reality of wanting someone so badly, feeling her right beside him, and having this night all to himself?

CHAPTER 3

THE RELIEF BUOYED HIM for an hour after ending the phone call to his in-laws. Shorat hadn't left him, at least not officially, wasn't ready yet to mail him divorce papers and ask a friend to pick up her belongings. But the blank he drew whenever he imagined looking for Shorat's whereabouts kept nagging him until he opened his computer to find this: "There is NO waiting period for reporting a person missing. All California police and sheriffs' departments must accept any report, including a report by telephone, of a missing person, including runaways, without delay and will give priority to the handling of the report."

Immediately he called the police again, and this time, the voice at the other end — a different one, sounding older and out of breath — took his report, asked him for a detailed description of Shorat. Indignant, Cal told this new voice how he had been treated the night before, but she cut him short. "Sir," the voice said, "I have no information on what you said and who answered your call. I suggest we focus on finding your wife."

Cal took pleasure in being able to describe Shorat perfectly. Her height, weight, the length of her hair, the color, which was never only one color but different shades of blonde and changed multiple times throughout the day. Her feet, her hands, her hips, he could describe them all, but what had she worn? The voice at the end of the line, after height and weight, was running out of patience with Cal. He didn't know. It didn't matter to him. He knew her whole wardrobe, had purchased many items himself. He didn't try to memorize her outfits whenever she drove to the grocery store. But wait, she had worn green baggy pants, not quite like harem pants, more bulbous at the bottom. The voice at the other end of the line was so quiet while he was describing them, he had to ask if she was still there. "Yes, yes, I'm still here. Green pants."

"And a gray t-shirt with a Buffalo on the front."

"Gray tee."

"Green sandals." He described the car she was driving, repeated the license plate number. He mentioned Shorat's purse, a canvas army bag he'd gifted her that spring, khaki. He wanted to tell this voice everything he knew, as though in remembering every detail he could create her in the voice's mind and bring Shorat to life right in front of that voice, and the voice would say, "Wait, I do see her now," and he would arrive fifteen minutes later and pick her up. But what if she hadn't worn that gray buffalo shirt? What if it had been the gray shirt he'd bought at the Tampa airport? Or the one that had no print whatsoever on it? Shorat would fail to materialize — like an improperly remembered spell, his description would have no effect at all.

His dean called in the afternoon, and he listened and agreed to raise class caps in some of the fall's courses. The budget had shrunk because of the pandemic — students hesitated to enroll or stayed home hoping to start classes the following year. The college had switched to online learning; the danger of spreading the virus proved too great in buildings with outdated and overmatched ventilation systems, narrow staircases, and creaky elevators. The dean's voice was cheerful, all business, and when she hung up, Cal kept sitting at the kitchen table. There was no friend of Shorat's he could call; his wife didn't have friends. Shorat's cousin Samiye, who'd been one of the bridesmaids, had discovered the fundamental Jesus and married a born-again Iranian businessman. What kind of business he had they'd never learned. A bitter and prolonged fight between Dariush's four sisters over a family vacation house at the Caspian Sea had slowly and irreversibly torn the families apart, and even Dariush, who didn't live in LA like his sisters, had been drawn into it. Shorat and Samiye, who had been close all their lives, hadn't talked in years. The bad blood between their parents had reduced their friendship to mere civility. They knew it wasn't their fight, but insults and insinuations in letters and emails and recounted over the phone many times over had made them choose sides.

Friends from high school had drifted away and loosely reunited on Facebook. Shorat peeked into her classmates' lives without interfering, like watching a model train make its rounds behind the large window of a department store on a wintry afternoon, lights unnaturally and beatifically bright, feet cold, without money or urge to enter the premises and get a better look or, God forbid, buy.

Cal had salvaged friendships with a handful of men and women, only one handful. Never had he and Shorat felt as isolated as they did in Northern California, where people were friendly and let you know right away that their lives were complete without you — they were so confident that Northern California was the best possible place to live that as soon as you mentioned another state, another region, they grew fidgety. Yet Cal and Shorat found Sonoma to be a cruel county, expensive and eager to get rid of you. It attracted tourists who sat on small black buses that carried them to wineries and tasting rooms, and unless you had bought a piece of that land early or had parents who owned some acreage, a beach house, a dry-rotting bungalow in the shadow of the 101, you couldn't afford to live here. Even people like Cal, who made enough money to last until the end of each month, retired elsewhere. You had either always lived in NorCal or you weren't welcome to stay.

Cal called Shorat's number yet again, and yet again the phone rang four times before the recorded message came on. His face twitched, his mouth was pulled open and wide, and no sound came. Only when he couldn't breathe anymore did his body finally relax. He sat at the table for another hour, unable to move even though his back grew stiff and started to ache, unable to think of Shorat and how he should find her. He poured himself a drink by the time the light had lost most of its heat, and after feeding the dogs, he went into the bedroom.

What he noticed was the eerie silence around him. His neighbors' children were not in the yard pushing each other off the trampoline. John, the retired car salesman, was not hammering away on yet another yard project. He hadn't heard a souped-up car or truck in hours. During the pandemic it had become increasingly difficult to know you were alive. What gave reality to every day were the people who noticed that your body was indeed present. If someone said, "Cal, I think you gained weight," or "Cal, your last book left me scratching my head," he could be certain he was still alive. Maybe Northern California had been hard to navigate because it didn't make you feel alive. It ignored you so well, without fuss or effort. Even in his fiction, Cal omitted Northern California because it felt like a graveyard, a beautiful graveyard where people gathered for picnics and bike rides and concerts, but you were one of the dead. You watched the colorful visitors, but they didn't return your gaze.

The pandemic had only exacerbated this impression. Now, you didn't even have a face, nobody could tell if you were smiling or mumbling epithets into your mask. How could he, how could the police, identify Shorat, when everyone was wearing a mask? Cal wondered if today's youth would one day think back on masks with fondness, wear them in the bedroom to feel aroused. Maybe they had already developed a secret mask language, color-coded, shape-conscious, cuts giving away intentions. But for him, masks had rendered him only more invisible.

He drank his crude Manhattan, and it didn't fail to cheer him, though after the first sips had settled and rearranged his body and mind, his existence still felt devoid of meaning. Of course, when your wife of twenty years had just left you, you might be excused for thinking life was meaningless, but he knew that Shorat's disappearance only lay bare what he had suspected to find all along, under the usual layers of daily activities, daily chores and pleasures. His life had come to a standstill. Or better, he couldn't read it anymore, grasp how anything he was pursuing was worth the effort. This knowledge was less shocking than he had expected. This was not the pained insight of a hardened detective who had chased the criminal for years only to find that the guilty party had always been himself. No, he was no Johnny Handsome finding the devil in his sitting room. His predicament was far less glamorous — his career had stalled, and should he die tomorrow, or tonight for that matter, nobody would even know who the man found dead in Coffey Park had been. His neighbors had never asked what he did for a living, his readers weren't interested in the picture on the back cover of the book.

Anonymity was a difficult ocean to navigate. More crushing still was the knowledge that he himself didn't much care for what he had written or whether or not he would ever publish another book. The satisfaction of seeing his work in print had ebbed. Books meant interviews with badly prepared interviewers, one after the other asking the exact same questions, and should a brittle soul endeavor to read all those interviews, they'd discover that the author had divulged nothing. At an earlier point in his career, Cal had been excited to share what he thought about the world with his readers, but the interviewers got in the way. The books were the books — any idiot could read them by themselves and make of them what they wanted, but the world was coming to an end. Something that had been clear to a young Karl in Berlin — that the environment would not be saved and that the superpowers would never stop threatening smaller nations and using dictators for their own means and to their own advantage; that the oil reserves would be depleted in the not-so-distant future, and that corporate greed made saving the planet impossible — all the very obvious truths a young Karl had learned, in the 1980s everyone, including Karl, had pushed aside in the '90s, willfully forgotten, and now the world was presented with the mess it had been busy worsening the last forty years. They'd created the mess over centuries past, but it was these last forty years that had decided the planet's fate. At least that's what vanity told Cal, who needed to believe, no matter how meaningless his own life, that he was living in important times. The point of no return had sailed past so quickly, nobody could remember exactly what it had looked like.

In a world at the brink of extinction, what could a middle-aged writer of bleak and sinister novels hope for?

That his pension wouldn't disappear because of another great recession? That his fame would outlast wars, famines, floods, melting ice caps, and pandemics? The world, especially one that based its literary judgment on sales figures and refused to ask a single writer what they thought about the state of affairs in a country ravaged by an incompetent authoritarian regime hellbent on abolishing all environmental protection laws as well as all checks on its own power; the world would not remember Cal or Karl or any of his books. The greatest prose and the best-polished sentence wouldn't stop a dictator. Even if the dictator were to be elected out of office, the interest in writing and what writers thought of the world would not be regained. This had been lost long ago, it was no use.

SHORAT AT THE TRAIN STATION

We'd spent five days in New York City, had met up with friends one night and gone to Coney Island, then Brighton Beach. We drank Vodka shots and afterwards roamed the water's edge, and only one of us was still able to drive and drop us off at the hotel in Murray Hill East early in the morning. That afternoon, we took the train to the Dia:Beacon and I've forgotten what we looked at or how exactly we got there. In fact, I've forgotten most of that day, but I do remember the picture I took of Shorat sitting on a wooden bench on the train platform. She looks relaxed, playful, she loves being in this city and she's taken off her shoes. I must be sitting on the ground in front of her, and with one of these early digital cameras I'm trying to capture her white, slender feet. Her left arm rests on the back of the bench,

*she's looking at me benevolently and without much
interest – the day is too warm, and her clothes fit her
too well to care for the camera in front of my eyes.
She's playful and allows this moment to slip past her
manipulation. Every time I look at the photo, I see
the real Shorat, the dream Shorat had for herself and
buried when she met me and became my wife.*

Cal hadn't noticed he'd fallen asleep until thunder woke
him; the time was four-thirty. The hopelessness he'd felt
while his mind was rattling off its grievances while slowly
shutting down, thoughts like tiny poison arrows, was still
with him. Yuuki and Vanya were too, Vanya now pawing
him, breathing hard at the side of the bed and dripping
saliva on Cal's arm.

He pulled away the curtains in the living room and
stepped out onto the patio. By creating more and more
life, humans were creating their own death. The planet
couldn't take such pressure, such depletion, the pollution of
resources the planet needed to survive. Even if all nations
came together and gave it their best effort, the catastrophe
couldn't be averted, and no country, and especially not
his adopted country, was giving its best effort. Instead the
populations grew and grew, driving animal and plant life
into extinction.

The failure to understand a certain situation and
act accordingly meant that even after all environmental
problems had been laid bare, people in city suburbs such
as Cal's own, produced kids, bought cars, watered lawns,
and poisoned weeds. They washed the cars in the driveway,
washed their clothes with non-degradable detergent, used
dryer sheets, and accumulated their own weight in trash
every other week. The situation the planet was in had to

be clear to anybody — you had to be a die-hard conspiracy theorist not to see the obvious signs — and yet life, the life our parents had lived, the life we'd dreamed up for ourselves even though the ingredients we had stolen from God knows where and couldn't recognize or defend, ignored that situation completely. The blue and green trashcans were the only hints Cal and his neighbors were even alive and listening to the news. But blue and green trashcans wouldn't save the neighborhood. They hadn't in 2017, when the annual summer drought, acquired by decades and decades of water mismanagement and other ecological crimes, had allowed the fires to romp through the city. The Coffey Park neighborhood had not resisted. The houses — siding slapped onto particle board — had not resisted. And still, still, still, here they were again, all of Cal's neighbors had returned to build bigger houses, buy bigger cars with the money they'd received from their insurance. They washed their trucks as they had before, they watered lawns and power-washed boats and driveways. Their minds lagged behind and would never catch up to 2020. They couldn't be retro-fitted.

Cal showered, the window illuminated by more and more strikes of lightning. Yuuki stayed hidden in Shorat's closet while Vanya sat next to the toilet hoping impatiently for Cal to reemerge. How could Cal stand in the shower watching lightning tear up the skies and believe that publishing yet another novel would help anyone?

Chapter 4

Annette waited for him in the dining-room after he had toweled off. She'd made coffee, put a saucer over his mug to keep it warm. "Strange weather," she said from one of the leather chairs. "This is a nice house you have."

"It's small," he said. She hadn't visited in a long time.

"It suits you. It's..."

"...calm?"

"Boring." She breathed a hint of a laugh.

"How are things? You have been released?"

"Just a year ago. On good behavior. I told you working for the library would cut time short." She still looked the way he remembered her, though the prison uniform had been replaced by jeans and a long-sleeve shirt, both black. Meeting her for the first time, he'd been amazed at how small and slim she was — he'd imagined a much bigger woman, one who could make a disinterested observer forget that she was six or seven months pregnant.

"Where is your wife?" Annette asked.

"She went to visit her parents."

"During a pandemic?"

"She's wiping down the door handles of her motel rooms, the nozzles at the gas station. She's packed a cooler with food so she won't have to enter a store."

Annette's smile grew a bit more wistful. "You want me to tell you where she really is?"

"Later maybe. Maybe later." He lifted the saucer to find perfect crema just below the rim of the mug.

"The way you like it," she said.

"How are your children?"

"Good. We're close. They haven't given up on me."

"Are they still in contact with your ex-husband?"

Her laughter wasn't pretty, he could taste the bile. "He married again. He was never charged. Funny how you can know exactly what a person might do without knowing much about them." She paused, replayed the words in her head. "What I mean is, even when we don't love each other...even if we *do* love each other, we often can't know what a person is thinking, feeling — about you, about their life, anything really. Yet when it comes down to it, we've observed them for such a long time that we know what they're going to do under certain circumstances."

"I didn't see it coming."

"But you knew she was getting out from under you."

Yes, yes, he had known. Despite the drinks on the patio, despite the support during the Covid quarantine, he'd sensed all along that she was emerging, or maybe transforming. Perhaps it was time to shed the seven-year skin and become someone else. Maybe he hadn't developed in synch with her or he had been too slow, too fast, or he hadn't anticipated her course corrections and new developments and missed the moment when she'd seen him in a new, unflattering light.

"Oh no, she's seen you in that unflattering light for quite some time. Love can keep that in check — none of us are too likeable. Other things can keep what we know in check too. I was afraid of my husband. A *Staatssicherheits* officer — he could get anything he wanted. I was no longer allowed to see my family, my friends. The only people who ever came to visit were his colleagues and his colleagues' wives. Some seemed happy enough, but most wives were as quiet as I was until later in the evening, after we all had too much to drink. It got louder then, and the wives started to talk until one husband or another shut her up or went to grab both their coats." Annette's hair was still dark, only a few gray strands showing at the temples. She was his age, almost exactly, but they had grown up on different sides of the Wall. When he'd found out that they had come of age together in a divided Germany, her case had for the first time made sense. And maybe, just maybe, he had made sense to himself for the first time. He and Annette were not the same — she would have set him straight in her sternest voice had he ever suggested it — but they were different answers to the same question.

"She doesn't have any friends," he said.

"See, it's what men do. Some men anyway. You're the jealous kind, aren't you?"

"I've been hiding it well."

"She's not been doing anything to make you suspicious. You've been keeping her close. Though that made her less interesting as well."

"I've been supportive."

"Yeah, yeah, but that's just money. It doesn't cost you anything. You've isolated her."

"She's done that herself," Cal protested.

"You worked it that way, didn't you? A 'what, now?' here, a 'I'm too busy' there. You don't have to shout in order to get your way. You've learned that from your mother who always got what she wanted, not that she saw it that way. You've been a drag on Shorat's life. She would have had children as well, if not for you." The lightning illuminated her face, a charming, open face. The skin, however, seemed to have been hurt by dozens of small cuts. Were these old acne scars? What else had happened that could explain them? He'd never asked. Then there were her teeth, badly repaired and only visible in the briefest moments when she lost control and laughed.

"I'm too selfish," he said. "I did my children the biggest favor I could and didn't have any."

"Isn't that petty?"

"The world is too crowded as it is."

"True, but were you really concerned about the world when you had a vasectomy?"

Of course he hadn't been. In Berlin, at twenty-three, with no control over his life, it had been one decision he was allowed to make. Something of importance, something irreversible. He'd wanted to impress his girlfriend who complained about having to use birth control, which diminished her arousal. He'd volunteered, vanity getting the upper hand.

Cal had told Shorat he couldn't have children early on, he hadn't deceived her. But in recent times, she'd begun to wonder about her life after Cal's death. He was eight years older than her, and men died at an earlier age than women in any case. She'd be alone, without anyone feeling obliged to come for dinner on Sunday nights or invite her for Thanksgiving. Like ghosts, Shorat's second thoughts had taken a seat at the table with them and stolen into their bedroom at night.

"Are you happy you had children?" His question was meant to hurt. Why was the discussion all about his own failures?

"Of course."

"So why didn't you allow for more?"

She hadn't shrunk from his questions when he'd visited her in prison a decade ago. It'd been an hour's drive from Berlin, in an indifferent town in a landscape that gave no signs of having any distinguishing features. This was Germany, where so many towns looked too sober to allow the eye to rest and find solace.

"I didn't want them to meet my husband. I didn't want them to enter my world." After giving birth to a son and a daughter, she had given birth nine more times, killing each baby in vodka-fueled somnambulism. Each of the nine babies she'd buried in large flower pots and fish tanks and kept around in and outside her home. Her husband claimed to not have known about the pregnancies, though the babies were his and they'd never lived apart. Prison had finally separated Annette from him. "Do you want me to tell you now where you can find your wife?"

"In a bit, in a little bit." He emptied his cup, asked if she wanted a refill as well.

"Sure. Why not? This weather you have. It will start all kinds of new fires."

The dogs, despite thunder shaking the house, didn't come into the living room to join him. Usually they lay down at his feet no matter where he went. Strikes of lightning danced about the walls, dervishes in bright costumes, all staccato.

When he'd filled the cups, and before he turned away from the espresso machine, he felt an absence attacking his own form, there in the kitchen, as though that absence could dissolve and melt skin, flesh, and bone. He had nothing to fight it and when he faced the dining table again, Annette was gone. She'd left him a note. "You're not as nice as you think you are."

CHAPTER 5

Cal drank both cups of coffee, located his phone, texted his friend Joaquin. Usually, it took him a while to answer, but on this morning, his lines flashed on the screen seconds later. They agreed to meet in San Rafael at the usual coffee shop — this time to-go cups and masks.

For an hour, Cal watched the rain — a miracle during a California summer — then he got into his car and turned onto the 101 South. Occasional showers blinded him, traffic slowing to a crawl. San Rafael, however, had used the time Cal spent in his car to towel off and wipe down outdoor seating for people who couldn't live without buying coffee away from their homes. Cal and Shorat hadn't eaten a single meal they hadn't prepared themselves in five months — it felt outlandish and nearly dangerous to buy a cup a stranger had touched. What if the virus hid on the paper surface?

He didn't have to wait long. Joaquin Lobo was never late to a meeting and here he appeared, impeccably dressed, hooded eyes hidden behind sunglasses. They elbow-bumped, then entered the coffee-shop and ordered. No one else was inside, which calmed Cal. "How are you?" Joaquin said while the barista was working on their drinks. His voice was low, pleasurably accented. He spoke with great solemnity, always, as though there'd never be a time for a rushed remark and an unconsidered phrase. In Joaquin's presence, Cal felt safe.

They'd met in the San Francisco airport a few years prior, had shared a row and several Bloody Marys on their plane to Mexico City en route to a crime writers' conference in San Luis Potosi they'd been invited and paid to attend. There'd never been any awkwardness between them. Cal, who never felt relaxed with anybody he liked — how much easier it was to tolerate people he had no feelings for — trusted Joaquin. He'd never had a brother — his only sister lived in France, and the two, though surely entertaining sympathetic feelings of a nature Cal couldn't understand and left uninvestigated, shared no interests, no world views, no family history they could agree on. They didn't even share their parents, since it was only his sister who still visited Germany every now and then. Since Cal hadn't grown up with a brother, he wasn't sure how his friendship to Joaquin compared, but Lobo called him brother in his emails and when they had coffee together, and that was enough.

For the first few minutes they reported on how they had lived these past few months, how their schools had reacted to the pandemic. Coffee in hand, they walked toward the Mission San Rafael Arcangel. Joaquin asked him if he knew a good watch repair shop. The gold Omega he'd inherited from his grandfather — he'd found it in an old cardboard box nobody had opened in years — was losing five minutes a day. "How is Shorat?"

"She is well, I think. She quit her job, and as of late, she's started to work with Islamic patterns, geometric art. I think it suits her — she works much longer hours ever since she's started to focus on these patterns. It appeals to her sense of order and organizing things. It gives her a precise framework to work with, and her paintings are lovely. Very pedantic in the best way."

"I would like to see them," Joaquin said.

Cal exhaled with an awkward whistling sound, as though his throat were leaking air. He imagined standing on the tower above the diving pool, walking toward the end of the springboard. He closed his eyes, "She left."

Joaquin turned to face him. Cal couldn't be sure what his exact expression was because of the mask. "For good?"

"Maybe." Technically he couldn't be sure she'd left at all. No break-up note, nothing that said she had no intention of coming back. "The police have my report. I mean, there's a possibility she drove somewhere, had an accident, and nobody has found her..." He had to cough as though he'd smoked dry weed. His eyes watered, and he took a few cautious sips of coffee to be able to breathe again and find his voice. "But something doesn't feel as though that's the case."

Joaquin nodded. "I'm sorry. You know why?"

Cal shook his head. "I was told I have a controlling streak."

"We all do."

"She married me when she was twenty-five. She's never lived abroad. She's never traveled by herself outside of conferences she attended for work. Now she's quit work, and I think she notices all the things she hasn't lived because she was living with me."

Joaquin didn't interrupt, though Cal was momentarily out of words. There was something else he needed to say, and it took time to find it. "I lived my life oddly goal-oriented. Not without detours, but I always thought I needed to reach certain points. As if this were a cross country road trip, and I needed to hit New York, Chicago, the Grand Canyon, the Rio Grande, Los Angeles. But I never got off the highway, and in the end, all I have are picture postcards, but no trip. Or better, my trip consisted merely of sitting in the car passing eighteen-wheelers. That's what I remember — the tediousness, the boredom, the stiff back after another day on the road, the cheap motel room towels, which once were white but haven't been in a while. They're threadbare and scratchy, and you unwrap the hard sliver of soap and go to sleep on a sagging mattress. The maids haven't switched the pillow covers, because they looked fine enough this morning, and you're too tired to really have sex, so you do it anyway, feel little, and she feels even less but understands that's how it's going to be and she likes you well enough and doesn't interfere with your moves. Even after you switch off the lights it's not dark, and you hear footsteps in front of your window all night, because they gave you a room too close to the staircase, and new travelers lug up their oversized suitcases, others have been to a bar and get into a loud argument over who the child actor was everybody remembers from the time they themselves were young. In the morning, your back hurts badly because the mattress sagged so much, you pinched a nerve, and you both know that this day won't be any better than the last, and you don't even want to see Yosemite anymore."

"Oh man. I hear you."

"We had so many days on the road, and I never felt I could take a sightseeing day or two and maybe stay a week at the Grand Canyon, hike, take a raft trip, read a book sitting on a giant bolder two feet away from a free fall.

"Does she feel the same?"

Cal couldn't say. "She hates Northern California. She doesn't know anyone."

"It's true," Joaquin said. "I've lived most of my adult life in San Francisco but I know very few people. It's hard to make friends. It's a cold city. So what are you going to do, my friend?"

Cal shrugged. "I don't know where to start, where to look. If I look here, she will be there. If I travel in the wrong direction, we might never see each other again. If I wait at home, she'll never return. If I leave to search for her, I won't be there when she comes looking for me. Whatever I do, it will be the wrong thing, the thing that makes it impossible to find each other. We once had a fight, a horrible fight in the middle of the town where we lived, out in the open, on the busiest street. It was fall and getting dark in the late afternoon, and I thought she couldn't understand, didn't care the way I wanted her to care and I left her there on the sidewalk and stomped off. And after thirty yards I stopped, and she was still standing in the spot where I had left her, and I opened my arms, I wanted her to come flying toward me, and she didn't. She didn't move. And I ran off, ran away from my love. Later, much later — maybe at the dorm room I rented, or maybe we already had our first apartment in town — much, much later that evening, she arrived wherever I was hiding, upset and in tears, asking why I had left her behind. And I said, 'But I turned to you and opened my arms. I was waiting for you.' But Shorat is very near-sighted. She had not seen me, couldn't see me and my wide-open arms. And so I feel that whatever I do now, Shorat might not be able to *see* me and will think that I don't care, never cared." Cal stopped for a moment, and the whistling sound returned. He had exerted himself and felt as though he was suffocating behind his mask. "The worst thing is that right now, I don't think she wants me to search for her at all. Right now, I think she's happy to have escaped my orbit, exploring the life I have denied her."

"It might be true," Joaquin said after a moment of silence between them. "She might need time to be away from you. But may I give you some advice? I know you don't need it, but it might help anyway. Two things could happen. Maybe Shorat will discover that being without you suits her. It happens. We grow and sometimes we outgrow the other. That's the first thing. The second is this — maybe your absence will make you visible to her again. When you live together for such a long time, we render each other invisible, we fuse in places and become one organism. Maybe her absence makes you visible again, and maybe she learns to see and appreciate you. Maybe not as her husband — you need to be prepared for this. But it's too early to tell."

"How do I find out when she won't let me know where she is?"

"You need to reappear her."

"How?"

"It's a dangerous path, but then, all meaningful things are dangerous. Don't search for her, not if she really has left you with the purpose of living on her own. Don't get in your car and look for the Shorat you've lost. Instead focus on who she is in your life. Remake her. Rebuild her. Conjure her, and maybe, maybe, she will be returned to you. You can't find what you have lost, you need to find what you desire.

"When I was a young man, I was kidnapped outside of Mexico City. Three guys jumped me and threw me into their car. We drove to some rural area, and when we stopped, I struggled, and one of the men stabbed me in the chest. I managed to escape, but I have this scar on my chest, an ugly, jagged scar I will forever carry with me, and I know that the stabbing truly killed the man I was. Or maybe he took off in another direction, and I will never be able to locate him again. I will never find the man I was before the kidnapping. I can go look for him forever. Maybe I catch a glimpse of him next to the orchestra stand in a plaza, maybe I see him from the corner of my eye sitting with a beautiful woman in a coffee shop. But when I focus to get a better look, he's gone. The only thing I can do is conjure the man I want or need to be. When I look at my scar in the mirror, I can make this new man appear. He might be me, and the more I focus, the more he looks to be me. Yet he doesn't remember the dead man. There's a before and there's an after, and there's no bridge between them. There can't ever be. The dead man's memories aren't mine anymore, and so I have to imagine this new man and invent his life with what I know life can be. It's not a natural process, it's pure artifice, but it's something, the only thing I can do for him and for myself. There's not a single day I feel whole because I'm such an imperfect sculptor. Every day I notice missing pieces, flaws in what I have assembled, faulty parts. But I'm not giving up. I can conjure a man. I'm putting together a life.

"My friend, your Shorat might never return. But if you ever want to see her again, you might have to let go of the Shorat she was until now. You have to conjure a person without past, without memories of who you both were. The Shorat you loved will not return to you. You can't reanimate her. Don't let sentimentality get in the way, don't let longing be your guide. Think of who she has become, who she must be. Maybe then you'll see Shorat again."

Chapter 6

When he got back to his Lexus, the smell of the old, cracking leather discomfited Cal. He found it hard to breathe; the coffee he'd consumed after drinking many cups earlier that morning left his stomach blind and inflamed.

That he had to live his own life was a painful realization. It hurt to have your own mind, worse still, to become visible to other people through your imprecise and fumbling actions. How helpless he felt without guidance. How stupid his every move felt. Being Cal felt all too real, like the scratchy woolen coat he'd lost in the fire and that wouldn't ever let you forget you were wearing it.

How much better to imitate other people, movie characters even. You could reach points when you felt you were close to having an authentic moment in that particular character's skin. That was Hollywood, inviting everyone to build lives after dreams, a benign form of living. You could buy clothes and foods and cars your favorite character drove, choose the music composed for a movie as the soundtrack to your own life. Cal found these fictions more helpful than the true stories relatives had told him when he was a boy. Why would he want to be like the people whose lives he abhorred and despised? What could these people teach him?

Cal had looked for guidance and people he could look up to, but he'd encountered none. Even the ones he clung to for a while turned out to be petty and cruel, with blind spots in which other people could fit whole existences. People were disappointing, but characters in books, contained as they were, offered some kind of hope. Yet those characters never found themselves teaching creative writing in Northern California, their wives having left without a note or hint at their whereabouts. And if you didn't know what your favorite character would do, because that favorite character had never been described having your exact experience, how did you make a decision? No matter what you decided, you had to feel alienated, estranged, oddly uncomfortable, because you suddenly stepped out of the shadow of that character. Hit by light, you were exposed as a fraud, your skin as white as a caterpillar's, your features softer, harsher, less gratifying than those of your avatar.

In his books, Cal had burrowed into other writers' worlds. He wasn't exploring his own, he felt, but creating beautiful echoes, laced with opaque references to those original works. He'd never had his own compass — he needed an already existing framework to see what he was doing. How could he evaluate his own writing if he didn't adhere to someone else's rules? No, he'd inhabited older molds, added maybe a new flavor, a new twist. Maybe he had advanced one or the other technique in the process. Maybe he had been so bad at imitating other authors that the result looked to be his very own.

Marketing looked for comparisons, of course. No marketing department accepted books that weren't new versions of this fad or that tradition. Readers didn't like to decide for themselves. They wanted to know what to expect, they wanted to stay within the one realm they had chosen as their playground. Yet Cal couldn't excuse himself by pointing at readers or the marketing people within the publishing industry. He knew that he had chosen to follow certain paths for the comfort they provided. He'd incorporated elements of his favorite works in every single book of his. He'd tied his lines and paragraphs to the books he'd admired. Only these ties allowed him to find a way forward, because without that guidance he would have flailed, thrashed, and ended in ugliness. Cal, the Cal without traditions, fictions, beloved characters, was so ugly that the world shuddered at his sight. No, no, even that was vanity. He was ugly in an entirely unconvincing way, not a monster, just something you didn't need to look at a second time. Negligible. A full trash bag a crow had ripped open to get to old chicken bones; the dried and dusty fur of a rodent by the side of the road; a white belly spilling from below a dirty shirt; a zit ready to burst; spoiled milk. He didn't know what to make of his life if he couldn't liken it to a book or movie. He couldn't see it. Only a story could make sense of Cal.

The weather took another turn for the worse. Lightning split the skies, thunder wiped out whatever the newscaster was saying, but it wasn't raining yet when he pulled into the Costco parking lot in Rohnert Park. Cal wanted to buy new dog beds, he needed to do something festive, something affirmative. He'd get new dog treats, wet dog food, and for himself fried mozzarella sticks. After parking his car, he fastened his mask, hurried toward the entrance. Wearing a hat and a mask afforded him almost complete anonymity as long as he stayed six feet away from the other shoppers — which was easy when you had time and no kids were waiting for you at home, or worse, running around the store with you and away from you, appearing every other moment with something new they begged you to buy. Lost in his anonymity, Cal didn't turn in the direction of the voice speaking somewhere near him. He had failed to hear what the voice had uttered in the first place; it could not possibly be him the voice was addressing.

"Karl, it's you, isn't it?"

He straightened, only now noticing that he had stood hunched in front of the dog beds, lost in a reverie, unable to decide between the cheaper round beds and the more pricey square ones. Would Yuuki and Vanya care about the shape? Were the thicker, square beds really more comfortable for them? How did you decide whether to spend thirty or fifty dollars when you had the money for either choice? It was the same question he'd already asked himself in the canned food section. Atypically, Costco had stocked two kinds of canned, wild-caught, skinless and boneless sardines. One cost nine-ninety-nine, the other, with the help of a three dollar discount, six-ninety-nine. But which one was better? Was it better to choose according to price or attractiveness of the package? The more expensive can's brand was named Safe Catch — did this indicate environmentally safe fishing practices, or was that the equivalent to the baseless 'all natural' claim on processed foods? He'd bought both kinds to avoid feeling as though he'd failed and was tempted to buy one round and one square dog bed, not to decide later which one was better — he already knew he wouldn't have a sardine taste test — but to get through this day feeling he'd done respectably well.

The woman who had asked stood six feet behind him, tall, short blond hair, dark eyebrows. Her mask said "This Was Preventable," and her legs stuck in black cotton stretch pants. Her shoes were cotton, an off-brand, her ankles thick, and her shirt light-blue denim.

"Yes?" he said, before grabbing two square dog beds. "Yes?"

"It's me, Katia."

"Katia?"

"From Berlin. We went to acting school together for a few months. We...that was a long time ago. I'm wearing a mask. I'm sorry, I can't take it off without getting thrown out." She laughed, and he thought he remembered this laugh that made her head bob up and down. It looked silly, though not in a bad way. Cal was embarrassed for this woman and yet didn't mind continuing the conversation.

"From Berlin?"

"I'm living in Sebastopol now. Sebastopoo we call it."

"We?"

"Sven and I and the kids. They came up with that name."

"Oh," he said, entirely unsure of what to make of that information, still searching his memory for the woman's face.

"What are you doing in Rohnert Park?" the woman asked.

"Sven? You were dating a guy named Sven back then, weren't you? Living with him when we..."

"The same one. Yes, we're still together. We have a boy and a girl." He imagined her smiling behind the mask, but her eyes didn't give anything away.

Cal remembered her now, though hadn't she been dark-haired and shorter? The woman who'd dated Sven — a man he'd only seen once, at a party at Katia's apartment a year or two after they'd made love for a few cold days in February — hadn't she been much different in appearance?

He remembered her as a fist closing around him; he'd dreamt of her often. In his dreams he had forgotten where she lived, had forgotten her number. What was her last name? In his dreams he looked at column after column in the thick Berlin phonebook, and yet no last name rang true.

"You might mistake me for someone else?" he asked, though he could hear how outrageous that sounded. "What I mean is..." But he couldn't find what he meant. "When did you move?" he asked instead.

"Two years ago. If I had known..."

"So you missed the fires...the Tubbs fire."

"Yes, we got here the following year. Were you...did you...?"

"I moved here in 2015," he said, avoiding what she wanted to hear. "I'm teaching at the college."

"I'm teaching German to small kids. On the weekends. There's a German community here, and they always need teachers. We're both teachers."

"German," he echoed. Their conversation, so far, had been conducted in English, and Katia did not have the accent he could hear in recordings of himself reading from his books. "God."

"It's so good to see you," she said. "I wish..." She motioned, extending her arms in an air hug.

"Yeah, me too." He wasn't entirely sure he meant it. In the past five months he had developed an aversion to even thoughts of hugging other people. Hugging could mean death. In the 1980s, he'd sometimes kept himself from coming too quickly by thinking about how likely it was that having unprotected sex with the girl he was making love to would give him AIDS. It was a successful strategy, but it also turned making love into something else, something more mechanical. The release still felt good, but the regret over not having used condoms was instantaneous. And soon questions kept nagging him — if he died, would the sex have been worth his death? Before making love, the answer had always been yes.

"Is anyone with you?" Katia asked.

"Is anyone...no, no, I'm alone. How about you?" His eyes and his memory were still looking for clues that he really knew this woman. The Katia he remembered had spoken more softly, her fingers had been longer, her nails had been longer. They'd dug into his back, leaving bloody tracks behind. Her forehead had been larger, her skin the color of peanut butter. Cal's eyes moved up and down the aisle as though that woman he remembered must appear and take this new person's place. And hadn't her name been Birke? It had been Birke. Birke and Sven.

"Do you have time? I mean, I have a little bit of time. I needed to get out of the house — Sven has been working from home, and the kids haven't been to school since March. I think they'd be happy if I stayed away a little longer."

"We could...if the weather...maybe we could get Starbucks and meet at a park? The distancing, the distance...."

"Sure. Sure?" She started a kind of laughter that was altogether too loud. "Isn't that a bit silly?"

"To protect your family from my Covid?"

"Yeah," she said. "You are right. I'm pretty much done here. How about you?" There were tortillas in her cart, large jars of Nutella, a plastic clam-shell of shrimp in a Costco-made sauce, diced tomatoes, six bottles of Rosé wine.

"The shrimp?" he asked.

"Will survive. I have a cooler in my car."

Her car turned out to be a Chevy Tahoe, slate gray and brand-new, something only a certain type of German could buy, the kind that wanted to embrace this new world and suppress the memories of better-made German cars, because these better cars also felt oppressively sober and bureaucratic, invented by people who mistook precision for passion, tenacity for temperament, vigor for vivacity, and simplicity for spirit. To buy a Tahoe you had to repudiate the old world and believe that shoddy quality and a thirst for gasoline were American rites as sacred as barbeques, fireworks, baseball, and the pledge of allegiance. The Tahoe stood close to the entrance, and Katia pointed in its direction and pressed the key fob, the lights of the vehicle responding with trained tenderness. But the weather had changed yet again. It was raining, pouring really. "No park for us," he said, hoping that maybe this Katia he still didn't recognize might give him her number and disappear. He would delete the number from his phone, forget he'd ever met her, and in the future visit the Santa Rosa Costco instead.

"What a shame," she said. "We could sit in my car, maybe. I can sit up front, and you in the back. We can keep our masks on."

"Sure." But how long had his dogs been cooped up inside? He checked the watch on his left wrist, an Orient diver. "I need to head back. The dogs." He nodded toward the beds in his cart. And then he surprised himself and said, "Why don't you stop at my place? I can make coffee, and we have more space to properly distance."

She hesitated for a second, then her head bobbed up and down in agreement. "Okay, yes, I can do that." She typed the address into her phone, with two thumbs that

were quite pretty, waved once more at him, and said, "I'll
see you in a few."

"Give me ten minutes," he said.

"Will you vacuum? Hide dirty underwear?"

"Let out the dogs."

"I'll race you," she said. "I know where you live."

Chapter 7

The rain let up as soon as he turned onto the highway, though lightning and thunder still performed their duet. Cal was humming, he was pleased with himself. He had shaken this impersonator and remedied his odd flub of an invitation by giving her an old address from the weeks after the fire had destroyed his house and he and Shorat had lived in a duplex in Burbank Gardens, where houses were three quarters the size of real houses, residences for children and dwarves. The scale was disturbing, and Cal still had nightmares about walking through the narrow streets. The windows of the house next to their apartment had been covered on the inside with sheets of aluminum, and once in a while the mailperson had still delivered letters to the front porch. But nobody had seen the owner in years, though people living on their street swore they could hear him on quiet nights stomping about.

Katia would wait in vain, and then she would give up and hate him, and he wouldn't have to think of Berlin and Germany again. Anyone from Germany was a potential chink in his armor. Anyone from Germany would bring with them the smell of marzipan, stollen, bratwurst, and cheap eau de cologne. He'd amputated his German past so successfully, there were brief moments in which he forgot he hadn't always been Cal. His novels had long discarded

Germany and memories of folk legends, a sinister past, and any and all relatives he'd ever met during birthday parties and family reunions. Cal was the bastard child of Molly Ringwald and Han Solo, he'd come into existence more cleanly and absolutely than through the messy biological way of birth. Cal had willed himself into being, and he wouldn't allow for any cracks.

By now, Katia would be sitting in her slate-gray Tahoe, waiting for his car to appear. Or maybe she had already rung the doorbell and maybe, maybe, a new tenant had opened and asked her what she wanted. She might be on her way back to Sebastopol, and Sven, that nice-looking if bland guy who had shaken his hand vigorously at that party decades ago, not knowing that Cal had slept with his girlfriend, would ask her why she looked so distressed. "Schatz," Katia had called him, he remembered it now.

Once home, Cal got rid of the old dog beds, smelly and grimy as they were, and Yuuki immediately plopped down on one of the new ones, apparently satisfied with his choice. He opened the door despite patio and yard still being wet and went into the kitchen to mix himself a drink. It was one-thirty, a halfway decent time for an illicit Manhattan. He hadn't come any closer to finding Shorat, and his sense of duty and a sudden burst of sentimentality made him check his phone and dial her number again. This time, his call went straight to voicemail. He didn't leave a message, dialed again, and had to wait four rings to hear her voice. Shorat's message hadn't changed. He'd read about people who played a loved one's message again and again, but for the life of him he couldn't understand what kind of solace this provided. He knew the message, he knew his wife's voice. There was nothing comforting in listening to a pre-recorded message meant not for him but for anyone who dialed her number.

The storm held its position. The dogs, ignoring the open door, sat with Cal on the couch. He was quite comfy. A second drink made him lose sight of the strange encounter at Costco, the Katia who wasn't the Katia he remembered and whose name had been Birke. In his Berlin, she had been Birke and he couldn't recall, no matter how hard he tried, why they had lost sight of each other. It was maddening how dry and brittle memories became with age, how they lost cartilage and wouldn't connect properly anymore. A bag full of bones, out of order and with no explanation on how to put them together. Whenever he arrived at their last meeting in Berlin, their last meeting as lovers, he remembered the odd fumbling, the half-hearted attempts at lovemaking on the loft-bed of hers, and the kebab he bought for breakfast near the subway station on his way back to the district of Wedding the next morning. He remembered the pale meat — the grill had just been switched on — and the abundance of red kraut, the browned lettuce. The bread hadn't been toasted, hadn't been fresh, and yet, yet, he remembered the ride home on one of the subway car's green vinyl benches as special. He'd known even then that he would never return to Katia's apartment, but why? How could he have been so sure?

Later in the afternoon, the sky washed out by all the commotion, empty and sagging, he awoke and fed the dogs, mixed himself another drink. He checked his university email account, sent replies to students looking to add classes, to faculty asking about the availability of office supplies (since the outbreak of the virus, they had not been allowed back in their offices). The dean had sent him a message about cutting yet another class, and he replied to that one as well. It was five-thirty, his day was complete. But Shorat had not returned, had not sent him an email to his private account or a text to his phone. If she's found dead by the side of the road, he thought, they will look at me, count the drinks I had, and kill me. It will be just punishment. I could have been a much better husband, and I should be searching...he stared out the window at his neighbor's boat, which said neighbor had bought with insurance money after the fire (his old boat had blocked the street post-fire, after pirouetting into the air once the gas tank exploded). He couldn't imagine where else to search, so he took the phone and dialed the numbers of all Santa Rosa hospitals again. It was satisfying to be disappointed again, and after the last call had ended, he went into the kitchen to make some coffee. The doorbell rang.

Only two parties ever rang that doorbell in those days of the pandemic. The Amazon delivery guy and John, with whom he shared seven panels of fence in the back of the yard. John was in his seventies and one of the intrepid spirits who can't ever sit still and read a book. Instead he built things, trimmed things, maintained machinery and cars. He took trips to Home Depot and bought lumber and built a gazebo because his contractor had refused to provide any kind of cover for the back patio, which got direct sun all day. He supported his wife's gardening by building raised beds, installing latticework and new drip lines. The rest of the day he spied on his neighbors and dropped off tomatoes and zucchini, the two staples of their vegetable efforts. Cal liked John.

He opened the door without pushing aside the curtains in front of the window pane first, a mistake he realized all too soon, because behind the person standing on the red carpet Shorat had bought for their entry way, stood a slate-gray Tahoe. "Hey," Katia said. "I know you gave me the wrong address but you're easy to find. I read that essay of yours, the one after your house burnt down. It mentioned the address."

Cal didn't say anything, but his face was hot. "I just made coffee. You want some?"

"That'd be nice." She stepped inside the house, slid out of her green raincoat, which he took and hung up in the hall closet, a closet Shorat had cherished almost as much as the pantry. Katia didn't wear a mask. He didn't either. And somehow, just by entering his house, they were past the point of wearing masks and protecting each other from the virus. "It's nice in here," she said.

"Calm," he said.

"Yes, calm." It hadn't rained since mid-day, and yet her hair was wet. And he couldn't have anticipated her full lips and her teeth, which were large and nearly translucent. Her eyes sparkled, and because he could now see the lower half of her face, the upper half of her face made sense. No, he didn't recognize her, he still didn't, but somehow he knew she wasn't lying, and even though the woman he remembered was smaller, shorter, more delicate, and went by a different name, he accepted that this woman had taken Birke's place and that he was safe with her. Now that she had entered his house he was safe.

She kissed him after he had poured her a cup, and he responded. How tall she was, how beautiful it was to touch someone so substantial. He hadn't touched anyone but Shorat in months; the shock took away his breath, made him burrow deeper into her. Then they took their cups to the sofa, sat facing each other, exploring each other's lips after drinking some more of the hot liquid.

"You meant to give me the wrong address."

"I was startled."

"You're not living alone here. You're wearing this." A finger came to rest on his wedding band.

"She left."

"When?"

"Why did you come to see me despite having the wrong address?"

"How did you end up in Northern California?"

"Where did you tell your family you were going? And for how long?"

"How long have you lived in the States?"

"Will they miss you?"

"Do you miss Berlin sometimes?"

"Is your husband working for one of the tech companies?"

"Do you miss Berlin springs, the first warm days with fragile green appearing and the skies are so archaically high, they echo with voices, and people are still pale and sitting in cafes along the canal and the waiters and waitresses are snooty and when your coffee arrives it has no foam and is lukewarm and yet you've never tasted anything better and afterwards you sit on the grass near the water and you haven't shaved your legs and little hairs are poking through your pantyhose and you don't care, because the boy next to you doesn't care and though you don't really like him all that much and might never call him again, he has the kind of hands and fingers you adore and you want to see them move over your skin again?"

"There'll be fires tonight. The lightning has started them all around here, and by tomorrow we're going to see smoke billowing into the air. We can't smell them yet, we wouldn't find them if we looked, but they have sprung up and will threaten the area."

"Yes," she said.

"Yes." The dogs came through the open door and sniffed the visitor, and Katia was greeting them too loudly, her voice full of sugar, a kindergartener's voice, and the dogs let her pet them, and Yuuki licked Katia's face. Cal reached for Katia's foot and pulled it toward him, pulled off her sock, and when he saw that the second and third toes were of the same length, he finally remembered her. Yes, her ankles were much too thick but her foot was solid in a way that calmed him; he wanted to hang on to that foot.

They left the dogs in the living room and lay down on the bed. Shorat had slept here but chose not to interfere now. As though she sensed the presence of his wife, Katia asked, "Is this okay?" and he thought about that for a long time without letting her slip from his gaze and nodded. Her shirt he unbuttoned. The bra had been washed many times, her belly showed marks from giving birth. The skin below her neck was rough and aged. He took his time to say hello to every patch of skin he discovered. He was so easily scared, easily shaken by the violence of nudity. He didn't expect perfection, what he looked for was harmony. He needed to connect the different parts of the body as though they might be pieces of a story. Something that wouldn't fit — a too-short thumb, a birthmark of the wrong shape — could kill his interest. He had no standards of beauty, no fixed shapes in his head that lovers had to conform to, he only needed to make sense of their parts. He needed time to fall in love with each limb, each scar, each bump. All the while he was afraid to be found lacking. What if the person he was holding in his eyes was aghast at what she found below his shirt?

But he'd known Katia before, they had been lovers before, and he believed and wanted to believe that her belly button, her hips, her neck and cheeks would all fit together again. And there was no haste. They had lived for decades without each other, why rush? No, there was no haste, and so he removed her bra and made her face turn serious. She got up on her knees and pulled his shirt over his head, and each inspected the other.

"What is that scar?" her pointer traced the red line on his arm.

"A particularly bad day."

"You did it yourself."

"A hot knife."

"You're still vain."

"I'm still vain."

"I liked that about you. You weren't nice. You were kind of a dick."

"Not to you."

"No. Not to me." She pulled him close then, and they both knelt there on the bed while the light, a guest wearing out her welcome, slowly left the room. She was dragging her feet, reluctantly making space for a new darkness, a darkness that caressed corners, spread on the furniture and wiped down every ledge and window sill.

They undid each other's buttons, pulled off pants without laughing. This was a serious matter and it required silence and stern faces. Too much depended on these moments and movements to taint them with smiles and laughter. It wasn't laughter Cal was craving. And when they had joined each other with an ease that surprised him, he remembered the silence in his apartment in Berlin the first time they'd made love on a cold day in February, the coal oven warming their skin, the courtyard below his window echoing with the shuffling of old people's boots, the banging of doors, music from behind half-open windows, and shrill children's complaints. He was a bit disappointed already, too familiar already, as though his body had memorized her every moan and move, and yet he was letting himself fall, slide, tumble, and kept falling at a speed that made it harder and harder to breathe. He listened to her lips form silent words into his ear, felt her teeth mark his skin, and now there were no more decisions to be made, retreat was impossible as long as he could breathe in the smell of her skin. Maybe this, maybe this would be enough.

Chapter 8

He woke again at two o'clock in the morning, Yuuki by his side. The house was so dark and quiet, he felt an enormous peace. Instead of going back to sleep he stumbled out into the living room sniffing for the last hint of Katia's presence, Katia who was lying in bed at home by now, after maybe making love again to her husband to dispel the memory of Cal's body. Or maybe she was up like him, searching for small bruises, patches of an unfamiliar, newly familiar smell. Maybe she was curling up on a couch away from the bedroom because there seemed to be no air left next to her husband.

Cal opened the patio door, and it took him a few seconds to realize the fires had started. Of course they had. Dry lightning in a region experiencing annual droughts. Of course lightning had lit more wild fires. He closed the patio doors, switched on the lights, and went into his office where he checked on his go-bags. He gathered his iPad, his phone, chargers and extra batteries, his reading and computer glasses, and filled a backpack with these items he collected from tables and counters around the house. He had a tendency to let his things spread where he used them. Without Shorat to look with anger and disdain at the small piles of gear, he had created a natural path through his day, time expressing itself in spaces used. He followed himself through this everyday, picking up what he would need should the fires arrive at his doorstep.

Afterwards he opened his laptop and searched for news. There was maddeningly little, only brief reports of fires near Napa to the east and near Forestville and Jenner to the west. In his bare feet he walked out the front door and stood in the street, sniffing like a dog, head raised, fear raising the hairs on his neck.

"Too real, huh?"

Jamie, his neighbor from across the street, stood in the driveway, wearing pajama pants and a white muscle shirt. He was bigger and taller than Cal, but they shared the same body structure. Straight cut, shoulders and hips nearly the same width, with a bit of a stomach, arms long but not big. Cal didn't like Jamie much, especially disliked the mustache and strange leering smile, but they had suffered the same, knew what the other knew about losing a house and all the evidence of your life. If another fire broke out, Cal counted on his neighbor to hammer on his front door before taking off.

"Way too," Cal said.

"Got gas earlier. The truck is all packed up."

"I got my bag packed too."

"If the fire comes through here again, that's it. Colleen and I will move to Washington. At least they have rain up there."

"I won't rebuild again."

They stood and stared into the sky. A third neighbor, Kevin, was making his way down to them. "Got the Nixle too?" he asked.

Jamie and Cal shook their heads.

"Evacuation warning for Guerneville. East of here too."

None of the men wore shoes. "You guys want a beer?" Jamie asked and without waiting for an answer went into his dark garage. Cal could hear a refrigerator open, the clink of bottles. He didn't wear his hearing aids, but he was among men of his age who were all a little deaf and raised their voices habitually. They kept standing in the middle of the street, which, on a Saturday morning approaching four o'clock, lay deserted. The temporary light poles still stood dipping the men into uncertain light. They talked about their preparations for the fire, the generator Jamie had bought, the large battery pack Cal had ordered, the air purifiers from Amazon. They stood far enough away from one another, though none of them wore a mask.

"It's all new stuff," Kevin said, referring to his furniture, his clothes, appliances, plates and glasses and silverware. "Doesn't mean shit to me."

The others nodded, drank more beer. Then, without Cal being able to say why, they all fell silent, handed Jamie the empty bottles and went their separate ways. Maybe they needed to check on what was going on beyond their street. Maybe they needed to get ready to leave.

Fires had sprung up everywhere in the Bay Area. Cal read about them after cooking himself some breakfast, a scramble wrapped up in a tortilla. The dogs were still asleep, too tired to come begging. Yuuki occupied the space Katia had vacated after ten o'clock. They'd kept silent, as though any word would be the wrong one. No goodbyes, no promises. They'd kissed, and then Katia had stepped outside to be greeted by her car's eager lights. There wasn't anything amiss, nothing anyone could add without tipping the scales. The moment required discipline, and for Cal it meant closing the door without watching Katia drive off.

He now went into the garage, stood surprised by his wife's car's absence, that open space. He retrieved the three air purifiers, set them up around the house and kept them running on the lowest setting. The whirring noise was pleasant, rendered his day more important. Again, he checked on the contents of his go bag. Cal had bought this piece of luggage as a promise to himself and Shorat that they would travel again once the house was rebuilt. The bag was small — they'd agreed to only ever take carry-ons to their far-flung destinations — and all he'd been able to fit was his favorite coat, an M-65 army coat made in China, a Seiko dive watch, his passport, and a change of clothes. Because the coat was so bulky, he'd been forced to pack a second, less important bag — more clothes, and several watches he didn't want to lose. He'd emptied the contents on the floor to remind himself of what exactly he'd taken off his shelves and hangers, when a sudden thought made him abandon his task and enter Shorat's studio. It was the only room that Katia's scent had not yet entered, and neither did it smell of the approaching fire, as though Shorat was still here, fighting off the changes and pushing him and the intruding world away.

There were her markers, her boombox, her diary — which he had never, not once, opened — her sketch pads. But he couldn't find what he'd come looking for, and when he finally opened the doors of Shorat's closet, he knew that his first search had been inexcusably careless. Her camera, a Leica, her most prized possession, was gone, and so was her green carry-on bag, the one she'd picked to travel the world. The discovery deflated him over the next hour or two. It was a small puncture, but he had no means to stop the flow, and by early afternoon he had taken refuge in bed, pulling the curtains and blocking the dogs from joining him. He'd failed miserably, foolishly. When he'd first searched her room, why hadn't he thought of the Leica? How could he have overlooked something so important? The defeat came at his own hands, and yes, it added insult to injury. Nothing terrifying had happened to his wife — Shorat had finally had enough and decided to leave. He wasn't included in her plans; she hadn't even informed him of those plans he was excluded from.

The bitter irony of his most desperate hours had always been that they provided Cal with the sweetest dreams. Once he had closed his eyes and let himself be lured to sleep by the air purifiers' tireless whirring, he held the contract for his new novel in hand. Shorat was at his side, wearing a dress that revealed her white neckline. She was flirting with a man in a tuxedo — where had he come from? — but that didn't inhibit his deep joy. On the contrary, the man, who now put an arm around Shorat's shoulders and kissed her neck, squeezed his heart in a painful yet pleasant way, and soon he found himself entangled in limbs, watching Shorat open her mouth with a new deep thirst. He was holding her head, stroking her hair and forehead while she began to moan.

Cal woke up briefly to relieve himself, vaguely aroused by the dream. He kept any thoughts at bay, dove under the blankets again, and found himself in another dream, in which Katia was coming to visit him and Shorat. He'd just published his new manuscript and together they celebrated and ended up on the bed in which he now lay buried under pillows and comforters.

Dusk muted the colors in the bedroom when Vanya's paw banging on the door awakened Cal. His mouth was dry, his head felt like a bucket full of soot. He walked into the living room, and the strength of the smell took him by surprise. Alarmed he rushed to the front door and, stepping out onto the stoop, he caught a last glimpse of the setting sun being swallowed whole by orange, brown and black smoke. He stood in awe, not unlike the man who'd slung his arm around Shorat in his first dream. The sublime could even be evoked by things that destroyed us. If the sublime showed us there might be a god waiting in the wings, directing our pitiful performance on this planet, then it must surely also reveal the biggest evil, the kind beyond our imagination. Annette's murders had always struck him as larger than what people could fathom, allowing him a glimpse of despair and fear on a scale that appeared unearthly. The smoke clouds knew no fear or purpose, yet the spectacle touched him with such violence that he was ready to believe in higher powers.

"It'll be a long night." Just like this morning, Jamie stood across the street, staring up at the sky.

"Yes, yes," Cal said. "How close is it?"

"Five miles away. It's on its way to Healdsburg, but if the wind turns, it might head our way." Then he grinned and pointed to the roof of his neighbor's house. The previous year, Francisco had installed garden sprinklers in front and back, when the Kincaid fire had forced the neighborhood to evacuate only two months after Cal and Shorat had moved back. They were watering the roof again, making sure hot ashes wouldn't ignite another fire. And ashes were raining down on them, white and black flakes settling on Cal's shoulders and arms, he could feel them touch his face. He stretched out his hands the way he had as a child when snow had fallen on icy nights, single crystals landing and melting on his mitts.

"Yeah, it's kind of pretty," Jamie said.

Cal spent the next hour loading his car. Joaquin had told him not to look for Shorat, and he decided to heed that advice. If he wanted to conjure Shorat, the way she was, not the way she had been, he couldn't stay at home waiting for her return. Who wanted to return to someone who couldn't take care of himself and his own life? There was still a week left before the start of the semester, and in any case, instruction and meetings had moved fully online. As long as he kept his iPad charged and had access to Wi-Fi, he could do his job wherever he might go.

Around 10:30, he took a last walk through the house. The purifiers had been switched off, all the windows and doors had been closed. All the items he felt he couldn't or mustn't live without, from his high-blood pressure medication to his running shoes, he had loaded into the backseat. It hurt him to leave behind what he'd worked so diligently to build and already he felt his resolve weakening. To dispel his longing to stay and keep the place intact for a life that had ended only two days ago, he quickly called the dogs, strapped them into their harnesses, then led them into the garage. Vanya, all fiery breath, jumped into the back first, whereas Yuuki took her time stepping into the vehicle, placing herself neatly into one corner and looking somewhat disapprovingly at Cal.

He made sure to watch the garage door close behind them, assured himself that he'd switched off all the lights, all the gas burners. He'd even watered the plants in both front and backyard one last time. And yes, he had his phone, his hearing aids, his glasses, the dog food, the dog dishes, and two gallon-jugs of water. He pulled out into the street, drove slowly toward Dogwood, turned onto Banyan. He might never see this neighborhood again.

Shorat in Saqqara

This picture I took from the backseat of the 30-year-old Peugeot taxi we'd hired in Cairo to take us first to Gizeh and then to the step pyramids in Saqqara. The shot shows the windshield and some dusty fields beyond, but is focused mainly on the oversized rearview mirror. In that mirror, the driver is to the left, I'm in the middle, my face blocked by the camera, and next to me sits Shorat, her hair covered by the scarf that was her constant companion.

We have left Gizeh and are making our way south, but every few miles, the car has to stop at a checkpoint. Our driver is talking with deference to the soldiers, defiance when there seems to be a problem with his papers. We don't speak each other's languages, and on the way back to Cairo, a few hours later, a song will play on the radio but I won't get an answer, won't be able to find out who is playing it, and instead he'll be switching to another station.

The driver is young, he's borrowed the car for the day. Before taking the photograph, we huddled over the maps in our guidebook, showing him the step pyramids which seem to mean nothing to him, and maybe he's just not sure about how to get there. We say things we know the other won't understand, we use hands, arms, and faces to try to make the other understand, and the atmosphere is relaxed. Once we've left Cairo, I'm not sure we'll ever get to Saqqara, but once we've left Cairo, that no longer seems important. We're in a country so foreign, we become ourselves again. We are not who people have made us, but we are who we dreamt of becoming. I look at Shorat's reflection in the mirror through the lens of the camera, and it's a woman I recognize and who isn't my wife.

Chapter 9

T_{HE FIRST STOP HE MADE} south of San Francisco, to let the dogs pee and to pee himself at a rest area that only offered bathrooms and vending machines. The vending machines were placed behind iron bars, like convicts, to protect them from vandalism. All the compartments and slots were empty, and someone had spray-painted the machines despite the iron bars. He found this jarring yet again, this display of utter contempt for everything public, things that weren't owned by individuals but meant to be used by everyone. Cal and Shorat had visited Japan ten years earlier and had been embarrassed by the utter lack of vandalism in the streets of Tokyo and Kyoto. Bike seats hadn't been slashed, vending machines worked without fail, trash didn't line the sidewalks, public bathrooms were spotless, and no bottles and fast food bags were left behind on park benches. How could one culture embrace public spaces so thoroughly while the other showed only contempt for them? Why could America not enjoy what it didn't personally own?

Vanya ate some old poop before Cal could interfere, and Yuuki showed her distaste for another dog by baring her teeth and growling viciously. After making sure that the men's bathroom was empty, he led both dogs inside and relieved himself. If he had left them inside the car, they would have started to unpack his bags with their teeth.

The long stretch going south on the I-5 made him drowsy, especially after Vanya had finally calmed down and fallen asleep. Cal listened to a podcast, but his thoughts couldn't follow, got stuck before translating what he heard into something he could digest. Music didn't help, opening the window only refreshed him for ten or fifteen minutes. When he finally saw a sign for Starbucks, he pulled off the highway and into the 24-hour drive-thru lane. The cup he received was only his second beverage since the virus had shut down schools and businesses and stranded him at home; it still felt dangerous to trust a stranger's hand with his drink. Cal parked the car in the nearly empty lot, got out and started to stretch. This was an old routine of his, which he had learned in his acting days in Berlin. He hadn't kept up that routine, but it came back to him quickly, and between sips of coffee he lowered his center of gravity, fencing and karate-style, feeling his muscles slowly accept the tension and bend to the new sensation, this rediscovered pain. How old I have let myself become, he thought. How and why did I ever stop using my body in these messy ways? How did I give up on the discomfort of feeling horribly stiff, awkward and clumsy?

He pulled up to the drive-thru window a second time, bought another venti-sized latte, and soon reached Valencia. Even though it was Sunday morning, the traffic thickened. Cal let himself be carried forward, jittery and sweaty enough to stay awake and grin at the sea of red taillights who pulled him toward Los Angeles, the only place he'd ever deeply loved. He rolled down the window even though Vanya awoke and began to breathe his noisy staccato, and sucked in the air smelling of he didn't know what. Surely refuse, trash, and the sighs of people who had been stranded on this desert island, sun and wealth bleaching their eyes, and flowers and hedges blooming in obscene colors. Smog, despair, and the lunacy brought on by winds, sun, and evictions and broken contracts had never succeeded in dissuading Cal. The city had forgotten him, no, it had never noticed him in the first place, but that didn't matter. His love for LA was too pure and ungainly to depend on reciprocity.

The hotel he'd chosen stood on Franklin Ave. He'd requested a room with a city view and balcony and had paid the dog deposit online. He handed the keys to the masked valet, too tired and cheerful to explore the self-park options. Nobody with a heart could afford current parking rates — what did they offer to your car? Snacks, massages, and pedicures? But Cal did what he'd always been good at: he excused inexcusable expenses with personal emergencies, real and imagined. The dogs, too, were too tired to offer any resistance. The masked receptionist offered them brightly-colored treats and, after handing Cal two room keys, assured him that there were dog dishes in the hall closet of his room.

Waiting for the elevator, he noticed the paintings in the lobby and hotel bar. They were large, photorealistic renderings of naked bodies, suggestive without being erotic. Most canvases were black-and-white, some sepia-colored. He thought he recognized the style — together with Shorat, he had visited galleries most every week, for the art and the free booze on opening nights. Back when they had lived in Koreatown, in a fifth-floor studio apartment overlooking 6th Street, they'd been constantly broke. The Big Recession killed businesses every week, and the only entertainment they could afford was of the free kind. They'd left Michigan and their jobs at the beginning of the downturn, and by the time they'd found their bearings, Shorat lost her job, and his work as a freelance editor for schoolbooks dried up. On the weekends, they got into their old Ford Escort wagon and drove to Bergamot Station, Culver City, La Brea and Fairfax, to drink cheap wine and, at posher galleries, cocktails. For a few brief hours they imagined they were part of the city and wouldn't go entirely unnoticed. They bought art too, at the galleries that served two-buck Chuck, happy to live on less money and more hot pockets and spaghetti. Fright diluted their pupils, and at night they sat on the roof with Starbuck, the Chinook, and the helicopters provided the musical backdrop, supported by the massaged exhaust pipes from so many Infinitis.

Where had he seen this style? Fortunately, Yuuki and Vanya were intimidated enough to be on their best behavior. They followed him from picture to picture, until he stood among the high tables of the bar area, his eyes recognizing the picture that hung between two windows. Without even looking at the small white card affixed to the wall, he knew its title. Paulina had named this picture of Karl's chest "7:10 Tuesday Morning." It had been available as a postcard all over Berlin for a year or two, in the days when many souvenir stores still sold art postcards. It had been a photograph back then, not a painting, but there could be no mistake. Cal approached the picture, lowered his head to read that small white card anyway. The artist's name was Paula Rhein, and the title of the oil on canvas was "Tim visiting my studio." The insult stung. "Tim?" he asked out loud. "There was no Tim."

He pulled the dogs toward the elevator and, once inside, waved his key across the pad, pressed 9, and watched Yuuki and Vanya freeze as the cabin began to move. "Tim," he said again, shaking his head. But the real news was that Paulina had to be in town. He hadn't seen her since a minor fight in front of a movie theater back in Berlin, a year or two before she had left the city for good. Was she living in LA now? In Berlin, where she had attended a private photography school, she'd been Paulina Rheininger, driving a yellow VW Bug, her accent heavily southern. They'd made fun of her, they'd all been in love with her, at least for a few days or weeks. In their circle of friends, loosely arranged around self-exploitation, coal-burning ovens, artistic leanings, and sexual availability, Paulina had stuck out – her family was wealthy, and despite her awful accent, hers was a beauty that felt untouched by strife, high school hazings, or heartbreak. They listened to her stories about a harsh father and terrible boyfriends politely, sometimes even compassionately, but they couldn't bring themselves to pity her. Too unblemished was her skin, too silky her hair, too clinically sterile her photographs. And just to be near her, women and men let themselves be photographed no matter what Paulina asked of them.

Cal found room 923, took off the dogs' harnesses. His luggage had already arrived and been neatly lined up on the floor. Before feeding Yuuki and Vanya, he went out onto the balcony, replete with table and chairs, made sure he really looked out on Franklin and the city grid beyond. The dogs followed cautiously, reading the air, getting excited about a table leg. When he went back inside to find the bag of dog food, he saw the flyer on the bed. It was a high-gloss announcement of the new art show's closing reception at 5:00 pm; the artist would be in attendance. Masks were required, refreshments were complimentary and could be consumed only by the hotel pool.

Feeding the dogs required walking them, and after ordering room service for himself, Cal took Yuuki and Vanya down to the lobby, passing Paulina's pictures on the way out. Did he like them? They were undeniably impressive, but would he want male hands cupping breasts on his walls? Male hands on female hips indicating doggy-style sex? A naked woman holding a burning teddy bear in one hand? What kind of lives invited such paintings into their apartments and houses? He'd often wondered about art buyers and their homes, and seldom had he set foot into places filled with original art, art produced by somewhat well-known artists instead of by the dilletante home owners or their adolescent children. He couldn't stand the art of hobbyists who were proud to display their smearings even in the bathrooms. It made Cal physically ill, he couldn't help it. Art, he contended, required commitment and sacrifice, and the products of fun outings to the park and the helpless collages of middle-aged disappointment reminded him too much of his upbringing and the boorish taste of his family and their friends, grounded in resentment and ignorance. Such helpless smears choked him, cut open his stomach, bled him dry. But where did Paulina's paintings end up? Who were these people? Would he recognize them? Would they see him?

Franklin was crowded and loud, peaceful even with masked faces surrounding Cal. How he had missed the city, how he had missed even the trash collecting in the gutters. The dogs were too scared to defecate, so he turned into a side street, walked up deeper into the hills. By the time they both had pooped, he was lost, and by the time he'd found his way back, his breakfast, wheeled into his room and coyly covered by aluminum and plastic wrap and an added layer of plastic, was cold. The scrambled eggs were runny and he fed them to the dogs. But toast and bacon were acceptable, though they oddly shared a similar consistency. He fell asleep soon after.

At five o'clock Cal stepped out of the elevator. The bar was open but handed out plastic cups. Food was delivered only to outside tables. A smattering of people, well-distanced and masked, stood inside the lobby, but no one was looking at the paintings. Paulina sat at a small table, a stack of books next to her arm, a pen next to her long fingers. "Paula" was printed across her mask, her lips. How clever.

"Hello," he said. "You must be the artist."

"I am," she said. "Thank you for coming tonight."

The books in front of her contained photographs of her art. *Recovered Bodies* it was called. "May I?" he asked. Paulina produced a bottle of hand sanitizer from a bag near her feet and pumped some of the clear gel into his palm. Cal rubbed his hands together, silky was the feeling, and he reached for a copy of Paulina's book and opened it.

"Do you live in LA?" he asked.

"Eagle Rock," she said. "You?"

"San Francisco." Vanity kept him from telling her who he was. He wished to be discovered, remembered, known. "Can I get you something to drink?"

"I'll have a Vodka Tonic," she said.

New arrivals lugged bags into the lobby, people lined up in front of the elevators to wait their turn, anxious not to overcrowd them. Cal felt a tinge of panic at being among the many bodies multiplying like cancerous cells. He ordered the drinks from a well-coiffed bartender who asked about his preferred brands, then produced Paulina's drink and an obscenely large Manhattan. Slowly, carefully, Cal made his way back to Paulina's table. She still sat by herself, now leafing through her book.

"Have you sold any?" he said.

She thanked him for the drink without answering his question. "How long will you be staying?"

"A week, maybe two. Hard to tell."

"Why is that?"

"How long have you been living in California?"

"How bad are the fires up north?" she asked.

His vanity was still holding, though he couldn't tell why. What was it that made him angry at Paulina? Because it was anger that stole into his questions. Nothing he could explain; Paulina had been annoying at worst, and he'd always remembered her as a minor fixture of his Berlin years.

"Well," he said now, "enjoy your evening. Like your paintings." And with that, he walked past the bar toward the pool area and carefully stretched out on one of the lounge chairs. His drink was still full enough to last for several more minutes. The air was turning cooler, and when he closed his eyes, he forgot that the city had welcomed a pandemic into its streets and boulevards like a tempestuous lover. Resolve to expel the virus had weakened, it wasn't so bad, was it? It didn't come to blows all the time. Yes, people were in love with this dark threat, secretly enjoying the bad news, the drama, the flare-ups and botched responses. Unprecedented — what sway this word held over the country.

A waitress stopped by his chair, and Cal ordered another Manhattan. It made him lose track of Paulina, her exhibit, the unfortunate coincidence of meeting her in his getaway hotel. He'd come here to find a way to make Shorat see him again, and instead he'd run into a friend who, once he looked at it more closely, had never been one of the dear ones. Yes, they'd made love once, when a teacher at the photography school had broken up with Paulina and she needed someone to console her, but the intimacy hadn't lasted. It hadn't been him she was after.

Still, he had modeled for her several times after that, had enlisted his changing girlfriends to pose whenever Paulina had a new assignment that asked for bodies, or a new idea for a potentially lucrative erotic photo shoot. She never shared the money she received, but that had never bothered any of her friends.

"You mind?" She sat down on the lounger next to him. "I didn't want to be rude," she said.

"That's quite okay."

"It's been a week, and now I'm here, and nobody came for the reception."

"I came to your reception," he said.

"Yes, yes. Right. But you weren't…I know, I'm…."

"No, I wasn't going to buy, it's true. I had seen your name and thought I'd recognized it."

"And?"

"And what?"

"Did you recognize it?"

"I'm not sure. I'm still searching my mind."

Paulina kicked off her shoes. Why was he so intent on calling her Paulina when she had changed her name to Paula? What if she had insisted on calling him Karl? Her toes were painted red; her feet, he remembered, had always been a disappointment to her. Too flat, toes spreading awkwardly when she walked across a room. He hadn't minded back then.

She took off her mask to take a sip and smiled at him. "Do I recognize an accent?"

"Swiss," he lied. "I grew up in Geneva. My father was a watchmaker in La Chaux-au-Fonds, but my mother, a lawyer, worked in Geneva. I stayed with her most of the time. They weren't unhappy with the arrangement, I think." He wondered if his lies were at all convincing, and to test the waters, he took off his mask as well.

"And what do you do in San Francisco?" she asked.

"I think I can hear an accent too?"

"Sweden," she lied. "I grew up near Stockholm."

"What brought you to the States?"

"Love." She was holding the straw with two fingers, closing her full lips around it. Her lips hadn't suffered. With age, they'd grown to appear more realistic. In Berlin, they'd resembled two large worms, incredibly fat worms. No one had injected their lips back then. "And you?"

"Money." His disappointment over Paula's refusal to recognize him had faded. He was interested to know what would happen next.

"How about I give you a private tour of my paintings?"

"I would very much like that." He watched her get up unhurriedly, refastening her mask. She hadn't been changed much by the intervening years. Her skin, her skin, of course, had lost its plumpness, but she was still as slim as ever, her movements of a gangly, awkward elegance. Time had been patient with her, or maybe she had harassed time, pummeled it, bullied time into letting her be and turn a blind eye to her pursuits. He followed that slim, middle-aged woman back into the hotel lobby, where she took position in front of the first large canvas, a group of three nudes, one male kneeling in front of a woman, the other standing behind her, shielding her breasts with his left arm.

"What's the story?" he asked.

"They were both sleeping with her, but only one of them knew. The other believed that the girl was true to him. He's the one kneeling."

"You told him to kneel?"

"I told him to kneel. He was just a boy, naïve, arrogant, not very pretty, not very special, but the girl had loved him for a while. He needed to kneel, because he was worshipping her."

"The boy behind her?"

"The whole time they posed for me, he had his hand, the one you can't see, all over the girl's buttocks. He dipped his fingers inside her, and she didn't make a sound so as not to give him away. She was already pregnant with his child, but she had only told the kneeling boy, who would later go with her to a clinic believing he was the father."

"And you painted them when?"

"I photographed them. A long time ago, while I was an art student in Paris."

"Paris?"

"I lived there for several years. It's how I got my start. I believed the photos had been lost during one of my many moves. But I recently recovered them, and I felt I needed to feel them again, paint them, remember what I had known about them."

"And these three? What happened to them?"

"We lost touch."

"But here they are, still bound by love. They still don't know what will happen to them."

"That's right."

"What about this next one, the one between the two windows?" Cal pointed at his own chest.

"That is Tim again."

"Tim again?"

"He's the kneeling boy. Though this picture was taken later, after the clinic, after he had left the girl. He'd become less wide-eyed, slept around, trying his hand at acting, though he was a poor performer."

"You saw him perform, then?" Cal felt an odd calm, something akin to hatred, so quiet and brittle it would take a surgeon to extract it whole. Instead, it would more likely break into the tiniest shards, each burrowing into his flesh and keeping him awake at night. Allergies, he might say when awakened by that itching sensation, but he would know better.

"Oh no." She laughed delicately, but mask and eyes didn't give away a thing. "I wouldn't have done that to myself."

"What's the story of that picture?"

"He came one afternoon. He'd been dumped by a girl, and I took pity on him, and to get at least something of value in return, I made him pose for the camera. He pestered me for a long time, until I told him in no uncertain terms to leave me alone."

"And that painting near the entrance?"

"That's Tim again."

"Tim again?"

"He hooked up with one of my friends, a beautiful woman several years older than him."

"The photo is blurry, as though they are...moving."

Paula laughed again, something so light it seemed to escape from behind her mask like an insect, hungry to sting and feed itself. "Yes, he is supposed to move as though the two of them are having sex. Her legs are slightly raised, and I have asked him to move his pelvis in an exaggerated way, so the camera will capture the up and down. But he gets carried away, and halfway through the shoot he is no longer pretending. But he isn't ruining the photo, he still performs exactly according to my instructions, and so is the woman. They pretend I'm not noticing that they are no longer pretending and they never miss a beat, and in the end, I get my photo, and they get the memories."

"You think they remember?"

"Of course. Vanity never forgets. I swear, Tim still thinks about this moment today."

CHAPTER 10

THE SIDE EXIT LED CAL and the dogs toward the hotel's parking garage, where two valets in uniform were smoking, one standing with his bowtie dangling to the side, the other seated on a rickety metal folding chair. He greeted them, hurried past approaching cars toward Franklin. He chose not to see Paula again, not to run into whoever she had hired to take down the show. One should never have his memories verified, he thought. What an odd thing to let other people guard what belongs to you. He could see now how his whole life might vanish one day, not because people didn't remember enough of him, but because they misremembered, believed in their own puny versions of the stories he had strung together for himself from artifacts recorded and recovered in his head. After his death, what horrible distortions would survive? Tim. Tim, not Karl. Had Paulina recognized him? Had her lies been a test? An offer to reveal himself? Or were they both still such children they couldn't let go of the ambitions they'd had for themselves all those long years ago!

Tim. But she had titled the image before she could ever have known he would appear at the closing reception. Tim. Was that her way of telling her own story, give those random things she'd encountered meaning? Or had she simply forgotten his name and come up with something that fit the ambience of her recollection?

Yuuki pooped. Vanya pooped twice. He ran out of bags before he was back at the hotel. And still he couldn't feel the dogs, couldn't feel himself. All he saw were Paula's paintings and how she had banned him, Cal, from them. She'd exorcised him completely, not by getting rid of him, but by reinventing him.

Cal had turned past friends into characters over the years, had used likenesses in his work, given them different names to cover his tracks. Was that what Paula had done as well? Yes, some lovers, some friends he only remembered by the names he'd invented. He was a bad guardian of memories, because his work was about pulling memories apart and refurbishing them, turning them into digestible units, making them more colorful than they had been. And Paula's recovered bodies? Did she really believe she'd taken pity on him back when they'd made love on the blue carpet in her apartment? And what would happen if he rang up all those former friends tonight? How would they remember him, if they remembered him at all? What ugly fabrications would they sell him as memories?

He grew panicked, and not even Vanya's rambunctiousness could dispel the fear he felt. His life was taken away from him. The people who should have kept him in their hearts were murdering him instead, altering his life, betraying anything good that might have occurred. They turned him into a grotesque creature, a monster, a helpless idiot, a stranger. They didn't bury him quietly in their backyards, without a stone, without a marker, no, they dragged him out into the open, mangled beyond recognition. Embellishments and falsehoods were draped over this corpse, to be used as a scarecrow in beer-fueled stories. He couldn't do anything to stop his former friends from stuffing him with straw. He didn't own the copyrights to his life.

Cal grew ever more agitated, asked himself if he'd taken his high blood pressure medication that morning when he'd stood in the Starbucks parking lot outside Valencia. He walked on, dragged the dogs along without paying attention to their sniffing and pulling until Vanya stumbled and briefly crashed to the ground. The dog soon stood again, panting and embarrassed, it seemed, by the mishap, but it was a sign that Cal had ventured too far. Vanya was tired, his bad legs were giving him trouble.

Back in his room, he sat on the green plush sofa, his feet on the coffee table, Vanya now asleep beside him, Yuuki already on the bed and keeping an eye on him. He understood that his fear went far beyond Paula and his former friends in Berlin. Shorat had left. She was the keeper of his memories, the only one who knew all his stories about the divided and reunited city, about the Wall and his apartment on Turiner Straße, about his first girlfriend and her pregnancy and how each time he recounted that particular story, he grew more doubtful that he had indeed been the father of her child. Shorat had seen the few pictures he'd saved from stage productions, from trips to East Berlin, photos of his former girlfriends. She hadn't been the jealous kind. As long as he'd handed it all over to her, she was content. Only she had seen all the old photographs before they had burned in the Tubbs Fire. Now his witness had left him. Whatever his mind decided to displace or discard would be irretrievably lost. Worse still, the twenty years with Shorat would fade too. These, he thought, were his most important years, though they seemed perhaps less exotic, less frantic, less lurid.

Their picture albums, their tapes, their CDs, all of it had perished in the fires. Without Shorat, these twenty years of his life would wilt and warp just like his memories of Berlin. And what name would his wife give him in ten or twenty years, should she ever bother to spread him onto a canvas?

He opened the balcony door, let noise and exhaust take over the room. He didn't hear the telephone until much later, as though waking from a dream. He listened to the receptionist, then left the room and took the elevator to the lobby. Paula, and with her the paintings, was gone. The walls appeared like overconfident nudists, the absence of decorative material was a shock. The receptionist left her desk once he had identified himself, and returned from the baggage room with a large parcel sheafed in brown paper and bubble wrap. He thanked the woman, then took the elevator back to his floor. He showered, even massaged some body lotion from an impossibly stiff little bottle into his skin before looking at the parcel again. She'd written "Tack för drinken" onto the bubble wrap, and why did she thank him in Swedish? Because she was still playing her role? Or was she mocking him? Had she not recognized him, or did she know that he was Tim, her Tim, the character she'd given that name? No phone number, no address. This was a parting gift, not an invitation. But Cal felt no gratitude, he had a mind to fling this canvas — whichever painting it would turn out to be — from his balcony. Its presence felt threatening; it was her story against his, and accepting the painting would feel like disavowing his own memories. The parcel was a Trojan horse, a mole, a chicken pox blanket, an anthrax envelope. He banned it to the hall closet and even then required another thirty minutes to calm himself.

Yes, he'd knelt in front of his pregnant girlfriend, but he hadn't known about her pregnancy. He'd known about her betrayal, though much later it turned out that sleeping with their friend had neither been the first nor the last time she'd cheated on him. How laughable "cheating" sounded, like something you did playing cards or Scrabble. It didn't capture her desire to be free of him at times, to shake him off like an itchy coat or dress.

Yes, he'd made love to the woman who was several years older than him in front of the camera, and he still doubted Paulina had become aware of it while taking photos and giving instructions. After completing the shoot she had disappeared into her darkroom right away, and he and the woman had finished unobserved, unfulfilled. The woman had not been Paula's friend; he had introduced them. She was the one with the burning bear in her hand. Yet even while he corrected Paula's stories in his head, he could feel that the damage had been done. His memories were already shifting, taking on new shapes. So many people believed that the past was the past and couldn't be altered, but he had always understood that this was utter nonsense. The past was constantly being rearranged, and not merely because our memories worked to make ourselves look better and find a thread we could follow, connecting fragments into a plausible story, but also because we always learned more about what we thought was enshrined in our recollections. Just as his girlfriend's infidelities had cast serious doubt on what he'd initially thought of as happy years, so too did Shorat's absence question everything they'd experienced together. What had he overlooked? What had he misinterpreted? What was it he misremembered?

It was past midnight, and the light on his nightstand was still burning, when he fell asleep. And there was Paula waiting, in a room full of paintings, many more paintings than she had shown in the hotel lobby, and she smiled exposing her prominent teeth, inviting him into her studio. She said, "Let me show you how you really were. Let me show you what happened. You were much worse than you think, and all the moments you thought were yours — they belong to me and the others, and we've decided to kick you out of our memories. Everything you see here in the paintings you will forget. This past is none of your business. And besides, I never liked the way you smelled."

He awoke around four in the morning, his mouth dry, his tongue glued to the roof of his mouth. He took his time in the bathroom, switched off the light, made sure that he could feel Yuuki's butt against his back, and fell asleep again. And this time, Paula's studio was empty, and Paula was nowhere to be seen, and no matter how hard he tried, he couldn't remember any of the paintings that had covered her walls.

Close to eight, Vanya started pawing him, and Cal fed the dogs, then took them for a stroll. He tried to remember the three prominent players on the Buffalo Bills team of the early nineties, and after much searching, after dead ends and divination, he finally said their names. Andre Reed, Thurman Thomas, Jim Kelly. He felt an odd sense of despair over needing almost thirty minutes to remember names he could have rattled off fifteen years ago, but something inside him started to settle. He was glad the night was over, glad there were names he could look up on the internet, glad that someplace somewhere you could still replay those games the Bills had all lost. How calming such trivial information was when everything else could be misremembered and purged.

Every life, every religion, every belief, every union, depended on a hollow at its core, the one thing everything revolved around and that couldn't be questioned, examined, not even looked at. The center was either a paradox or an absolute, something that seemed silly, really, when you said it out loud sitting at your kitchen table with the lights burning and the smell of sauteed onions wafting through the house. God was omnipotent yet didn't interfere when people died in alarming numbers during a pandemic. God loved all humans yet hadn't intervened to save millions from Hitler's genocide. God hadn't wiped Germany off the map, nor had he ever clarified whether or not Jesus was really his son, whether or not Muhammed really was his prophet; he had refused to appear in the past few thousand years. If you were a believer, these questions could not be asked or had to be dismissed, sometimes in the form of long-winded explanations that sounded like apologies for a cruel dictator. Each system of philosophy suffered that same hollow, the system carefully arranged around that core as if to shield it, protect it, hide it from curious gazes.

Every love story worked according to a similar principle. You couldn't ask whether the other person loved you. What kind of answer could you hope to get? Surely nothing sincere. Once Cal had married Shorat, he learned to accept that their love was religion. You didn't question it. You couldn't examine their bond and the substance it was made of. He'd had to trust that Shorat was in love and content with her decision. Any doubt would have led to madness, jealousy, sleepless nights, and a quick divorce. No, you had to trust your faith, and you had to trust the other's faith in what couldn't be explained. If he'd exposed the hollow center, his marriage would have spun out of control. Now that Shorat was gone, it was hard to see why he could have believed in a bond built on next to nothing. Attraction, curiosity, some feeling we had named love but couldn't quite explain nor expect to be the same for everybody. Shorat had stopped believing. She had left their religion, their philosophy. What would bring her back? How could he restore himself in her eyes? Losing faith was not at all like losing your purse, your home, your memories. Losing faith was to lose your old self. You were free to choose a new one, but things couldn't be rushed. Such things took time. And maybe somewhere Shorat was looking for a new self, someone to replace the woman who had been married for twenty years. Cal had once replaced Karl. Paula had replaced Paulina. What would Shorat's name be if he ever saw her again?

Later in the day, after a long, miserable breakfast by the pool and two Bloody Mary's, he walked to a branch of Wells Fargo and checked the balance of the account he shared with his wife. He still trusted her not to hurt him, and he was right, though looking at their savings account also diminished any hope he might have had about Shorat returning to him with one of the explanations favored by the movies — amnesia or kidnapping. The chances had been close to zero — you didn't take bag and camera to suddenly suffer amnesia, and yet, the heart was not a logician. The missing $40,000, two thirds of their savings, said she wasn't going to hurt him, but she was also not going to make it easy and disappear without a trace. She wasn't sentimental, she'd never been.

<h1 style="text-align:center">Chapter 11</h1>

Back at the hotel, he transferred the rest of his savings into an account they didn't share — an old account he'd never bothered to close. This felt immensely petty, it smudged the high opinion he had of himself when it came to financial matters. He logged into his university account and changed the information for his direct deposit and while he was still typing, he felt his process of grieving Shorat's absence changing with it. He was still upset, sad, nostalgic, he felt all the emotions that such words were trying and failing to conjure, but he also needed to plan his future. The house belonged to both him and Shorat in equal parts. He earned enough money to pay the mortgage, but he wouldn't be able to pay her half of the equity. Their new house was worth a lot more than the one that had burned down; they wouldn't have been able to buy it at its current value. That was one of the many ironies of the fire. Their savings, too, only existed because of them losing everything; the insurance had paid for their lost property, and they had not replaced solar panels, bikes, paintings, and other valuables. Their savings were for travel, that's what they had decided.

He drank the first Manhattan on the balcony, feeding the dogs treats from an outsized bag of Beggin' Strips. They weren't healthy but the only bribe the dogs accepted without fail. Was he afraid of losing the house? The alcohol allowed him to listen closely to the smaller signals he received from somewhere that he thought of as 'inside.' Alcohol made him patient, and after spending a good ten minutes pre-feeling his reactions to a possible sale of his home, he was satisfied and started on the second Manhattan. He wasn't afraid. Yes, he might be inconvenienced, but he had never cared too much about belongings, about space and conveniences. He'd be able to buy a condo near the university, in one of the lesser neighborhoods, where buildings were always at the end of their maintenance cycles. He could move to Vallejo, a city that everyone shunned for its violence and poverty. He'd be closer to San Francisco, he wouldn't be stuck in a provincial town without any distinct features or atmosphere, where most people were terribly old and culture was second-rate. He didn't mind Santa Rosa, he'd grown oddly fond of it, but at times voices licked his ears about streets lined with cafes and bars and restaurants, its patrons neither old nor scuzzily clad, where no diesel trucks with right-wing stickers and American flags in the bed stood parked outside. Academics lived where they got a job, that was the whole truth, but if he had only to worry about himself and the dogs, he could live anywhere. He wouldn't have to pretend he needed quartz kitchen counters and nice cabinets, he didn't need toilet seats that lowered themselves slowly onto the bowl, he didn't need any of this. The dogs didn't need these things either.

He was drunk enough by then to try a Beggin' Strip himself, and yes, it was as he had secretly suspected for a long time — they were quite good. In ruggedly handsome spirits, he managed to put the harnesses around the dogs' chests, tie a mask to his face, and in a few minutes they spilled through the glass doors onto Franklin Avenue. He hadn't forgotten the poo bags.

Up into the hills they walked. It made Cal happy to see the dogs entertained by new smells, watch Vanya mark post after rock after hydrant. Where did dogs store all that pee? And what control they had over their bladders. They could go twelve hours without relieving themselves, they did so every night.

Up and higher he walked into the hills until the street ended in a sandy parking lot, a curious-looking apartment complex to his right. He turned around and froze, barely breathing, assaulted by the view the alcohol had made him forget was waiting right behind him. While making plans to rent shabby apartments in downtrodden districts, the only kind he'd be able to pay for, he'd been blind to the Los Angeles grid set ablaze. What beauty, what infernal noise, the 101 shrieking below him, the city traffic pushing ever more exhaust into the plume of smog browning the horizons.

"Are you looking for Anton's place?" a voice behind him asked. "You can follow me, if you want."

The speaker was a slender woman with very short blond hair and a foreign accent, large sunglasses masking her eyes. But her mouth was unmasked, and looking at her lips, which seemed amused by his slow, wide-eyed response, he decided that yes, he was absolutely looking for Anton's place. The dogs followed him obediently, Vanya because he was getting tired, and Yuuki because she appeared to have fallen for the woman. Her snout was raised, her tail up high, and she pulled with vigor.

"He might have a crowd tonight. It's not the final cut, yet. I think he'll show two different endings."

"Fantastic," Cal said. You couldn't go wrong with that word.

The woman stopped, took a second look at the dogs, crouched, and began to pet Yuuki. "They're adorable," she said.

"She's a big fan of yours."

The woman shouldered her bags again and led them up a flight of stairs to a small courtyard. "Your first time here, right? It's an old nunnery. See that dome? That used to be the chapel. I don't know how Anton scored that apartment. I'm still trying to get him thrown out so I can take over his lease. I think he's set up everything by the pool. I'm Lena, by the way."

He introduced himself and the dogs, then followed her down another flight of stairs to the pool area. He was relieved to find that the crowd was indeed large, so large that his presence wouldn't even be noticed. While some guests wore bathing suits, and several men and women had ventured into the pool, everyone was masked. Even Lena now donned one, with a giant open mouth printed on the black fabric. Cal pulled out his own and took up a seat in what looked to be the quietest corner. He pulled the dogs close, entertaining them with small crumbs from slightly soggy Beggin' Strips he carried in his pockets.

The sun had sunk below the hills a long time ago, but it would be another hour before the movie could be shown on the large canvas stretched in front of a windowless wall. Nobody seemed in a hurry to watch it, and scanning the crowd, Cal wondered which one of the many trim and tan people might be Anton. Posters for the movie were taped to a few columns, something quickly photoshopped and printed on 11x17 paper. "The Accuracy of Time." And Cal wished he hadn't brought the dogs, who began to get nervous, casting anxious glances at the shrieking guests. Los Angeles pool parties — how he had dreamed of them during the years he and Shorat had lived in Michigan. They had never materialized. His books had never made it to film, and a TV series based on his most successful novel had died twice, only yielding a script for the pilot. Even though they had spent five years in LA, he had not cracked the circle of people with access to, or ownership of, a pool. It was a stain on his record, a stain on his life, and he wouldn't live long enough to rub it out.

A growl from Yuuki made Cal leave his chair and make his way to another staircase and leave the pool crowd behind. He wasn't sure where he was when the walkway in front of him widened and opened up onto a large terrace. None of the party guests had ventured here; Cal had the terrace to himself. The view was terrifying. There were no guardrails, no fencing protected him; Cal felt as though he had been pushed into the city and was falling toward the 101 and onto the hood of some freshly detailed Land Rover. Two helicopters flew toward him, one beginning to circle near the Capitol building. The traffic noise made him lightheaded, how excited he was, how close to death he felt.

He was pulled back, how he couldn't figure out until he could hear again, see again, until the dogs began to bark at the woman who now raised her hands as if to show she meant no harm. She was wearing a mask demanding, Vote!, and for a few moments she and Cal stared at each other, rendered helpless by the apparition of a face they couldn't read.

"I thought you might fall," the voice said.

"Oh no, no," he said quickly. "But thank you."

"It looked dangerous." She wore a beach towel wrapped around her. Obviously she was one of the pool guests. "Will your dogs bite me?" Her feet were dirty, her toes painted yellow.

"What? No, they're more afraid of you than you are of them." He'd tried that line before, and so far it had failed to work every single time. And it did again, eliciting nothing from the woman. "I'm dripping," she said several beats later, grabbing her dark hair with both her hands and wringing it like a towel.

"Do you live here?" he asked.

"I wish," she said. "How about yourself?"

"San Francisco."

"I know some people there. They're snooty, no offense." She undid the towel to dry her hair, then fastened it again, this time around her waist, like a long skirt. "I need some dry clothes," she said, "otherwise I'm going to get cold. You want to walk me to my car? Your dogs can protect me."

She took a different route toward the street than the one Lena had showed him, and once they had left the compound, the woman took off her mask. "We're outside, right? This will keep you at a safe distance from me." Her laughter exposed an overbite and slightly yellowed teeth. The contours of her lips appeared to have been sharpened with a razor blade. She was in her forties perhaps, late forties likely.

Her car turned out to be an RV of an older vintage with lots of chrome and fake wood. She unlocked the door, said, "Thanks for guarding me, see you at the party," and blew him a kiss before vanishing inside. Cal took the opportunity to find his way back to the hotel, feed the dogs, and retrace his steps toward the old nunnery. By the time he arrived at the compound, he was glad he'd brought a jacket against the chilly night air, and several wrong turns later, he was back at the pool area. By now, everyone had left the water and was staring at the screen. The sound from the loudspeakers was tinny but clear, the faces of the crowd as earnest as though the death of a dear friend had just been announced.

The movie had started a while ago, it seemed, and this made Cal happy. It was an old game of his, one he'd been playing since childhood. Could he piece together the plot and identify the conflict? Could he find out who the characters were and what the relationships between them were? Could he figure out what had happened until now? This wasn't unlike coming to this party, though less fraught with anxiety. You didn't owe characters anything, you didn't drink their wine, didn't get entwined in small talk and friendly chatter. You just watched, without having to interfere, without even having to react.

A man who looks to be in his forties is driving a car through the desert. He is wearing aviator sunglasses, his dark hair being blown into his face by the wind coming through the open window. It is an older car, of course, though none of the usual suspects. A Mustang or GTO would have been too simple, too cliché. This one is a Lincoln Continental from the 70s, all black and battered. The man seems to be searching for a woman, her picture appears in front of him every time he lowers the visor. She is youthful, with short blond hair. It's an old photo, wrinkled, as though he's been searching for a long time, showing it to people along the way to ask if they have seen her.

The man turns off the highway, his land yacht bouncing over dusty trails ever deeper into the desert, past rattlesnakes, tumbleweeds, and bleached animal skulls. These are cliché markers, old friends telling you the same story over and over again, and you don't mind. After several minutes low mountains appear in front of the man, and once he's come close enough to make out rock formations and sharp outcroppings, he also sees an RV shimmering in the violent sunlight. He cuts the engine, steps out, and walks the rest of the way toward the vehicle. The door is flung open, and a woman emerges with a rifle.

Cal watched heads in front of him turning, craning, and yes, there she was, sitting at a table close to the screen. The woman who'd pulled him back from the edge of the terrace, the one whose mask said, Vote!. Somebody was whistling now, a few people clapped. And the RV she had exited on-screen just now, stood in the parking lot of the apartment complex.

"How'd you find me?" the woman in the movie asks. And Cal realized that she is indeed the woman in the wrinkled photograph, though she is wearing her hair long now and it is no longer blonde. She's clearly older than the woman in the picture.

The man says, "You can disappear easily in this country. It's easy to take a new name, change your address, your looks. But you can't change who you are, and your patterns will betray you, your habits will reveal you. If you watch and listen long enough, you can pick up the rhythm of a person, and if you're patient enough, you can follow that rhythm to its source."

The woman puts down her rifle, reaches into the RV to extract two camping chairs, and under the retractable awning, the only shade available in this place, they sit and look at each other, familiarizing themselves with who the other has become.

"How was your life?" she asks. "Are you happy? Has it been what you wanted it to be?"

The man removes his glasses, the obvious attempt at honesty, and yet the actor is pulling it off without pulling the viewer out of the movie. Cal wasn't sure if the lead actor had been introduced as a sympathetic figure, but he didn't feel much goodwill towards this man who clearly knows that he looks the way leading men in Hollywood are required to look — chiseled chin, full hair, nice long muscles playing whenever he reaches for the beer the woman has offered him, or his glasses, or to put a stray strand of hair back behind one ear. Still, Cal was already invested in finding out what this man, who has clearly aged at a slower pace than the rest of the population (you can tell he's well into his forties without seeing it), has been through and what he hopes to accomplish out here in the desert now that he has located the woman. Locating someone is one thing, finding someone quite another.

"It feels as though I've always arrived too late, too early. I've never been in sync with what was going on around me. If I were to fill a sheet of paper with bullet points, I think mine would appear to have been a rich, fulfilling life. But it doesn't feel that way. I wanted to buy a diamond ring and all I could afford were rhinestones."

The camera pans to the woman's hands, detecting a gaudy ring. "It was a nice gesture," the woman says and smiles, unafraid of her overbite, and really, it's endearing, making her look vulnerable. Without it, she'd be too beautiful, boring even. "Though it was never the real thing."

"And how about you?" he says. "Have you found what you were looking for when you left?"

"You've never understood me, and perhaps you've never understood yourself. I've found what I was looking for. I found it back then, after buying the house, the car, the dogs and filling our lives with things that didn't fill us. I found it back then, that's why I left. And I've kept it close all these years. Am I happy? Maybe, though I don't care about happiness much. As long as I wrestle with what I found, as long as I bite and claw and harass it, I don't worry where or how long I live."

The lines are stilted, oddly solemn, but the actress makes their edges disappear. When she says them, they sound convincing, as though she were just thinking them now. The stiltedness enhances her struggle to explain how she feels.

"Out here? In an RV in the middle of heat and dust and nothing?"

"Today, yes."

The man smiles. "Today, yes. Today I have found what I was after."

"But it's not what you wanted. You can't build a life around loving another person."

"What else is there?"

"I'm sorry you've never found out who you are," the woman says.

"There's still time. It's not over yet."

"Yes, yes, it is." The rifle has appeared in her hand again, and she shoots twice, without hurry. He's shocked, his handsome face ugly now. The actor drops his own prettiness, and for the first time looks shockingly real. The woman keeps sitting in her chair, drinking her beer, and when she's done, she drags the lifeless body of her husband toward his car, manages to install him in the passenger seat, then gets behind the wheel. Kicking up thick clouds of dust, she takes a narrow road up the mountain. Up and higher she drives, until the road levels off and reaches a plateau. Without slowing down she approaches the cliff, pushes open the door and lets herself fall to the ground. The camera pans back, lifts off into the skies and reveals a very blue lake just beyond the cliff, the black Lincoln driving into thin air and arcing toward the lake's surface. The audience doesn't hear the splash, just watches as the car bobs in the water for a few seconds and slowly sinks out of view. Then the camera is back on that plateau, watching the woman dust herself off and walk away. The audience just stares at her walking, watches as she becomes smaller and smaller, the heat blurring her figure, dissolving it finally.

The movie had ended and applause started up slowly, people still shaking off the dream they had been following, but after a few seconds of fuzzy black and scratchy sound, the crowd by the pool was watching the man drive up to the RV again. Cal remembered Lena's remark about an alternate ending.

This time, he gets out of the car, but there's no one there to greet him. He opens the door to the RV. It is a cozy place, what people might call bohemian — colorful scarves draped over lamps, a colorful bedspread, colorful knickknacks one might find in esoteric bookstores. The man hears the honk of a car and rushes outside. The woman is behind the wheel of his car wearing a bathing suit; the passenger door is wide open.

He gets into the car, and the woman takes off in a cloud of dust. "How did you find me?" she asks.

The man looks at her, takes off his sunglasses and says, "I'm not sure I have found who I was looking for."

The woman laughs, exposing her overbite. "You're smarter than you used to be." She turns onto a narrow road leading up the mountain. She's going too fast but seems perfectly comfortable. "How will you find out?"

"It'll take time," he says.

"There might not be much of it left." She doesn't overemphasize the line, and when she looks at her passenger, her face is almost blank. She isn't threatening him, she's just stating the truth. The man nods in response — he doesn't seem to understand but nevertheless accepts her words. He knows she's not playing games. The car reaches the plateau, and the woman brakes, shifts into neutral and revs the car. "We have always lived in two different times, you always ahead, planning, thinking things through before they had a chance to happen, making sure time was not going to hurt you. Look at your face! Time has been gentle, you've always dived under its waves. Me? I've always been a bit late, never fast enough to dodge the waves, always getting caught up in them, getting dragged across the ocean floor, getting pummeled again and again. But since I left you, I've learned to neither dive under a wave nor get hit by it. I'm right on top of the wave and it's dangerous, never safe, never easy. It costs you a lot, maybe too much, but there's so much more to see and feel."

"Where are we going?" the man asks after a brief moment.

"We'll find out how much time we have left." With that, she shifts into gear, and the car lurches forward with an angry snarl. The camera pulls back, up and higher, and the Lincoln drives over the edge of the cliff, hangs in mid-air before descending toward the lake. But before it hits the water, the image freezes. The sound of the car crashing into the lake is audible while the image dims and fades into black. The credits start rolling.

This time the applause was louder, more prolonged, and after it had started to wind down, the male lead appeared below the screen, holding a glass of wine. The applause picked up again and intensified to a staccato. "Anton," somebody shouted. The man shielded his eyes, then waved toward the female lead sitting by the pool, and shouts of "Vera" erupted. Hand in hand, the two stood among their guests until Anton shouted, "I love you guys," and the last few claps were soon overtaken by chatter and clatter. Music was starting to play on a wireless speaker.

"Where are your dogs?" Vera asked some thirty minutes later, her shoes in one hand, a glass in the other. Cal was leaning against the hood of her RV, nursing the rest of his wine.

"In my hotel room, or at the pound if they started to make a ruckus during my absence."

"I'm that important? Should I be flattered or write you off as a bad person? How'd you find me?"

"You can disappear easily in this country. It's easy to take a new name, change your address, your looks. But you can't change who you are, and your patterns will betray you, your habits will reveal you. If you watch and listen long enough, you can pick up the rhythm of a person, and if you're patient enough you can follow that rhythm to its source."

"So you like that ending better? I'd have to agree, but I think he's going with the shorter one. They might survive together. There's still hope."

"Hope is such a tease, it tires you out," he said.

"Big words. Are you going to hurt me, or is it safe to invite you in?"

"Very safe."

"Don't sound too boring. You were always a bit boring. You come on strong, and then you switch to your everyday mode. You're damn good at that everyday mode." She unlocked the door, leaving it open for him to follow.

The inside of the RV looked every little bit the way he'd just seen it in the movie. It was a charming place, tight and yet not of the choking kind.

"So, how did you find me?"

"I didn't. I came to watch a movie."

"Huh, sounds highly implausible."

"You changed your name."

"Don't be boring already. That was twenty years ago, nobody remembers who they were twenty years ago. I hardly recognized you."

"I have changed."

"No, no, that's not what I meant."

"What did you mean?"

"Would you like something to drink?" She opened a cabinet, took out two clear-plastic tumblers, opened another cabinet and lined up several bottles on the narrow counter. "I even have ice," she said and started to fill the glasses. "Stirred, not shaken." She was using her finger. "You don't mind, do you?" then, "Did we have fun back then?"

"Some," he said. "When I wasn't boring."

"Don't pout. You've been waiting here for at least an hour, so we must have had fun. I must have made an impression. That's good to know. Even if you should hate me now, I once made an impression." She took a sip, took another. "What's your favorite memory?"

He thought about that, but then it dawned on him why she had asked the question. "You don't remember me."

"I do. I do. Otherwise I wouldn't have asked if...."

"But you don't know which of your memories I am?"

"I have been a naughty girl."

"And you don't know anymore which ones belong together."

She fluttered her lashes. "If this is a quiz, can I get a hint?"

"I should be pouting."

"Was I that important to you? I had no idea. But if I really was that important, you must give me a hint."

"Washington, DC. Van Gogh exhibit."

"Oh, we must have met in Buffalo. I was staying with my mom, and you had lost your apartment and were staying in the attic of that same house, without the landlord knowing."

"You had cheated me out of the lease."

"You wanted to throw me out. I had to defend myself. I visited you in your attic, and we made love on your terrible mattress."

"You were homeless."

"I had my car. And I did want to see Van Gogh, but I thought you wouldn't come, so I bought these handcuffs and once you were next to me inside the car, I handcuffed you to the door. You were stubborn. We stayed in some fleabag, I'm sure, some awful hotel that I can't remember because I stayed in too many awful motels to remember the particulars. But we did go to the exhibit and all the tickets were gone. They were free but limited, and a scalper sold me one, but we couldn't get another."

"You decided to leave me by the entrance. You asked me to wait for you."

"But I didn't, I grabbed you by the hand and dragged you to the ticket counter, and I said, "This is my dear friend. He has terminal cancer, and we drove all the way from Buffalo to see the exhibit, but there are no tickets left. And you stood there all miserable, you didn't even have to act because you were petrified, and they looked at you silently for a long time, and even I pitied you then. I got you the ticket."

"You still don't know who I am, though."

"I am very tired. My movie just premiered, and even though people were nice enough, it won't be a major success. Anton has appeal, I like him a lot, maybe a bit too much, but he is no major talent. He's good, I give him that, but all his movies look like indie versions of other, higher-budget movies. There's a certain flair to them until you notice that this je-ne-sais-quoi is just the lack of production value and that none of the actors — except for me, of course — ever stood a chance of starring in a major Hollywood feature. The stories are derivative and only look fresh because the editing is bad and people speak in strange ways because the writers were underpaid. Or overpaid. Or not paid at all, and half the scenes Anton wrote after watching his favorite movies."

"I'll have to go now," Cal said.

"Will you tell me your name? You have an accent, I can hear your accent."

"Goodbye, Vera."

"You are really something. One more hint. Puhlease."

"You tried to run me over with your mother's car."

"I must have really liked you."

"We stood inside a Burger King, and you suddenly lost it, you said you didn't want burgers and fries but nice little salads. You wanted your own kitchen and you wanted to prepare nice little salads, and finally I left the restaurant, and you got into the car and almost killed me in the driveway."

"But I didn't succeed."

"Goodbye, Vera."

"Don't be sad. I must have liked you for a while."

"You said I made your heart blast off like a rocket."

"Oh my."

"Goodnight."

"Say hello to your dogs. I'm glad you didn't jump."

Cal turned at the door. "Excuse me?"

"On the terrace. You wanted to jump. I pulled you back."

He nodded. "Good night, Vera."

Cal was crossing the parking lot, when behind him he could hear the door of the RV fly open. "It was your ring. The ring in the movie, you gave it to me. You bought me this awful white prom dress and we spent money on a marriage license."

He looked at her standing in the door, her face dark and hidden by the light behind her.

"Yes," he said. "Yes." And because her voice hadn't changed at all in all these years, his heart broke again at the memory of throwing away that dress, the dress that should have been the wedding dress, and how it had sat on top of the other trash in the dumpster outside of his apartment complex near the Peace Bridge to Canada. "Yes," he said again. "That was me."

"Then why do I not remember you?"

Chapter 12

THE DOGS WERE BOTH lying on his bed, raising their heads without much interest when he stepped into his room. He fed them, walked them one last time, then mixed himself a stiff drink with what he found in the minibar. It was nearly two o'clock, and he should have been tired, but the memories Vera had stirred up stood like visitors about the room; it was too crowded to catch your breath, and nobody was wearing a mask.

"I would have married her too," he told Vanya and Yuuki. She had been his first American girlfriend and his last, because Shorat had never gained girlfriend status; he had married her right away. Vera had been the last in a string of lovers who tried to hurt him or themselves, and from the first moment he'd seen Shorat, he had known that she was Vera's opposite in most every way. She was as stubborn and headstrong as Vera, but even before he had ever talked to her, Cal noticed what he could only describe as an energy that left no space for darkness; Vera's features had been full of soot.

The year was 1999, and Cal had finished a Master of Arts in American Studies and started another one in Humanities. He was biding his time, staying in school to stay in the country. Once school ended, he'd have sixty days to return to Berlin. He'd been accepted into the

MFA in Creative Writing Program at the University of Michigan, and after the summer he would leave Buffalo for Ann Arbor. In the meantime, he still had a job in the Office of Admissions at the University at Buffalo. He was responsible for assisting international students with application materials, and he sat by himself in a windowless office, dressed professionally in case he needed to help out with drop-ins who'd brought their parents to have their questions about dorms, recreational activities, and academics, answered. He only had three dress shirts, all of them frayed at the cuffs, and two ties, and his pants were too baggy and his shoes scuffed.

On June 1st, he left the apartment he shared with two guys he didn't care for and walked toward Delavan station. Buffalo had only one subway line, connecting downtown and the old South Campus. The downtown stations of that subway, whose trains looked and drove like streetcars, were above ground, and Delavan was the fourth station underground. The trains were slow but sounded like the nuclear-powered super train the *Weekly World News* was promising its readers. The girl with pig-tails and a tight white shirt stood by the ticket machines when Cal entered the station. He walked behind her down to the platform, and, after the train had pulled into the station, made sure to enter the same car. He watched her the whole train ride, praying she wouldn't get off the train at Amherst Street or La Salle. He tried not to be obvious, he tried not to stare. The girl with pigtails wore leopard-flecked eyeglasses and wouldn't, not once, look his way. Like him, she got off at the last station, University, and he was happy to see that she too was headed for the Blue Bird shuttle bus to North Campus. He watched her walk toward the waiting bus, then lost sight of her while getting in line to board.

All the seats had been taken, and after he'd come to stand near the back of the bus, he searched for the girl with the pigtails. But she hadn't taken a seat, nor was she standing in front of him or among the people toward the front of the bus, and he finally spotted her sitting on the bench of the shelter outside, waiting for the next empty bus.

Cal never asked women out. He'd tried once or twice in his life, but it hadn't worked. Whatever and whoever he wanted, he thought, could not be obtained directly. He was cursed. He couldn't choose, so instead he let himself be chosen. That's how he'd met Vera; Vera had started talking to him in a bagel shop on Elmwood and had left him her number. But today he was standing at the back of the bus, and the bus would close its doors and start pulling away any moment now. He needed to be at work by nine, and he was already late.

Cal watched the girl waiting outside, and something told him with a clarity he couldn't explain then or later, that if he didn't get off the bus right there and then, he would forever regret it. He fought his way past the bodies blocking the aisle. His knees were shaking, and when he finally had made it to the front and exited the bus, the hardest part was still ahead of him. The girl with the pigtails did not look *nice*. She was beautiful, and she wasn't part of the darkness Vera belonged to, but she was definitely not *nice*. He was late for work and sat down on the bench next to her and asked, "Do you have time for a coffee?"

She turned, her face stern, and answered, "But I don't know you."

And Cal said, "So what?"

Shorat took a piece of paper from her bag, wrote down her name and number, and handed it to Cal. She didn't have time, she needed to get to class, but maybe they could meet another day. On that first date, he told her he had a girlfriend, and she told him she was living with her boyfriend of four years. But six weeks later, two weeks after he'd left Vera and just minutes after her boyfriend had moved out for good, he asked Shorat to marry him. He wore his only suit jacket, got down on his knee and offered her a red rose. And she was still crying because breaking up with someone you'd known for four years wasn't easy, and she said yes.

Chapter 13

The next day he moved from the hotel on Franklin Ave to an Airbnb in Long Beach. He took Vanya and Yuuki to the Marina and felt at home watching the Potemkin-village oil islands rise up a quarter mile off the coast, with their tall cement towers, waterfalls and palms, oleanders and sandalwood trees. At night they shone with bright Vegas-style lights: orange, yellow, red, and blue. LA was exciting, a prickly diva, but Long Beach was ugly enough for Cal to freely love the city. Tankers and freighters from China and around the world lay waiting beyond the breakwater, and on bad days a toxic smell from the port or the oil refineries entered the city. He'd lived here with Shorat for four years and he was giddy now with anticipation, though he couldn't say what he expected to happen. He doubted Shorat had moved down south; something told him that he was wasting his time, and yet, and yet, the smell of seawater, diesel, refuse, sulfur, car exhaust, and dead fish was welcoming him.

The apartment had a balcony overlooking the bike path along the beach, a luxury they hadn't been able to afford back then. But what he loved best about Long Beach was that its memory still held, that nothing had happened in this city that turned his recollections sour.

He wasn't sure why, but his past was never a gentle one. There were people whose minds snipped off the endings of love affairs, the fights with friends, the nasty things that followed the better ones. Cal's mind wouldn't let him forget that most of his friendships and nearly all his love affairs had ended in neglect, or worse, ugliness. And not only those. Books he'd written, projects he'd seen through, plays he'd starred in — had they not ended in heartbreak, harsh words, and disappointment? What was it about him that he couldn't hold on to anything? Even the things he owned turned against him in the end. They witnessed a fight, witnessed him at low points, witnessed his own bad behavior and that of those he'd called friends. They witnessed too much, knew too much, and every time he picked up any of these items, he dropped them quickly enough — he didn't want to be reminded. Cal was only loyal to new friends, new things, never the ones who'd known him for years. He didn't trust relationships that lasted an inordinate amount of time. He knew nothing would last, and so he poured himself into beginnings, the early stages, the honeymoons. When his clothes had burned, his mementos, his desk, a stack of handwritten stories, his computer, his blue sofa, his watches, his photos of past girlfriends and of past friends, his photos of Shorat walking out onto the salt lake; his photos of Shorat naked in a bathroom stall in an artists' building in Toronto, her breasts heavy, her stomach round in those days when they'd first had jobs; his hats, his cartoons, the birthday cards Shorat had drawn for him, the graphic stories she had drawn for him, his shoes, his whiskey glasses, two cans of fresh paint for the deteriorating siding of their house which was nearing the end of its maintenance cycle, his pens; his scarabs he'd bought from a young boy in

Saqqara, whose mangy dog would rub against Cal's pant legs; his glasses, his hearing aids, his electric toothbrush, his underwear, the white shirt Shorat had worn on the day he first met her; the one t-shirt he'd kept from his years in Berlin, his camera; the paintings they had bought together in small galleries while drunk on cheap wine, celebrating their acquisition by having sex in the back of their Ford Escort station wagon off Pico Boulevard; when all this had burnt, he'd felt secretly relieved, and beneath the pain and the urge to remember it all and hold on to the memories until the hour he might leave this planet; beneath the sadness that made him cry loudly in the aisles of Target because there were so many new pens and he could only think about the ones he had lost; beneath the pain he felt relief. His old life had been eradicated, and he was allowed to build a new one in which he could be whoever he chose to be. No witnesses were left. All the lies he could tell about himself were true. All evidence had been turned to ashes.

Later though, he noticed that his bad memories were not replaced by new ones. Holes appeared and grew wider. New things he bought, mainly at Costco because he couldn't face the task of choosing appliances, dishes, silverware, it all seemed so silly; new things he bought didn't attach themselves to him. They failed to register, failed to move him. Even expensive items — furniture, new paintings — barely registered. He had been weighed down by his often oppressive memories, but with only new things surrounding him, he felt as though he was in the early stages of Alzheimer's; the things that no longer existed felt more real than what he could touch and did touch every day. He didn't recognize the items he bought, they seemed to have no value, they were all equally old. He hadn't moved from state to state with them, he hadn't bought them in a Lisbon boutique, in a Tokyo convenience store, in a Cairo market. They were all the same, saying the same exact thing. He was lost.

There was the "before the fire" and the "after the fire." At times, Cal felt certain that his former self had split off and was still continuing on his old path, living in the old house with the woman Shorat had once been. At times he thought he might come home from work and find not the new house they had built together but the old one, and he would walk into that house and find Cal and Shorat from before the fire. They would look at him, maybe invite him in for a drink, but they wouldn't recognize the man Cal had become. They wouldn't understand his jealousy, his anger, they would be bewildered by the ill-fitting clothes he was wearing, the expensive car he was driving, the air of aloofness he couldn't shake. They wouldn't like him very much, though they'd be too polite to say anything on that account. After an hour or two he might no longer insist, he might say his goodbyes. He would leave the old green house and not ever find the new one again. He would never find Shorat again. Because when their house had burnt down, it had also burned down the definitions of who they were. The fire had turned them into new people, people free to choose their own lives. Three years later, Shorat had finally found a thread she felt she needed to follow, and following that thread required her to say that she was going to the grocery store and leave Cal and the dogs and the new house and the backyard full of weeds.

His past was a burden to Cal, but now, that the last person that tied him to that past was gone, he felt so little he grew afraid of himself. He made himself another drink, showered, went out onto the balcony again, but he wasn't sure he was present. Someone was walking in his bare feet out onto the balcony and surveyed the glittering lights of the ships beyond the breakwater, ships sitting on the horizon as though that horizon were a brick wall, but he wasn't sure anymore if the person watching and the person observing the person watching were still the same. The woman on the balcony next to his said, "Would you make me one too?"

It was Lena from the night before, only now she introduced herself as Kathy. She wore a dark-green, silky shirt and bikini shorts, and her hair was longer tonight, reaching down over her shoulders and playing with the open collar of the green shirt. "Take mine," he said and reached over the balustrade, and their fingers met for a brief moment, and then the glass had passed into her hand. She shook herself after the first sip, and he asked. "Not to your liking?"

"It's good," she said, "but strong. Very medicinal."

"It's the bitters," he said. "I'll be right back." And she was still where he had left her when he returned with a drink for himself. That was his test — if she was there when he stepped out onto the balcony again, then she had to be real. Because he knew already what was going to happen. At times he'd met people that had allowed him to look into the future as though it were a memory, and now that he raised his glass and she giggled by way of an answer, the next few hours opened up in front of him like a passageway, and as long as he didn't break the spell by not following the script he was able to read as though it were lying on the small table on his balcony, he could walk out securely into that passageway; Kathy was waiting for him.

"You left Western New York," he said.

They clinked glasses. She smiled, maybe a bit wistfully. "I only ever felt real in New York. I understand the people and I understand their bodies. They aren't pretty, they are not exceptional bodies, but people live in them, they fill out their skin, they are greedy and lusty and during the first days of spring after winters that are always too long, they crowd the streets with their pale bodies full of feelings they have no appropriate names for, but you can see their skin crawl with excitement. I don't understand California. I can't see it. No, I do see it, but I can't feel it, it all sits under glass; I'm at a jeweler's and nothing I reach for I can touch." She held out her small hand, and he leaned over the railing and held it. "But I do like the air, and the cool evenings and the ocean smell."

At her request, he later climbed from his balcony to hers, the gap between them was so tiny, there was hardly any danger of falling to his death at all, and once he had managed to land next to her with something approaching grace and without spilling his drink, she embraced and kissed him, drinking him, biting and pulling his lip, then pushing her tongue deep into his mouth. She got up onto one of her chairs, which were identical to his — up and down the building's façade all balconies and chairs and tables were identical, though no one else was occupying them — and now was triumphantly taller than him, held his face with both her hands, and pushed even deeper.

His hands reached under her shirt, found her small breasts, pulled down her shorts. She was so slim, she didn't weigh anything. Once Kathy's legs had tightened around his waist, he carried her into the apartment, where she told him to undress and lie down on the massage table that stood in the middle of the living room.

"You're still a massage therapist," he said rather stupidly.

"Not anymore. My wrists are too brittle. But once in a while I do friends a favor." She too undressed, walked into the kitchen and returned with a bottle of organic extra virgin olive oil from Greece. "I'm allergic to most other oils." She was naked now except for thick black socks, and she started on his back, moved to his legs, and by the time she was done and told him to turn over, she giggled and closed her hands around his erection. She flicked his nipples feeling him pulse, then spread oil on his chest and poured herself over him.

"You had a pet duck," he said.

"That was a long time ago, before you left me and before I tried to kill myself."

"Yes," he said.

"You sang 99 Luftballons to my duck. That was nice of you."

"You were still living with your parents."

"You were still in love with someone else."

Later, he stood in front of the table, his feet still oily, her body glistening. She lifted her legs, pulled her ass cheeks wide, entered herself with slick fingers. He began to pull off her socks, he needed to see her feet, but she said, "No. Don't. They're ugly."

"Please," he said. "Please." And she finally relented, and he pulled off the black socks. Her feet were tiny, with long toes, and he sucked in Kathy's toes before oiling them as well and putting them around his cock, then pouring oil onto her ass, and she said, "Yes, fuck me in the shitter." Grabbing her feet, she pulled them toward her until both ankles lay crossed behind her head, creating a pillow from which she was able to watch him. It was a feat Cal had never witnessed before. He drizzled more oil onto his cock, pushed deeper still, and her fingers went to work on herself and she made sure he was watching too. She asked him to pull her nipples hard, it was the only way to feel them.

No, harder, she ordered, harder than that, and after she'd come, she pushed him off, she couldn't take it anymore, she said, and she rushed into the bathroom. When she re-emerged, she was wearing the black socks again, and she wiped him with a Clorox wipe, then washed him with water, then dried him with a paper towel, then oiled him again, got on all fours, and said, "The other hole."

Since he hadn't taken the keys to his apartment with him, he climbed over the balcony a second time at five in the morning, after waking up next to Kathy's diminutive body. They'd showered together the night before after drinking champagne in her kitchen. "It wasn't your fault I wanted to die," she'd said and slung her arms around him and kissed him. The champagne glasses were showing smeared prints, their bodies were still silky with oil, and it was good that no carpets covered the blond bamboo floors. She said, "Did you like it?" and he kissed her again.

He walked the dogs, Vanya turning again and again to sniff his legs and feet. They walked into the Gay Ghetto, where Cal and Shorat had lived, and Cal bought two coffees and Raisin Danishes at Broadway Doughnut, and on his return rang Kathy's bell, then knocked on the flimsy door, but nobody opened. He drank both coffees and ate both Danishes as well before brushing his teeth, drawing the curtains, and falling asleep once more.

At seven in the evening, he stood again at Kathy's door ringing the doorbell and knocking on the cheap wood; he hadn't seen her on the balcony. He'd ordered Thai food and it would arrive shortly. He'd also bought more bourbon, more champagne, more wine, more olive oil. A man in his fifties wearing a mask and holding a vacuum cleaner in one hand opened the door. "Yes?" he said. No, there was no Kathy, no, he wasn't the person renting out this apartment, he had been called to clean up, he was really sorry. And as if to show how bad he felt, he let Cal take a quick peek inside. The apartment was exactly as he had left it that morning, minus the massage table, but it felt dead already, as though what had turned it into an apartment had been extracted. The smell of dust and Lysol covered every surface.

That night, more fires erupted all across the state, and by morning the smoke wasn't the diesel exhaust from waiting ships, nor was it the stench coming from the oil refineries to the west. Catalina Island had disappeared from the horizon. It was time for him to move again.

Chapter 14

THE QUESTION OF whether or not to have children had cropped up intermittently. Though his own tubes had been tied a long time ago, other men were donating sperm every day to provide women and couples everywhere with the opportunity to become parents. Cal and Shorat could have adopted, but each time they had seriously considered inviting a child into the life they had formed together, that life seemed to disappear and leave them despondent. Shorat was afraid of growing a child and squeezing it through an opening that seemed too tight and small for that purpose. She was afraid of carrying around an entity that fed on her for nine months. For Cal, the thought of highly regulated days dictated by the screaming needs of a baby, a baby who would then become a walking invitation for disasters, small and big, and grow into a soccer-playing, ice-cream slurping, broccoli-hating, smartphone-abusing pre-teen, was too disorienting to be fully entertained.

After Shorat had turned forty, they had talked less and less about possible offspring, but Shorat, on certain overcast days, at certain times of the mornings, which were difficult to navigate even on the best of days, fell silent in midsentence and stared at her plate or the weed-infested backyard. He knew, because he had pried it from her on previous occasions, that she was thinking of the time after his death when she would still have ten, twenty, thirty years to live. Who would be left then? Who would she talk to? Who would come to help out? In those moments he felt defeated and guilty. He had led her down his path, and of course he wouldn't be around to see her in her oldest age. He would abandon her, it was basic biology. Eight years her senior, Cal stood little chance of accompanying his wife to her grave. He'd isolated her, Annette had been right. He'd done his best to take her away from her family and he had not been able to start their own. Of course she had agreed to this — if she had insisted, he would have taken the plunge and adopted a child — and yet, how selfish to provide Shorat with just himself. He should have offered her more exquisite lovers, more exotic travels, better meals, children, more love, more square footage, more acreage, nicer cars, expensive coiffures — he'd been cutting her hair for over sixteen years — more friends. She had no friends, no friends at all in Northern California. She had been lonely and let him know many times, but academic jobs didn't grow on trees. Of course it was patriarchal nonsense, chauvinistic grandeur, to blame solely himself for Shorat's lack of friends, but in a black wrinkle of his heart, in a wrinkle where Annette was a common guest, he knew he'd wanted it that way. In that wrinkle he knew that he'd never had the confidence to hold onto Shorat or any other woman he desired. Cunning had to stand in for courage; he had to make her smaller in order to fit his life, he had to cut Shorat down to fit his solitude. Only then did he feel safe that she wouldn't leave him. Only then was he certain she wouldn't find him lacking.

After two years of marriage, Cal had suspected Shorat was falling for one of his peers in grad school. She was too friendly, laughed too much when he was around. Back then she had been so shy, she sat quietly through every party, every dinner, every get-together. People thought her rude at times, snobbish, disinterested, but Tad had made her talk, smile, and even got her to tell him about work as a project manager for a company partnering with GM on a hybrid system for its cars. It had pained Cal to see her loosen up, because Tad seemed to have powers he was missing. He started to talk badly about Tad in the small apartment he and Shorat rented on Liberty Street, but she wouldn't have it. She defended him, she defended even his wooden and sentimental writing. For a time, Cal had expected Shorat to run away, or worse, betray him and keep living with him out of sheer convenience. When this fear had faded he couldn't remember. What he did remember was an evening at the small lake not far from town. They had sat together on the dock in darkness, and he'd asked if she still loved him, still was in love with him, or if she wanted to leave. He couldn't recall her answer or if she even had answered at all, but grad school had ended, Tad had moved away, he and Shorat had moved away. Had they moved so Cal would have her to himself? Was that why they had left their jobs and moved to LA during the Great Recession? Was that why they'd moved to New Mexico and moved again to Northern California?

The possibility of having children had slowly evaporated, a problem solved by indecision. By now, Cal had a distaste for younger friends and colleagues who didn't adopt children but needed to see what their own genes might look like. With age, he'd realized how selfishly people behaved, even people who pretended to have a social conscience and were outraged by systemic poverty and the Republican war on social justice, people who recycled, composted, gave money to charity, and spent time with therapists to mine the darkness of their own childhood. No matter how progressive, how politically active — before nature could render sperm and eggs impotent, they went at it, then told everyone around them that they had rediscovered life.

The problem was that the root cause of all the problems the planet faced, from famines and extinction of animal species to garbage patches and climate change — and here he was, heading north under orange fire clouds on the I-5 — was overpopulation. The planet was bursting at the seams, but his friends organized gender-reveal parties in their backyards, baby showers, and then popped out another contribution to global misery. Especially gender-reveal parties irked Cal, because these were held by educated people with enough money to buy pyrotechnic gimmicks that caused wildfires and who were too afraid to say 'sex.' Gender was a social construct, and babies didn't have gender. What they had was sex, biological markers. But the word 'sex' had become too obscene, and those friends of his felt it to be more appropriate to say gender, even though it was ridiculous. They wanted to sound educated, elevated, socially conscious, but they had it all backward. These friends didn't care about climate change at all, and neither did they care about their children's future, because to have a future, the planet needed less humans, not more, and in any case, these friends of Cal had two cars or more, commuted for hours, and polluted this very planet their children would inherit. They did nothing — aside from dropping Greek yogurt containers in the recycle bin — to save the environment. Where did they think all those Pampers went? All those shiny plastic toys? Why did they have babies when they knew for a fact that climate change was burning down California right now, all of it, up and down the coast, plus Oregon and parts of Washington?

Why did they have babies whose output of waste, whose hunger for meat and vegetables, whose need for electricity, gasoline, clothing, picture books, tumblers, milk bottles, and breast pumps, insured that nothing would get better, would make things only ever worse?

The root cause was overpopulation, and nobody did anything against it. Nobody. All the nice gestures toward environmentalism, the memberships to the Sierra Club and NPR, the private vegetable gardens and drip lines, were bound to fail. They only served to make everyone feel good enough not to do anything of importance. We needed fewer people, fewer cars, fewer private residences, less of everything, but that message would not be heard. It had been ignored in the 80s, when Karl had expected to die young of nuclear war or environmental disasters, from acid rain to droughts and famines; it had been forgotten during the 90s and early Aughts; and now it had been warmed up again, because he was driving north on the I-5 and he couldn't open his windows to let any new air in, and the sky looked like the inside of a monster's stomach digesting him and everyone else after devouring the whole state in one swallow. There was no escape, there was no patch of blue sky anywhere, and he didn't have a respirator mask. After walking the dogs at a rest stop somewhere near Visalia, he coughed until his throat was raw.

No, he hadn't denied Shorat and himself children to save the planet, but that didn't excuse his friends who popped them out and did nothing to ensure that their children's lives would be sustainable or just merely possible. What were they hoping for? Some odd miracle cure for environmental damage? Some miracle weapon to freeze the polar caps back into shape? Children were not the answer because the parents hadn't even asked the right questions, not ever, not one single fucking time. Instead of breathing new life into this one earth we all shared, the only one we had, the only one we had, the only one, they gave more death. Giving life to their drooling offspring — and ooh, they looked like Daddy, say Daddy, Mommy, say Mommy — they made life on this one earth, the only one we had, impossible.

His house still stood. Cal hadn't consulted the newest fire maps and forecasts, but when he rolled down Hemlock Street, the neighborhood appeared largely unchanged if you forgot about the deep-orange sky above. Maybe because of that unchanged appearance, Cal felt like a stranger and was nearly speechless when his garage door opener worked and revealed an empty garage. Shorat had not returned and what was this house without her?

After letting the dogs out into the yard, he switched on the air purifiers again. It was some time in the afternoon, what time exactly you couldn't tell, there wasn't light enough. There hadn't been light enough since he'd left Long Beach. The house smelled of smoke, but after an hour, the purifiers and the AC took the sting out of his nose and throat. He lubed his eyes yet again, sat on the sofa, the dogs now sniffing their beds as though they'd forgotten they'd ever slept on them, and stared into the brown-orange skies. Because he was dead tired, and because he had mixed himself a drink whose color looked a lot like the sky, he felt calm spreading through his limbs, vacuuming his mind until there was no dog hair, no bread crumbs, no thought of paying bills and the coming semester left. There was quiet, and he missed Kathy's kind obscenity just enough to hum Jane Siberry, and the vibrations of his voice further calmed him. Vanya jumped onto the couch to be petted and then fell asleep next to him. Cal's body drained of all its edges, knots, hardened muscles, excrements, bones, tissue, until he was featherlight, so featherlight he couldn't explain why he wasn't floating toward the ceiling. The humming continued even after he had stopped humming, and he sat and stared at the sky while California was burning to the ground around him.

Shorat in Kyoto

She's wearing a thick, colorful robe in the small hotel room after we have returned from the bath off the lobby on the first floor. She looks regal and relaxed. Behind her, buildings are dotted with lights while the sky is clinging to the last hints of the day. I took the photo with Shorat's Nikon; her robe is opening below her tummy revealing a bit of leg. Childlike wonder makes her beam, and we're drinking sake and eating sushi from the Seven-Eleven down the block. Before the trip, we went to REI and bought backpacks and warm layers. Every day we're discarding a pair of underwear and socks — our backpacks are getting lighter. We're smoking cigarettes on our walks around the city, careful to collect the stubs and discard them properly; we try noodle shops almost every day. There is so much to discover, we have little time to think about ourselves. Our eyes and ears are so full, we forgive each other every moment of impatience or neglect. Shorat beams at me and says something I have forgotten.

Chapter 15

Drink and heartburn ruined his night hours, and waking up to a sky full of smoke that kept the sun from shedding any light left him disoriented. His sinuses burnt angrily. Shorat's absence, maybe for the first time, felt permanent. She wouldn't return. He'd known right away, he now believed, even before he'd left town, even before he'd gotten into the car to drive to the grocery store and getting rear-ended, even before then. She was gone and would stay gone if he didn't make her appear again.

I can't make her appear unless I myself become visible again, he thought, and this made sense to him, though when he looked more closely at what it might entail, he couldn't say. I have to live as though she'll never be back. I have to live as though she's gone forever. I don't have to forget Shorat, but she won't ever recognize me again if I stay hidden behind my love for her. There's a chance that nothing I do will make me visible to her again; my actions might lead me to new places where we can't and won't meet. In the end, this means death. If I want to be reborn, I have to undo the old and rebuild. But there is so little left of me. What kind of foundation can I build with what's left of who I am and have been?

Work kept him occupied and tight-brained for the next two days. Emails full of paranoia and shards of anxious rhetoric snapped him out of his melancholy but produced nothing but anger, hectic activity at the keyboard, an endless cocktail accompanying him around the house. The smoke forced him to stay inside. The dogs grew restless without walks, Cal grew restless without walks, and on Thursday afternoon, a week after Shorat had left him, the air quality index was at 298. He was overwhelmed by the feeling that he did not want to start anew, that he indeed liked his house just fine, and despite feeling and sounding like a chain-smoker at midnight, he now believed California suited him. He was still a stranger, but wasn't that part of the appeal, an accomplishment even? He'd given up his home country, he'd gladly given it up and resisted becoming a citizen in his adopted country. He loved to feel adrift, or better, to feel as though he could change plans at a moment's notice. The Stork, friends had called him back in Berlin, because he only ever put one foot down while pondering his next step. He and Shorat had moved often, never quite satisfied with what and who they found in the places they settled in before his career or the desire to be somewhere else whisked them away again.

Could he become someone new if he stayed where he was? How he hated and looked down upon people who stayed where they were. Those people were his parents and their friends who settled down after landing a decent job, had kids, went on vacation once a year, and died at fifty-one of cancer. Grown men with toy trains in the basement and home improvement projects every weekend, women who berated their husbands once everyone was inebriated enough to loosen up a bit. They died early, and the partners they left behind married widows and widowers, took on more kids and more mortgages and stayed perfectly the same, getting smaller every day, finding God and giving up booze and staying put in the small town where they didn't have to explain anything, because the whole town had witnessed their deaths, their toy trains, their cancer, their second and their third marriages.

This smallness Cal had sought to escape, but how well had his plan worked out? Was his life so vastly different from the one his parents had led? His expectations of what life should be had exceeded those of his family, but how far had he come? He was the chair of the English Department, writing books and teaching writing and literature at a regional college instead of being the head of the dessert department at a large regional dairy plant. Inside their heads, Cal and his father might see different reflections of the world, but in that outside world, would a hypothetical onlooker spot the differences? The house, the yard, the marriage — they didn't look so vastly dissimilar. Northern California did not resemble the flat fields of Northern Germany, and yet, Santa Rosa had maintained its rural character, and inside his subdivision, the architectural styles didn't reveal anything about Cal's precise location. The view from his back patio didn't scream, "California!" All too often, when walking Yuuki and Vanya through the neighborhood, he had the distinct feeling of being nowhere at all.

If he settled down and stayed in this city, would he finally become his father, the man who had insisted on taking Cal's girlfriends out for walks and who put his arm around them, hugged them, kissed them; the man who'd asked his son to spend time alone with Shorat and whom Cal had cut out of his life thereafter? The man who was now in his eighties and suffered from macular degeneration and could barely see or read anymore, the latter only with the help of a strong loupe; the man who'd suffered a stroke and been diagnosed with stomach cancer? Maybe Cal was truly different from that man, but why did their lives resemble each other so much from the outside? Cal's ambitions, looking back at them, felt so ordinary — only good enough for replicating the life he'd meant to outgrow. He hadn't dreamed big enough, obscenely enough, ruthlessly enough. He hadn't dreamed viciously enough to escape the middle-class, middle-class morals, a middle-class level of education and a lifestyle that might allow him a few good years after he'd finally retire. That he lived with a wife of twenty years in a house in a subdivision of a mediocre, mid-sized city not in his home country but a foreign country he had entered at age thirty, did that count in his favor? Did that make him different enough not to die of some cancer or other?

Maybe he'd never tried hard enough to advance in his career, maybe Cal had only wanted to belong. Acting in Berlin had been about community and the right to sit with people you loved and admired in cafes along dirty streets in Kreuzberg and Neukölln; about following a woman home to her apartment and rehearse a specific scene for a workshop and make love to that woman sometime later, after she had fixed them a tomato salad, fruit flies settling on the rim of the bowl, the big spoons, the plates; about finding stretchmarks on her breasts and loving them, about kissing the dirty soles of her feet, and about seeing her the next morning on the stage of that small theater where the workshop met for a week, and play that rehearsed scene and forgetting for the ten minutes they shared the stage, with everyone else watching from below, that he knew that woman at all, forgetting her legs and breasts and the way she kept her eyes half-closed while he was moving his mouth along her hands and arms, and seeing a very different woman and feeling himself be changed into somebody he barely recognized and yet intimately knew.

After his dreams of the stage had faltered, withered, taken too many hits for Cal to recover, he'd returned to university, but studying literature had not been enough. He'd tried his hand at writing stories himself, because again, he wanted to feel he'd earned a small spot among the people whose work he devoured while riding the yellow subway trains, sitting on green vinyl or blue vinyl benches while the wheels screamed in their tracks at every turn; he wanted to live among the writers he admired, not study them from afar. He wanted to perform his stories at small events and that woman with short hair and miner's hat approach him later and ask him to sign her book, and by the way, some of her friends would be meeting soon at a nearby bar and would he care to join them? Writing, like acting, Cal perceived as his portal into a world safe from cancer, mortgages, toy trains, and drunken parties in the backyard gazebo. After coming to Buffalo and starting to write in English for the first time, making up sentences in a language he'd been learning for years but had never used in artistic ways, and after making it to Michigan and after publishing his first book, a dark and nasty novella, he'd seemed to have stepped through that portal into a world where toy trains and groping the neighbor's wife while your own wife was being groped by that neighbor, where plaid acrylic shirts and socks in sandals, where perms and bike rides with the whole family did not exist. The portal, after stepping through it, had closed and allowed Cal to feel safe, safer than he ever had. Yet after the first two successful books, the market had moved elsewhere, or no, he had moved elsewhere, because how many books that were different yet felt exactly the same could Cal write? The market had not followed him, the interest had waned. He'd landed a good position at a regional college in New Mexico and then a better position at a better regional college in California. And it seemed as though the landscape he had once stepped into through that portal also had a back door, and what Cal found behind that door was not a community of artists but a community of little-known scholars and writers full of resentment over not landing a position at a first-rate research university. The well was poisoned and the taste of the water middle-class.

If that hypothetical observer of lives were to take a look at Cal now and compare him to his father, would Cal be able to convince him that he indeed had turned out differently? Would trips to Japan, Egypt, Portugal and Mexico count? Would the books he'd written count? Would the women he'd known and loved testify for him? Would his friends side with him and lobby that observer?

No, nothing Cal had done could hide how thin his life was, his soul a half-eaten lozenge. No amount of work and obsessions could hide the loneliness which lurked just beyond the noise, beyond his CV, beyond the clipped sentences in his stories. He'd lured Shorat into that loneliness, fooled her for twenty years. But she had finally discovered what he had feared all his life, that there was nothing to him. His looks had helped him for a while, but at fifty-four those looks ran stale. No, nothing more interesting had emerged over the years; he was stuck where he'd lived his whole life — afraid of being alone, unknown, unrecognized, unloved. He'd chosen isolation to preempt what he feared most, and Shorat had been his willing companion. Now she had finally grown into herself, she had changed in this last year, he'd been able to see it. She had grown a new face, developed a new gait, a new body, nothing reminded him of the shy girl he'd met at the bus stop in Buffalo in the last year of the previous millennium. She was her own person. She didn't fade and become less, instead she cut away the parts that had never suited her and grew and polished the ones that were truly hers. He loved this silent and stark transformation, but he hadn't been able to keep up.

Where would he start? What could he do to reach her again? And would either of them be able to recognize the other? Love each other? Or would his own growth mean that he would even lose the memories of her, his love for Shorat, his wish to come home to her sitting bent over the work table coloring one of her patterns with a devotion that struck him as nearly religious? Was he ready to give up on the nostalgia for having coffee with Shorat every morning on their brown leather sofa, her face knitted and grouchy on most days until after they'd listened to the news and had their second cup? Was he willing to forget her bumping him in the grocery store, gently, one arm around his waist, looking with him at all the candy options? Was he willing to forget Shorat?

CHAPTER 16

HE CALLED THEIR REALTOR in the morning. Chloe's voice sounded as though she had been waiting for this conversation ever since the night their house had burned down. They'd almost become friends once, but the moment had passed; their lives didn't overlap. Now she asked how he was, had he bought enough air purifiers? And yes, she was praying the fires wouldn't hit Santa Rosa again. After these first pleasantries, her tone suddenly changed, and in an excited, conspiratorial stage whisper, she asked, "So, what did you forget?"

"Forget?" The question perplexed him, his mind went blank.

"Yes, did your lovely wife forget something? I just got off the phone with her. Did she give me the wrong date? I'm really sorry you're selling, but I understand. It must have been strange to move back into the same neighborhood."

"Oh," Cal said, swallowed. "Yes, yes it was weird." The shock turned his mouth dry, and for several awkward moments he cleared his throat, coughed, apologized. What he didn't say was that his fears about moving back to the spot where the old house had burned had proved unfounded. He'd expected nightmares, anxiety seeping into his dreams like formaldehyde, but no, the new house had welcomed them, felt protective of them. They had slept soundly from the very beginning.

Maybe sensing his unease, Chloe filled the silence. "And your contractor. Did you see they booked him and his wife and daughter for fraud? It made me so happy, maybe there's justice after all."

Cal slowly recovered, said empty lines about no hard feelings, about how he had worked around the builder's bankruptcy and how they'd got lucky because he'd had the summer off and had organized the rest of the rebuild himself. "No, I'm sure Shorat covered it all. I just wanted to make sure you didn't need anything extra from me."

"No, not right now. You both have to sign later, of course, but I still have your emails, so all's good."

"Will you come and take pictures of the house?" he asked.

"No, the ones you guys took are marvelous."

"Oh, I'm glad." Cal's ears and mouth were full of flies, he couldn't hear or speak. Shorat had prepared her departure for a long time. She had taken pictures after cleaning, after rearranging, after he'd left the house to walk Kurt or get tomatoes and cucumbers at Costco.

"The resolution is incredible," Chloe said. "They'll be up tomorrow or Monday."

He coughed again, had to drink some water, poured it down the wrong pipe. "It's nice to be working with you again," he finally said.

"So where are you going?" Her voice dropped again to a whisper. "Shorat was a bit, um, vague about the details. Is it the job, the fires, the president?"

Cal wondered just how vague Shorat had been. "A bit of everything," Cal said. "After a few years we always get antsy." Had Shorat mentioned at all that she and Cal hadn't seen each other in a week, that he didn't even know where she was?

"I hope you find what you're looking for. You guys are so, you know, artsy, cool. I always loved working with you."

"Same here," he said. "So what *did* she tell you?" He hoped he didn't sound too awkward, too probing. But Chloe didn't miss a beat.

"Oh, just that you wanted to explore some more, that some opportunities had come up. And I didn't want to pry, she was a bit shy about it."

"She's pregnant," Cal said, not knowing where he took his words from, which script he was reading. "We want to be closer to her folks. The kid should have grandparents."

"Oh my god." Chloe made the phrase sound like one word. "I'm so excited for you guys."

"Don't tell her I told you," he said. "She's a bit superstitious, and it came, I mean, this happened, you know, it came out of nowhere. Kind of a miracle. So she's a bit spooked. Happy, but spooked."

"Okay, got it. I won't say a word. Oh my God, that's such great news. I always thought you would make great parents."

Cal thanked her, though he couldn't imagine why anyone might think such a thing, and he doubted very much that Chloe had taken the time to imagine that scenario before this very call.

"So you need a bigger house, or...?"

"A place without fires, without earthquakes, without madness, if possible." He didn't name the president. Chloe was a conservative, and though she wouldn't argue with a client, there was no point in pushing the issue, no convincing possible. It seemed that the time for debate and exchanging arguments, changing viewpoints, changing minds, had largely ceased to exist. It was us versus them all the time, and every small issue became a focal point in the fight for and against what was left of democracy. Whether or not to wear a mask during the pandemic became a question of whether or not you stood with the racist, xenophobic, authoritarian president.

"I hear you," Chloe said. "Well, don't leave before you've met my husband. We'll have you over, masks and all." Chloe's husband was ill, suffering from a disease Chloe had never explained. He couldn't work anymore, and going out wasn't an option. Even though they'd met with Chloe socially for a few months, she had never invited them to her house. Every time they'd seen Chloe at a party in Kenwood or a dinner in Rincon Valley, she dished up yet another excuse why the husband couldn't make it.

"Of course." Cal thanked her, hung up, stared at the walls which had immediately ceased to feel like home. In the five or ten minutes of his call, the house he so intimately knew had lost its meaning. It had happened so fast, it left him dizzy and heartbroken. The past was never the past, it could be changed at any moment, without notice, build-up, or warning. No, unless he took out a second mortgage, he would not be able to afford buying out Shorat. He'd lose this place. And where was she? Where had she be calling from? That she hadn't told Chloe about the separation filled him with hope, and yet that feeling only lasted a minute or two. Shorat wasn't one to confide in people — not mentioning how things stood meant nothing. What alarmed Cal was that she hadn't even sent him an email or text about putting the house on the market; she expected him to go along with it because he had no other options.

He walked out onto his small porch, sat down on the concrete stairs and let smoke fill his lungs. The sun was orange even though it had risen over his neighbor's house; the haze blurred the properties at the end of his street. Shorat was destroying his life and she had every right to do so. He was outraged on the surface of his mind; anger over having been blindsided made him close his eyes and shake his head, but below the commotion he was neither surprised nor alarmed. His life was breaking apart, and the call to Chloe hadn't changed anything, only confirmed the obvious. The question was, would he stay in the area, keep his job, endure the pity of his colleagues and teach classes until his heart gave out in the middle of a lecture about point of view?

He could leave California, he could leave the States and live in Portugal, France, Italy, try his luck there. The sale of the house would net enough to allow him to live for two or three years without a steady income if he was careful; the world stood suddenly open. Cal blinked, inhaled the smoke deeply and thought about his options. Too much static made it difficult to concentrate. One moment he was overcome with sadness, the next panic quickened his breath. If he left today, before the semester had even started, a meagre pension would kick in, making it possible to live maybe an extra year without having to find a job. But what would he do? Was there anything he desired more than the life he already had?

That night he dreamed of Berlin again, about the apartment he still rented, the one he'd forgotten about. He owed several months' worth of money, but he still had his keys, and the mail was still delivered to his door and dropped through the slot onto his hall carpet. Through all these years living in the States, he'd kept that tiny apartment on the fifth floor of the old building, looking out on trees and, beyond the foliage, more apartment buildings. He only had a few briquettes left but got the coal-burning oven going, and soon it was cozy, warm enough to take off his coat and sit by the window and think about why he'd been gone so long.

The dream came in its habitual gray and yellow tones. Cal's dreams were black and white on most nights, but when he ventured back to Berlin, the palette changed to accommodate his feelings of dread and longing. This dream also developed, progressing like an alternate life he was leading. At times, Cal thought of sleep as a portal, a giant slot machine that dropped him in one or the other life. In one recurrent dream he went to high school again, trying desperately to finish his degree after flunking math repeatedly, though he wasn't young anymore. Over the years, Cal, in that particular dream, had aged and now looked at his life in horror. He was fifty-four and still living with his parents in the small northern German town of his childhood. He still lived in the room he'd grown up in and clung to the hope that soon, soon, he would move out and get his own apartment.

Another dream, one he hadn't visited in years, but which still lurked within him, just out of reach, was that of learning how to fly. At first he had flailed, catapulting himself into the sky to the point where coming back to earth meant certain death, but then he had learned to breathe in the right manner, avoid panicking, and instead lift himself off the ground with a peculiar cunning and grace he lacked in real life. Once he'd mastered the ability to fly without disappearing into the clouds and beyond, he'd often awoken believing he might truly levitate after stepping onto the cold floor in front of his bed. Soon after, the dream had been mothballed, his mind had pursued other nightly lives.

Berlin, though, Berlin had survived and prospered. Cal, in this dream, had lost sight of Shorat, though how he couldn't fathom. Sadness colored the situation once he'd lit the coal-burner and taken a seat overlooking trees and apartment buildings. He couldn't return to the States, he couldn't remember Shorat's address, and no matter how hard he tried, couldn't convince his fingers to punch in the right phone number. His adult life had vanished and he was back where he had started, in the city that had once meant home but now felt nightmarishly small, provincial, dirty, and desolate.

Each time he had dreamt this life, he'd come closer to finding and talking to his wife, and then one day he did talk to her, but she refused returning to him. She wasn't mad because of a fight they'd had, not disappointed in him. Her tone was loving and detached. He watched Shorat speak, watched her lovely figure move, and the yellow tones darkened until he could feel her warmth. He was in love and upset. He hadn't been enough for her, she said, she was done with him.

Tonight, though, he slipped back into his Berlin life to advance its story. He was in the arms of another woman, the woman he loved until, after some time, he pulled away and recognized that he'd mistaken her for Shorat. No, not mistaken — he'd believed this woman could replace his wife. He had sought to forget it wasn't her. Now however, holding her at arm's length, the face wasn't Shorat's, the body wasn't hers. He'd fooled himself. All the warmth he'd felt left him, and he rushed out of his apartment to search for his wife. Yet down in the courtyard, hoarse voices coming from an open window above him, he realized once again that he was stuck in Berlin and his flying suitcase had been burned. He'd never be able to return home to California.

What lingered in the morning was not the memory of Berlin, but the knowledge that Shorat had not left him in a fit of anger or at the spur of the moment. She had taken her time to get everything in order. She had acted without haste. Even while living together through the pandemic, cooking meals together or running through the neighborhood most every morning, she had planned her exit. That knowledge hung about the house like the smell of burnt toast. Making coffee for himself and watching the dogs stand in the yard, looking curiously into the haze from the fires that the sun couldn't pierce, the finality of Shorat's decision stopped his breathing and he had to sit down and wait for the sobs to ebb and subside. By then his coffee had gone cold, and he drank it anyway, and after a call to the university, he retrieved the black and yellow storage boxes from the garage and began to pack.

There wasn't much he could lay claim to; most of their belongings he found to be pleasant and wouldn't remember within two weeks of not seeing them. He took a box of watches, enough shirts and pants and underwear and socks to last him a week. In the end, what he thought he needed wasn't much more than what he'd packed for his trip to Los Angeles. Car title, extra pairs of shoes, several memory sticks, two flashlights, a knife, a lighter, two hats, two knit caps, two baseball caps, several running outfits, his M-65 coat, his denim jacket, copies of his books. The rest of what was left in the house filled him with disdain. He couldn't remember the person who'd bought furniture, carpets, light fixtures, and appliances. The last thing he squeezed into his SUV was the coffee maker. Then Cal put spare keys into a padded envelope, addressed it to Chloe, and put it in the mailbox.

For the next two days he talked to retirement specialists, his dean, two colleagues, to his doctor, his vet, to his audiologist. He saw the ad for his house go up on Redfin and Trulia, and long before Chloe had a chance to plan an open house, he put Yuuki and Vanya in the back of his car, pulled out of his garage, and turned toward the highway.

Chapter 17

What he felt was his left leg aching, the food from the drive-thru igniting his stomach, his right arm falling asleep, his eyelids gaining weight. Yuuki was quietly asleep, Vanya still fighting the large dose of travel pills, poking up his head but unable to keep his eyes open. They were long past Reno and Cal hadn't spotted a town since Lovelock, so when signs announced their arrival in Winnemucca, he pulled off the highway and checked into the Super 8. The site lay to the south of the fancier motels, away from the noise and all-night brightness of truck-stops. People in the parking lot loading and unloading their vehicles didn't wear masks, but inside the foyer Cal was happy to greet covered faces. He received the room key, dropped off his travel bag, then led the dogs outside and walked with them along the Winnemucca cemetery — many people seemed to have lived and died in this town he hadn't known about, a thought that scared Cal —and toward the KFC on Winnemucca Boulevard, where he later, after returning the dogs to their room, bought them all dinner. They shared chicken tenders and fries, and only the mashed potatoes he kept for himself. Vanya, still drowsy but excited about the food, slobbered all over himself before falling asleep on the bed. The television was turned to a baseball game, functioning as a window into the world when the actual window in Cal's hotel room revealed nothing. He didn't want to die in Winnemucca. Right here on the bed with his dogs, his biggest fear was dying in Winnemucca and being interred in the cemetery down the street. Nobody would ever find him here. Nobody would remember him. Then he thought of Shorat.

For the first time in months he felt that odd diminishment of being in a place that didn't know him. Even though he had little illusion about his own importance in the world, his house, his work, and even Santa Rosa, afforded him the feeling of being seen and recognized. Some people would notice his absence; his inbox was already filling with emailed questions about why he was leaving his job. Everything he owned, even the things he hadn't considered packing, all confirmed that he was, indeed, alive. Chloe, once she came to arrange the house and remove unnecessary or unwanted items, would feel his and Shorat's presence lingering. But if he died in this motel room, Winnemucca wouldn't turn its head. His dogs would be thrown in the pound, he would be buried in a shallow grave without anyone saying a final word. Then he thought of Shorat.

Since he couldn't know where she was and where she wanted to be, he allowed himself to follow his instincts. That's how they'd met — he had lived thirty-three years on two continents in haphazard fashion to finally meet her at the shuttle bus near Buffalo's University station. What had been the chances of it ever happening, or of him noticing her? Of him talking to her? While many times since leaving Santa Rosa he'd scolded himself for not having a better plan, he believed that only chance could bring them together a second time. There was no guarantee, there was no true method, but if he lived the way he felt he needed to, then maybe he would see Shorat again. His call to Chloe had given him hope, despite receiving the news that his wife had long turned against their shared life. Shorat had called only moments before he'd picked up the phone. Maybe their connection wasn't lost. Yes, it was silly to bank on what was surely coincidence, but it was better to believe in coincidence and chance than to stay in a town Shorat had already left. Cal was entirely certain that his wife had placed the call to Chloe from someplace else in the country. He couldn't be sure if he was inching closer toward her now or widening the gap between them, and he would doubt himself every hour of every day for however long it took to see his wife again, but he'd continue moving.

The dogs woke him in the middle of the night, their usual rhythm upended by car ride and drugs. Outside the motel, the noise from the highway was still audible, the parking lot glaringly white. He wished for cigarettes; he and Shorat had always smoked during their long trips together until an eye-doctor had told him that this could contribute to macular degeneration, the condition Cal's father was suffering from. As a Northern European, his eyes were prone to that condition, the doctor had said, and Cal hadn't touched a cigarette since. Only once, but he didn't want to think about that.

In the morning, Cal raided the paltry buffet and fed Yuuki and Vanya biscuits, waffles, and sausages stiff with salt. The coffee was bad but did the job of giving him the jitters. He was ready for another day on the road. They stopped near the Bonneville Salt Flats and Cal took a selfie, posted it on Instagram in black and white. It was his first post in a week; he'd checked that Shorat was no longer following him, but that didn't mean she wouldn't take a peek occasionally. His was not a private account. He'd leave a trail, like Hansel and Gretel, and maybe Shorat would pick up on it. Or would she avoid him if she checked? The quandary took forty-five minutes, and in the end he decided once again that he couldn't allow himself to think about what Shorat might or might not do. By then he'd deleted and reposted the photo of him in front of the white expanse several times.

Shorat on the Salt Lake

This one pictures Shorat during our first road trip, a few months before our wedding and right before my move to Michigan. We drove 6,200 miles in ten days, and on our way back to Buffalo were interrogated separately by US customs agents at the Canadian-American border. She was born in Iran, I was born in Germany — why were we traveling together, the agents wanted to know.

The photo shows her in a white shirt with spaghetti straps; she's wearing my Ray-Bans to shield her eyes from the sun. Shorat is rail-thin, her face wide and strong-jawed. There are only a few pictures among all those I have taken, in which I captured more than her lovely face or her figure. On this day, she's playful, awkward, self-conscious. She doesn't know me yet and feels at liberty to try on different selves. She is trying a new pose in every new town to challenge me. What I capture is Shorat trying to fit me into her life, trying to fit her body into the new role of soon-to-be wife. Shorat is laughing, she is still a stranger, the stranger I love and fear and who's decided to become my wife without knowing who I might turn out to be. Yes, I fear her because I have made my intentions known. The moment I asked her out for coffee, I lost control of the situation.

When I look at my selfie in front of the Salt Flats, I only recognize my age.

The night they spent in Rock Springs. He'd continued on despite getting tired and moody, because he remembered the short story of the same name. Rock Springs, he imagined, looked nothing like the town it had once been, but despite staying in another Super 8 and calling a local pizza joint for delivery, his spirits lifted. He'd picked up a six-pack of beer, and getting drunk while feeding pizza to the confused and tired dogs made him inexplicably happy. For this night, he took leave of his life and turned into a fictional character with fictional dogs and a fictional pizza. Anything was allowed to happen, though nothing much ever happened in Rock Springs.

Near midnight, a knock on his door was repeated, repeated again before he had a chance to find a shirt and pants.

"I thought it was you when I saw your name on the registration slip."

"Oh?" he said, and spent the next two minutes tearing Yuuki and Vanya away from the door. Making sure he had his key, he stepped into the hallway.

She walked ahead toward that side entrance he'd used earlier — by now he was a connoisseur of side entrances — and soon they were at the far end of the parking lot, where somebody had placed an old rusty picnic table and a few crooked chairs. She pulled out a pack of cigarettes and offered.

He shook his head. "Can't do that."

She pulled out a cigarette for herself, lit it with a green Bic. "I think I wouldn't have recognized you if I hadn't read your name first."

"That bad?"

She squinted, maybe because of the smoke. "Not bad. Not really. Very different."

"You see me all the time in my dreams."

"You look different when you are asleep. Softer, more fragile. In your dreams I can never hold on to you, and yet you never leave."

Cal inhaled the smoke, was on the verge of asking Sophie for a cigarette, then thought better of it. "How old is your son now?"

"Sascha is twenty. I got pregnant the year you got married. Funny, isn't it?" Her laughter had always been a bit vulgar, had always confused him. Was the real Sophie the soft-spoken, loving woman, or the loud, loutish one she became when she was around friends, drinking and enjoying the attention of men, men that had nothing in common with Cal?

"Paulina lives in LA now," he said. "I saw her last week. She's painted pictures of our old photos."

"Oh God." More laughter drove the smoke from her lungs, and she coughed and turned away until she could breathe again, her eyes watery now.

"It was upsetting to see them."

"You were so young. I'm sorry for what happened."

"For what you did?"

"For what happened. You were an active participant, though sometimes I get sentimental and start missing you. Sascha."

"What about him?"

"Never mind." She stubbed out the half-smoked cigarette, lit a new one. "She's left you, hasn't she?"

"Word travels fast." He pulled the sturdiest of the chairs onto the asphalt and sat down. The air was full of Diesel and shallow breaths, full of dew and odd yearnings. Sophie wore flats, and the little toe on her right foot poked out. It curled over the adjacent toe; years earlier she had been thinking about amputating it, a doctor's recommendation. "What are you doing in Wyoming?"

"Driving through." She pointed to something behind her. "Helmut was invited to a conference in Chicago, and we decided to make it a vacation. "Sascha is studying at UCLA, so that's where we're headed."

"And you saw my registration slip?"

There was this laugh again; he meant to smell her breath, a mix of fried food, chewing gum, whiskey, and cigarette smoke. "I thought I saw you with two dogs. I asked at the reception."

"So you did recognize me?"

"I couldn't be certain, but the manager was nice." She still wore her hair in Eighties' fashion, though not asymmetrical anymore. It was very fine, sparser than he remembered. She had turned sixty-one this year.

"Where's Helmut?"

"Asleep. Sitting in the car tires him." She took a chair and pulled it opposite of Cal's. Sophie was wearing a sundress, no sleeves. The large, silvery pendant of her necklace swung forward while she lit a third cigarette. She kicked off her flats and put her feet in his lap. He didn't dare touch them, not yet. After Sophie, he had never again tried to get back with a girlfriend he'd left, or who had left him. It didn't work, couldn't work. The betrayals, the warmed-up passion. He remembered the night he'd tried for the last time, walking down Turmstraße to her apartment, where they had lived together for a while, the apartment they'd rented together, furnished together, though he wasn't the one she'd made love to first in their bedroom. He'd been certain that this time it would work, that this last time was the right time to get her back. Sophie had let him in, had made love to him without a word, and only later told him that she was no longer taking the pill. He hadn't blamed her, simply hadn't understood; she was seeing another man by then, a lawyer she worked for. Why had she stopped taking the pill? Why hadn't she told him before making love? A few weeks later she called him with the news that she was pregnant, and he accompanied her to the abortion clinic. She cried the whole time in the taxi to the clinic. "Do you really want me to give it up?" she asked. Maybe it had been his child. Maybe it had been his.

"You were like a soft rain," she said, her chin raised, blowing smoke away from him. He recognized that gesture, that way of talking to somebody in front of you while looking sideways. They had rehearsed it together, back when he had been seventeen and she twenty-four. "So soft, I never got wet."

"Yes, that's what you told me."

"I wanted to take a hammer and drive a nail into your forehead, it was so high."

"And you hated when my hips got wider than yours and I couldn't wear your pants anymore."

"I hated when you wore my clothes."

"But you liked putting make-up on me."

"For a while. But you liked it too much."

"Are you happy?" he asked, finally putting his fingers around the sole of one foot. The toes were awfully short, like fat little children. He immediately missed Shorat's long, even feet. "How has life treated you?"

The laughter didn't last this time, and a new bitterness crept into it. Or was she mocking him? "I can't complain," she said before blowing more smoke into the night air.

He didn't ask if she loved her husband, since he'd long ago decided that he wouldn't believe either answer. They'd been staying together for thirty years, proof that they shared enough to get into bed together and forgive the other's slackening neck, loosening arms, the small pains and slowing movements. If you could forgive these signs that you were well on your way toward your grave, you had enough in common to stay until you attended the funeral. Cal had never liked Helmut, not even before he'd started sleeping with Sophie.

"I've read your books."

"You did?"

"Wasn't really sure what to make of them. I guess some people find that sort of thing interesting. Are you chasing after her?" She was on her fifth cigarette.

"You can't chase somebody who has disappeared," he said. "What is your son majoring in?"

"Political science. He wants to be a lawyer like his dad."

"Like his mom."

Her laughter broke midway, and ash dribbled onto her dress. "It was your child."

He didn't say anything but kept his hand around her foot, bending her toes backward.

"No, it wasn't," she said. "But I was hoping it was. I wanted it to be."

He kept quiet, watching her lips quiver, her face losing its resolve.

"Let's go." She pulled away her feet, stepped into her flats and stomped onto her half-smoked cigarette. She'd never been a graceful walker; he watched her crossing the parking lot on short, sturdy legs, then holding the door open for him. She slung one arm around him before he could enter the hallway, pulled him close, pressed her lips against his. He acquiesced, pushed her dress up and ran his hands over her belly, her buttocks. He unzipped her dress and slid a hand between fabric and skin, both warm, both soft, smelling the same at this moment. Something, maybe a sound in her throat, maybe the sound of feet on gravel, maybe the air brakes of a truck passing in the distance, made Cal hesitate for a second, and in that second, whatever he had thought might happen next became impossible. He pulled away, walked quickly through the door into the hallway of the Super 8.

"Such a soft rain," Sophie said in his back, and he heard the zipper of her dress. "But it was yours." He didn't look back, though. He didn't look back. He ran toward his room, pulled out the key with trembling fingers, and there were his dogs, his dogs. There were Yuuki and Vanya, and it would take days to get rid of the smell of fried foods, whiskey, chewing gum, and cigarette smoke, and he wished he'd made love to Sophie one more time and he wished he'd never kissed her. He wished for the purity of Lysol and Clorox and bathroom tiles. He wished for fresh sheets and more soap and for his nose to be swabbed with alcohol. He wished he'd never set foot in Berlin, he wished he could burn down his memories the way the fires had destroyed his home. If only he'd taken Sophie to his room.

Chapter 18

After tossing for an hour, he packed his things and led the dogs to the car. By noon they were in Cheyenne, in another parking lot of another fast-food chain. Yuuki and Vanya had no green space to poop on, and Vanya barked incessantly despite the drugs, despite being hardly able to keep his head up. On the spur of the moment, Cal looked up dog-friendly bed & breakfasts, found one near the Frontier Days Old West Museum, called ahead, and fifteen minutes later pulled into a graveled parking lot. He paid the outsized dog deposit, and yes, they had something ready, he could move right in.

The room was conveniently located in the carriage house and one of only two, each having its own entrance. He took the dogs for a short walk, made sure Vanya pooped twice, then fed them, drew the curtains, and went to bed. His last thought before falling asleep was that if someone were ever to break into his brain and image all the recorded moments of his life, his thoughts and impressions, they'd never suspect how much he had loved his wife. His love was so outsized, maybe he'd drowned her in it.

Vanya woke him, pawing insistently. It was eight o'clock and high time for his last meal of the day. In the back of the room, hidden by a thick curtain, Cal discovered a door to the outside that opened onto a small yard surrounded by thick bushes hiding a rusty chain-link fence. He let the dogs out, who sniffed and explored, and, after a few initial barks to intimidate whoever might be hiding beyond the property, fell asleep on the grass. Cal dragged a chair onto the lawn, and in the light coming from an apparently newly-installed LED lamp whose shape was meant to cut down on light pollution, he opened the guestbook he'd found on his nightstand. The first entry was from three years ago, October 9th, 2017, the day his house had burned down. He read the date again and again, took a picture with his phone and posted it on Instagram, rubbed the ink with his finger until it slightly blurred, and yes, he hadn't misread. On the day his own life had turned upside down, Ellie and Ben had stayed in this room, and Ben had given Ellie "a mighty tongue-lashing." This first entry set the tone for the following paragraphs. A couple from Mankato, Minnesota, called the fenced-in yard their "Garden of Eden," where the husband had tasted the "juicy apple of knowledge" again. A few pages later, a woman — it seemed that only women wrote these entries — complained that after the getaway weekend with her husband (one pair of grandparents were watching over the children who were finally old enough to be left in the care of relatives for a few days), had left her more exhausted than her job and children combined. "I had forgotten about his stamina. I hope we didn't wake the upstairs guests too many times."

There was no dearth of terribly mundane thank-yous and praise for the breakfast, the room, the generosity of the owners, but the farther he got into the black leather-bound book, the more Cal was convinced about the growing competitive nature of the entries. They became more graphic, describing certain positions, the size of certain organs and appendages, the length and depravity of the enjoyed intimacies. The bedposts featured prominently a number of times, as did the gilded mirrors Cal had hardly noticed. Apparently they could be moved so that lovers had a full view of themselves from every angle.

Curious as to what had happened the night before his own arrival, Cal skipped ahead. What he saw made his body feel as though he had been submerged in arctic waters; his breathing stopped. He closed his eyes for several seconds but got so dizzy he opened them again. He'd recognized the artist long before seeing the signature at the bottom of the drawing. Depicted were the three gilded mirrors and Shorat reflected in them from the front, from the left and right. It was one of her quick drawings in which she showed a verve and edge she often denied herself in her paintings. She was kneeling on the bed, the only color in the picture being the gold of the mirrors' frames and of her hair. Her body was rendered in black-and-white, almost cartoonishly, her square face dominated by the frames of her eyeglasses. Her breasts were bouncy, her buttocks supremely round. Yes, yes it was Shorat, there was no doubt. It was Shorat who gazed intently at him from three gilded mirrors in this particular room in a Cheyenne bed & breakfast near the Frontier Days Old West Museum, and behind her rose the contours of a man, cut off just above his belly button, his hairy legs cut off below the ankles. No face, no feet, but he was there, his hands resting on her waist.

Later, much later, after the second time he switched on the lights again because sleep wouldn't come, he tore the page from the guestbook and buried it in his travel bag. Yes, the drawing was signed "Shorat," no last name. Shorat had stayed in this room the previous night and left before he had arrived in the early afternoon. Had she made fun of the other guests' entries, or had she drawn what she'd experienced here? Cal went through the drawers of each nightstand, inspected the closet, the dresser, the bathroom cabinets. Nothing spoke of his wife's presence. Nothing had been left behind in the trashcan or under the bed.

Before eight in the morning, Cal stood at the reception desk, pulled a watch from his pocket — he was going to miss it, he was certain, should he have to sacrifice it — and asked about the previous guests who had occupied his room. Had they left an address? He'd like to send them the watch he'd found in the nightstand, just beyond the bible.

One of the owners, a heavy-set woman in her sixties, heard him out, smiled, and offered to send the watch herself. He had to be reasonable, she couldn't divulge her guests' addresses.

"But you see," said Cal, "it's kind of funny. I'm a bit of a watch collector and have been looking for such a piece for quite some time. It's no longer being produced, and I would like to get in touch with that person. I'd like to ask if he or she might be willing to sell it. Then neither of us would have to send it."

"We could certainly get you in contact with that guest, if you'd like to leave a phone number."

"Would you? How gracious, I'd be much obliged. Quite a coincidence, wouldn't you say?" Where had he learned to be so treacly sweet, so utterly spineless? "Has the gentleman not yet inquired about his watch?"

But the owner didn't take the bait, just smiled, said no, nobody had inquired about it.

Cal left her a phone number he'd received via an Internet provider, associated with his phone, a local Santa Rosa number he was certain Shorat would not connect with him. But would she call because of a watch she'd never lost in the first place? Wouldn't she smell the ruse? A Santa Rosa number, a watch?

He thanked the woman and left in worse spirits than before. He was an idiot, he felt, and he hadn't gained anything with his ploy. He hadn't learned if Shorat had been alone or if she traveled in company. He didn't know where she was headed. What under different circumstances would have felt like a miracle — staying in the same room his wife had used just the night before — now only seemed unusually cruel. He picked up the poop in the small backyard, then walked the dogs around the leafy neighborhood, ate breakfast in the dining room of the main house — a lukewarm frittata he abandoned after finding a long hair in it — then walked toward the museum. He dreaded the prospect of yet another day inside the car, the dogs emanating the faint urine smell of fear and discontent.

Growing older hadn't scared Cal until it had taken his appetites. In the beginning, he and Shorat had sanctified every piece of furniture in every room in every apartment they had lived in. They did it in the car, on the hood of the car, in car ports and garages, in entryways and elevators. And though things between them had become more complicated after the first two or three years — though he wasn't willing to think about that now in his depressed state of mind — his urgency hadn't abated. Age, however, had slowly drained his lust. Age and routine had been working hand in hand, conspiring against Cal's wish to never get enough of Shorat. His body had started to stiffen, his muscles took longer to recover. His mind had started to stiffen as well, refusing to get excited about the things that had once given him a childlike joy. Cars, road trips, all-you-can-eat buffets, candy stores, malls, movies, they all failed to rouse him now. Disdain crept into how he viewed his former pleasures, but he'd failed to replace them. Now his eyes refused to read books without glasses, the words blurring beyond recognition. He could still drive without enhancement, but his ears needed aids throughout the day. Spontaneity, never the strong suit of someone who was scared of change on the best of days, died quickly once you needed glasses and hearing aids every time someone sent you a text or called you on the phone.

Worse still, his appetite for himself had evaporated. He was used to his face and body, he was, and he didn't dread staring at what time and too much food and drink had made him, they had all been gentle. But he no longer took any pleasure in looking at himself; on good days, he was relieved he didn't look any worse. It wasn't ugliness he feared, it was something harder to pinpoint. What he feared was becoming less. Not different, not ravaged, just less. And what he saw on the rare occasions he lingered in front of the mirror after putting away his toothbrush or razor, was a thinning of features, a blurring of lines. He'd grown less of who he had been, and nothing new had emerged. Some people, after being beautiful in young years, developed aristocratic features, or plain scuzziness. They let time whip them, carve them, chisel deep crevices after losing their chiseled chins. But Cal, when he appraised his reflection, only saw his face and body fading. Youth had become him, turned a somewhat generic look pleasant. In the end, though, he'd failed to become something more interesting than young. He hadn't found himself, hadn't found what made him special, because, and this was as liberating a thought (on good days) as it was depressing, he was nobody special. There was nothing special to him. His tastes, his accomplishments, his lifestyle, his favorite foods and fun things to do, they were all exceedingly normal. There was no Cal — time and age had gently removed the disguise. Now, in those rare moments when he moved closer to the bathroom mirror, only Karl was left. Fifty-four year-old Karl, his figure threatened by extra pounds, his face fading into obscurity. It was a face you easily forgot and mistook for somebody else's. The high forehead, the widening lower face, jowls moving into his jawline, the loss of his dark, long lashes, the coffee-stained teeth — yes, it was still him, watered down, pleasant enough in its refusal to become anything of note. Ashamed, he'd look away.

His appetites were gone, and when was the last time he'd been overcome by the joy of randomly breaking into a run, sprinting down a street as fast as he could just because? It'd been a while. It'd been many whiles. He'd run a marathon the previous year, together with Shorat, but that was endurance, not wild joy. He'd lost his appetites, for excessive meals and excessive drink — his stomach wouldn't have it and needed meds whenever Cal wouldn't listen — for naked shoulders and deep-cut necklines, for shiny cars and long days of staring at straight highways and mountains in the distance, for reading while lying on a couch and nibbling on pretzels and drinking coffee, for himself and for everyone who wasn't him, for greed and for asceticism, for complaining, whining, and for stoicism. How boring the world had become. How boring it had always been, in all those years when he hadn't noticed. And how all the fun in the world had ruined this world. How small Cal had become, how utterly unrecognizably normal. A gentle older man with stooped shoulders and a laugh that could awaken the dead. Who? Who? Who was he really? What was left of him?

"Karl."

He had paid the admission fee and entered the poor, cramped displays of Cheyenne pride, something between ignorantly racist and folkloristically delusional. Yes, here was the bronze statue of a shooter, over there was the stage coach, and yes, they had installed a totem pole and a few native headdresses, though Cal very much doubted their authenticity.

"Karl?"

After the first shock, Cal opened his mouth, but he'd forgotten the words that fit this occasion. The man in front of him was ten years older and rather incongruously wearing a Cowboy hat, white. The grin though, Cal recognized. "Thomas." For several years they'd worked together in Berlin. Thomas had been a director, a teacher, a friend, a mentor to Karl, and then, after many years, an antagonist. Not of the unforgivable kind, but of the kind that stopped all calls and all conversations.

They'd struggled through a burned-down theater, an abandoned show, shows without an audience, an acting school falling apart after a year. Thomas, with his Vienna accent; Thomas of the stylish clothes and tobacco-yellow fingers; Thomas, the gifted actor, gifted in a way Cal would never be; Thomas who had lost the love of his life to AIDS and refused to talk about it; Thomas with an impeccable taste in literature and contempt for people who agreed with him; Thomas who told Karl that he was given a role simply because he knew so little; Thomas who enjoyed and derided Karl's vanity. They'd spent days and days in rehearsals, acting sessions, in cafés. They'd stuck together through smaller and larger disasters until Karl had pulled away. It had been a betrayal or a justified reaction to an earlier betrayal on Thomas' part, or maybe they had just disagreed over which path the acting school should take.

After the split, nothing. Another of Karl's friendships had turned ugly, had become a memory he'd rather forget because he could not hold on to the good parts, the rare sold-out shows, the nights spent in East Berlin's vibrant theaters, setting up their stage for another show, sitting in a coffee shop on Nürnberger Straße and discussing their next play. No, no, he did remember all the good moments, but his mind didn't stop there. Unfailingly, each moment of closeness and friendship led to his failure to hang on to his friend. And yet, here he was, Thomas, in a white Cowboy hat and a grin that hadn't turned old. "How have you been? You're looking good."

Cal returned the compliment. "And how are you?"

They embraced, and it was good to finally feel Thomas again. No, his friend hadn't grown younger, but he was still there, still around. They looked at each other's faces, Cal smiling now. He still didn't have any words, and he didn't care, held on to Thomas' arms until they both let go, and Thomas said, "Servus," and left. Cal watched him disappear into the parking lot and get into a rented Nissan Altima, then proceeded to the next room with plaques and old signage, a few weapons, and a history of the Cheyenne Rodeo.

There had been nothing to say. There was no bad blood, no, but they would never sit in a café again, never work on a project together again. There really wasn't anything more to say. Before noon, Cal was back at the hotel, took the dogs to the car and pulled out of the graveled lot of the bed and breakfast. In a few more minutes he had entered the highway, letting himself be pulled along by semis and pickups and a never-ending stream of single drivers training their eyes on some point in the future, some place they expected to be in due time.

At a rest stop somewhere, somewhere, because for the life of him he couldn't tell what day, what time, what country, he fed the dogs, and Vanya refused to eat from his dish. He was drooling profusely, eyeing the food, but he wouldn't come near the dish as though the dish were haunted, and so Cal sat down on the ground, on the oil-smeared, cigarette butt-marked asphalt, and fed Vanya by hand, and the dog took the kibble from him, handful by handful, and by the end, Cal was calm, almost calm, almost happy, and he felt relaxed enough to train his eyes on the road for another few hours, on some point in the future, some place he didn't expect to ever see.

CHAPTER 19

THE MIDSECTION. His was expanding, and he tried to keep it from becoming soft and extending beyond what he thought appropriate, and it was always the midsection, wasn't it? The midsection is where you got lost, where the urgency stalled and you had to shift without causing disruption, where you had to shift into higher gear or deeper depths, where readers tired and writers lost their way, where marriages fell apart, where you remodeled your house or bought a new one just to escape the boredom of what you knew and what had come before. The midsection was the one that bloated life, flattened its meaning beyond recognition, the steamroller of life, the desert of diminishing expectations, the desert of meetings, administrative duties, college funds, sagging butts, shrinking dicks, more food than a body could hold, more bad food than you ever thought existed, crushed goals, crushed dreams of threesomes with the neighbor's wife, threesomes with the two women who had looked your way at the hotel bar in Vegas, threesomes with the brawny neighbor who would probably turn out to have a bigger dick and be a better lover than you, threesomes with fat women, skinny women, old dudes, young dudes, women and men of every color and complexion and size, and that was only scratching the surface, because after all the threesomes had been exhausted, it would be time to think about the foursomes, the orgies, watching your wife have sex with three or four or more men, watching yourself being penetrated inch by fat inch, getting fisted by your wife who turned out not to be your wife, passing around women and men, getting passed around, getting pity-fucked by some young woman, getting cuckolded by this guy with the super long dick, it was so long you could only compare it to a cucumber or a footlong sub with teriyaki chicken, it was the mid-section where things turned messy without ever turning better, just more expansive like the tastes you had for food and bodies, whatever gave you a rise, whatever saved you from Viagra and sheer boredom, whatever saved your marriage; it was the mid-section that turned into the graveyard of clarity, of vision, of things you'd really wanted from this time on this dying planet you'd swooped down on you didn't know why and without any chance of ever finding out while you were still able to get it up and shove it into an asshole, a pussy, or just your hand. It was the mid-section that invited you to rant and invent new desires when you hadn't even fulfilled the old ones. It was the mid-section of this country, the giant section of stretchmarks, having given birth to too many corn-fed, AR-15 trained, huntin' n fishin' lovin', bible totin', gun totin', XXXL-Tshirt totin', football throwin' children; it was this giant stretchmark Cal was now entering that flattened his thoughts, made him question his trip, his selling of the house, his retirement, and even the love for his wife and dogs. What in the world was he doing in this car, a day beyond Cheyenne and days away from entering a state he might consider blue-ish, what was he doing here? Why had he come to look for America? What was this midsection? And what was he hoping to find should he ever make it out of here? Would he be just so many days closer to death? So many miles closer to something he couldn't even name yet? It was the middle where you lost hope and got sidetracked and ended up in complex and complicated situations that you would never be able to resolve. It was the midsection that extended and caused heart failure, diabetes, and impotence. It was the midsection where your spirits died. Death didn't kill you, it was the midsection that did you in.

It was in Des Moines that he checked into the next Super 8, paid the dog deposit, and curled up in a heap of tired clothes, bones, skin and sinew, and slept and slept and only came to sometime the next morning, close to noon, when the cleaning personnel opened his door by mistake and roused the dogs. It was here in Des Moines, in the great state of Iowa, that Karl looked out of the window into an overcast sky and felt the weight of his grandparents' and parents' history bear down on him. It was in Des Moines, while outside his room a family pushed and dragged their many suitcases toward the staircase, that he saw his grandfather again, a kind, old man who had once owned horses and who had idolized Hitler, because the Führer had pushed through land reforms that benefitted small farmers like Karl's grandfather Willi. He saw his grandmother, a woman he'd feared because of her loud voice and habit of spreading butter on black bread before applying black cherry jam, and who had been the village's highest party official. And he saw their farm, the farm where Karl's dad had grown up and where once prisoners of war had been forced to work and where one of them had been killed. He saw his mother's mother, pummeled by depression after losing her husband in the war and coming to the post-war West from East Prussia. He saw them all in their "good living-rooms," that odd German institution of expensive upholstery and dark wood, where heavy clocks chimed incessantly and barometers were read and where the good China was excavated once a week and for Christmas, and where everybody ate butter cake after someone in the family had died. Karl could smell the low ceilings, the acidic coffee that burnt through your stomach walls, the mothballed smell of Sunday's best, and the smell of too much cologne and hairspray. The sins of the grandparents had been suppressed by his parents, their childhood memories of war had been laid to rest in outsized freezers in the basement, right next to enormous quantities of meat, bread, peas and beans. His parents had buried their memories in the icy coffins, only referring to their childhood as "the bad times," and the bad times were off limits, couldn't be talked about, mustn't be talked about because they made Oma cry and then made Mom cry in response to Oma's tears, and afterward Sunday was ruined, and who knew when Oma had to return to the madhouse because of her affliction and how many days she would be put to sleep, to rest, to forgetfulness, because what Oma had lived and seen, Germany didn't want to re-live and re-see. It wanted to bury the past in the freezer of the wirtschaftswunder, it wanted to bury sins of grandparents and pain of parents under frozen pizza, frozen soup, frozen sausages, frozen stew and cauliflower. All the mental constipation of the post-war years had caused Karl and his sister Fredi nightmares; the guilt, never faced and never talked about, resurfaced in their notebooks and afternoon adventures. Not knowing why, young Karl feared Jews and the Commies; he dreaded his grandma's kisses for fear of contracting the same affliction that forced her into the madhouse; he feared the ghost of his mother's dad who was killed at the Russian front and who drove Oma into the madhouse; Karl crawled into his sister's bed at night, because his grandparents were shooting prisoners on their farm; Karl kissed his sister's cheek and neck and shoulders because it was better to fear your sister's breasts than be shot by your grandfather. Karl was a coward, Karl was a coward, there were too many ways to die at the hands of your family, of getting bombed on your escape to the West, of starving in a small room on a farm owned by a stranger who reached under your skirts or threw small stones at your head. Karl was a coward; there were too many ways to be left behind at the front, to drown on the transport ship across the Baltic, to be shot to pieces in Latvia, to be shot to pieces in Königsberg, to be shot to pieces because you had lost faith in the Thousand-Year Reich. Your uniform was stiff with dirt and torn, and you were bleeding, and you hadn't had a meal in days and had brushed your teeth, if at all, with what you found in puddles. There were so many ways to die, and his family had tasted them, his country had inflicted them, and all the rhetoric of blood and soil had led to exactly that, blood, more blood than you could ever measure soaking into the soil, and Karl had been able to smell it, smell it every day, outside his house during the day, and in his dreams at night. There had been so many camps, you always lived in close proximity to the one or the other. And later, later, in the days when his grandma had escaped from East Prussia, the enemy hadn't been forgiving. The enemy hadn't forgiven the women for their husbands' crimes, because, you see, in the end, in the end, Karl, Karl, in the end you are all to blame. The nannies and artists and bakers and janitors and housewives and teachers, in the end you all are to blame because you all were needed to stop the nightmares and you all kept quiet instead and let them proceed. You were all cowards, and how much easier it was to gas and shoot people than to stand up and say, No.

And now, now that the wirtschaftswunder has erased the last traces of the war, now that silence is coming back and seeping into your ears, but not into the ears of those who perpetrated the crimes but into the ears of the children and grandchildren, and it's so loud, vastly louder than even the factories Karl worked at in his years in Berlin, the noise is so overwhelming he is losing his ability to hear anything but the din of his parents' nightmares, the ones they fed him like scraps, the way you feed leftovers to your dogs; his parents had fed them the nightmares they vomited up at night, and Karl was afraid. He'd always been afraid. He'd always been afraid of dying without being known. He'd always been afraid of being shot to pieces on the front, of drowning in the Baltic, of being buried in an unmarked grave. "I'm Cal," he said into the skies above Des Moines in the great state of Iowa. "I'm Cal," and the dogs huddled around him.

But he wasn't Cal, it wasn't that easy to turn himself into an invention. The seams showed, his accent showed, he resembled his dad, this man who had wanted to be alone with Shorat, who had announced to everyone in the living room that he wanted to spend time alone with Shorat; his sister Fredi had looked at Cal and seen her dad, a larger, younger copy of the man who lusted after young girls, who always had his hands on their backs and legs and rubbed their arms and shoulders and then asked to be touched back; his sister Fredi denied everything that was so obvious to even blind people, she too was eating everything she had been fed and trying hard, trying her hardest to keep it down and not let the world around her know the nightmares that were now forcing blindness on her father. The father who had never grown up, had never understood what growing up meant, had never understood how to be a parent, because he was still the boy scared by what he'd seen in the war, by the man they'd shot on the farm, the tinsel being thrown from planes to counteract the radar, the beatings from his dad in the good living room with the Führer watching from inside his wooden frame. The father who had never understood who he was, who still thought that as long as he smiled he could ask to be left alone with Shorat. Karl looked exactly like him, and his feet and hands grew cold every time he thought about how he'd never escape his childhood, how he could never unsee his dad's hands all over the half-naked bodies of small girls, his smiling dad calling them girlfriends and scratching their backs after they had lowered the tops of their dresses for him. His mother watching, always watching, always denying anything had happened. There had been so much silence all their lives, they were blinded by it, blind to everything, blind to themselves, blind to their children.

There was no Cal that morning in the great state of Iowa, and after he had left the bed and sat on the lid of the toilet for some time, and after he'd showered and brushed his teeth and slathered deodorant under his arms, he felt nothing. Shorat had left Cal, and now Cal had left Karl. Here he was, the byproduct of a war, a byproduct of his Oma losing her home and being driven west by the advancing Russian army, a senseless byproduct of millions and millions dying, being tortured, being killed, being shoved into unmarked graves. Karl was meant to eat the sins and nightmares of the previous generations and just as he'd been told, he'd always finished his plate. Always; he'd never left anything uneaten. The wirtschaftswunder was the blanket under which the killers went to sleep.

It took two-hundred miles for him to breathe again, to regain his highly polished fiction of Cal the writer, Cal the writer from California searching for his wife Shorat. But he wasn't searching anymore, he was too afraid to find his wife and for her to no longer recognize him. He was merely driving now, driving away from who and what he'd been and losing layer after layer of who he had become in this country. Cal was his own alternate history, that toy thing of so many books and TV series and movies these days. Near Davenport, he finally understood the appeal of the many what-ifs, of the odd tumorous outgrowths of invented history, of the Nazi-killing troop sprung from Quentin Tarantino's brain, of the man in the high castle, of difference engines and the rhetoric of the current president. Wasn't it better to be ruled by the victorious Nazis rather than having to live through the decline of your own democracy? Wasn't it better to carve up Nazis than to look at the reasons why your country had not interfered in the war earlier? And driving past Davenport, Cal looked at his own fiction, and yes, if repeated often enough it seemed real enough to be sold to people who didn't investigate what you told them. He wondered if his former students understood the difference between *Inglorious Basterds* and what had really occurred a lifetime ago. Was alt history slowly becoming history? Had it ever been different? If his followers believed any of the lies the current president was dishing up to them, was it so difficult to believe that history was already being rewritten and rewritten every day? Were the camps already being deleted? Was the genocide against Native Americans already being re-revised and made smaller, made less significant? Was slavery being deleted, or glorified again? Did it really take just four years of a ruthless, lying president to change the history of a country and make people forget the sins of their forebears?

Cal had no forebears, Cal didn't even have parents. He'd come into the world fully formed and clothed, untethered by family relations, cut off from the country he no longer visited and whose products he no longer bought. He'd never lived in Germany, he'd never crawled into his sister's bed, he'd never seen his father fingering half-naked girls. Cal was not weighed down by memories, Cal was much smarter than that. Cal, alt history to the core, enjoyed a better life, a life more real than Karl's. This was true, it had to be, because Chicago rose on the horizon, and Karl needed to believe in Cal to not let go of the steering wheel, close his eyes and apologize to his dogs. Karl needed Cal. To drive and look for the woman he loved, Karl needed Cal to kill him, to euthanize him, to bury him in the backyard, to drown him in the bathtub of the next Super 8. Karl needed Cal to be more plausible than reality, more attractive than reality, to be *more* than reality. He needed Cal to lead a life for him. Only if Cal squeezed him to death, was life possible. Of course Cal wore two watches, one on each wrist. Killing the person who had dreamed him up required ruthless work. It depended on accuracy, time and time again.

By the time he could see Lake Michigan stretching out and away from him, Cal had reconstituted himself, reconfigured his presence from the tiny dead pieces of Karl's life and the experiences Cal had catalogued in his twenty-four years in this country. The catalog was thorough, yet the holes had been getting bigger and wider ever since the fire had destroyed the smelling salt for his memories, the photos and trinkets of twenty-four years, the reference points of a life lived by a fictional character named Cal. Inside the car, it was Cal who was in control, Karl a tiny mass like a lump you could feel under your skin that made you worry about tumors and cancers and your own mortality. Karl had been deflated and rolled together tight, packed neatly under Cal's skin. And Cal was driving, his image complete once again, his presence without flaw. If someone had looked at him now, behind the wheel of his white SUV, the dogs asleep in back, they would have seen a clear image of a middle-aged man, his eyes tired, his features large and somewhat pleasant. Had they followed the car on a whim, their suspicion aroused by something fleeting, something they had no words for just yet; had they seen this man climb from his car a few moments later at yet another Super 8, this one in Evanston, the first town he'd stayed in after landing in Chicago twenty-four years ago with a scholarship to attend the University at Buffalo; if they had cared to look at this man with California license plates and two drugged-yet-excited dogs jumping onto the pavement, they would have rubbed their eyes and sworn they'd noticed the pixilation.

Chapter 20

CHLOE SENT HIM A MESSAGE the next morning, she had three potential buyers for the house but suggested to wait a few more days and drive up the price. Maybe there would be a buyer from Silicon Valley tired of paying out of their nose for a cramped space in San Francisco. Wine Country was in high demand.

"Wine Country is on fire," Cal said. The TV in his room was on mute, flames destroying vineyards and senior homes and private residences.

"The wind is already turning," Chloe said. "The air is much better today. In a few days, nobody will remember we had to evacuate."

He thanked her, hung up, wolfed down two slices of pizza from the night before, and fed the rest to the dogs. A half hour later, he parked in a nearly empty lot by the lakeshore and together with Yuuki and Vanya — the dogs suspicious of the empty space in front of them, Yuuki's tail between her legs — advanced toward the water. In '96, he had kept his distance from the other scholarship recipients, the ones who after the three days of orientation would fly to large cities and fancy schools. At thirty, Karl, still a few weeks away from inventing Cal, had been the oldest in the group of about forty students, and no one had envied his assignment to Buffalo. While he followed some of the others to the beach in the afternoon, he didn't take his shirt off and didn't take a swim, feeling awkward, too pale, too unattractive. He couldn't stand the chatter, the excited voices, the advice of those who had lived for longer stretches of time in the US before. And he couldn't stand their talk of going back to Germany the coming year to complete their degree and become a scholar or teacher. Cal sat among the groups of confident baritones and expert sopranos and felt lost. Unlike them, he had no plans of going back. There was no future waiting for him in Germany. All he needed was in his one large backpack and the other, much smaller one. They were easy to carry, held next to nothing. He wished to be as light as possible, as new as possible, as vacant and blank and untarnished as possible, and this was not an easy task when you were thirty years old and surrounded by people who still remembered their high school graduation, still talked about it on the shores of Lake Michigan. Karl swore a solemn oath that after these three days of orientation, he wouldn't speak another work of German. Not ever. Not ever. Not ever.

He let the dogs off their leashes, a gamble, but one he was willing to take because he carried some left-over pepperoni in his pocket. Yuuki and Vanya took off, fighting each other, chasing each other, and it had been a long time since he'd seen them so rambunctious. Watching Yuuki, a Chinook most people mistook for a Greyhound, getting chased by Vanya, inelegant but tireless, was the most beautiful sequence of movements he could remember seeing, he was quite certain of it. Unchoreographed and uninhibited their chases were, and then, whenever Vanya was threatening to catch up or cut her off, Yuuki lowered herself and began to fly. Yuuki, the ground-effect plane, the Ekranoplan. Cal could hear her swooshing sounds.

He had no plans for the evening, spent the late afternoon in the outside area of a coffee shop, jotting down descriptions of photos he'd taken of Shorat and lost in the fire for good. Next door, he had bought a six-pack of college-ruled notebooks. Maybe he would fill one or another. Time was running out on his memories, you couldn't herd them, and the coyotes always came at night and even during the day to carry off one and another. Notebooks could burn, all his notebooks had, in fact, burned in the fires, but he wouldn't trust a computer with his memories of Shorat. Did his cataloguing mean that Cal believed he would never see his wife again? Perhaps. He wasn't certain, and at times he felt like dumping the notebooks in one of the city's trashcans even though they were still wrapped, but he continued one photo at a time. If he did one or maybe two photos every day, by year's end he would have an album of Shorat. Would his words be good enough to help him remember Shorat's features years from now, in days he would spend in a nursing home, in a hospital bed, in a hospice?

Around seven o'clock he returned to his hotel room, walked with the dogs across a mostly empty university campus. It was dark by now, colder than California nights at this time of year. He'd soon have to buy scarves and gloves, all the attire of winters in the Northeast. He wondered what the dogs would make of the white stuff they hadn't seen in years. Yes, he was looking forward to short days and long nights with the dogs, to yellow snow and walks through snow drifts. But was he really going to settle down again? Was he going to stay in one place again, trying again to grow roots and become part of a community? Was he really up to that task?

Shorat after the Haircut

In 2001, we lived in a house on Liberty Street in Ann Arbor, Michigan, not far from downtown. It was a short walk to the restaurant A Moveable Feast, and in another three or four minutes we'd be at the Fleetwood Diner, open 24 hours every day. A one-bedroom apartment on the second floor had been the first we shared, after Shorat had finished her degree in Buffalo and joined me in Ann Arbor. The space had been cramped, but after a year, one of the downstairs apartments became available, and we never grew to love it, but we did have a larger living area, an extra bedroom, and the light during the day was nearly green because of the trees outside the large front window. I'd been trimming Shorat's hair for some time, and on this occasion, she wanted it much shorter. She sat down on the purple wooden chair, a chair I had found and painted before her move to Michigan, and she wore nothing but her panties. Her blonde hair – of various and varying shades, from stark-white to the color of the dust you gather when swiping a finger along the window ledge of a beach house, she had dyed a light rust brown, and she wanted it short on the sides and slightly longer on top, 80s style.

The light in the room was green, brighter behind her because we kept the curtains of the front window half closed, but the window to the side of the house had no curtains, and in the afternoon, the sun brightened the area for which we would buy a yellow sofa later on in the year, after receiving a check from the government to restart the economy after September

11. But on the day I took this picture of Shorat, the sofa her parents had given us and which her dad had built himself, was still in the apartment and giving both of us back aches. Pretty it was, with its striped cushions, but we needed several pillows each to make it pain-free through a movie. Shorat sat on the purple chair, but maybe it was one of the metal chairs we had already bought, the surplus chairs from the university which you also found in army offices. They came with green or gray vinyl upholstery and despite their spartan looks were oddly comfortable. I prefer to think she sat on one of the metal chairs, a green one, because the light was green, and behind her the light was much brighter, no, not much, just enough to render it three-dimensional, to distinguish Shorat's drawings we'd hung on the wall, drawings from her years in art school before she decided to enroll in computer science and start all over again.

Shorat is sitting on the green chair, enough light coming through the trees and the half-open curtains to illuminate her face. She's squinting slightly from behind her glasses, and because her glasses have thick lenses, her eyes appear small. She's squinting into the light and a trace of a suspicious smile appears on her lips. When you look closely, it seems to disappear, but when you shut your eyes for a second and open them again, there it is. She's suspicious, because it's the first time I haven't just trimmed her hair, taken maybe half an inch off its length, but really cut it, styled it with scissors and shears, and she hasn't seen the outcome yet. The hair I've taken off has accumulated on her shoulders and large breasts, and before she can get up and swipe at the hair, fine rust-

brown hair clinging to her skin, I take my camera, an old Konica SLR I once bought in Denver for forty dollars, and take her picture. Her face is wide, her jaw strong, and her hair is bracingly short. Her skin, so incredibly soft, is tinged olive even though she's as pale as the moon. Her chin shows some red spots, pimples she hasn't grown out of yet; that will happen once she turns thirty. For now she still has acne, which embarrasses her and which I secretly adore, I don't know why. Her suspicious smile doesn't keep her from looking almost aggressively into the camera, but her shoulders and breasts make her vulnerable, and the hair on them makes them look even softer than they truly are. Shorat is vulnerable, ready to say something harsh, but she lets me take the picture, one she will never like much, and beyond her, way beyond her, hangs a mirror, and you can see the back of her head and the half-open window in that mirror. She'll never like that picture, but I will keep it, will keep it every time we move, every single time. It will always travel with me until it burns in the Tubbs Fire in 2017. She'll never understand why I like the picture, nor will she like my hands on her breasts. She doesn't even like her breasts, because they remind her of her mother's cancer. She finds them too large, too cumbersome, she doesn't like my attention, my touch. She'll barely tolerate a kiss, won't tolerate her nipples between my lips, my teeth. Her smile is an act of defiance, but she doesn't stop me from taking the picture. Later I regret taking it, as though I've stolen something from her, but when the prints arrive, it's the one picture where she fails to hide, where she is open, where you can see how little she trusts me, how *little she expects from my efforts as a hairdresser and photographer. Her smile says, I don't know you, I still don't. It says, We've been married for nearly two years, and I'm still not sure I actually like you.*

In the morning he caught a bit of a high, an acceptance of what had happened so far in the fifty-four years of his life on this planet that still bewildered him. In one of his books he'd ventured into cyberpunk, the not-too-far future, but in everything else he'd ever written, he'd stayed in the near-past. It was the present he didn't quite understand and that made him suspicious. He didn't trust the things he saw and touched, didn't believe in reality as it presented itself to him. He didn't trust people's faces, people's intentions, he didn't trust people who had left the room to say and do what they'd promised to say and do. So much could derail a day.

But this morning, because he had opened his email and found a message from a student asking for advice about her writing after college, and because he had already started on his response in which he suggested looking at MFA programs, he stopped himself in mid-typing and thought, No, the straight path is the boring path. Cal remembered some advice from a horology podcast host — doing tons of research before buying your first expensive watch in order to get it right — and felt the urge, and gave in to the urge, to rewrite the response to the student and advise her against looking at MFA programs just yet. There was no need to get it right the first time. In fact, getting it right the first time was the most stifling possibility he could think of. If he had gotten things right the first time, he would still be living in the small town in Northern Germany, be close to retirement, live in a comfortable home he shared with the girl he'd met around the time of high school graduation. His kids would be in college, and he would be teaching high school and bike to work. His wife would have died of cancer two years prior, and he'd be meeting women he'd encountered via OkCupid on weekends in Hamburg or Bremen.

Maybe, because he had been doing a lot of research beforehand, he would have studied in Marburg or Göttingen, maybe in Kiel, and instead of trying to become an actor for several years, he would have studied English right away, gotten his Ph.D. and taught high school in Lübeck or Eckernförde (he had been in love with his substitute high school teacher in 11th grade and she with him, and maybe, if he had gotten things right, they would have taught high school in Lübeck or Eckernförde together, and she would be sixty-five by now, and they could retire together and live in a town on the Baltic Coast and have their children over for dinner, vacation in Italy and Japan, and own a subscription for the Hamburg Symphony). If he'd gotten everything right, he'd be one-hundred-and-eighty pounds right now, would have a glass of wine every now and then, play tennis with his friends, drive an Audi, and own ten acres of land behind his old-but-remodeled farmhouse. When was the last time he'd thought of Kirsten?

No, no, there was absolutely no need to get it right. Cal sat down and wiped out his previous message and assured the student that there couldn't be any wrong choices. Or, well, if they turned out to be wrong, they could help her steer towards something that seemed better and more promising. An abundance of not-quite-right choices was unavoidable if you were a curious human being, but oh, how Cal had sometimes envied those four or six-year-olds who picked up a violin — or into whose hands a violin was placed — and who committed themselves to their art from childhood to coffin. It was admirable and seemed so much easier than the hodgepodge of choices Cal had made and regretted and cast off. All the women he'd met and loved and fallen into and abandoned, all the women who had abandoned him. And yet, and yet, on this particular morning it seemed like a richer, more turbulent, more colorful, more lived life than marrying your high school love and playing the violin until neck pain and deafness forced you into retirement. If you did everything right the first time, what was left?

Then he thought of Shorat who wouldn't answer his calls and wouldn't even let him know where she might be. Hadn't his marriage been the one good decision he'd made? The one thing he'd never questioned? Never long enough to feel he should leave? Never long enough to pack a bag? And maybe that wasn't entirely true, maybe it wasn't, but on this morning in Evanston, Illinois, he didn't want to dwell on that and swiftly wrote an upbeat email about making tons of mistakes, because at least his student would have stories to tell. A lifetime of right decisions wouldn't yield a single story.

CHAPTER 21

HE'D BEEN SIXTEEN, unloved in school, but growing out of the need to be accepted for things he wasn't. Growing tall had helped, too. Four inches in the previous year, and suddenly he was 6'2", and the other students, also growing and discovering what their bodies wished to do and how to use them around other bodies; the other students looking for things they might love enough to pursue for the last two years of high school and beyond; the other students lost their loathing of Karl the loudmouth who always raised his hand because that was his way of not falling asleep and falling behind in class, and who would never do his homework. Karl the brownnoser became more or less just Karl, and he found his way into the drama group and a circle of friends who drank tea and ate cookies in the afternoons, and even though he didn't smoke, they allowed him to stick around.

Kirsten had been as tall as him, as thin as him, her dirt-blonde hair much longer than his. She'd been the second substitute teacher that semester, and his class had a reputation, and on her first day, they'd initially shouted her down, interrupted her every sentence. Kirsten had fallen silent, stayed silent, until after about thirty minutes, everybody had fallen silent with her. They'd opened their books and had started with their English lesson, and the noise never returned. They'd all been in love with her, but Karl had only noticed how much on the day they all drove to a café to bid their substitute teacher farewell.

He'd written her letters after that, and she had responded, and within a week they had declared their love for each other, their wish to make love. By then she was living up north again, near the Baltic coast.

"Would we have stayed together?" He'd expected her to come to the coffee shop and sit down opposite of him. He'd been filling the pages of his notebook, drinking a latte, feeling immersed in life without the need to take part in it.

"You were just a high school boy."

"I've always regretted writing that letter to you," he said.

"That last one."

"Yes. And I've always regretted the letter you wrote me, saying I was just so young."

"You'd met Sophie. She was real, not just a letter."

But Kirsten's letters, he knew with a clarity only hindsight, with its many editing tools, could afford, had been far more real than anything he'd ever done with and to Sophie, and even back then, when touching Sophie still had felt like worship, he'd noticed how Kirsten's letters were more vivid than any of the love notes he would receive from Sophie, his girlfriend of five years. And now he was relieved to finally tell Kirsten about this. About her letters, about the dreams he'd later had of finding her again, of knowing her.

She let him finish, there was no rush. "I had forgotten about you." She still wore her hair long, though by now it was different shades of silver and gray. Her figure was still the same, the lines of her face clear and deep. "It was one of my first jobs. You had that magic about you, this aura of a first awakening."

"I never forgot," he said.

"Maybe you've never grown up. I met my husband a few years later, had two children. There was too much life to think about brief episodes of the past, no matter how sweet they were. Unconsumed."

"The ones you don't consume..."

"You like that thought of yours, don't you?" Her laughter wasn't scolding. There was no need for it, because he'd never meant that much to her. "But if we don't forget what we don't consume, because we never tasted it fully, how come I don't recognize your features? How come I no longer recall what you looked like, or what your letters said?"

"I still wish I could have visited you. Sometimes I think you were the key to a world that never opened again for me. A way of participating in the world that wasn't about vanity and success, but about appreciation, studies, teaching, raising a family."

"I was never a key." The waiter came and Kirsten ordered an Americano. "I wasn't an instrument. I wanted you. Your enthusiasm was touching, and I let myself get caught up in it. You were pretty, and loving you could have landed me in prison, too. So maybe I wasn't quite what you later thought I was. Maybe what I did back then was as juvenile as everything you later did."

"You raised a family."

"But you only have my word for that. Maybe I never became a fulltime teacher. Maybe I never married. Maybe I'm living off welfare in Kiel, in a small studio apartment. Maybe I received a small inheritance when my parents died. Maybe I have just enough to last me until I die. You were a mistake."

"I wasn't a mistake. Not seeing you again was a mistake."

"You still haven't grown up. If you still have room to think about what might have happened, what does that say about who you are and what you've done?" Her parting kiss felt cold on his cheek, her hair brushed his face, and she let him hold her hand for a second longer. "She gave you Berlin," she said. "Sophie did. What would you have done in the small towns where I taught cute boys like yourself?"

That evening, Cal sat on the beach with his dogs and fed them Beggin' Strips from his coat pocket. Their drool turned his hands sticky. They licked his fingers and face, and he looked at the horizon, which wasn't really a horizon, because night and lake had merged, and he felt some knot finally giving way like sutures dissolving after surgery. The dogs lapped at his face, and their voices silenced his own to anyone who might have walked past. Sand in his shoes, sand in his pockets and socks, he arrived back at the hotel. He made himself some more coffee even though he was out of milk and sat on the bed, burning his mouth on purpose. Yes, the knot had come undone, and it left him undone as well. In the morning, he only walked the dogs after they both started to complain, and after returning to the hotel he slept, and when he didn't sleep he stared at the window and his clothes on the sofa, at the dogs lying on the carpet.

Starting a new life as an immigrant, even a privileged immigrant who didn't enter the new country because of strife or persecution or poverty, left you naked. Even if, like Cal, you hailed from a country that wasn't unlike this new world. He'd arrived with nothing, exactly how he'd wanted it. Still, on an October day in Evanston, Illinois, in a badly lit room in the Super 8, he felt as though his first thirty years had been taken from him. It wasn't new, this feeling, but now that he had only Yuuki and Vanya as companions, who would be witnessing him from here on out? Who'd keep track of his whereabouts? When he'd arrived in Buffalo, thirty years had been erased, and he'd been happy about it. Life, for him, hadn't meant continuation but reinvention and this also meant giving up on being known and understood. New people he met told him of days in Munich and nights they had partied in Berlin, but their eyes filled with impatience when he tried to explain the German high school system with its three tiers and different degrees. Leaving Germany meant leaving everyone he'd known, the language he had known them by, the endearments they'd exchanged. At the time he had left the city, Berlin had felt crowded with his mistakes, bad relationships, false starts, and failures. But in quiet moments like the current one, when no one watched and interfered, he could feel the emptiness his move had caused him, he could feel the emptiness spreading, devouring his years on this continent as well. When I'm gone, he thought, I'll leave behind nothing. I'll be gone for good. The few friends I've made will keep me in their thoughts a few moments longer, but that will be all. They've known so little of me, for so few years, nobody remembers what I looked like as the sixteen-year-old, when I was in love with Kirsten and she with me. That moment, edited and worked-over, altered and refurbished, only lives inside myself and is therefore gone. Soon, my years in America will be gone too. If I don't find Shorat, my whole life will have vanished. This was a beautiful thought, how clean and benevolent it appeared. He hadn't left any architecture, infrastructure, no invention, not even a large heap of garbage. At this very moment, he existed only in the eyes of his dogs. He wished to fall apart, to burn apart and leave nothing, not even his car in the motel parking lot, and the thought soothed him and made him miserable at the same time, because he had no control over any of this. Despite being alone in an acceptable motel room outside Chicago, his life, unless he was hit by another car or dying of an as-of-yet undiagnosed disease, might continue for another twenty, thirty, even forty years, and he had no plans for such a time, none at all.

Was this self-pity? he asked, and of course it was, but even so, he didn't feel he was wrong. He had kicked away thirty years of being witnessed, and now another twenty were gone. How would he ever piece his life together again? Even if he were to write a meticulous autobiography, six or ten volumes of minute observations, how much would he fail to remember? How much would get lost by a reader, even if that person read every word of every sentence? How much had he retained of the books he'd absorbed?

To leave your country was to forfeit the past, and much of the present as well. The past couldn't be explained to new friends and acquaintances who only wanted to talk about Hitler, beer, soccer, or the Autobahn. The present meant nothing and couldn't be explained to the people who'd known you in your first life. Your life only ever had half an audience, and your voice only spoke with an accent. Cal was no longer fluent in German, and twenty-four years in the States had mauled his pronunciation. Yet his English had never become American enough to fool anyone. The German accent was all people heard when he was introduced to them. "Do I hear a German accent?" they'd say and be proud of themselves for guessing right. They were so proud and smug, and for him the conversation was over.

As an immigrant, you couldn't work yourself into the fabric of those who'd known one another for twenty or thirty years. Academic circles had been welcoming mostly, but those circles broke apart quickly; moving came with the profession. Cal had never been able to hold on to friendships, and in his last position, his colleagues had held their jobs for so long, they hadn't needed a newcomer in their lives. They were nice, they were friendly, sometimes even supportive, but they'd been in academia long enough to pull away from the institution. They taught and left the building. They commuted and didn't come to readings, holiday parties, or student events. In five years in Northern California, Cal and Shorat had not been able to make friends at the university. Nobody would remember him for very long. His project of reinvention had failed, his plans hadn't been large enough, persuasive enough, or maybe he hadn't put enough energy into fulfilling his promise. He hadn't reinvented himself, he'd just smudged his outline, blurred what people who looked his way saw, blurred himself past recognition. He'd left his old country and had not been able to become visible in this one. But now it was time to take the dogs for another walk.

Chapter 22

"We never met here, even though we could have."

Cal felt relieved that it was Bobbie he'd run into and that no one else had stopped and taken the time to recognize him. He'd come to hate Ann Arbor, a town so smug it gave him nightmares. It was a club, a large country club of academics, auto industry managers and engineers, and pseudo artists still waiting for their break. People behaved as though they had been chosen to live here by an important deity, they basked in the glow of the university and imagined their restaurants to be supreme. They loved their Art Fair, their Wolverines, their coffee and bagels. Everything was better here.

"No, we didn't. Four years. I could have been your teacher."

"You could have."

She had three children now and lived in New York City with her husband, a video editor. "Why are you here?"

"My friend Claire is getting divorced and she wants us all to celebrate, all her friends who came to the wedding."

"And your kids?" he asked.

"Are with my mom and Ben."

They'd become friends many years later, after they both had left town. They'd been in a reading a mutual friend had organized during a writers' conference. They'd stayed in touch, watched each other buying houses, getting settled. They sent each other their work, and he watched her kids grow on Instagram and Facebook. She watched him getting tenure. There'd never been any awkwardness between them despite, or maybe because, their age difference.

They took a walk with the dogs in the Arboretum, then had coffee downtown. She was staying at the Bell Tower Hotel, and he at the Red Roof Inn. Tonight, she'd go have drinks with her friends, maybe dance at a club near Detroit. But she had two hours before she needed to get ready.

Something in Bobbie's demeanor had changed. He couldn't tell at first; she hadn't gained weight and she wasn't wearing sensible pants and shoes either. And yet her face was overcome with a new harshness, or maybe her sadness had taken permanent hold of her lines and tightened them. She looked like a lost scout, desperate to believe she still knew where she was headed. Maybe three children had the power to rework a face that had once been melancholy and soft. Or maybe it was him she was reacting to, maybe it was his confession that he had lost Shorat that pulled at her face.

"Where are you headed?" She was on her second bottle of Perrier; caffeine threatened her stability.

"East. For now."

"Will you find her?"

He shrugged, couldn't tell if he believed he would. "There's a chance."

They held hands for a while, as though this was the better way to read each other. "It's getting cold," he said. "I don't remember winter."

"You brat," she said. "In the Upper Peninsula they had their first snow. What's happening to your house?"

"Is it Friday?" he asked. "Monday. Monday, the realtor will make a decision. If I'm lucky, I'll have enough money to buy a house in Western New York. Something small, maybe something with a bit of land. A barn. If that's what I feel like. I've never been good at knowing how I will feel before I get somewhere, do something, touch somebody. I can't think things through before they happen to me."

They walked along Main Street before turning onto Liberty. "I wish I could have that freedom to move wherever I want to be. It seems so romantic. You can be anyone you like."

"You don't mean that," he said. "But yes, it looks romantic, because you don't imagine that I will only have the dogs to remember me."

"I remember you."

"The part you've seen. For a little bit."

"Yes, the part you've let me see." Then she said, "My mom is losing her mind. She can't remember a thing I say, she can't remember a thing she says. And she talks non-stop. She asks me if I'm going to kill myself, she talks nonstop to the kids, and they are frightened. When she leaves for a few days, they look traumatized. They stare blankly at walls and cry at small things."

"She's looking after them right now?"

Bobbie stopped to search his eyes. Was he accusing her? "Ben took the weekend off, well, sort of. He can do some stuff from home. I wouldn't leave them alone with her. She might forget she's looking after them. When I was little, I stayed with my grandmother in Mackinac. She had a large house; my grandfather had died a few years previous. I might have been five or six. My mother was in the hospital, she'd just given birth to my brother and had suffered a hemorrhage. Dad had to work. So I stayed with Oma. One morning, we went shopping, buying some groceries for dinner, and when we came back to her house, she took the groceries from the backseat, locked the car, and went inside. I had been sitting right next to that bag, but she didn't see me and she didn't remember me. I banged against the car window for a while, I shouted for her, but she didn't hear me. The locks, they didn't work from the inside if you locked them from the outside. It was an old car with lots of kinks — I couldn't get out. Hours later she unlocked the car because she thought she'd left her sunglasses on the dashboard. She was wearing them. She saw me, took off the glasses, and stared at me as though she was going to scream. "Don't ever scare me again like that," she said.

They stood in front of the State Theater. The air had cooled, his sinuses asked for warmth, but they both stood without moving, without even looking at each other, just staring down the street toward the quad.

"If my mom loses her mind, I will be lost too," Bobbie said. "My dad doesn't speak. He can't bring himself to talk about memories, good and bad. He's not the type. It's as though Mom is doing his talking as well, as though she were having their conversations by herself. And she's having them *at* me. But there's nothing there, no space where you can find me in her words. Does that sound selfish?"

He made a sound in his throat to reassure her, refused to look her way. If he looked, she might take the chance and leave and join her friends to celebrate the divorce.

"If she loses her mind, I will be sitting in that car again, and no one will be able to find me and let me out. If her mind refuses to know me, I'll grow translucent."

"Yes," he said. "Yes."

"My parents sold their house in Bay City, the house where I grew up. Two years ago they sold it and bought a house in Virginia instead, to be closer to my brother. They never asked me before they put it on the market. I hate them so much for giving up that house. Whenever I visited them, I had the feeling I knew where I had come from. And — I don't know, but I always had the best sex with Ben there. I really don't know, but I was somebody else, everything meant something else. Everything meant *something*, there were no dead spaces, no empty spaces, no fog. I knew my place and I didn't need to be explained. I was Bobbie, I belonged. Now the house is gone, and some other family lives there and has remodeled the place, rearranged everything. Even if I could go inside, I wouldn't know who I was."

He made another sound, watched two women cross the street holding hands. A skateboarder went past them, forcing Bobbie to pause. "It doesn't help that I have Ben and the kids. It doesn't help that I know you. She's wiping me out."

Cal looked at his shoes as though his gaze might warm his toes. Some thirty minutes later he sat in the Indian restaurant on Main Street in a booth by himself, studying the menu, a glass of red wine in front of him, House Merlot. Cal sat by the window, looked out at passers-by, himself shielded, he hoped, from curious gazes. There was something wholesome about fall season back East. In California, the Halloween decorations and Christmas ornaments felt as though they had been brought from basements and garages at the wrong time in a communal act of nostalgia. Snow had never threatened LA or Santa Rosa.

Cal ordered samosas and lamb biriani, he still had an hour or two before having to return to his hotel to walk and feed the dogs. He wasn't sure what had made him look up — maybe the food was too hot to be enjoyed yet, or maybe he had been reaching for the wine glass. Something had drawn his eyes outside, past the group of students standing by an orange VW. He pulled out his wallet, left too much money, and ran toward the entrance, pushed through the door. There she was, on the other side of the street. It was her gait, it was her hair, it was her purple winter coat they'd purchased at the ACE hardware store in Sebastopol, a year after the fires. Shorat had her hand in somebody else's, a man's hand. He was tall, wearing a black wool cap, walking with an assuredness that made Cal long for the food he had abandoned, so empty and cold his stomach felt. South they walked, toward Palio's, and Cal followed in what he thought was a large enough distance for them not to hear his footfall, not to sense how upset he was, and large enough for Shorat to not recognize his face should she turn around.

Yes, they were headed to Palio's, the Italian place where the food was passable and you could drink at the outdoor bar on the second floor. They had hated the place when they lived in this town; why was she now entering it with the tall man? Cal hoped to see his face, but no, people exiting the restaurant prevented him from catching a glimpse. He counted to one-hundred, hopefully giving Shorat and her companion enough time to step away from the entrance. They wouldn't wait by the door if they couldn't get seated right away, they would venture upstairs and get drinks first. Why he was so certain he couldn't tell, but at one-hundred-and-twenty-one, he pulled open the door, and he had been right. It was in that moment, when he felt relief over not running into his wife and her male companion — he couldn't bring himself to think the word boyfriend or beau or lover — that he recognized his madness and shouted, "Shorat." Of course that's what he should have done, why had he been so afraid? She was his wife still, his love, the woman he'd lived with for twenty years. Cal didn't mind the stares, shouted, "Shorat" once again and went through the entire restaurant to look for her, before the maître d' had a chance to stop him and ask if he'd made a reservation. He checked the dining areas twice, then hurried upstairs to the bar. Where was Shorat, where was she? She was here, she was, she was, she was, but no, he couldn't spot her, not after crossing the patio three times and checking on every face. But there, down there on Williams, there she was, the black wool cap right next to her blonde hair.

Cal reached the spot where he had seen his wife some thirty seconds later. He couldn't see her ahead, though he ran up Williams for several minutes. He looked into alleys and driveways, into cars and parking garages, and when he was sweating so much that his whole body was growing cold, he yelled her name, and a group of young male students howled like a wolf pack in response. Where was she now? Which restaurant, bar, or hotel, had they entered?

He arrived late at the Red Roof Inn. Yuuki had torn a pillow to shreds and destroyed two of his books. Vanya, sweet Vanya, had overturned the bags, found the food container and bitten through the plastic lid. The container was empty now, and turds dotted the carpet.

Cal didn't feel the tiniest morsel of anger. He cleaned up, received a new pillow at the front desk, then walked the dogs until Vanya had pooped several times more. Everywhere Cal looked, he hoped to see his wife, and much later, he loaded the dogs into the car and walked through downtown, up Williams, down Liberty, up Washington, and along Main and State. He walked until midnight, when he spotted Bobbie among her friends outside a bar. They were wearing masks, wearing colorful dresses, no coats. He didn't have the heart to cross the street and say hello. He had no heart.

CHAPTER 23

THE FOLLOWING DAY couldn't make Shorat reappear. Cal walked the dogs through downtown, sat with them outside of coffee shops and delis. She wouldn't appear for him. By mid-afternoon, her presence he'd felt all morning was fading, then gone. The town felt empty, foreign, it meant so little you could have swept the remaining crumbs onto the tiniest of dustpans. Cal paid for another night but was kept awake by dreams of pursuing Shorat and finally catching up with her. It was in Ann Arbor that Cal and Shorat had started running together and since then, they'd run thousands of miles together, he on the left, she on the right. Most mornings they had coffee first — coffee was always first — then put on their running gear and left the house. They'd explored every new town they moved to on foot, using the long weekend runs to look at new neighborhoods, find new restaurants, hidden corners, tucked-away parks. Running without Shorat at his side felt not like running at all. In his dreams, she was wearing shorts and a tank top, and after many turns and missed chances he caught up with her, panting, and she turned to him with a smile, and said, "I'm faster now than you. I'm faster now without you. Ever since I left you, I'm just so incredibly fast." Each time Cal woke, he was overjoyed to have finally heard her voice. Sadness would set in a few seconds later, when he'd found his bearings and it was Yuuki sleeping next to him, not his wife. And quickly, oh so quickly, he closed his eyes and started running after Shorat yet again.

When he arrived at the Lenox Hotel on North Street just before dark the next day, he felt an overwhelming sense of relief. He couldn't explain it properly, though he'd tried from time to time, but he felt as though he understood the people in Buffalo in a way he'd never experienced again after moving away. People's faces, their skin, their manners and mannerisms, their paranoia and disillusionment, their physical presence, had felt erotic to Cal. People stranded in Buffalo he experienced as hot breakfast, greasy slices of peperoni pizza on the way home after a night out on Chippewa Street; they were puppies, nightgowns, foot rubs, hot soup, scarves and facials, fingers drumming on your spine, the smell of dog paws, rainy spring days, a book read in front of a dark window, a book read on a couch with a cup of tea on the table beside you, a book read out loud while your love was making love to you and hanging at every word you uttered. Cal felt alive in their gaze, alive in their memories even though he didn't figure in their past. He couldn't get lost in Buffalo. Each new face felt like a kiss, carefree and unhurried.

In the morning, electronic papers waited for him in his inbox. He signed them, and somewhere else, in some other room in a different hotel, or inside a living room, car, or plane, Shorat added her signature as well, and by the end of the day, the deal had gone through. The buyer was paying in cash. "We're rich," Cal said without joy, and the dogs looked up from the couch they were sharing only to lower their heads again and gaze longingly at the window. Cal celebrated by ordering two large pies from Just Pizza and drinking a Genesee 40. He sat between his dogs on the sofa and shared pizza and a few cupped handfuls of beer. Then they walked up Elmwood and into the neighborhood where Shorat had lived when they'd met in 1999. Too much pizza and sadness threatened to choke him, but he also felt a strange gratitude. No, this town wouldn't heal him, but here he was allowed to cry. It didn't matter how ugly his face turned, it didn't matter how ugly the sounds his throat produced were. Shorat had lived here, right here on the second floor, and as if they understood what Cal was seeing, the dogs sat down on the pavement and waited until he was done and had wiped his face on the sleeve of his jacket.

After breakfast the next morning, Cal drove down to Ithaca to see his friends Elliott and Therese. Twice he drove past their driveway, but on his third try he managed to spot the mailboxes and turned onto a graveled path. The ascent was steep; after a quarter mile he arrived in front of a large house overlooking a meadow. The couple had sold their house in Hilo and given up on retiring in Hawai'i and instead bought one-hundred-and-forty acres of mostly wooded land. The dogs jumped greedily from the car, and Cal didn't bother to leash them. Yuuki dashed off, Vanya giving chase for a bit before standing dumbfounded by this new vastness, without the confidence yet to bark at birds.

"You found it." Elliott wore a plaid flannel shirt and jeans. He stopped after taking a few steps toward Cal, his hands in his pockets, his shoulders high, and laughed quietly as though he were still thinking about a good joke he'd heard that morning.

Elliott was Cal's first American friend. Together they had taken Irving Feldman's creative writing classes, and Elliott had given Cal a ride home on most nights, dropping him off on the corner of Main and Lisbon. They'd become and stayed friends, surviving moves and fights, running two marathons together, reading and critiquing each other's work. He'd been Cal's best man.

"Living the dream, I see" Cal said.

"Well, you should see our tax bill."

"You wanted some land."

"I know, I know. You've got a bit of time?"

"Enough for a stroll, but not for an expedition. I have to get back to Buffalo by five."

"By five? Well, you need to come back sometime and stay a day or two. Therese is in her room writing, but she'll come downstairs later."

The dogs joined them, and, after barking once or twice at this man in his flannel shirt, gave in to his outstretched hand and let themselves be petted. "I sold the house. Shorat and I did."

Elliott wasn't one for big feelings, so he just looked briefly at Cal before shaking his head. "That's a shame. I wouldn't have quit the job, if I were you. What are you going to do now? Where are you going to do it? You want to buy five acres from us and build your own house?"

"I might," Cal said, even though living twenty minutes outside of town wasn't what he was hoping for. He wasn't one for woods, trees that robbed you of your sight and wouldn't let you determine where exactly you were. Living near friends was tempting, however.

They took a path through the meadow, turned once to look back at the house, then continued down towards the woods. "This will be your first winter. Lots of snow."

Elliott shrugged. "We bought the previous owner's old F-150, comes with a plow. The Bimmer has all-wheel drive; we'll be fine. Really, though, what are you going to do? You think you can patch things up? Do you want to?"

Cal thought about how he should answer the question. He didn't want to tell his friend that he'd spotted Shorat in Ann Arbor, didn't want to mention why he had to return to Buffalo so soon. "She planned it for a while. I find it hard to believe that someone who plans carefully to leave you can be easily persuaded to return." He paused, because the next thought came unplanned, uninvited, unloved. "How would we stand living together after she left without giving me any reason for it? I feel as though she hasn't broken up with me yet, so before getting back together, we would need to break off things first. I guess what I'm trying to say is — since I don't know why she left, I can't know what it would take for her to return. Maybe I wouldn't want her to return. Maybe I would hate her reasons for leaving me. Maybe her reasons would make me detest her. Or they might make me detest myself. And I'm not sure I know what person the Shorat who left me is and I can't be sure who the person that might return could be."

"You've been married for twenty years," Elliott said.

"I'm afraid I have lost all these years. I'm afraid they're gone and I won't ever be able to reconstruct them, remember them, make people understand that we were close and had a life with nooks and crannies and secret passageways. But who would return to me after leaving me like this? Who would do such a thing? Do I want to welcome back that person?"

"I left Therese as an undergrad, before heading off to Harvard. And forty years later I found her again, and we've been together for sixteen years now."

"I'll be dead in forty years," Cal said.

Elliott grinned, did the math. "With a little luck..."

"I'm wearing hearing aids already. How will I ever hear a word she's saying at ninety-four? And she won't be able to see me anymore. We could be together in the same room and not know about the other's presence."

Back at the house, Therese sat on the deck with some tea, receiving kisses from Yuuki and excited barks from Vanya. Getting out of the Adirondack chair appeared to cause her pain, and her smile was replaced by a toothy frown before reappearing more forcefully. Yet the next second, the corners of her mouth dropped again. "I'm so sorry," she said. "Elliott told me everything. I hope you're okay?"

"He's left California for good," Elliott said.

"Will you be staying here? In Central New York?"

Elliott brough a thermos with motor-oil coffee out onto the deck and handed Cal a mug. "He'll buy land from us," he said.

"Oh, really? How wonderful. I hope you're keeping the dogs? They'll love it here."

In the evening, Cal drove out to Chef's, the old Italian place on the corner of Seneca and Chicago Streets. He'd made a reservation for two and was seated at a tiny table with a draft chilling his feet and neck. He didn't have to wait long before Shorat sat down on the other chair, half-smiling, studying the menu, her eyes only an inch or two away from the small print. "What are you going to have?" She was wearing a sleeveless long blue dress that hugged her form, but she wore it as though she wasn't aware of it at all and would have scolded Cal had he pointed out how lovely she looked. She hated compliments, or better, she craved them but wouldn't believe any and instead felt pitied and insulted.

"Spaghetti and meatballs," he said.

"Then I'll have baked spaghettini."

A waiter took their order, and they tied the bibs behind their necks, laughed at how awkward they looked. "I've missed you," he said.

Her eyes and face didn't give away how she received his words. She looked directly at him, and only when the silence became so thick it threatened to turn visible, she said, "What do you want me to say?"

"Nothing. I just wanted to say that I've missed you."

"What are you going to do with your half of the proceeds?" she asked.

"I'm not sure yet. I thought about buying a house around here, something small with a bit of land for the dogs. I'd like to have two or three more dogs if possible. I'd like a barn or big garage. I've been thinking about buying a wheel and kiln and focus on pottery." He laughed at his words, because he imagined they sounded stupid coming from someone who only ever had thrown mediocre bowls and plates, and only for two years anyway. And yet, it was the only thing that appealed to him at the moment. "You?"

"Don't know yet. Though I think I will travel. I'll have time to visit my family. My brother's daughters are growing and I hardly get to see them. My parents are getting old and I want to spend more time with them. I don't know how much longer I get to have Mom and Dad."

"Yes," he said. "Of course."

"You never wanted a dog in the first place, and now you want more?"

It wasn't entirely true. He'd wanted a dog as a boy, yet once he moved to Berlin, a dog was out of the question; the city had also taught him to detest dogs and their owners. "I lost my taste for traveling. Maybe I'm too complacent, but I think I enjoy company more than looking at new places, staying in hotels that are all a variation on the same theme. I don't know, I miss being a stranger in Tokyo, Seoul, Mumbai, but I've been a stranger all my life, and for once, I want to get to know people. Let them hate me, like me well enough, let them think I'm a loonie. I want to see the same faces every week, become part of the fabric."

"I never really left. I never really was a stranger." Shorat took a sip of red wine from an impossibly small glass. "I'll be going to England soon. As soon as we have a vaccine, I'll be studying Islamic patterns in London. I want to see Paris. You never took me."

"I should have."

"Yes, you should have. Have you looked at real estate yet?"

He shook his head. "I need to take a few days. Haven't been back in Western New York in such a long time. I'm not sure I can take long, cold winters anymore." He tried to turn his answer into a joke, but Shorat didn't laugh or smile. "I'm really hungry," she said.

Bread arrived, and she emptied the small basket by herself. The pasta was brought to their table only a few minutes later. Shorat looked at what the waiter put in front of her, poked a fork through the thick layer of browned mozzarella, pulled out the fork, and stared at the strings growing longer and longer.

"We can switch," he said.

"Yes, let's switch." With relief, she received his spaghetti and meatballs and was done with her meal long before him.

"Who are you traveling with?" He hadn't been sure he would find the courage to ask this question, and once it had left his lips, he winced.

"He's fun," she said. "He'll take me to Paris. He promised. He'll show me the Eiffel Tower, Les Halles, the Centre Georges Pompidou, the Champs Elysees."

Eating baked spaghettini now felt like a mistake; his stomach protested, couldn't handle the aggravation. Sadness on top of melted cheese was too much to bear. Nothing good would follow. "Where did you guys meet?"

But Shorat wouldn't answer. Instead she finished her wine, ordered more, rummaged through the purse he had bought for her in Sebastopol, a purse made from soda can tabs. "I'm getting stoned later. I'm so glad I went to the dispensary before I left. New York is so behind the times."

"You haven't told me yet why you left."

"I haven't," Shorat said.

"Do you think you'll ever want to be with me again?"

Shorat looked at him as though he had spoken with a full mouth, or maybe she thought the question ridiculous. Maybe she hadn't understood what he'd said.

"You didn't really break up with me, but you planned everything. Do you want a divorce?"

"I don't want to think about that tonight." Her teeth were stained red. Her neck had loosened in the past few years, lines had formed running from her nose past her mouth and down to her chin. She wore no jewelry tonight.

"Are you happy?" he asked.

"You always did ask a lot of questions. Why do you have to ask so many questions? I don't know if I'm happy. But I wasn't happy in Santa Rosa, and now I'm somewhere else. That's it. I'll see how it goes. But I'm not going to waste any more time going after things that mean so very little. I've wasted twenty years working in jobs I didn't even like. Yes, they were easy and paid well, and I didn't hate them, but I can't live my life merely not hating the things I do."

"What about me?"

"What about you?"

"Did you merely not hate me?"

"That's a stupid question. God, are you trying to make me feel bad?"

He didn't and said so, but a moment later he wasn't so sure anymore. He'd never trusted his intentions. If Annette, who had murdered nine of her children, could have seen him, she would have said he was manipulating Shorat.

"I'm sorry," he said. "Maybe we should pay."

"Maybe we should." She looked at her watch, a large diver and a recent birthday present. "Yes, I should be going."

"Where are you parked?" he said.

"Somebody will pick me up."

"Oh," he said.

She took her phone from her purse and texted while he flagged down the waiter and gave him his card. "He's close, he says. Shouldn't be more than a few minutes." Together they waited for Cal's receipt, then he held her coat, and she thanked him. Cold wind from the lake greeted them, swept past them through the streets, pushing and prodding styrofoam cups and plastic lids and an old McDonalds bag. "Gentrification hasn't reached this part of town yet," he said. "Will you have a home base?" She didn't answer and kept her eyes on the street. She seemed to be in a hurry. "Is that your ride?"

The dark Audi pulled up to the curb. Shorat thanked Cal politely; he wasn't sure if her eyes, so small behind her thick glasses, were even looking his way. Then she opened the passenger door and got into the car. Cal lowered his head, trying to catch a glimpse of the driver's face, but Shorat's companion was already checking the wing mirror, looking over his shoulder. A moment later Cal was staring at the rear lights growing smaller. Behind him, someone was saying, "Sir? I think you forgot your coat." And yes, he'd forgotten his coat, his green army coat.

"Thank you," Cal said.

The waiter nodded, stared, grinned sheepishly. "I also wrapped up the spaghetti and meatballs for you." Cal looked at the styrofoam box, couldn't make sense of what the waiter was saying. Without thinking he reached out and took the container.

"Lunch for tomorrow. Or dinner," he said. "You have a nice evening, sir. Should I call you a taxi?"

"No, no that won't be necessary," Cal said.

"Maybe you shouldn't drive."

"I parked my car right around the corner." And as though he needed this waiter to believe him, he started to walk toward the old Lexus, turned once more to make sure the waiter, who was still standing by the door, saw the lights blinking in response to his remote key. He would have waved goodbye, but he didn't want to seem desperate.

Chapter 24

There is a lot to say about inefficiency, but maybe this insight had arrived too late in Cal's life to fully blossom and bloom. All his life, he had treated drinks, food, books and manuscripts he read, as hurdles, as though their only purpose was to slow him down and deny him — what? He ate fast, downed his drinks, finished his work early, wrote novels in brief summers. To him, it seemed as though these things had to get done in order to start — what? Ever since his forties he had asked himself that question and he still hadn't been able to find an adequate answer that unlocked the peace and patience he was craving. You could only grasp what your body understood, he believed, and no matter how many times he told himself that he could slow down his eating, his drinking, his love-making, his writing, he couldn't feel that time was available to him. He only understood haste.

In the past, he'd thought he needed to be done with whatever needed to be done just so that he was free to be with his parents and entertain them. Telling them stories about school, about his latest crush, the music he liked. They wanted to see him smile, they wanted to live through him because their own lives had ended sometime in their mid-twenties. They'd died, because they hadn't had a plan beyond putting food on the table and children on the chairs surrounding that table. That's what one did, and they had never understood nor questioned that concept. Karl's parents were post-war children, born in the late Thirties but getting their bearings only after Hitler had been defeated and pushed deep into the German closet. Self-realization had never entered their vocabulary, and art was something other, more depraved people, did. Art and self-expression were a source of shame, and they were ashamed for everything their neighbors might not like, and they were ashamed for their children who didn't turn out to be carbon copies of themselves, and in any case, they were always ashamed. Too ashamed to look for the reasons why they felt that way. In their world, psychology had never happened. Freud had never lived (though, Freud, Cal contended, had gotten it all wrong and was a misogynist to boot), Jung had never lived, therapy had never been invented, and mental illness only meant personal failure. Their world was intensely German, intensely post-war German, where food on the table excused everything past and present. There was food on the table, so much food, because so much had to be excused. And Jews were still to be distrusted. If Hitler had tried to kill them all, they had to be guilty of something. They had to be devious, debauched, degenerate. Oh yes, Hitler had been wrong to kill Jews. Couldn't he just have seized their belongings? Confiscated their money and belongings? Did he have to kill them? Food on the table made amends for all the shortcomings, all the historic failures, excused their own parents from any wrongdoing. Because how, how could you drive home to your parents' farm and accuse them of cruelty, conformism, and war crimes? You showed them your kids instead and told them the amount you made every month. If you could put food on the table, your parents' existence had been justified. Shame on those who still wanted to remind everyone of the Nazis and their terror regime. Shame on those who still claimed that their parents had kept Hitler's picture on the living-room wall long after May 1945 and only taken it down when British soldiers made an appearance on the farm and inquired about the Polish POW who had gone missing a year prior.

Cal's purpose as a child, as much as children had any purpose at all outside of being imprisoned by people who weren't sure they'd wanted these particular beings and would have been willing to swap them for other specimens if only they had been allowed; Cal's purpose had been to justify his parents existence and make them happy. If Cal existed and displayed obvious signs of being a happy and halfway-intelligent child, then his parents' life wouldn't be regarded as utterly futile and meaningless. If Cal played happy, his parents could have another beer or glass of wine or cognac, another slice of pot roast, without having to think about the meaning of their own existence. It was so easy — put food on the table and a smile on your kid's face, and you're golden. Never mind the Jews and the Nazis and the Neo-Nazis and the old Nazis in high positions throughout Germany's convoluted bureaucracy. Eat, smile! Karl, won't you eat and smile and make us happy?

But what was it that thirty-five years after leaving his parents' home still made him hurry through everything he did? What was it that stopped him from giving time to the people and the trifles he loved, the activities he loved? What was it that always told him to hurry and finish fast?

Connected to this haste was Cal's inability to admit how he felt in any given moment. At times, when a friend would ask, leisurely and without any intention to gain a firm answer, how he felt, and Cal would consider that question, he had to admit that he didn't know. Throughout the day, he suspected, there existed long stretches of him not feeling anything in particular outside a general mood. Monday mornings, this mood was often one of dread, because he feared opening his inbox. Early afternoons, his mood shifted routinely into one of general fatigue, a sense that nothing he had done or would do on this particular day mattered. Between noon and four o'clock, the world lost all its meaning and turned into the waiting room of a large train station, the air full of tired breaths, the faces of his fellow travelers indifferent or vaguely pained, their belongings bloating cheap suitcases and duffel bags or spilling from plastic bags. Sandwiches, made hastily at home the night before, were being unwrapped and chewed on and discarded half-eaten.

When he caught a glimpse of how he felt, it often displeased Cal. His feelings didn't correlate with the life he wished or ought to lead. His feelings embarrassed him and often pointed to what he perceived as character flaws, flaws in his lover's character, flaws in how he lived and perceived things. His feelings put him outside of what he deemed acceptable. How could he be attracted to a lover's sister? How could he be disappointed by a gift a good friend presented him with? Why did he consider the work of a colleague lacking? Why did he look at his wife and see her lines and how she had grown heavier? Why did looking at his own body fill him with shame? The watch he'd bought himself for his birthday looked and felt chintzy, but he couldn't admit it. His career had painted him into a tiny corner; he'd known it for years, but only Shorat's disappearance had forced him to acknowledge this. Worst of all, Shorat, after getting high in the evening and asking Cal to fix her a drink, reminded him of Sophie and her loud laughter, her vulgarity when drunk. Shorat reminded him of Sophie lying on the bed in the Berlin apartment on the fifth floor, not moving at all while they were having sex, pushing him off while making love as though he had turned into an attacker. Only weed allowed Shorat to feel anything during lovemaking, only alcohol and weed let her initiate sex, though by then she had turned into a different person altogether, one he didn't recognize nor love. And even though he tried every day to drop his feelings into an old shoe box and even though he never forgot to take that box out to the recycle bin on Sunday nights, Shorat made him feel grotesque, made him feel like a monster, ugly and despicable, something you could only endure after you'd given away your mind.

To live any kind of life that appeared happy at least if seen from the outside, he needed to disavow his feelings, and long practice had made him lose track of what he wanted. But it hadn't started with his marriage, not even with Sophie. He remembered his parents reciting, *Kinder die was willn, kriegen was auf die Brilln* — a very ungrammatical invitation to spank children should they ever *want* anything. You were allowed to ask for something — though most often that request was denied — but you were not allowed to *want*. The children of Nazis and Holocaust deniers had carried forth the seed of denying what was undeniably and very obviously true. What they hadn't been allowed to see and feel, they denied their own children. You felt what you were allowed to feel, what you were asked to feel. Everything else had to be denied until you couldn't feel it anymore, until you were numb to your own mind.

Spaghetti and meatballs were breakfast, and for the first time since talking to his eye doctor about macular degeneration, Cal bought a pack of cigarettes. While he was strolling through Delaware Park with Yuuki and Vanya, he smoked one cigarette after another, and after getting two venti lattes at Starbucks and drinking them both while smoking another three cigarettes, he felt much better. For the first time since leaving California, he admitted to himself that his life up to this point, up to sitting outside the Starbucks smoking cigarettes and keeping the dogs entertained with pieces of a somewhat stale croissant, was gone, and that the pain over losing everything would be with him for a long time. Maybe for the rest of how ever many years he would spend on this overpopulated, dying planet. He could die of Covid in one or two weeks, or of cancer, a car accident, an aneurysm. He would be miserable on days when Shorat would come to visit without warning, but he had Yuuki and Vanya, he had coffee and cigarettes and whiskey. He had money to buy a house. Cal forced himself to sit another hour on Elmwood, forced himself to smoke two more cigarettes before returning to the hotel, taking three Advil, drawing the curtains and falling asleep. He wouldn't hurry anymore. He wouldn't.

His mood carried over into the next day, and he followed his dogs, let them sniff, pee, and bark. He fed them treats and delayed his second cup of coffee indefinitely. He watched Yuuki contemplate small bushes, didn't interfere when Vanya went into a crouch on some late-blooming flowers — sometimes you needed to be a dick to others, but really, Vanya hadn't done much damage at all — and later sat with them in Delaware Park, Vanya's tongue reaching the ground, Yuuki offering him her belly to pet. Cal sniffed their paws, their ears, their fur, and they let him. Later, after dropping them off at the hotel, he sat outside Spot Coffee on Elmwood, then entered a bar on

Chippewa and ordered a Long Island Iced Tea, the drink Shorat had ordered one afternoon almost twenty-one years ago. She didn't appear, no dark Audi pulled up to the curb to drop her off. It was Olga who stepped into the semi-darkness instead, and who, without noticing him at his table by the window overlooking Chippewa, sat down at the bar. Olga dressed in a short black skirt, black stockings and heels, Olga's long dark hair now streaked with white, Olga with her prominent nose and slender hands.

He took his drink to the bar, sat down next to her, and could see from her face that she was seriously baffled by his appearance. "What are you doing here? I thought you lived in California." She got up to hug him, pulled him close, and held on for several long moments.

"What are *you* doing here?" he said.

"I'm waiting for George. He's paying for the trip, asked if I wanted to join him. So here I am." George had been her boyfriend when Cal met Olga. Although Cal had replaced him soon thereafter, George had never left Olga's orbit. They had both remained single and childless and over the past ten, fifteen years become a couple again. They didn't live together, and yet never lived without the other.

"Where are you staying?"

"At the Curtiss Hotel. Expensive, but I got a deal. Where is Shorat? Do I finally get to see her?"

Cal shook his head, tried to be brief. He didn't want any pity and was disheartened to see his friend's face fall. It lost its carefully decorated demeanor, and yet there was some odd glee in her obvious sadness. "You guys looked so perfect together. All the pictures on Facebook."

"Where are you and George headed?"

"That's not important. How did you lose her? What happened? You have to tell me what happened."

Cal ordered another Long Island Iced Tea. "Too long a story for a brief afternoon. Some other time. Where are you headed?"

"We didn't know if we should come at all, but George insisted." And off she was talking about Covid, the visa, requiring adequate travel outfits and several masks — she held up the one she'd worn on entering the bar — and bottles of hand sanitizer, medications for George, who couldn't walk all that much anymore because of his condition. Her sick older brother was still a problem, and her younger brother's girlfriend had now moved into the house their mother had left them, and they couldn't sell it because her older brother wasn't able to live by himself and where would he go? He'd never lived outside his parents' home. Olga hated her younger brother's girlfriend, who was rude, and who did she think she was moving in without asking Olga's permission?

Cal was glad to be off the hook, happily listening to the heartbreak of people he remembered and barely knew. He watched Olga, slim, elegant Olga, who had turned sixty earlier that year. When they met, he'd been twenty-three; Sophie had her abortion, and after leaving his former girlfriend, who was tired and disconsolate and without her lawyer boyfriend because he wasn't allowed to know, he'd made love to Olga in her small dorm apartment in the district of Wedding, half a mile away from his own. They'd met at a moment of darkness, and that darkness had never quite lifted. Now, looking at his friend, he could still see that darkness enveloping her.

"When is George coming?" he asked.

Olga shrugged, checked her watch, then took hold of Cal's arm to check his. "He should be here by now."

Cal had no intention of meeting George, who was a lazy, entitled, and resentful schmuck, complaining about bad breaks, bad systems, bad health, and believing that his work was done after dumping his bile in other people's laps. The last time Cal had visited Berlin, almost ten years prior, George had insisted on meeting him in a café at Steinplatz, and Cal had barely been able to squeeze in a word. Instead, George had aired the same grievances Cal had heard for years and years, either channeled through Olga or directly via phone at odd hours of the day, usually when it was night in Berlin and George was deep into his whiskey bottle. Cal remembered that this had been the first contact he'd ever had with George — drunken calls in the middle of the night, and Olga, naked and sweaty, taking the receiver from Cal and trying to talk her former boyfriend out of killing himself. How strange that this man, this George, had stayed exactly the same all his life, and how strange that he and Olga had never entirely separated.

"Let's check on him," she said now, pulling on her mask and reaching for his hand. "May I?"

They walked along Chippewa to Franklin, and they'd been here before, in his first year in Buffalo. She'd visited him, had stayed for a few days before taking the train back to New York. "How will you remember me?" he asked. "Will you remember me?"

"And what about you? What am I to you? Sometimes I believe your view of me is less than flattering. We didn't lack love, nor did we lack passion. What we lacked was harmony, common goals, common views. Now that so much business is done via Zoom, with people bending over laptops and iPads and showing you nothing but neck and chin, I've come to think that this is how you saw me, are still seeing me. We were never able to be at eye-level. Either you wanted me more than I wanted you or the other way around. We never matched."

"You didn't want me?"

"I didn't. Not at first. Things with George were difficult; I wanted nothing more than be alone. And then you came, and I let you in. But you fell out of love quickly. I never thought you could stay with anyone for twenty years."

Together they entered the impressive foyer and took the elevator to the fourth floor. "We booked separate rooms," Olga said. "I insisted. He didn't like it, but he really wanted me to go with him."

Her room was naked and comfortable, the carpet already stained, the air used and hot and very dry. Olga's suitcase took up one side of the bed. It was an old leather suitcase, black and scuffed, the airline tags still clinging to the handle. The window looked out onto Franklin, assuring the viewer that they hadn't left Buffalo yet, hadn't left the rustbelt and the dreadful architecture of the American downtown.

"Feel free to take things from the minibar. I'm not paying. I'll be back. I'm going to check on George. Don't go anywhere."

He sat down on her bed after taking off his shoes, pulled the suitcase toward him, and looked at its contents. The clothes were mostly black, by brands he didn't recognize, neatly folded and containing a smell he couldn't quite place, possibly an amalgam of suitcase, detergent, dry-cleaning, body lotion and Berlin apartment, that smell of dry rot, unaired spaces, rooms that were either too hot or too cold. The smell, above everything else, was prim and orderly, as though someone had captured the smell of a German public official's cubicle.

"He's asleep." Olga's appearance had changed, though how, Cal couldn't say. Maybe her smile seemed altered, or maybe it was the way she moved onto the bed next to him, fluid and willful as a cat. "Have you missed me?"

"How do you remember me?" he asked.

"It's been so long. The part you played in my life is becoming smaller and smaller. Sometimes I wish you hadn't left, or no, that's not right. I wish I had left too. Berlin was always my city, but it's giving me the cold shoulder these days. Yes, I wish I had left too. You left me and Berlin, and you seemed to gain everything; everything I wanted, you got so easily. I never married. Now Shorat has left you."

He listened to the effect her words had on him, couldn't quite decide if she felt compassion or satisfaction. She took off her sweater, revealing a sheer blouse and black lacy bra underneath. Her long legs lay stretched out next to his.

"At times," she said, "I look through the pictures we took of each other. I don't think anybody ever loved me the same way you loved me. There are so many pictures, and I'm naked in most of them. I still have the prints Paulina gave me, the one with the burning teddy bear — I find it really embarrassing now, even though the picture itself isn't terrible. It's just so...deliberately meaningful. I also have the photos of us making love in front of her camera." She looked for a reaction from him, laughed in fake embarrassment.

"Paulina lives in LA now. She's become a painter and changed her name to Paula. She's painting all our pictures, but she has misplaced our names and identities. She remembers us, but her memories won't lead her our way. She's given us false names and identities."

Olga moved to sit on his legs. Her face was not the face he remembered, but then, his own face he didn't remember either. Her sharp knees he recognized, her feet with the large gap between the second and big toe. "So we're getting a second life? How is she?"

He told her what had happened, how it had happened, and she listened, resting her torso and head in his lap. "Yes, our pictures are getting a second life, but she has forgotten our stories. Now her paintings only tell what she wants them to." Then he told her about Paulina's strange gift.

After Cal had ended, Olga said, "I can feel how you felt when I look at the images. I feel how my own body felt, and it really doesn't feel the same way anymore. My body has become a stranger, it won't let me taste the euphoria of the time we were together. We once ran down your street in the rain and you took off your shirt."

"And you said it was unfair and took off yours as well. We made love in the staircase."

"I remember how it felt to run next to you, your hands reaching for my breasts. I can feel how I could bend into any position you or I required. Let me see you."

"I'm not sure," he said, keeping his hand in her hair.

"I'm not either. But what are the chances we'll ever run into each other again? Really, what are the chances?"

"For you, I only exist in a span of a few years. I wish there would be more you could remember me by."

"For you, I ceased to exist. Sure, we spoke on the phone, but you would have gladly forgotten about me. That's how you always dealt with your guilt. You blocked out anybody you might have wronged, just to forget about what you'd done. And in due time you had turned them into the guilty party. Your mind is so fluid, it turns everything on its head. You know what bothers you most?"

He watched her intently, afraid he wouldn't be able to forget the coming moments.

She smiled like a schoolteacher who shares an important moment of her life, even though it will be wasted on the student. "What bothers you is that having me will mean you're not better than me. You think you can have me because you're convinced that I want you more than you want me, that you're the better catch. But if you reach for me now, it means that you haven't advanced, haven't moved into the new clean space you thought you'd found when you moved to the States. If you reach for me now, you'll admit that you're still Karl, and that the old relationships are still intact. You'll admit that I'm your equal. What bothers you most is that you still remember me at all."

The light coming from the outside was dimming until the window fell black, but Cal didn't rush. He wanted to have this moment, the not-knowing whether or not he should watch Olga strip away her pantyhose, take off her skirt and blouse and bra.

She said, "Sometimes I wasn't in the mood, but you were so determined, it made me want you. You would just stick it in and have your way with me, and more often than not, I loved that. I had more attentive lovers after you."

He took off his sweater, his pants, and everything else, until he felt as naked as the hotel room on Franklin Avenue. And how odd it was that after thirty years they'd spent apart, his body still knew and reacted to Olga the way it had when they both lived in Berlin. He'd always trusted her, his body had always trusted Olga's. "I'm not sure I really want to," he said. "George...."

"...doesn't own me. If Shorat hadn't left you, I wouldn't even be thinking about this. You haven't changed all that much." She let her slim hands glide over his shoulders and arms. She flicked his nipples and grinned. "Do you want me?"

Shorat on New Year's Eve in Chicago

We'd taken the 1985 Grand Marquis I had bought
in the summer for $500 off a rickety lot in Flat Rock,

Michigan. The car had coach lights and felt truly grand despite the ceiling liner hanging in tatters. I had bought new tires and put four sandbags in the trunk for better traction in the icy conditions.

Shorat always knew how to get deals to make her penchant for glamor and extravagance possible. She could go months saving money to pay off her student loans, but then might come home one day and tell me to pack, and in front of the house would stand a large luxury car she'd rented, and we would drive to New York for the weekend.

That year, 2003, she had booked a room in the Intercontinental, with free new Year's Eve dinner. We arrived in the early afternoon, walked through the frozen city, then gussied up for the occasion. I don't remember anything but dessert, which came in champagne flutes, and afterwards we were so full, we made love quickly and fell asleep right after. The fireworks woke us up. We had intended to walk toward the lake, but instead we watched perched on the couch we pushed up to the window.

Her hair is very short and she's wearing a pale-pink dress with a deep décolleté. It's a very festive dress. The picture was taken before we went to dinner, and she has used makeup, which she does on rare occasions. She looks like a cabaret singer, like someone who can tell you a dirty secret with a straight face and then purr into your ear. She looks as though she might go to the opera or the philharmonic without wearing underwear.

CHAPTER 25

HE CLUNG TO THE DOGS that night as though he might drown without them. He couldn't find a ready shape for what he had done; Olga didn't fit any easy mold. She still felt dangerous, after all these years, as though they were brother and sister and committing incest. By letting her see him and touch him, he'd lost control of his story. It had become hers too and she was free to tell her side and distort him whichever way she saw fit. And wasn't that what lovemaking was about? Meeting the other and gaining the opportunity to speak the other person, to say the other person's name with a recognition you couldn't fake? Wasn't lovemaking about changing the course of one's lover's life and remembering the moments they shared in unpredictable and ever-evolving ways? Now that he had shared himself, Buffalo was no longer his alone — what would Olga make of their encounter and how would she speak of him? Not for a second did he believe she wouldn't mention him to friends in Berlin. He shuddered, he would never regain what he'd given her.

Olga had been right, his worst fear was losing control of the story he had so finely spun for himself. Through failures and setbacks, he had spun the story of Cal, seeking to prove everyone who insisted on calling him Karl wrong. No, Karl had never existed. He'd always been Cal, always destined to live in the New World, write his own narrative and pity the ones that hadn't done the same. But this wasn't arrogance. He was too afraid to spend much time on arrogance. He wanted to kill who he'd been, and that meant pitying Olga and forgetting about her. Yet she was right — now they were equal, and his story was a lie. There was no Cal, there had never been such a man. He was still Karl trying on new lives and finding none that fit, none that disguised his ugliness and the years he spent flailing.

Had Olga filmed them? Had she kept her phone on the nightstand running? Was there a video of him, tired and overweight giving in to his past because he couldn't have the story he'd chosen for himself? And was this madness? Had Olga really infected him with the past? Were his thoughts about preserving his story the outsized ramblings of someone whose wife had finally put a stop to their marriage because she didn't want to have a bit part in Cal's narrative, this one-note piece of fear and anxiety? Was he so different from his parents who had buried their childhood memories because those had been too terrifying and shameful? Hadn't he done the same? Hadn't he buried his first thirty years in Germany and invented a life without a core? Without a credible protagonist? That's what he had done. He had invented someone too afraid to take root in his own invention. He'd been so afraid of the past, he'd never had the courage to believe in his own life. He'd never been alive, had always been looking for ways to start a life, and wasn't he looking yet again? Behaving as though he were sixteen and wondering where he might attend college? He had no baggage, there was nothing in his bag. However long he had lived, nothing had accumulated.

He packed that evening but couldn't bring himself to leave. Instead he spent the next day walking through the

Albright Knox Museum with a mask, walking the dogs through Delaware Park with a mask, having dinner on a curbside patio with a mask. He felt grateful for the masks that allowed him to be just a figure in a green army coat, nobody special and nobody you could possibly recognize. Seven days were left before the election. He could feel the frenzy, the anxiety, could see the fear on even masked faces.

Where would he go? Was this where he was supposed to live with his dogs and five-hundred dollars a month in pension money? Or should he keep pushing east, maybe cross the ocean once more and settle in France, somewhere near his sister and close to the Mediterranean? He could make his pottery there, sell it in markets on the weekends. Maybe he could teach English to French children and businessmen or even teach creative writing to expats and college students in the English departments. What would he do with Yuuki and Vanya? How would he care for them?

The realtor he called the next day picked him up in front of the Lenox in the early afternoon. Her ride was a small Cadillac SUV, the leather smell still thick, as though brought on by an infuser you plugged into the USB outlet. She introduced herself as Stacee and had to be a few years his junior. Since he was the only passenger, Cal took the seat next to hers. The inside of the SUV was icy cold with the AC running, as though it were a midsummer day. Cal noticed the leather seats squeaking with his every move.

"How is your room?" Stacee asked. Her voice was harsh, a bonus for a man with tinnitus and hearing aids; it cut right through to him. Yet despite hearing the question perfectly, he didn't understand it. "The room?"

"Did he screw up?"

"Who?"

"The manager."

He thought for a second. He always thought for a second before giving an answer. He wanted to be truthful, he wanted to make sure the person asking was getting what she had asked for. "It's a very...adequate room. The décor is old-fashioned, a bit behind the times. But the room is clean, they clean it as soon as I leave the building."

"Hah, I knew it." She laughed, slapping the steering wheel of the vehicle. "He's so proud of his clean rooms."

"He is?"

"He says you can lick the carpets."

"It's a clean room."

"He's going to be so pleased when I tell him. Maybe I won't tell him. He's my husband."

"Oh," Cal said.

"Yes. We used to live in Denver. In fact, we still own a place there. But then this gig came up, and I was in-between jobs and wanted to get my real estate license."

Cal grunted to let her know he'd heard her. The streets were broken from snow and ice, and the din of tires and suspension now obstructed her voice. He didn't want to tell her he was losing his hearing. To him, it equaled admitting he couldn't have sex anymore. He thought about that analogy for a second and then dismissed it. No reason to follow a bad analogy, even if it reflected what he felt.

"Are you staying in Buffalo, then?" he asked.

"We're looking for a house in the area." As though this answer had crossed a certain boundary, she added, "My husband's name is Steve. Eventually he wants to move back west."

"Back west?" Cal echoed.

"His dad still lives in California. Steve wants to be closer to him. Keep an eye on him."

"He's old then?"

"No, no. Well yes, but that's not the reason. If you're the indecisive type, I might have time to tell you." She was turning onto Lancaster Avenue, pointing to a house on her right before finding a parking spot a few houses down. The sky was hazy and the humidity still surprising after living for years in New Mexico and California.

Stacee opened the lockbox, fished for the key and seconds later opened the front door. But Cal was still standing at the foot of the stairs taking in the generous porch, the gray and red paint peeling in places. There was an optimistic grandeur about these Victorians that had never been surpassed, as though the architects, instead of imagining a race progressing to a gleaming future, had finally allowed themselves to build spaces for the kinky minds and obscene bodies of their clients, giving dark fantasies and moody minds a home. The nooks and crannies allowed lust, guilt, and longing to stay hidden. Even on the brightest of days, the rooms offered enough shadow and dark corners to feel consoled. This wasn't a world of productive, streamlined geniuses, but a place full of needy souls forever feeling displaced.

"So what is wrong with your husband's dad?" he asked.

She waited for him inside the hallway, and, once he had closed the door behind him, picked up where she had left off. "He's homeless, though he stays in the same place most of the time. He lives by the side of a highway."

"Homeless," Cal echoed.

"I know," Stacee said. "Doesn't it sound horrible? But he wants it that way. It's the only place where his tinnitus doesn't bother him."

Cal touched his right ear by reflex. Had he told Stacee about his ears? Had he mentioned his hearing loss? He didn't think so. No, he hadn't, he was sure of that. Had she spotted the wires in his ears?

"Tinnitus," he said.

"Yeah, he has this loud humming in his ears. Says it's like a swarm of mosquitoes. Or like rubbing two electrical wires together. When he's sitting by the highway, he doesn't hear it and he can sleep. He has a tent there; Steve is giving him money every month. And he's such a sweetie. He keeps several chairs, and last time we visited, he made us sit inside his tent and cooked for us."

Cal grunted.

"This house was divided into four units by a previous owner, but the last owner undid all the changes and converted it back into one single-family residence. He only stayed for a year or two, though. Everything is new. New roof, new furnace, new kitchen, new balcony upstairs."

"Washer and dryer?"

"In the basement. Brand new also. Only drawback — no garage." She climbed the stairs ahead of him to the second floor, opened a door leading from the narrow hallway onto the balcony. The light was failing already, but the orange hue illuminated her face, her dark hair, her rather large nose. She wasn't wearing lipstick; she caught him staring. "Steve's dad caused the biggest wildfire in California history. Well, the biggest before the most recent ones. Hundreds of thousands of acres burnt down. They never had any solid evidence it was him, but he was seen camping in the area where the fire started, and he insisted on defending himself in court and was sentenced to five years in prison, got out after three." She quickly glanced over to him. "Wild, huh? But you can look it up on the internet. Ever since his release, Steve's dad has been living by the highway. He once had a company and dozens of employees, but the state asked that he pay for damages from the fire, so he sold everything. Still, even that wasn't enough. He doesn't have a bank account anymore. Steve just sends cash to a P.O. Box. He'll never be able to own anything again."

Vocal fry allowed Cal to hear every one of Stacee's words. He closed his eyes briefly to get away from that voice. Of course it didn't work.

"How old is he?"

"Late 60s. Wait, no, he'll be seventy next year. So yes, very late 60s." She laughed.

"I like the house," he heard himself say, even though he hadn't set foot into any of the bedrooms yet. "Why don't we have a look at the bathrooms?"

She obliged, and together they looked at tiling, shower heads, sinks. "Will you be happy here?" she asked.

He shrugged, told her about the dogs, his dream of owning enough land to house a whole pack. A barn to house a kiln, a wheel, tools, and a car or two.

"I can show you the basement," she said.

"Yes," he said. "I would like that."

CHAPTER 26

IN THE MORNING, it was Cal who picked up Stacee at her office on Allen Street. The dogs were in back, curiously sucking in the smell emanating from this stranger. Instead of barking or whining, they were on their best behavior, cowed by this woman's presence.

"It's going to take a while," she said.

"Can you spare the time?"

"If you end up buying a house."

It was before they arrived in Hamburg that she asked, "How bad are your ears?" And when he didn't answer and only quickly glanced at her, as if to make sure she had really asked that question, she added, "Your hearing aids. I noticed them. I hadn't when I told you...."

"I'm afraid," he said, even though that had not been what he intended to say. "Every time I put them in, I'm deeply grateful to hear voices and music clearly, but every night I'm also afraid I will have lost more the next day. My world is getting smaller. My wife used to ask me, 'Do you hear the birds?' and I would listen and hear nothing. Or she would say something at the breakfast table, maybe turn her head to look out the window and keep talking, and I couldn't follow. I just couldn't make out the words."

"They suit you."

"They do?"

"I'm not trying...," but she fell silent and didn't say what she wasn't trying.

"My house burned down three years ago. The things that slowly leak from my head I'm only able to recall through music. Listening to music with hearing aids isn't bad, I shouldn't say that, but certain nuances go missing. I'm afraid my ears will wipe out ever more memories. And once you lose a certain pitch, a certain range, how do you remember it? My memories will become blunt, lose their magic. They will turn into facts. They won't be sensual anymore, just something you pull from a file folder. And I'm only fifty-four. What will be left to me when I'm sixty?"

The house she had on her list was near the water, a charmless structure. It did come with three acres of land and enough space to build a barn. "Would you visit me here?" he asked while they were inspecting the interior.

"No," she said. "It's not you."

Still, they drove the short way to the shore of Lake Eerie, found a public access beach, and Cal opened the hatch and took the dogs. "Do you have kids?" he asked.

Stacee smiled at him, shook her head. "We're taking our time. You?"

"I did them the largest favor by not having them," he said. "Tomorrow is Halloween. The day before the wild fires, we'd decorated our house inside and out. I haven't been able to look at ghouls and tombstones ever since. And do we really need to remind ourselves of our mortality during a pandemic? Why are you not wearing a mask?"

"Would you buy a house from a person you can't even see?"

"You didn't ask me to wear one."

"It's bad for business."

He stared at the lake in front of them, opened his mouth but the words seemed too jagged and uselessly cruel to taste them. Together they walked until the dogs had relieved themselves. The lake, Cal decided, was too big to be seen. What did you do with a lake this big?

The next house was a half hour away in Warsaw, a one-story Arts and Crafts building as stern as an elementary schoolteacher. Stacee hadn't visited the house yet, so they explored it together. "It's cute," she said, standing in the dining area, a finger running across the marbled table top. "At least it has a big yard. And a detached garage you could turn into a studio."

"Does your husband work on the weekends?"

She cocked her head. Her nose flared as though she were trying to smell what he was after. "Most weekends, yes, at least some hours. I often work Saturdays and Sundays as well. Open houses mostly, though since March, we've only been showing houses by appointment."

He settled on the red leather sofa, a staging item, he was certain, and tried to imagine himself brewing coffee on a Thursday morning in Warsaw, the dogs begging for their chow. Who else would be with him? Who would he call? Stacee sat down in front of him, on the sturdy coffee table The heat had been turned to low or off, and she was still wearing her coat. "Would you be happy here?" she asked. "I'd come visit."

"Is it *me*?"

"Part of you. The part that wants to belong and live among people who say Hello and How Are You and remember your name after the second time you've come to the hardware store and asked about a Makita or high precision steel balls. They'll help you install the kiln you order and even give you a huge discount on larger orders of clay. The neighbor's wife might bake you banana bread to welcome you to the neighborhood, and her husband will make jokes about the women who stay the night. The neighbors might buy your pottery for themselves or for an aunt in East Aurora, and they won't understand why you're asking so much for what they can buy at the Walmart for four-ninety-nine, so they won't buy more items unless you have a big feature in the local paper, and then they they'll buy six plates so they can tell their friends about it."

"How many times would you visit before complaining about the drive?"

"Twice. The second time there'll be people coming for dinner, and you'll introduce me as your realtor, not your friend, because you feel awkward about how we got to know each other. I'm not a writer — I Googled you, and you even have a Wikipedia page — and I'm not an artist, and I don't even like your pottery very much, and yet I'm still interested enough to come and see you, but that evening I won't like your friends, and they'll treat me like a foreign entity, like someone spying on their thoughts and conversations and they'll look my way with distrust. 'Can she really understand what we're saying?' they'll think and cast those quick glances, and I won't tell them that I graduated from the University of Colorado in Boulder with a Master's degree in American Studies and published my thesis as an academic article before deciding I didn't want to spend the rest of my life in a classroom. If I decided to tell them, they would become even more suspicious. What was wrong with me to leave a promising academic career?"

"You don't like academia."

"I'm an academia nut. Take off your shoes."

He hesitated, had she really asked him that? Ever since the days when he failed to understand what the students in corners or the last row of the classroom were saying in response to his questions, he'd learned to distrust what he heard.

"Take off your shoes," she repeated.

The request was so blunt he didn't hesitate, and after he'd done what she'd asked for, she said, "The socks too." Then she pulled his feet into her lap, inspected his toes, his skin. "They're nice," she said and licked the sole of his right foot. Her lips closed around the big toe, sucked on it. After a while, she pulled off her pants. "You can open your fly if you want. I like watching men do that." She put a hand on herself, her strong fingers going to work while she kept his toes between her lips. They watched each other, their voices visible in the cold. When he tried to pull her towards him, she shook her head. "Too complicated," she mumbled. "It ruins everything." They were quiet for a few seconds, before she reached over to close her hand around his. "Don't stop."

The third house was in Colden, and the village wasn't all that charming and a major road went through it, but it had a general store and a restaurant, and the house was cheap because it stood too close to that main road, and it had a huge barn, and a creek was running through the acreage beyond the backyard. "I could live here," he said. The dogs were running toward the creek before chasing after sudden movements toward the left. "Will you visit me?"

"Maybe," she said.

"You don't like it?"

"I do. But what if your wife returns?"

"You're married, too."

"We might be moving back west before the end of the year. Steve is going to fly out to Portland next week. If all goes well, we're celebrating the new year in Oregon. And no, I didn't know that last night."

"Should I take it?"

She shook her head. "You're not a potter. You need people around you, people who flatter you and tell you how charming you are, and that you look nice, and that your work means a lot to them. You're vain, Cal, and I like that about you. Here in Colden, what would make you get up in the morning? What would make you turn on the wheel? There's nothing here, you don't understand this world of villages in Western New York. They'll be nice to you, and you'll be nice to them, but they won't know you in a million years, because they have twenty books on their shelves and half of them are by Harold Robbins and the other half are old copies of *Reader's Digest*, and their favorite movie is *Driving Miss Daisy* and their second favorite movie is *Rambo*, and just because you're some artistic type from Northern California who speaks with an accent, they won't change their lives. You'll be fine, and on sunny days you might even convince yourself you were meant to live by a creek, but the world will forget you, this village won't even know you ever entered. For them, you're a tourist, a long-term tourist. If your pockets are deep and if you buy drinks, they won't key your car or set off M-80s in your front yard."

"How about dinner?" he asked.

"I know a place," she said.

They dropped off the dogs at the hotel. Stacee stayed behind in the car, and he understood and didn't comment on it. "Turn right," she said, "it's close."

Only four people were allowed to sit at the bar, and several tables had been set against the wall in back. Theirs was by the window, the cold laughing at the single-pane windows and nesting in Cal's sinuses. He didn't take off his coat. "The imperfect makes the perfect visible. The perfect numbs our senses."

"Am I that ugly?" she asked.

"You look lovely."

"But not perfect?"

"That's not what I meant," he said. "You're the first person ever to tell me to take my shoes off."

"Do our kinks match?"

"And you're leaving. I could live with the fact that you're married."

"You're awful."

"I could live with seeing you during my days, stolen hours, maybe a weekend when Steve visits family."

"You're truly awful."

"And I might never see you again, but tonight I get a taste of what is possible."

"I might not like that."

"Yes, that's possible too."

The bartender put the drinks in front of them, took their orders. "We might get our first snow tonight." He wore his hair slicked back and tied into a ponytail. His face was haggard, the features blurred as though they'd been finished in a hurry. "I've seen you before," he said and nodded toward Stacee. "Welcome back."

Once the bartender was out of earshot, Cal said, "Is this where you take your clients?"

"Don't be jealous. It's ugly."

"Sometimes I feel, in certain moments when I have to make decisions, that two Cals are being created, one who takes this way and another who takes the other way."

"By now there must be an army of you crisscrossing the country."

He laughed. "We only just met but I'll miss you."

"Isn't that perfection? To look at me now and not being able to have me? To never become weary of me, to never see all the brown spots on my skin, the little bumps, to never see my legs on days I don't shave? We'll have great food tonight, and maybe when you get up to use the restrooms I'll follow you, and in the darkness of the small hallway you can kiss me and feel as though you are losing something very important, when really, you don't know what you're losing out on. Isn't that perfection? You never have to wonder about me getting old, getting sick, wanting to see my folks, wishing to visit Thailand and South Korea. You never need to worry about my clients and the houses I take them to. You can just take what you can get, what I'll let you have, and soon you'll be rid of me because I'll be living in Oregon and you are trying to survive your first winter in Buffalo."

"Are feet really your kink?"

She shrugged. "They're yours though, for sure. You manscaped."

"You noticed."

"I don't think I have any preference, really. I can appreciate hair. But, you know, when you shave and trim, you let the viewer know that you've come prepared. That you expected to undress. You prepared yourself for being watched. It's lovely."

Their burgers came, and they ate in silence, drank in silence. The memories of the house in Warsaw, the coffee table, Stacee pulling down her pants and her shoe getting caught inside the pant leg, were beginning to melt, giving off small whiffs of steam, shrinking.

"I need to use the bathroom." He found the dark hallway, opened the door and stared at his reflection after he was done and washing his hands. Once he'd stepped outside, he waited listening to the chatter from the other patrons, dodged a middle-aged guy in a Polo-shirt who needed to relieve himself. Cal waited another minute, happy to wait for Stacee, whose face smelled of unpaid utility bills, of cheap hotel soap and dead flowers. The guy in the Polo-shirt exited, and Cal pretended to be on his phone. Finally he walked toward the front of the restaurant. Stacee's seat was empty. As soon as the bartender saw Cal, he approached the table, said, "Your friend got a call and needed to leave. She already paid, so you're all set. She told me to say she's sorry." His words were overly friendly while at the same time barely-veiled insults. "Everything okay?"

"Yes, yes. I'll call her."

"You do that." The bartender sounded unimpressed. He smelled that something wasn't right, smelled that Cal was to blame for his date's departure. And Cal felt the same way. What was it that had made Stacee leave him? What had he done to drive her off?

The bartender lingered. "You want another drink?"

CHAPTER 27

SHE SAT IN FRONT of his door, her mascara smeared, her cheeks red, and she didn't appear happy to see him. Cal could hear Yuuki and Vanya whining. "I'm sorry," she said. "I'm not in love with you, I don't even regret leaving you at the restaurant, but I don't want to go home, and it's kind of late to pick up some other guy and make sure he's discreet. Someone I can be interested in for one night. Don't send me away. I don't love you, I just want to spend a few hours with you."

He unlocked the door and let Stacee in. "I didn't see Steve downstairs."

"You're not listening to me. We'll be leaving before the election. I can't be home right now, it's going to kill me. Just be nice, take off your shoes, take off your clothes. Just be nice. We don't have to talk, there's no talk needed."

"I need to walk the dogs."

"Go walk the dogs, but hurry, people are waiting."

He expected to find his room empty when he arrived half an hour later. The dogs had relieved themselves quickly, as though they understood the urgency of the situation, but he had given them some extra minutes; he didn't want to appear needy, he wanted to be loved well enough. He gave Stacee time to regret her decision to seek him out again, yet there she sat on the bed, right where he'd left her. She pushed her phone back into the front pocket of her purse.

"Now be nice and just do what I say. I need it." She took off her coat, slipped out of her boots. She was heavier than he had taken the time to notice, taller than his arms and mouth remembered. Cal was afraid, not of Stacee, but of the messiness of what was to follow. He'd appreciated the perfection of her exit back at the restaurant — the heartbreak had been implausible and sweet, something you could replay in your mind on nights when you were in the mood for feeling lovesick. Stacee's return turned Cal helpless. They still had no future, but now she was making demands, now he was in the awkward position of having the upper hand and being required to acquiesce. He wasn't made for that position. But he did as he was told, he was too afraid of losing out, of harsh words, of not being put to good use. She said, "I don't need to see that. This, this is enough."

Three days later, Americans went to the polls and by midnight, the election still hadn't been called. Wednesday afternoon came, and Nevada and Pennsylvania were still counting mail-in ballots. Staying at the Lenox was eating into Cal's savings, but he still hadn't made up his mind about buying a house. He was getting used to life in one room. The dogs were getting used to their new surroundings, to North Street and Elmwood and Delaware. He was more afraid of the election outcome than he had first noticed. He hadn't seen Stacee since she'd left his hotel room and forgotten her purse and phone. In the large bathroom mirror she'd surveyed the damage, making sure Cal had left her unmarked enough to face her husband. Cal was holding her phone for long periods of time, not answering calls but staring at the faces appearing on screen once the phone began to vibrate. He read the incoming texts.

Thursday came and went without any clear results, but the sitting president could be heard and seen advancing his lies, claiming victory even though he was behind in the count. These were scenes Cal had watched many times since childhood, and they had always played out in countries you had a hard time locating on the map; in countries where you couldn't name even three politicians; in countries you neglected because the chances of ever traveling to them seemed negligible; in countries where military uniforms looked outlandish and threatening; in countries one should have known more about, one should have been traveling to; in countries you looked down on because they could be called republics only if you also mentioned a certain fruit. But this was America now, a stunning display of sound and fury, Mike Tyson ready to take a bite out of Evander Holyfield.

He was exhausted and unable to tear himself away from his computer, checking and re-checking results. By 1:30 Friday morning, the challenger had begun to pull even in three of four still-undecided races, and by 6:30, he was in the lead. A victory speech seemed only hours away. By 4:30 that afternoon Cal had rented a house on Ashland Ave, signed a year's lease, and after only one hour he already felt remorse and regret overtake him. To plan for a whole year seemed ludicrous when his life had come undone in a matter of days and more than one-hundred-thousand Americans got infected with the virus every day. What was he rebuilding for? What was he hoping to achieve? He felt bad enough about the empty house that was now his to furnish to order an obscene amount of pizza pies, and together he and the dogs watched the president-elect cautiously declare victory without ever using that word, while lying on the somewhat wobbly air mattress and sharing slice after slice, until Cal's stomach, despite Prilosec, warned him about the consequences.

Around midnight, he dressed to take a walk, and once he turned onto Bryant, his mind eased into a familiar and comfortable misery. He could permit himself comfort only in times of duress, which was maybe the reason why he wasn't entirely unhappy about his current life. Yes, he still wanted Shorat back, but he knew misery better than happiness. He feared happiness — this elusive and stupidly broad concept — because he had little expertise. Misery, however, seemed attainable. He could deliver misery, he was good at it, he had plenty of experience.

With those thoughts he turned left onto Elmwood. Ahead of him a tall figure was walking north, in the direction of Wilson Farms and, ultimately, Buffalo State College. Even though he couldn't yet tell why, Cal followed that figure and slowed down so as not to catch up with the man in the brown hat and woolen coat. It was a long coat, the kind you wore when you'd reached a certain age or position in life, or if you were young and had taken a chance on an item from the Goodwill store. But something told Cal that the man wasn't a student, his steps were too unhurried, too exact. They spoke of a certain stiffness.

The man crossed Elmwood and walked past Auburn to turn right on Lancaster Avenue. In front of the house Cal and Stacee had visited a week prior, the man hesitated. Yes, it was the house that had once been divided into four units but turned again into a single-family residence. New roof, new furnace, new kitchen, new balcony upstairs. The white post from the real estate agency was gone. The man went through his coat pockets and came up with a key chain, jingled his keys. Cal watched the man's profile, though it was too dark to make out more than a large nose and an unimpressive chin. From the man's posture, or maybe from the way he tenderly cupped the keys now, Cal knew that this wasn't proud homeownership on display. There was nothing arrogant about how he took in the house he'd just bought with cash, most likely, since it had sold within a week. Then Cal followed his gaze and understood immediately the man's silence, his tender awe. On the second floor, at the door that opened onto the balcony, the hall light stenciling her silhouette, stood Shorat. Maybe she had spied the man, maybe they were gazing at each other, anticipating the moment the man would climb up the stairs to the porch and unlock the front door. Their front door. Then her silhouette vanished, the porchlight came on, and moments later the door had been opened from the inside, and the man, after bounding up the stairs, entered the house. But Cal couldn't see anything more. The cold made his eyes water.

Chapter 28

The election was called the next morning. Relief pricked Cal's body, unstiffening his limbs after sleeping between the two dogs. He spent time walking Yuuki and Vanya and surveying his new neighborhood, he drove out to Costco and bought a mattress for himself, six dog beds, and food for two or three weeks. Later he visited the AmVet store and picked a kitchen table and chairs. He ordered a desk and chair online, plus lamps and rugs so the dogs wouldn't slide over the hardwood floors. Cal gave the dogs free reign of the house, and they chased each other from room to room, though once Vanya had made it upstairs and back again, he decided to stay in the lower half of the house. His legs couldn't be trusted.

Cal scrolled through job offers on Craigslist, cut and paste the ones that seemed demeaning enough to make him a viable candidate. A clinical trial for anti-depressants, a local enterprise searching for individuals able to write term papers for students whose parents had the money to buy them, a call for nude models for a private photographer. That last one specified that all ages and figures were welcome. Cal set up an appointment with the doctor responsible for the trial, emailed the academic fraudsters, and left a message for the photographer. He felt heartened by his initiative. He needed some income to stay afloat. He was old enough to be thinking about retirement but too young to seriously consider it.

Of course he went back to Lancaster Avenue that night, full of whiskey and pizza. The house stood in darkness, all sharp angles and harsh edges. Winter would sweep the streets soon. Maybe Shorat was already in Paris, or maybe she and her lover were having dinner somewhere along Elmwood. Cal kept walking east toward Delaware Ave, and once he'd reached the end of Lancaster, he turned onto Auburn where an acquaintance of his, someone he had called a friend to inflate his friend count, once had lived. They both had been grad students in the American Studies department, but David had come from money, driven a Volvo station wagon, and taken well-funded trips across the country. Cal couldn't remember the party he'd been invited to, couldn't remember which house David had rented. He couldn't remember what they had talked about. What he remembered was the feeling of shame. All of David's friends seemed to be well-connected, had brought expensive bottles of wine or whiskey and talked about vacations in French Polynesia, diving in Bonaire, culinary trips to Oaxaca. Cal had worn an AmVet sports coat and needed to check his account balance each time he went to the grocery store. Rooming with a hoof-trimmer in a small apartment had seemed like an achievement, but the party taught him otherwise. There was a level of worldliness he would never reach, not because he wouldn't ever be able to afford trips to French Polynesia, but because he hadn't even known about Bonaire and how wonderful the waters were for diving. He hadn't heard of Oaxaca and its cuisine. The other people at the party owned maps, the world was laid out in their minds. Cal only owned blank spaces and a ratty sports coat whose lining was beginning to tear.

He had liked his acquaintance though, who was now a watch writer and diver and motorcycle enthusiast. David called himself a hipster, which was the surest way to know a person wasn't a hipster, and on his podcast he talked about purchases and trips, vacations, and watches and motorcycles he'd bought. He had turned into a blowhard, but Cal still envied him — David would never know what a blowhard he was.

Auburn Avenue, even though it was Lancaster Avenue's spitting image, had always felt foreign to Cal, and not only because of David renting a whole house while Cal and his hoof-trimmer shared a two-bedroom apartment. No, Auburn had always seemed prim, the haughty cousin, the street that made you quicken your pace. A few houses before reaching Elmwood again, he saw another white post, another house for sale. His heart leapt into his throat and onto his tongue, his lips closed around it not to drop it onto the sidewalk. Quickly, he ran down the driveway and fought his way through tall weeds to the end of the backyard, until a creaky fence stopped his approach. But yes, yes, he was certain. Yes, yes, the house beyond the fence was Shorat's. It belonged to her and her lover. He turned away to take in the dark house that was for sale, and his mind made all the financial calculations and no, he had just rented a house and no, he shouldn't even think about this and no, he shouldn't torture himself. In short, he needed to buy this house.

The coincidence kept him awake until well into the morning, and when he finally fell asleep, he found himself in a subway car in Berlin, the wheels screaming over the tracks, people swaying while trying to hold on to poles or door handles. Two guys no older than nineteen or twenty were swapping headphones, moving to the beat of their music. A woman was watching Cal watching, several girls stood in front of a door and laughed about a story one of them had just told. Nobody, though, was wearing a mask, and Cal grew afraid of the half-open mouths, the loud laughter, the man who was blowing his nose right next to him, and if not for the photographer who returned his call just after eight o'clock, he would have slept past nine, when the real estate agency opened. For the first minute, Cal had no idea who was talking to him. His mind caught up when the conversation turned to copyrights, contracts, and a safe environment. Yes, Cal had time that evening for a test shoot, but no, he would not get reimbursed for the test shoot. They had to click, the man on the other end of the line said. If they did indeed click, Cal would be paid forty dollars an hour thereafter. He gave Cal an address on Hertel Avenue.

The real estate agent's name was Michael and he agreed to show the house on Auburn at noon. This left Cal time to shower, walk the dogs, and look halfway awake at the time of the appointment. Michael drove a Subaru, a choice Cal found disturbing in a real estate agent. There was something small-minded in a Subaru, something decidedly Puritan. Subarus were the sensible shoes of the automotive world. The cars lacked horizon, they lacked joy.

Together they traversed the house, which, during the daytime, appeared neglected and at the end of every maintenance cycle. The outside paint was an unappealing brown with black trim, the roof shingles were worn down like the hide of an old bison. The hardwood floors in the downstairs rooms were scuffed, the bathrooms in need of renovation. Once he'd climbed the stairs to the second floor, Cal was greeted by worn carpeting in a shade of brown approaching pink. Michael wore a mask and delivered his remarks in a voice that forced Cal to ask for repeats, which Michael did but without raising his voice or enunciating more clearly. Cal had the distinct feeling they were getting on each other's nerves. Because of the many larger and smaller repairs needed, he ended up making a very low offer, one that Michael received with a shrug and eyes that appeared decidedly angry. The down payment would eat at least half of Cal's money and force him to look for steady work within the next three months. It would curtail his ability to fly to Paris, Seoul, Egypt, or wherever Shorat might take her new companion.

He stress-ate at Manhattan Bagel, standing outside on the sidewalk with two egg-and-bacon sandwiches and a large hazelnut coffee. Eating made him feel in charge, because he knew he was definitely in charge of ruining his body, growing his gut, messing with his digestion, and jeopardizing his health. It was glorious, a strange kind of body modification that didn't require needles, ink, piercings, or surgery. It was open to everyone, and most everyone partook in it. He kept thinking about his photo shoot and how his stomach would gurgle while he was getting rid of his underwear.

The afternoon he spent with the dogs in Delaware Park, fishing for his phone every now and then to see if Michael had called or texted him. By now, the seller would have his offer in hand. Cal sat on a bench, the November sun warming his back. Vanya's tongue hung from his mouth while watching the mix of pedestrians, runners, and bikers. Cal wondered what the dogs were thinking about Shorat's absence, if they expected to spot her everywhere they went, or if they blamed him for her disappearance. Their lives had been upended, they showed signs of distress in their quiet ways — ever since moving to Ashland, Yuuki refused to come inside from the yard. Vanya shadowed him everywhere he went , except for the upstairs bedrooms, as though he expected Cal to disappear as well.

The photographer turned out to be in his early thirties, tall and slightly overweight, handsome in a '70s kind of way. His sweater fit snugly, his pants were corduroys, and hair and sideburns were long and dark. "I know this is awkward, or, well, I think it might be. It might be a weird project, but I want you to know that, I'm not, well, it's difficult."

The photographer, whose name was Weston, had lost his father the previous year. His parents had divorced when he was ten, and he had grown up exclusively with his mom, visiting his dad only a few times during his college years. "I have these memories of Mom and Dad together, of them sitting on the sofa, she in his lap, both of them laughing. I remember them getting drunk together and laughing. I hated my mom's shrill voice — when she drank she turned into a person I didn't recognize. Worse, she turned into a person who didn't recognize me, her only son. My dad was a sloppy drunk. He couldn't find the bathroom door and instead opened closets. He'd just laugh quietly, like God had told him a secret joke. Or maybe the devil. In any case, when my father died, of esophageal cancer, he left his home and his papers and everything to me. By then he lived near Lake George. I was in grad school, I had papers to write, art work to turn in, and the day before I was going to drive north and have a look at my dad's house, it burned down. The police suspects it was arson, but they never caught the guy who did it."

The apartment, a lower unit on Hertel Avenue, was cozy despite the traffic noise overpowering the old, single-pane windows. Cal had taken a seat on the black leather sofa, the only light in the living room coming from a red-shaded floor lamp. Area rugs covered the shabby hardwood floors. Bookshelves lined the walls, and books lay stacked on the coffee table.

"You want me to be your dad."

"You don't need to look like him. That's not of the essence. But I need to see him in you."

"A certain way of being."

"Since college, people have been telling me that I remind them of their best friend in high school, their cousin from Indiana, their lover from Switzerland. My dad was from Buffalo, but my mother is from Guadalajara. Her father was a diplomat. I look — well, this is the way I look, a distinct mixture of certain features. And yet, all my life, people have been telling me that they'd met or known somebody who looked just like me. I can't be certain how many others hear similar claims, but it has always been disconcerting to me. Do I really own such an ordinary face that nature has replicated it in great numbers? Or is it a face that never clearly registers with anyone, so that they mistake it easily for someone else's? I am a vain man, someone for whom everything he does is of the utmost interest, if not importance. And so I started to wonder if acquaintances were mistaken when claiming to know two people who looked the same. Maybe they remembered me but had forgotten my name. They had encountered me before, and were merely unable to connect the dots, turning one and the same person into two instead. Had I been in Rome or Berlin or San Bernardino without my knowledge? I know, this sounds preposterous, but the thought of random men sporting my face seemed more intimidating than the thought of being transported, maybe in my sleep, to other places."

"So you've been looking for the person someone might mistake for your father? And you want me to be that someone else, if all goes well."

"You don't look like him at all, if that's important to you."

Cal shrugged. "What do you have in mind?"

"I remember certain moments. No, not correct. I remember certain photographs of him. My mom threw out everything that reminded her of my dad. She has this firm belief that whenever a relationship ends, you either return the items that were given to you by your lover, or, if that's not an option, you donate them or put them in the trash. All the photographs of Dad — she chucked them. But whenever I visited him, he'd show me old pictures. I don't think he ever got over Mom. It wasn't him who broke it off. I mean, well, he did cheat on her, but he didn't want to leave her. I think they never matched up well. They loved each other, of that I am certain, but they never got to know each other well. They didn't *get* each other."

"You don't remember the specific occasions, but you remember the photographs your dad showed you."

"I made a list. It's not a very long list. Twenty-three pictures. I want to re-take them. I want them to be in my possession. I want to look at them and see Dad. I want to see my parents."

"What about your mom?"

"She hates the project. She doesn't want anything to do with it."

"You found a stand-in?"

"Yes."

"You're going to make memories. I always found that phrase infuriating, as though we get to consciously decide which events, which people we'll remember. But your project is exactly that."

Weston nodded, and for a while they didn't say anything, and the silence was comfortable. Cal rather liked the apartment, and the whiskey was good.

"Are you ready?" Weston finally asked.

"Sure," Cal said. "What do you need me to do?"

It turned out that Weston also owned the upper unit, and after entering it via another entrance and a creaky set of stairs, Cal understood the obsessive nature of the project. Even though he'd never set foot in Weston's family home and hadn't seen a single picture of the set Weston wanted to reproduce, he immediately grasped that the furniture, the lights, the books, the vinyl albums, were the exact same items he'd known as a kid.

"I just want you to be yourself," Weston said. "Please try not to act. No poses are required. If we end up working together, I assume I will direct you, guide you. But not now. Take possession of the apartment. I will follow you around and take photos." He walked over to a dresser and held up a camera, a Leica Q2, the model Shorat had bought for herself. "Whenever you're ready."

It was an odd request to be someone you had never met. For several moments, Cal just stood inside the apartment trying to get a feel for his surroundings. He took a seat on the blue sofa, he walked into the kitchen, opened cabinets, and looked for a glass. When he'd found a tumbler he liked, he walked over to the old-fashioned drink cart and poured himself some Laphroig. He sniffed it, took a sip. He walked into what turned out to be a bedroom, took off his shoes, bunched up the pillows on the bed and sat staring at the two paintings on opposing walls. The drink sat in his lap. All the while, Weston was taking pictures, deliberately, unlike the photographers Cal had known in Berlin, who didn't care about the amount of film they used and who were hoping to get the one right shot you couldn't plan for. No, Weston's shutter only sounded occasionally. At first it unnerved Cal. He liked the white noise of rapid shooting, but then he settled down, got off the bed and inspected the toiletries in the adjacent bathroom, put a dollop of shaving cream in one palm, and started to shave with an unused Bic. After finishing, he went back to the kitchen to make coffee, Weston in tow. Suddenly curious, Cal walked back into the bedroom and opened the large closet. He pulled off his own sweater, took a black shirt from its hanger, and tried it on. It fit perfectly. Now he took off his pants and stepped into a pair of black slacks he found folded on a shelf. The legs were a tad short, he felt, but otherwise he had no complaints. "You didn't specify weight or height in your ad," he said out loud, not expecting an answer from Weston and not receiving one.

Cal took a carton of two-percent milk from the fridge, poured some into a cup with the caption, "You're awesome. Keep that shit up!" The coffee had turned out weak, the way Cal liked it, and satisfied he claimed the blue sofa again, reaching for an old *New Yorker* before becoming aware of a photo album on the bottom shelf of the coffee table. It was one of the old-style albums with card-stock pages and some flimsy, sheer paper dividing them. You needed photo corners to keep pictures in place, and with great care Cal opened the album to the front page. What greeted him was a drawing, not a good one, of a couple sitting on a blue sofa, she on his lap, looking into his eyes. Her hair didn't reach her shoulders and was neither curly nor straight — the artist hadn't quite captured her face either.

"That's why I need photos," Weston said. "They are terrible. They only have meaning to me. They are stand-ins for what I intend to do."

"Stand-ins for the stand-ins." Cal turned a page, and in this new drawing, the man was positioned behind the woman and lifting her shirt. The woman's belly button was visible, and a corner of her bra. "Who took the original photos?" he asked.

"I think you should put the album away." Weston's tone wasn't sharp, neither was it friendly. "I don't want you to imitate what you're seeing."

Cal returned the album to the bottom shelf, took his mug, and sipped his coffee.

"My female model will need to meet you first," Weston said.

"Does that mean I'm hired?"

"For one evening, yes. For now. If she agrees that you are the right choice and that she can work with you, we'll be working on my project together, yes."

"She is more important than your dad?"

"Without meeting her, I would never have thought the project possible."

"What did you see?" Cal asked. "This last hour."

"You want to hear how well you fit the role?"

Cal thought about that. "Not really. I'm vain too, sure, but what in the way I did things convinced you I could be the stand-in for your father?"

"You're touching and holding things as though you're afraid you could hurt them, or they could end up hurting you." Weston paused. "I'm not going to tell you more. The less you know, the better the project will be."

"I must be your father's height, his weight. I'm wearing things you chose because he wore similar items, right?"

Weston was still holding the camera in front of his chest, reminding Cal of a schoolboy on a trip to the zoo or the museum. Now that this first meeting was nearly over, his ears again focused on the traffic noise, the rattling of the windows whenever a large truck went by on Hertel. "You look exactly like him. I'm sorry, but I think we're done here."

Shorat at Grulla

The dogs are visible behind her, running toward the white dunes where, maybe two or three decades earlier, a lake stretched toward the horizon during the winter months. No one we know has witnessed water here.

The Grulla Wildlife Refuge is a spot where light pollution approaches zero, and for long stretches of time we can't hear anything but ourselves and the wind in our ears. I have taken out my "ears," my hearing aids, because the wind savages them, turns everything to static. Yet even if I had perfect hearing, I'd detect nothing except for Vanya's loud breathing. In the 1840s, the U.S. Army established a camel corps, and the legend of the Red Ghost, a giant camel with a dead soldier strapped to its back making the rounds of desert ranches, is still alive. New Mexico was not haunted by this creature that refused to die and was spotted into the 1930s, and yet we're looking out for its silhouette to appear any moment now.

Her hair is long, though this must be my memory rearranging the facts. In New Mexico, she wore her hair short again, an inch maybe. But I see her glancing back at me now, and her hair appears as long as it was on the afternoon she left me. She's glancing back, as though to say, "Where are you? Why are you not keeping up?" She is worried because the dogs are off leash, which is forbidden, and what might they run into? If they spot a coyote, or worse, the Red Ghost, what will they do? How are we going to get them back?

We still have three dogs. Starbuck is still alive, leading the pack. He is a Chinook, and he's the most divine being I've ever seen. People are drawn to him, as though they are seeking his blessing, the blessing of a spiritual master and healer. That day, I still believe that he'll never die.

Shorat's face is relaxed, even though she wants me to hurry so that we won't lose track of the dogs. Her face is quiet, as quiet as the landscape around us. She hates walking off path, even though at Grulla no clear path is visible. There's no trail you can follow easily. Shorat will never leave a sidewalk for a shortcut across a grassy patch, she won't leave a trail to scout out the surrounding woods, she won't jaywalk, not ever. She looks back over her shoulder as if to say, "You got me into this mess."

CHAPTER 29

INSIDE THE CAR, he checked his phone for new messages. Michael, the real estate agent, had called. The seller was agreeing to Cal's offer, under the condition that the house would strictly be 'as is.' "I would have it inspected thoroughly. I'll be sending you the paperwork, and you should meet with a mortgage broker as soon as possible. Let me know if you need any help."

The news made his hands vibrate and he promptly ran a red light on Delaware. He couldn't feel himself, was dissolving into the moment and getting afraid he might not live long enough to move into the new house. "Just concentrate," he told himself, rolled down the windows to let the night air get in a few hard bites. He thought of his friend Joaquin. During their last meeting, while sitting in front of the Mission San Rafael Arcangel, a funeral procession had emerged from the church, six men carrying a coffin toward a Cadillac hearse. A very old man received the most attention, the most pats, and all the guests following this man wore masks because of the pandemic. The man's mask had slipped below his nose, he seemed to see nothing but the casket. No, his eyes did not see anything, Cal was certain.

Joaquin had asked him, "Are you afraid of death?"

Cal had stared at the procession dispersing, like sugar dissolving in tea. "I'm not afraid to die. I'm afraid of forgetting myself. As a small boy, I thought that after death I might be sitting in Heaven, looking down at the people I left behind, looking down even on my own grave and watching my loved ones water the flowers they'd planted. But one night, while my room was dark and my parents were still watching TV next door, I realized that there would be nobody left who could claim to be me. I'd be gone, I couldn't watch anything or anyone, there wouldn't even be a thought or memory left. There would be no thought left anyone could trace back to the person I had been. Everything I loved, everything I knew, would have ceased to exist because no thought, no memory, could ever lead me back to the person I had been. In other words, I had arrived at absolute emptiness. That feeling has never left me. I'm not afraid to die, I'm afraid of forgetting myself.

"One night, Shorat and I had eaten chocolate we'd bought at the dispensary. This was a few weeks after our house had burned down and we were staying in a rented duplex. Our neighbor had an autistic son and some nights, the boy would hoot like an owl for hours at a time. We shared a wall heater, and the sound wasn't muffled; it was as though the boy were sitting in our own living room. That night, I woke with severe heart palpitations. I thought, no, I was absolutely certain, I would die. Shorat was with me, but any ambulance would be arriving too late. And I remember I wasn't afraid of dying. I was deeply disappointed that it was going to happen in the dark, on a cheap mattress in this run-down duplex. All my thoughts would be taken from me, and I wasn't even dressed."

Cal let the dogs into the small backyard, filled their dishes with leftovers, sat with them drinking whiskey. It was true, he wasn't afraid to die, but now that his offer had been accepted and he had met Weston and possibly become part of the younger man's art project, he was afraid of missing out. He was going to move into the house sharing a fence with Shorat's, he couldn't wait to see her, watch her, run into her. What he might say, how he would explain his proximity, he had no idea. But he didn't want to die just yet. He poured the whiskey onto the lawn, then went inside to mix himself another drink.

The morning was taken up with calls. At noon he saw Marlena, a mortgage broker who had her office near the old train station. The rooms she occupied on the first floor on an old non-descript house with gray siding were full of smoke, and she kept smoking while taking notes, asking Cal for documents, proof of employment, bank statements. "You can wear a mask, that's up to you, but I won't, I just can't." It wouldn't be easy to get backing, she intimated, since he was out of work, but his down payment would pave the way. "You got a good deal," she said.

"You should see the house."

"It's the location, always is. Do you have money for repairs?"

Cal shook his head. "Pray that the furnace won't break."

"We have home warranty for that."

"I can't afford that."

"Michael will pay."

"He will?"

"He's my cousin. He's not as bad as he seems." She offered Cal a cigarette, and since he was inhaling her smoke anyway, he accepted. "Business has been slow," she said and held out her gold lighter. "Divorced?"

"No," Cal said. "No, not yet anyways."

"Complicated?"

"I don't know. Maybe I'm in denial?"

"Has she served you the papers?"

He shook his head again.

Marlena stubbed out her cigarette and lit the next one. "She left you for another man?"

"Maybe, yes. It seems that way, but it's strange. I've seen the guy, and yet, something tells me there's more to it."

She laughed loudly, pleasantly. "Yes, you are in denial. But you'll have a house on a nice street. This is not California, but you won't experience wildfires and droughts. Sinus infections, plenty of them. Everyone has them, all the time."

He signed what needed to be signed, then drove to the marina and walked by the water until he couldn't feel his hands and toes and his ears started to hurt, then went home to be with the dogs. Later that evening, he walked to the Food Co-op on Elmwood, bought greens — dark greens, which were good for his eyes — tomatoes, Persian cucumbers, meats, canned fish, and a large bag of rice. He cooked and ate, fed the dogs, drank too much whiskey, and around nine, Weston texted him to ask if he had a minute to talk.

"She has seen your pictures, and she has agreed to do a first photo shoot with you."

Cal was looking for a fitting reaction. Why was this woman so important to the project that Weston refused to make a decision without her? "Does she have a name?"

"She might tell you once the two of you meet. Do you have time tomorrow evening?"

After ending the call, he sat in the living room, Vanya yipping and twitching in his sleep, and tried to feel something beyond his confusion, the not-knowing whether or not he would indeed move into a new house;

the nagging suspicion that Shorat and her lover might not spend much time in Buffalo, especially in the winter. And really, had they bought the house for themselves or for his ailing parents? What did he really know about why they had been inside the house on Lancaster Avenue?

Twenty minutes later, he went up the porch steps to that house, searching for a name on the mailbox, a letter in that mailbox. The driveway was empty, the windows dark. Where was Shorat? Was she already asleep? Were she and her lover already in Paris, taking a bateau-mouche down the Seine or climbing the steps toward Montmartre? Where was she? These questions were enough to make Weston's art project look insignificant, they robbed Buffalo of all its charm. Yes, Buffalo had only ever been the city where he'd met his wife. Beyond that, it had little significance. Cal sat down on the stairs, waiting for something to tell him he was doing the right thing.

If you removed a certain memory from an object or place, were object and place still the same? They couldn't be, it was absurd. Walking home along Elmwood Avenue, Cal wasn't even sure that anything in his life, once Shorat would have been removed from the very center of his thinking by elapsed time and the end of his denial, would feel or remain the same. Already his coffee consumption had dropped, because she no longer sat with him on the couch, the front porch, the back patio. Mostly he drank cold coffee these days, a full carafe lasted two to three days. If he really wanted it hot, he warmed it up in the microwave. His car had lost its charm — it had been their crazy purchase after the fire, a twelve-year-old Lexus they barely needed — because she no longer sat in the passenger seat. Even America itself, the whole country, had lost its meaning. Maybe another woman, maybe some event, could restore the luster, but it would be a different life, a different country, a different car.

Some objects in his possession, like the Vostok Amphibia GMT, had meaning because of when and why he had bought them. This was, of course, a common thing. People bought jewelry for birthdays, weddings, career achievements. They bought watches after landing a job or welcoming a baby into the family. Often these objects were expensive, once-in-a-lifetime purchases. They held monetary value, and that monetary value was the reason they had been chosen for a specific occasion. Without that monetary value, the occasion would fail to appear as momentous as the buyer of the object wished it to be. In return, the occasion — now marked as important by the price the buyer was willing to pay — endowed the object with meaning.

Given the possibility that the owner of said object might fall on hard times and sell the item, would the next owner be aware of its previous meaning? Most likely not, because even an engraving might not tell the full story. The object would become merely a valuable, or previously valuable, commodity.

But you didn't need to fall on hard times to have your objects devalued and rendered meaningless. Nothing he still owned from his life with Shorat meant the same anymore. At this moment, these leftover souvenirs delivered a low-level pain, like a paper cut or broken toe; sometimes cut and toe acted up. Soon enough, though, his army coat, his watches, the few items of clothing he'd packed, would merely be objects, not unlike burned-out light bulbs perhaps, or empty batteries. From the outside, they might look unchanged, but their usefulness had ended. No, Cal thought, not quite. Yet even though his logic was faulty, he rather liked that last comparison. Army coat, pants, and shoes would not fail as objects the way a dead battery failed as a useful contraption, but the meaning of his personal belongings lay *not* in their ability to shield him from the cold or tell the time; the meaning lay in their ability to make him feel at home, to remind him of who he was. That alone was their primary goal. With Shorat gone, with Shorat having chosen a new partner and a new life, the objects surrounding him were dying quickly. And Cal himself was dying with them. Like them, he was still there, but he had no meaning left. He was a body, unrecognized, unnoticed, unknown. Nobody would pick him up and put him to use again.

Chapter 30

"The homage, or the fake, is more evocative of the real thing than the original." Weston sat opposite of Cal in the downstairs apartment on Hertel, a Diet Coke in his hand. Stubble was spreading across his pale face, his hair needed a wash. "It leaves us unfulfilled, thereby forcing our mind to conjure the original at every turn. It's a painful scenario, because you wish you owned the original, and yet were you ever to own it, you'd lose sight of it."

"You don't trust your mind to hold on to the memories."

"The mind changes everything that's set before it. It rearranges, it blurs, it glosses over. Whenever I revisited the photos of my parents, I was astounded how wrongly I remembered them. My drawings are only approximations, but I want to fix in place as much as I can. You have two choices when you can't have the original — you forget and let go of the pain of not owning it, or you can keep the pain and the desire alive. In any case, I have decided, for my own sanity, that if I were to have saved the original photos, my hunger for them would diminish. By owning something, you forget about that item. The homage, however, reminds you of how much you lost, and of how much you'll never have. The near-miss is the best way to be reminded that perfection exists."

"I'm the near-miss."

"You're not my father, but you move like him, you share some general physical traits."

That morning, Cal had learned from his sister that his own father could barely walk anymore and had stopped chemo for his stomach cancer. Restrictions and safety measures at the clinic, established to curb the spread of the virus, were taking too much of a toll on his body. Cal had been pushing the news around and aside all day, and yet there was nothing he wanted from his father before he died, nothing he wanted to give. All day he'd been irritable and impatient with the dogs. A call from Marlena about a delay in his application's approval had caused him to hang up on the mortgage broker. The first thought after reading his sister's email had been, So it looks as though he'll die first. For the past years, he'd seen it as a competition. If he were to die first, Cal thought, his father would have won. What the prize was he couldn't say, but yes, he was still afraid that his father would outlive him. Was his father the original, and he the near-miss? Cal's sister had always maintained that her brother resembled their dad not only physically, but that he'd also acquired the same mannerisms, facial expressions, even speech patterns. She would always see their father in him, never see Cal. He was only evocative of the real thing, but himself a fake.

The front door to Weston's house opened, but instead of entering the downstairs apartment, the newcomer ascended the stairs, unlocked the apartment door. They could hear hard-heeled steps crossing the space. "She has arrived," Weston said. "She'll call when she's ready."

"She has her own key."

"It's more convenient that way."

After ten minutes, Weston's phone lit up, and a few moments later, the two men walked up the stairs. Weston knocked, waited until they heard a woman's voice say, "Come in."

She was sitting on the blue sofa with a glass of champagne in one hand and a cigarette in the other. "Shit," she greeted Weston, "you look tired." She got up to kiss him on both cheeks, peered at Cal while doing so. "So who is this?" she asked. "Introduce us." Her name was Kai, and she had chosen one of the outfits Weston kept in the bedroom closet, a lace floral slip dress Cal imagined had been fashionable in the 90s. Her own clothes she had folded and placed next to her on the sofa. She nodded after Weston introduced Cal but failed to extend a hand or otherwise acknowledge him. "Did he get tested?"

"Did you?" Cal walked past Weston and Kai toward the kitchen, took a glass from the cabinet, and poured himself a drink.

"He looked younger in the pictures," Kai said to his back. "He's wearing hearing aids."

Weston didn't respond. He pulled the camera from its bag and as though he had cast a spell, he seemed to disappear into the background. They could still see him, but he was no longer accessible.

"What are you having?" Kai asked.

"Whiskey, Angostura bitters, Fernet Branca, Amaro."

"Can I have one too?"

"If you get yourself a glass." He watched her walk over to the cabinets, open a door, and carefully picking a tumbler. Her shoulders were slightly rounded, as though she were trying to make herself smaller. Maybe she was working in front of a computer all day.

"Tastes like medicine. Harsh," she said after sniffing the glass first and then taking the tiniest of sips.

"You can throw it out."

"No. No, I like it." Her nails were a shade of brown, maybe with a faint pink hue, not unlike the carpeting on the second floor of the house he was trying to buy. Her lips were red, her eyes showed mascara but little else. She saw him watching her and offered, "He said not to imitate his Mom."

"This is only the first session."

"For you, yes. For me, it's number four."

"You dismissed three candidates."

"You're good at math."

"What was wrong with them?"

She thought on that with her eyes staring into the overhead lamp. "I didn't want them to touch me." And after Cal kept his silence, only taking another sip from his drink, "It's an oddly intimate proposition. I'm married to someone, or pretending to be. I don't need to be in love with the other model, but I can't feel self-conscious every time they come near me."

"You're not an actress," he said.

"I'm just picky. And Weston wants me, so he has to play by my rules."

They heard the click of Weston's shutter, and Kai turned and blew him a kiss. Then she took Cal's free hand and said, "You are really pale, we'll look goofy together." It was true, Kai's hand made his own appear devoid of color. "Should we inspect the bedroom? Which side of the bed do you prefer?"

"The left one."

"We might get along then. At least for tonight."

She didn't let go of his hand while they looked at the apartment together, even after it turned sweaty. Or maybe hers was the sweaty one, who could tell? Kai told him about improvements she would make, colors she would switch. He thought they needed new appliances — a Japanese coffee-maker, a rice cooker, a Sanyo toaster oven. All the while, Weston kept following them though never drawing near. Like a very large, overweight child, he followed his parents around.

They stood by the window together, looking out onto the balcony and Hertel Avenue beyond. "What's up with your ears?" she said.

"I'm losing the high sounds, the breathy ones, the ones I most cherish. I call the hearing aids my "ears," because without them, everything turns dull. I can still hear okay, but I'm underwater listening to what people are saying above the surface. They also help against tinnitus."

"I like the wires," she said. "You can barely see them, and they're kind of hot." She got up on her toes and kissed his ears, careful not to make a smacking sound. He put an arm around her waist, kept it there. She didn't shrink from his touch, didn't lean into him; she seemed to be tasting the sensation the way she'd tasted her drink. Behind them, Weston kept taking pictures. Cal wondered why he refused to silence the shutter. Would that have turned him into a voyeur? Or would he have lost control over his subjects? Why did he want to remind them of his presence?

Cal woke late the next morning, Yuuki jumping onto his bed to lick his face, Vanya barking from the bottom of the stairs. He searched for Kai's scent but had to do with the summer-smell of Yuuki's paws. By the time he had dressed and opened the door to the backyard, Kai's presence, so vivid in his dreams, felt ghostly. Not enough was left to cheer him up on a cold, foggy day in Buffalo. Later, when Marlena called to congratulate him, he said all the right things without feeling any of them. His call with Michael was short, and the agent dropped off a small, black, pre-lit Christmas tree in the afternoon, plus a bronze key-chain with Cal's new address engraved on it. "Isn't that a bit premature?" Cal asked, trying to feel excited about this purchase.

Michael shrugged. "I'm moving to North Carolina next month, so I won't be here for your closing. It's now or never."

They bumped their elbows, said a few words that meant little enough, then Cal watched Michael walk back to his Subaru, close the hatch, and drive off. The tree was a nice touch, though, and tenderly he carried it inside, plugged it in, and watched the dogs sniffing this new appliance. Next week would be Thanksgiving.

Chapter 31

THE SITTING PRESIDENT was still refusing to concede the election, even though the margin by which he had lost was decisive. Instead he claimed voter fraud had kept him from winning. "I won the election," he tweeted; his surrogates spoke of a landslide victory. He fired administration officials responsible for keeping the election safe, threatened state legislators and administrators who wouldn't repeat his lies. He denied the new president-elect the daily briefings necessary for the transition of power.

Two vaccines against the virus were promised by year's end. Their effectiveness, the trials said, were at ninety-five percent. But without the president giving his successor access to task forces, government agencies, and money to fund setting up offices and start assembling the new administration, the vaccine distribution was already in question. Taking photos in Weston's apartment was madness, but in Buffalo, Cal was only risking his own life. Who would take care of the dogs if he died? He didn't allow himself to think about that scenario. He still hadn't heard how much time his father might have left, but ever since his sister's message, his moods were like old stains on a shirt, barely recognizable, yet visible enough to cause embarrassment. Since Vanya wouldn't come up the stairs anymore, he watched jealously over Cal during the day, sleeping at his feet or next to him on the couch. If Cal forgot to pet him, Vanya pawed and swatted his arm until Cal relented. Just before Christmas, he'd be able to move to Auburn Street if the deal went through, and he would have to find a new renter for the house on Ashland. Cal posted ads on Craigslist, on Facebook, even on Instagram.

On his trips to grocery and pet stores, Cal wore a mask, but he'd already broken safety guidelines so many times. He'd been reckless. Were any of his encounters with old friends and lovers worth the risk? What was his life worth? And what was worth saving? Then he thought of Kai. He wasn't in love, though he was looking forward to seeing her again. He wasn't in love, not with her hair, her neck, her fingers, her feet, he wasn't in love with her nose, her cheeks, her eyes. He wasn't in love.

That night, Weston called, and an hour later he was going through the closet in the master bedroom, looking for something that would make him feel comfortable while Kai was standing in front of the bathroom mirror applying lipstick. She was wearing slacks and a bra, and for the first time Cal saw her back and ribcage, and he couldn't make sense of Kai's body yet. It looked like a sketch, unfinished; some lines seemed to be missing. Her hips were boyish, her feet — she wasn't wearing shoes yet — unremarkable. She was more beautiful than him, younger too, and he was ashamed of his gaze that turned a body into a checklist. He watched her put in contact lenses.

"What do you see without them?" he asked.

"Little. I wouldn't know if you were checking out my butt or picking your nose."

"None of the women who lived with me had good eyes, none of them. Sometimes I thought that nobody with good eyes could."

"It sounds vain."

"It might be. But don't you find it strange that all women who were ever attracted to me needed to wear glasses?"

"The less you see, the more you can invent." She paused. "And just to be clear, I'm not attracted to you."

Cal was prepared to do another improvised photo shoot, but tonight Weston gave them instructions. "You're cooking together. Kai is going to heat up tortillas, and you, Cal, are frying up rice, meat, fish, veggies, and mixing it with tomato sauce while drinking cocktails. Dad called it the ghetto paella. You're listening to music, I don't care what you're listening to. You're having a good time, both of you, and you haven't been married for long, I'm not even a thought yet."

"Who took the picture?" Cal asked.

Weston shrugged, a hint of impatience pulling his lips straight. "Some friend. A good friend, they weren't shy around him."

The instructions, as unspecific as they were, kept Cal from focusing on the simple task of cooking. His body felt stiff, uncomprehending, it wouldn't belong. The magic he'd felt during the first two nights was gone. He neither liked Weston nor Kai very much, until she started to fiddle with the old boombox and the Strangler's "Golden Brown" began to play. The music pulled at his face, squeezed water from his eyes. Moments later, while the oil was heating up in the pan and looking for routes of escape, Kai slung her arms around him, feeding him her body. He gave in to her reluctantly, unwillingly. "You're freezing," she said. The Stranglers faded, and never had Cal been so afraid of a next song. What would come next? What did she have in store? It was true, he was cold, but at the same time he was sweating now and afraid it might show, afraid she might feel this and be repulsed. And he didn't want her enough, not yet, he hardly knew her, he'd hardly had the time to sniff her out, to feel a leg, a knee, a shoulder. What would the next song be?

Songs in narratives were a liability, of course they were. Who was going to remember "Golden Brown"? Who still owned the album *Feline*? But what would come next?

Kai had chosen "Bulletproof" by Radiohead, and the ice in his body melted. He kissed her, told her to start frying the onions, very low heat, he'd be right back, and he went into the bedroom and changed his shirt, chose a black button-down, rolled up the sleeves, and this time it was him who slung his arms around her, one hand grabbing the spatula from her and turning the onions, his lips searching her neck below all that curly hair.

"Will you make me a drink?" she said, "One of those medicinal ones? What are they called?"

"It's a Hemlock." He left her in charge of the cooking, poured drinks, added ice, looked for and found an apron, handed her the glass. "My turn," he said.

The next song was "Echoes Remain Forever" by Anne Clark. "You know," Cal said, "Have you ever thought about what would make you turn around and leave after going on a first date with someone and following them home?"

Kai tasted her drink, appeared satisfied. "Like what?"

"You just walk into their apartment or house. You might have been making out at the bar or restaurant where you met, and your attraction to that someone is really strong, and you trust that they're not a creep, and they open the door and — what kind of discovery would make you say, 'Sorry, this was a mistake. I'm really sorry, but I should go now'?"

"A dead body?"

He laughed, drank too much of his cocktail. "That too, but no, what kind of furniture, what kind of knickknack would stop you cold?"

She shook her head. "Hummels. If that person were into collecting Hummels, I'd leave. If they were into collecting anything, I'd leave. What's yours?"

"Tommy Hilfiger sheets. I imagine walking into the bedroom. If she has Tommy Hilfiger sheets, or worse, Tommy Girl sheets, I'm done. Can't do it. Wrong person."

"You're kind of judgmental."

"Never said I wasn't."

"Maybe I don't like you at all."

"I'm a collector."

"No. Gah! Don't say that." She was laughing by now, coughing a moment later. She put down her glass and he held her, running his hands down her back, feeling one buttock.

"That's mine," she said. "Don't touch that."

"It's mine now. I married you."

"That doesn't mean you own me."

"Sure it does."

"I'm the boss here, and I get to decide. You go back to cooking." She put a hand under his waistband and squeezed his butt. "Not bad, old man. Still perky."

The ghetto paella needed his attention, and for the next few minutes she sat on the kitchen counter with her drink. "I started reading one of your books," she said over David Bowie's "Holy Holy."

"Which one?"

"You have a foot fetish."

"It's fiction." He looked at her face to search for a reaction. Somewhere out of sight stood Weston with his camera. "You want to show me your feet?"

"They're gross." But she took off her shoes anyway, wiggling her toes as though to ascertain that she was still in control of them. He turned the heat to low once again, even though the meat was already browning and he needed to add the rice. He took the left foot in one hand and studied it. Small it was, narrow, the big toe large, the arch flat. One day she would develop bunions.

"I once worked in a running store. We watched people walk to see what kind of shoe they needed. But in order to see their feet, they had to take off their old shoes first. They were allowed to keep their socks on, but whenever I was interested in a person, I asked them to take their socks off too."

"You're a pervert."

"I am, I really am. They always agreed, though. Feet give away so much of your personality. The way we treat them, the way we care for them. Even anatomically, you can feel whether or not you will like the person or not. It was quite an astonishing discovery for me." He turned around quickly to add the rice, mix it with onions, meat, and vegetables, then poured tomato sauce over the mix.

"What kind of feet do I have?" she asked.

"The careless type. You don't love your feet, but you're good enough to treat them adequately. You don't feel naked when you let me see them."

"What does that say about me?"

"You're using your body like a Swiss Army knife. You're not in love with the shape or its looks, but it does all kinds of cool things you appreciate."

"Like what?"

Cal pulled her knees apart to make space for himself, and she locked her ankles behind him. He kissed her nose, her eyes, her ears, and what he loved best was the smell of nutmeg, the smell of running through an October night, the smell of burned toast and an open window on a summer morning, the smell of her putting a hand into his hair. Her eyes were searching his face now, and he couldn't tell what she might read or if he was revealing too much of himself, but she did answer his lips, and he did push up her shirt and unclasp her bra, and she did not comment on the burning smell coming from the frying pan, her tongue did not let go while he reached over to shut off the gas.

CHAPTER 32

THE PROLONGED RAIN kept Cal and the dogs inside. Twice a day he put on his coat, a hat with a wide brim, and walked Yuuki and Vanya around the block, Ashland to Summer to Norwood to Bryant and back. He had no love for Norwood, but the dogs were too loud and frightened by the Elmwood traffic to allow for another route. He signed all the papers Marlena had sent him electronically, and now he just needed to wait. After dinner, despite getting his coat soaked twice already, he visited the house on Lancaster Avenue. Each time, though, the house remained dark, and he couldn't detect any changes. Christmas lights hung scattered about the neighborhood, men were climbing ladders to mount light chains while kids watched them from the safety of the porch. Snow was starting to mix in with the rain, and on some lawns, specks of white appeared.

For half an hour, he sat on the stairs of Shorat's house, not sure what he was waiting for, unsure he was waiting at all. In her absence, the house was enough to evoke a sense of belonging and familiarity. Cal greeted the sadness, the pain that robbed him of sight and air whenever he was able to conjure Shorat's image unadulterated, without sentimentality or adornments. The way she'd looked when doing yoga in her studio after two in the afternoon, sweaty and not pretty, but focused. He'd felt never farther away from her than in those moments he walked past her door to his own office. Or Shorat walking Yuuki in that slow and deliberate way the dog preferred, ready to stop and sniff for a minute or two. Shorat getting into her car, starting the engine, then plugging in her phone. How often he had stood by the door to the garage until the music came on, too loud and upbeat to let him linger.

Later he stopped at a bar that hadn't attracted any outdoor business but hadn't closed yet either. A young woman in boots and a red nylon jacket asked for his order and returned a few minutes later with a Manhattan. He paid and sat in the cold, watching the young woman shut off the lights inside, one by one, before coming outside again to lock up chairs and tables. "You can stay if you want," she said. "I won't chain your seat to the others."

The poet Paul Celan had once written that, "Only in the mother tongue one can express his own truth, in foreign languages the poet lies. Cal considered this while sitting at the tall table, its top mounted on an old barrel, one half reflecting the lights of Elmwood Avenue in a sheen of rain. After Karl had arrived in Buffalo twenty-five years prior, he'd kept family calls to a minimum, purged all German books and magazines from the house, and read Kafka in English translation. Memories of past conversations had come to him translated — his parents admonished and scolded in perfect English, even though they had never learned the language. All his memories were stealthily switched, in sweeping fashion, to English. Each time he accessed his past, he found that new areas of his mother tongue had been erased.

Much later, when he was asked to translate his own novel for its German publication, he squirmed. He hadn't thought or written in German in more than twelve years

Karl had been invented by his parents, his teachers, his high school friends, he'd had little say in the matter. Karl's mother tongue kept pressing a pillow onto his face while cooing sweet nothings.

No, you didn't lie in a foreign language. You might fumble and thrash about, your truth might be ugly, might sound hoarse or crude, but the new language let you breathe. Cal was a crude invention, but it was entirely his own. And maybe, Cal thought, to honor his current situation, he needed to invent another truth. He should no longer use English but learn to write in a third language to speak exactly who he was and what he meant. A third language might free him of mortgages, SUVs, whiskey, and creature comforts. A new language might bring him closer to the person he needed to be in the coming years.

Chapter 33

THE NEXT PHOTO SHOOT was delayed time and again by bad weather. Weston apologized but insisted he didn't want to change the succession; the photos needed to be taken in the right order, and the next time they'd meet it would be outdoors. On Thanksgiving, he called in the morning and asked if Cal could come right away.

An old Grand Marquis stood parked in the driveway of the house on Hertel Avenue, its open trunk revealing a globe, a green parasol, camping chairs, stuffed animals, and several outfits from the upstairs bedroom closet. Weston and Kai sat on the porch with a bottle of champagne.

"It's a bit of a change today," Weston said after handing Cal a glass. "I'm bringing two cameras, one is for you. What I'm trying to do...what we're trying to do..." He stopped, lifting his gaze and staring into the sky, face scrunched up, his mouth slightly open. "Only my mother is in the picture. There were several rolls worth of pictures, Dad told me, but he managed to save only one shot. Technically, I could do this shoot with Kai alone, but it was a very private one, and my mother reacted the way she did because she knew and loved the man holding the camera. So I want you to take pictures, Cal, but I will also be there, shooting both of you. Well, mostly my mother."

Cal looked past Weston at Kai, but she didn't pay him any mind. Her lips appeared glued to the rim of her champagne flute, her eyes blind to the two men beside her.

Weston was driving the old clunker, photo equipment stashed away in the passenger footwell and seat. Kai and Cal were relegated to the backseat. "Where are we headed?" he asked.

"Downtown," she answered without looking his way. "It's a good day for this shoot, there won't be much traffic. We can't have any daily commuters or tourists show up. I only wish it were warmer."

Weston said, "My dad took the pictures in their first years of marriage. At the time he suspected that my mother had fallen in love with someone else. Living together and waking up next to each other every single day was still a new thing, the whole concept of forever and ever weighed on them both. As my dad put it, they were stuck with each other, and Mom lashed out at him numerous times for little or no reason."

"You married?" Kai asked.

"Used to be," Cal said in an attempt to cut that part of the conversation short.

"You're still wearing your ring."

"I always will." He was surprised by that statement, surprised too that it was the absolute truth.

"She left you."

"She left the person I have become."

"You don't look so bad." Kai put a hand on his knee, squeezed it. "She could have done worse."

Near the Statler Tower, Weston entered a parking garage. The lower levels were half-filled, but the higher they climbed, the fewer cars were parked in the oil-dripped spots. On level four they passed two idling cars, windows rolled down, the drivers passing things that fit into a fist back and forth. When they reached the sixth level, dirty clouds attempted to block the sun, and a wind that hadn't been noticeable on Hertel Avenue blew the smoke from Kai's cigarette into Cal's eyes and made them water. He had a view of the lake and the highway cutting the city off the shoreline. No other car stood parked on this level.

Weston opened the trunk. "My mom dropped caution at some point and gave herself to what was happening. I think she conjured another character, another persona, and she felt comfortable."

"So what am I supposed to do?" Kai asked.

"I'm not part of this anymore. Don't ask for anything from me." He handed Cal a Nikon SLR, explained lens and camera quickly. "Just shoot away. You direct her. It's just the two of you. Really, forget about me." He stepped away from the car.

Kai pulled her hair into a ponytail. She was wearing Ray-Bans now and smoking a second cigarette. "So, how do you want me?"

"Take off your shoes."

"Fuck you, it's not that kind of weather."

"It's my shoot and he's paying you. Take off your shoes."

"And then what?"

"Don't worry about the globe and chairs. Just try on the dresses, see what fits, just do what you feel."

"What I feel?" She took off her sports coat, a tweedy thing a few sizes too big for her, and pulled the dress she was wearing over her head, revealing green panties and a black bra. "This is a bit weird. I mean, she's supposed to love you, right? But she isn't sure you are the right one?"

"No, she isn't."

Kai nodded. "I don't know, you're a bit creepy when you talk from behind the camera. She must have felt that too."

"Creepy?"

"Does your ex-wife know what you're doing right now? How would she feel if she saw us like that?"

"Like what?"

"You're pretending to be another man taking pictures of me pretending to be your wife. We don't even match up in age, and I'm dressing and undressing in front of you. You're twenty years older than me."

"It's Weston's shoot. We don't have to obey him. We can stop anytime. You're in charge. I'm not forcing you."

"What if your wife finds out?"

"I don't know," he said. "It's not the photos she'd mind, I imagine."

"You don't think she would look at these and feel jealous?"

He kept taking pictures, followed her moves only through the viewfinder. "You're Weston's mother, not my wife."

Kai wouldn't have it. "She never loved you."

"How do you know?" he said.

"I can feel her," she replied. "She was afraid of you. Always."

"I never hurt her," he insisted.

"No, you wouldn't," she said. "You're not a bad guy. But there's something you won't trust anyone with. Like you have this horrible secret you won't confess to anyone. And if someone came too close, you would obliterate them."

"Obliterate them?" he echoed.

"She was afraid she would stumble over that secret."

"What kind of secret?" He tried to laugh, but it sounded squeaky and forced. And while changing into a drab green dress with adjustable red elastics at the shoulders, waist, and legs, she began to tell him what she thought of his camera and the whole project. She called him things that made Cal shake, but it didn't keep him from taking pictures. Kai opened the green parasol, sat down on the hood of the old monstrous car, put on the dark sunglasses again. She grabbed the pack of cigarettes and insulted Cal for the next hour, the way he looked and acted, the quality of his photography, the ridiculous task of completing the set of pictures. She took the globe from the trunk of the car and rolled it across the parking deck, ran after it, followed it around, sat down on the concrete with the soles of her feet dirty, a cigarette in the corner of her mouth, and Cal didn't stop taking pictures, never stopped, and his eyes were so full of Kai, he had no idea how to get rid of her, how to ban her from his thoughts and his mind and his body. When his eyes were so full he couldn't possibly take another look at her, Cal took the globe from Kai and got on his knees, his hands fumbling with the belt, his hands so cold she screamed. Into his ear she hissed, "I'm your wife and you don't even like me. You don't even like me." Behind them, Weston was taking pictures even now. Even now, he did not interfere.

CHAPTER 34

ON BLACK FRIDAY he bought decorations for the black, pre-lit plastic tree Michael had gifted him and unpacked the many boxes in his living room. Yuuki and Vanya clamored to be allowed in the backyard, and Cal obliged. Maybe it was him, maybe it was the new house, the new smells and surroundings, but the dogs, whenever it didn't rain, spent all their time outside. Cal felt neglected but unpacked the red bulbs he'd purchased, the stars, the strange mix of shiny animals that had been on sale already. For lunch he ordered take-out from the Great Wall and drank two cans of Sapporo beer. He scoured Craigslist, sent off older short stories to newer magazines, searched for discounted pottery wheels. Panic filled him like helium and he had no escape valve. Not even an afternoon walk to Lancaster Avenue and a look at the dark windows of Shorat's house could release the pressure. He didn't dare visit Auburn Avenue.

Around seven and on his way into a bottle of Four Roses, the doorbell rang. For several long moments he wasn't sure what was happening. Nobody had used it before, and the angry humming sound only managed to vaguely alarm him.

"Merry Christmas." She was wearing a red faux-fur coat, fishnet-stockings, and a black beanie adorned with a bear. In her hand she held a small fake fir tree, lights in the shape of toadstools wrapped around its branches and glowing. "Battery," Kai said. "Obviously."

He took tree and coat and pointed to the sofa, the only place to sit, asked what she wanted to drink.

"You smell like whiskey. I'll have some too. I thought all old guys have heartburn."

"Old guys have Prilosec as well."

She was wearing a black, velvety dress, black shiny pumps. "You have a depressing place, but I like your tree. It goes well with my tree. They had pine-needle spray at the store, but I didn't want to splurge. Do you like the toadstools?"

The dogs were standing by the backdoor now, and against better judgment he opened it and watched Yuuki bark at the visitor and bare her teeth. But Kai wasn't impressed, and after Vanya had sniffed black pumps and dress and found the visitor to be harmless, Yuuki gave in and let herself be petted, returning the favor with a kiss.

"You didn't tell me you had dogs."

"You didn't tell me you were coming."

"How can I resist a guy in sweats and some weird acrylic sweater?"

"Performance fleece. Keeps you warm on runs."

"How often do you run?"

"Most days. When I'm not moving across country or buying houses. Are you hungry?"

"I could be."

"I could make an odd stir-fry."

"I don't eat meat."

"Fish?"

"Maybe."

"Smoked trout?"

He changed in his upstairs bedroom and, turning away from the closet, was surprised to find she had been watching him from the dark hallway. "My ears," he said.

"My feet." She raised the hand that held her pumps. "You have love handles."

"You hadn't noticed?"

"You're half-deaf, I'm half-blind."

"I'm afraid to come near you. You might find you've been mistaken about me this whole time."

She watched him cook from atop the dishwasher. "Weston would like to be done by Christmas, New Year's at the latest. He didn't consider the weather, the lack of sunny days, but he says most sessions will be indoors, so our clothing can reflect the seasons."

"How did you guys meet?" He'd poured them Manhattans, sipped from his glass while cutting onions, mushrooms, broccoli, carrots. He was heating water for the pasta.

She hesitated for a half-second, and Cal was sure that this detail was important and also certain he'd forget it soon enough. "An ad. He thought I was perfect."

"Does it feel weird to be impersonating someone's mother so perfectly?"

"It does. And I never met his dad, so it's weird to meet you, but in Weston's eyes, you're not you. You're someone else."

"What do you see?"

"I see you, but I'm also looking at his dad. I'm making out with his dad. I don't like to think too much about it. Grosses me out."

Cal tossed the pasta in with the vegetables, added the smoked trout and several sauces, let it simmer for a few more minutes, fixed them another drink. The dogs were already bored with their humans and lounging outside again.

"What do you do when you're not playing Weston's mother?" he asked.

"I was singing in a band and I used to bartend. I haven't done either since March. We were really close to getting a contract. Album, tour, everything. I teach the piano sometimes, because parents only want the best for their children, and the little fuckers don't get the virus anyway. As long as I wear a mask and wear latex gloves, they're okay with me yelling at their offspring. I also design websites. I got a computer engineering degree, just to be safe."

They ate on the couch, each in one corner. She didn't compliment his cooking.

"Do you have family in the area?" he asked.

"They moved to Arizona. Tucson. My dad got his degree there ages ago and idolizes the place. I think it was his first time of being alone, away from his folks and their prying eyes. This year my mother finally caved. She hates the summer heat but figured in times of the pandemic, heat was safer than the cold."

After they had finished eating, they seemed to have run out of things to talk about as well. They sat staring at each other, unmoving, listening to the furnace turn on again and again. "The parking garage," she finally began.

"Yes," he said. "I thought that's why you were here."

"Has he talked to you about it?"

Cal shook his head. "Has he complained about me? Have you?"

"Weston got what he wanted. I think. Though you can't be sure. Not really."

"What about you?"

"I haven't decided yet."

"And you've come to find out?"

"You really are full of yourself. I like that about you. You're an exhibitionist. You've done all this before."

"In Berlin, nudity wasn't a big deal."

"You're so suave. You're so European."

"The public swimming pool had a nudist area. People came with their kids. Nobody cared."

"Don't you find it strange to impersonate someone's parent? To have sex with the person who is supposed to be your wife even though she could be your daughter? Out in the open, the people behind the windows of the Statler Towers cheering you on?" She put the empty plate on his coffee table, then got up on her knees and scooted over to his corner. "Seriously, you could be my dad. Almost. I mean, my real dad is older than you, they waited a long time before they had kids, but you could have fathered me in your very early twenties." She sat down with her back against his chest, her hair tickling his nose. "You can't tell Weston I visited you. I don't think he would appreciate my initiative. Something about the artistic process."

Sometime later, he came downstairs again to feed the dogs. He loaded the dishwasher, cleaned up the coffee table, folded her clothes. And when nothing more needed his attention, Kai was still asleep, and he watched her from the doorframe. And only much later did he find the courage to get under the covers and even then sleep wouldn't come. When it finally did, without him knowing, he found himself in the bathroom of the university, a cavernous room with showers and long rows of sinks, and none of the men were wearing masks, and he was certain that this time, this time for certain, he had contracted the virus.

Chapter 35

"Why do you wear two watches?" Yuuki was lying at Kai's side, staring at the toast on her plate, the mandarin orange she was peeling just now.

"It keeps me sane," he said.

"How?"

"It ties me to reality and the material world. It actually feels as though I were strapping on the world. I know how bombastic and silly that sounds, but it works. It kept me from thinking of the fires. Whenever Sonoma County was covered in smoke, it kept me from panicking."

"I've never seen anyone sleep with two watches. You sure about the sanity?"

"You want to try and take them off?"

They showered together, and she soaped his body and rinsed it off, and he washed her hair. Then they had sex again; Yuuki made off with the last piece of toast. Crumbs were stuck to Kai's back when she finally got up to look for her clothes downstairs. Piano students were waiting for her masked lessons. Cal watched her pull on the black velvet dress and turn herself back into the woman from the night before. By the time she was ready to kiss him goodbye, he barely recognized her. "Don't tell Weston about this," she said again. "He might call this whole thing off."

He followed her outside, and while she climbed into her Toyota, he checked the mail. Forwarded letters and bills and magazines had finally found him, and he carried a whole stack inside and sat down on the sofa to sort through them. A postcard from Lisbon had been sent to his current address, an impossibility, he thought. How had Shorat found out about his rental? Or had her companion followed him home one night?

The card read, "She looks cute. You could do worse. Lisbon is lovely this time of year. You'd find it melancholy, but I think it's quite cheerful. I broke a tooth and got it repaired for fifty Euros. The hotel has a chocolate fountain." Her name sat squeezed into the corner, barely legible. The card had taken ten days to arrive. Where was she now?

What looked to be a coup attempt by the sitting president floundered. He hadn't mobilized the military to overturn the election results, instead he'd filed dozens of lawsuits alleging voter fraud. He clamored for recounts and second recounts, he sought to intimidate election officials, state legislators, judges, and the attorney general. But by December 1st, his efforts had fizzled, judges had summarily dismissed all outlandish claims of vast international conspiracies to block him from serving a second term. Meanwhile, the president elect introduced his new economic team and new members of his cabinet. He put together a taskforce to fight the pandemic and, after his inauguration, distribute the vaccine.

There was no news from Cal's sister or mother about his father's health. He wasn't sure he wanted any, but at times he thought he might feel better once his father had died. He wasn't holding his breath, nor was he wishing for a speedy demise of the old man, and yet, he didn't want to be remembered by this father who'd never been much of a father. These past months, he believed, had all been about preserving what little was there of Cal in this world. He was scraping together memories his friends and lovers owned, hoping they may amount to something more than random thoughts. There was no plot to his life, there was even less plot now in these days of waiting, in these days of new beginnings, in days where he needed to put old things to rest. This was his transition from being Cal to becoming another, as yet unnamed person. This wasn't about plot but about disentangling himself from the web of second rate memories, plans, and ambitions. No, he wouldn't be sad about his father's death, merely relieved. Whatever his father thought he remembered about his son Karl was of no importance. Worse, it was dirt, garbage, soot. All lies. Wasn't it sad that the people who should have known him best had no clue about who had lived with them for nearly twenty years? All his father's memories of Karl, they would be gone, and Cal would feel lighter, a bit more like himself perhaps. It might be easier to start a new life.

Shorat in Toronto

Because I was a writer and cited Hemingway as one of my main influences – in a time when citing Hemingway as an influence was met with frowns and blank stares – Shorat booked the Hemingway Room in the Omni King Edward Hotel in Toronto during our stay in the city. We lived in Ann Arbor then, and Toronto was only a four hour drive away. For the first time in our lives we had the money to fulfill odd desires and spontaneous whims, and she booked the room on a Thursday and we arrived

Friday afternoon to do nothing more than drinking the wine we'd brought and walking around Toronto neighborhoods, wherever the subway would take us.

I felt intimidated by the presence of Hemingway, though I had my doubts that Hemingway had truly stayed in this particular suite. Even so, as a writer who hadn't even published a book yet, did staying in Hemingway's room amount to a jinx? It felt presumptuous, but it also felt grand; Shorat and I got drunk together and took pictures of each other sitting at the room's desk. But Hemingway's room is not what I remember from that trip, and in any case, what I remember best might not even have happened during this particular stay in Toronto, because we visited often. It might have happened during a winter shopping trip or a trip for no reason at all.

What I remember is discovering a building that housed artists' studios on its two floors. The neighborhood was foreign to me, no memory could lead me there again. Some of the studios were open, artists working on large-scale paintings, but it was a Saturday and many doors remained locked. After a stroll through the hallways we went together into one of the bathrooms, and because the light was just so, and because the door could be locked, and because we had only been married for two or three years and our bodies still didn't feel familiar at all, I asked her to pose in the nude for me. I had an old film camera from the time before we'd met, one of these odd possessions that made life feel more precious and glamorous than it ever had been, and Shorat, shy and usually reluctant, agreed to take off her coat, sweater, and bra, and keep on her necklace and jeans.

We were both overweight at the time, because having money for the first time also meant that our fridge was always stocked and that we tried new restaurants every week. Shorat was twenty-seven, maybe twenty-eight, and looked even younger, and the extra weight added to her beauty. Her belly and breasts were taut, the way water bends when you overfill a glass. She stood in the corner of the large bathroom stall, a window set high in the wall toward her right.

The memory of our trip doesn't strike me as a happy one. We were still fumbling about, and looking back, I feel as though she was already leaving me, even then. Maybe I was too blunt, or maybe I wasn't blunt enough. Our years seem like a succession of misunderstandings, of false leads, faulty assumptions, and only in rare moments did we achieve harmony. We were devoted, I think we were, but we were badly matched in experience and temperament. Most often, we were out of sync. Only sleep and alcohol made us lose sight of that.

In the picture she's not wearing glasses, and her eyes are probing the failing light in the section of the room where I stand with the camera. I give directions, but minimal ones, there's nothing I can do to make anything better. She is the most beautiful woman I have ever loved, and her slight awkwardness, the shame she's feeling, casts its own light. She doesn't want to give in to feeling pretty or desired, and that gives her stance and the way she keeps her arms at her sides its poise. The picture is in black and white, and her body seems to be lit from within.

We made love in that bathroom stall afterward, of that I am sure, but I only remember the picture I took. We kept it in an album only the two of us were allowed to see. I remember this picture alone. This very picture.

Walking home after a brief shopping trip to the co-op on Elmwood, he meant to recognize Shorat's companion sitting at the very same outdoor table where he had thought about Paul Celan and what it meant to write in a foreign language. The memory filled Cal with shame, the way most memories did. But instead of giving in to self-doubt, he approached the table wearing his mask and asked if he could sit down. The man wore a black mask with white lettering — This Was Preventable, it read — and after quickly glancing at Cal, nodded. It was hard to read a friend's face obliterated by a piece of cotton cloth, and impossible to make sense of a stranger's expressions from behind a mask. Cal wasn't even sure this was the same man he'd seen walking up to the house on Lancaster Avenue. Yes, he was wearing a hat and looked to be tall, but Cal had never been able to get a clear view of the man's face. "We're going to get more snow soon," he said.

The man nodded. He was looking at his phone, scrolling through his Instagram feed perhaps, or looking at the most recent death statistics. The virus had infected over 200,000 people just the previous day and killed 2,700. Over 100,000 people were being treated for the virus in hospitals around the country.

A waiter, dressed in red flannel, took Cal's order, asked if the other man wanted a refresh. The man said yes, and could he have a burger and fries, please?

"Great idea," Cal said quickly and ordered the same, he couldn't help himself. He asked the man, "Would you know where the closest liquor store is located? I'm new to the area and I don't think I have seen one yet."

"I'm new to the area myself, but I think there's one near Summer. I might be wrong." Now he took off his mask, letting it dangle from one ear, and took the last sip of his beer. "Labatt's," he said. "I'm a sucker for bad beer."

Cal took in the man's features. His nose was large and listed to one side, his lips were full. Stubble covered a slackening jawline and an adequate but unremarkable chin. Maybe he was Cal's age, maybe a bit younger or a year or two older. How could one tell? Cal checked the man's hands, his long, even fingers, which tapered hardly at all, and still he couldn't be certain. They were not the hands of a young man, that much was clear, but they hadn't turned gnarly either. This man, much like himself, was muddling through the vast emptiness of middle age. "I'm a big Miller Lite fan myself," Cal said. "Have you moved here recently, or are you just visiting?"

"A bit of both," the man responded, replacing his mask once again. His voice seemed pleasant, though Cal was sure he wouldn't be able to recognize it again. It was devoid of anything distinctive.

"I'm looking at houses in this neighborhood," Cal volunteered. "You think you're going to stick around?"

The man shrugged. The waiter brought their food and drinks, and both men took off their masks and placed them in their coat pockets. "We're not supposed to do that," the man said.

"Not supposed to do what?"

"Mingle with strangers."

"We're outdoors," Cal said quickly, he didn't want to lose this opportunity to talk to Shorat's companion.

"Still," the man said. "It's a risk." He looked around and there were two open tables in the outdoor seating area.

"Sorry, I wasn't thinking." Cal grabbed his plate and glass and carried them to the next table.

"I appreciate that," the man said. "I don't want to infect others."

"Your wife."

The remark elicited a smile that exposed long teeth and deeply creased the man's face, and this smile convinced Cal that he was indeed looking at Shorat's lover. Despite his best intentions, he rather liked the smile. The man's face wasn't one you'd pick from a crowd of strangers, it lacked a certain something to be memorable, but the crooked, way-too-wide smile carved out some character. Once it had dissolved again, an utterly forgettable fifty-year-old began eating his burger.

After dark, Cal drove up to Hertel Avenue. Weston and Kai were already in the upstairs apartment listening to the Youth Underground. He would have loved to pull Kai in for a hug but knew better. "It's hot in here," he said.

Weston nodded. "That's because you're taking a bath."

"I am?"

"Those are my directions for tonight. But take it slow. It doesn't matter how soon you get there, or even how you get there. You're taking a bath, is all."

"In solitude?"

Kai made a face. "I'm right here, silly."

"I was wondering," Cal said to Weston. "Are there any shots where you were present? Or which you took as a boy?"

He could tell immediately that he'd asked the wrong question. Any expression disappeared from Weston's face, as though whoever lived inside that body had left.

"That's not the project," he said.

"You want to see your parents only the way they were without you? Like peering into your neighbor's windows and imagining what is going on between them? I was thinking about your project, and there's something voyeuristic about it. And not because we're naked or because we're making out, but because the one who takes the pictures knows his subjects well, and yet in those photos they don't know him yet." He stopped for a second, trying to gather his thoughts. "Maybe there are some photographs from a time, taken by someone else or by your parents, where you were already born. But the moments you're after, they betrayed you in those. They forgot about you. They had their own fun. It's a beautiful thing to watch the people you love when they're not thinking about you at all. I once saw my wife buying shoes in a store. I saw her clearly through the store window, but she didn't see me. And she was clearly flirting with the shoe salesman. I watched her, pretending to look at the window display, and it was odd to see her have a life outside of the one we shared, independent of me. It hurt like hell, but she was so beautiful."

"Should we get going?" Weston said.

"You're a fucking creep, Cal." Kai stood up, kicked off her shoes. "Will you please make me a drink and shut the fuck up?"

"When my parents had parties at our place, they of course made us go to bed at a certain time. They didn't want me or my sister around. They wanted to have their own fun. But how can you sleep when the record-player is blaring at full volume while the drunk voices of your parents and guests turn shrill? I hated their laughter the most, the drunk laughter that ripped me from my sleep. I once went downstairs under the pretense that I needed something — maybe a glass of water. Or maybe I just wanted to tell my parents that I couldn't sleep. My mom was wearing a red wig. Her face was red too, and her eyes were watering from all the laughter, and when I pulled at her sleeve she looked my way and couldn't recognize me. Her face was without any worry or warmth, she couldn't understand what I was trying to say because the music was too loud. My dad was dancing with the neighbor's wife, her face resting against his shoulder."

Without waiting for a reaction, Cal went into the kitchen and mixed drinks. Kai appeared behind him, putting her arms around his waist. She was his wife again, his pretend-wife, Cal her pretend-husband. "Want a cherry?" he asked.

"Would love a cherry," she said. "What happened?"

"It's Monday. It's December seventh. Everybody behaves strangely today. I behave strangely today. I have this feeling of foreboding. Can't explain it. Tomorrow is my parents' wedding anniversary, fifty-eight years, and my father is dying. I don't like him, I really don't, even though I wish I would, but there's too much history, and he just isn't the guy I'd choose to like."

She held him closer, much closer now, walked with him toward the refrigerator, bent down with him while he was scooping up the ice, walked back with him toward where their glasses were resting on the kitchen counter, never once relinquishing her grip. "You want to take a bath?" she said. "A really, really hot bath?"

To his astonishment, that was exactly what he wanted. He wanted to take a hot bath, and he watched her pouring it, testing it with her slender hand, then taking off her glasses because the steam rendered them useless, while he was undressing in the bedroom. "I smell."

"That's okay," she said. "I haven't showered all day."

He was grateful for that piece of information, immensely grateful, and whatever it had been that bothered him — he knew all too well what these things were but he no longer felt the urge to keep track of the ways the world kept getting in the way of him creating perfect order; whatever it was that bothered him, melted. He didn't mind Weston and his Leica anymore, he didn't mind that Kai had to keep pretending that she hadn't spent the night with him. She hadn't showered, she hadn't washed him off. He was forgiven, he was accepted, he wasn't something that needed water and soap to be forgotten. "Yeah, me neither."

He failed to mention Shorat's lover; how inappropriate and unnecessary it now seemed. Then the scalding water made him yelp and her laugh. "Slow," she said. "Take it easy. God, you're such a baby." He remembered a photo of himself that Olga had taken in her apartment in Berlin, of him lying in the soapy water and looking up at her, half questioningly, half in love, and what he remembered about that picture was how vulnerable he seemed, how unguarded. Not even in his sleep — and Olga had taken photos of him sleeping as well — did he look this unguarded. And remembering Olga's photo of him, he slowly sank deeper into the water, until the heat framed his face and all he could see was Kai gazing down at him, planting kisses on his nose and forehead. "You're kind of pretty sometimes," she said. "You look like a girl."

Chapter 36

THE SECOND TIME he talked to Shorat's lover was the following day, December eight, on a park bench opposite from the Albright Knox Gallery. The man sat wrapped in a long, brown woolen coat, a coffee in his hand. When Cal asked what was going on with the construction, the man seemed to have forgotten about their brief conversation the previous day. "They won't open until 2022," he said unmasked and without recognition softening his gaze. He only seemed somewhat annoyed. "They opened a different space, Northland, but it's closed because of the virus."

"I wonder what Paris must be like in December," Cal said. And yes, the man did the double take he'd anticipated, though his face grew darker still.

"I wish I hadn't left France. Our president still says he won the election by a landslide even though he lost by six million votes. People have lost their minds. His supporters believe whatever he tells them. The election officials he's smeared are receiving death threats. He fires the people who kept the election safe. He fires the people who keep the country safe. He will be gone in a little more than a month and he's trying to leave the biggest mess he's capable of so his successor might fail. But what gets me, what really gets me every day, every single day, is the willingness of almost half the electorate to swallow lies, endorse racism,

311

and deny simple facts. They deny the election results. They deny the pandemic. In previous years I often wondered how some people could deny the Holocaust. But now it's happening in front of our own eyes, in real time. This is not a memory. This pandemic is still spreading and killing thousands every day. But if you believe in the President, then three-hundred-thousand deaths have never happened, and he won the electoral college and the popular vote. Please understand, I'm not a fool. I know that racism and stupidity have always existed and will always exist. But how can over seventy million voters get behind a president who tells forty lies a day, denies that the virus is a problem, and claims that mail-in ballots are fraudulent? How is that possible? How can people believe that the opposition party operates a pedophile sex-ring and worships Satan? How is any of this possible? People are evil. I accept and respect that. But how can they believe a word the president says? How can they deny he lost?"

Together they walked east along Nottingham Terrace until they hit Meadow Road and entered Delaware Park. They didn't wear masks, but left enough space between each other to be safe. They avoided moms with baby carriages, runners, bikers, men in puffy coats walking their dogs. "I didn't mean to sound like a moron," the man said, "but it's so damn hard to explain how I feel in this country. Right now. I'm wearing a brown coat, but if the president says he doesn't see the coat, then his believers won't see it. It disappears. How can they accept this president as their messiah?"

"We'll have a new president," Cal said.

"But how will those seventy million people who voted for racism and corruption react? What will they do? No, I think I'll have to leave this country. I love it, I never wanted to feel as though I had to escape, but this country scares me. And it's not the president I'm afraid of. It's the people who had four years to observe his madness and are still siding with him."

"Will you be going back to Paris?" Cal asked. "I've been thinking about leaving myself. I'm torn. I'd like to buy a house here in Buffalo, but I'm scared as well. I'm afraid of the future this country will see. Like you, I'm not afraid of the president. I fear the hatred that has destroyed our trust in facts and a shared reality. What does your family think about leaving the States?"

"It's just two of us. Just the two of us. I think she's excited about the move, wherever we decide to go. We get antsy whenever we stay too long in one place."

"You do?"

"We don't like to get comfortable. We want to be strangers as often as we can."

Something very important Cal had wanted to ask, something that involved Shorat, a sure-fire way to get a more detailed and revealing answer from this man. And yet, even though that question had just been filling his mind, it was now gone. All he managed to say was, "Dogs don't enjoy new things."

"Dogs?" the man asked and stopped to take another look at Cal's face.

"Mine enjoy change only in small doses. They like getting into the car and going to a new park, but they don't enjoy traveling. They don't enjoy the house I rented, they're suspicious of my motivation. If I buy a house and move again, they'll lose their trust in me altogether. We sentimentalize dogs, we say they love us unconditionally, but that's not true. They're great manipulators, they push the boundaries. Their goals are nefarious and always self-serving."

The man didn't say anything in return, not an uncommon reaction. Cal had rarely found someone willing to talk about dogs in depth and at length. He now feared he had lost the stranger's interest. "What do you do for a living?" he asked. "Does it allow you to move wherever you wish to go?"

"I'm a writer," the man said. "I can indeed write wherever I go."

"Fiction?"

"Yes. Yes, I'm a fiction writer."

"And your wife? Is she a writer too?"

"No, she's an artist. But as long as she has a room to herself where she can spread out her markers, paints, and sketchbooks, she's okay. It's a universal language."

"You write in English, then?"

"I used to, but I have started to write in French. I find that the less vocabulary I have to worry about, the more I can concentrate on what is really important to me. I don't like choices."

"Choices?"

"When I go to a supermarket and see rows of jams and cereal boxes, cheeses and meats, my heart sinks. I can't focus on my shopping list anymore, I get lost in the glut of similar and largely indistinguishable choices. How do you decide which raisin bran cereal is better? What are the criteria that matter to you? The better I speak a language, the more lies become open to me. The more fluent I become, the less urgent my sentences feel. I learn idioms and proverbs. I can't stand it. I want my language to come from a convenience store. Limited choices, less excess. You buy what you really need, nothing more." The man had stopped again, this time in front of a parked car; Cal recognized the Audi.

"So you will leave Buffalo again soon?" he asked.

The man opened the driver's door. "As soon as we can. My wife has family in the area; we'll see how everything goes." He nodded, waved. Cal stared at the disappearing vehicle, then at the empty parking spot. The empty spot felt much more substantial than the car turning onto Jewett Parkway.

That night he dreamed he was at a hotel swimming pool. It was extraordinarily warm, and people sat dangling their legs, drinking from plastic cups, massaging sunscreen into one another's bodies. Cal was trying to get a drink at the bar, fighting his way through the crowd. It was only when the bartender finally turned to him that Cal remembered the lockdown. He couldn't smell or taste anything.

In the following days he noticed that he was forgetting plans, intentions, small necessities. He'd be deep in thought one moment, only to discover he'd forgotten to refresh the dogs' water. The next moment, whatever he'd been thinking about vanished, without any chance of retrieval. Before he could write down something that just a short while ago had struck him as profound, it disappeared; all the crumbs had been eaten by birds, and no path would ever lead him down that thought again.

"Age," Kai said. "Covid. You're traumatized. Your wife left you, you left California, our country is not the same anymore."

"I'm becoming afraid of myself. No, no, I'm afraid I won't be myself much longer."

She laughed, and what a gift her laughter was. "I'll hit you until it hurts, until you can feel yourself again." She had arrived late, just before midnight, and he had already been in bed. Now it was seven-thirty in the morning, and they hadn't slept at all. They were sweaty, they reeked, they needed a breather, they needed breakfast.

He watched her walk about the house, letting the dogs out and in again, filling their dishes with kibble. He wasn't in love with her, he told himself, he wasn't in love. Their bond was something else, something less fraught, cleaner, less tangled and devoid of the desire to own the other. That's how he explained it to himself; Kai wasn't seeing a life partner in him, and he wouldn't ask her to move into the house on Auburn. They were free to let the other have a taste, bodies and company were on loan. Cal was a loaner, he'd always been good at that. Marriage, even though it had lasted for such very long years, had turned him self-conscious. Marriage had worried him, the responsibility had turned his performance stilted and overbearing. He'd never wanted to be in charge of anything, especially not in a patriarchy. This old creaky system forced men into roles Cal, for one, did not cherish. Men were the shoulders to cry on, the ones who left the house in the morning, the ones who were responsible for repairs, oil changes, barbecues. Worst of all, you were not supposed to complain. Men didn't whine, didn't cry, didn't show weakness. You could tell men everything that bothered you, but they couldn't return the favor. Who wants to confess to the weak person, after all? In order to confess, you need to feel that the person you're confessing to can take it without exploding or being rendered helpless. The moment you cry on someone's shoulder you've silenced that person. If you had previously played rock to your spouse, how could you suddenly admit weakness? No, every frustration had to be silenced. It wasn't a lack of commitment or emotion that silenced men; they were playing the role they were given. Cal remembered a thriller from the nineties, an erotic thriller that had caused quite a stir and had later been made into a movie — in America the ultimate compliment for a writer — and the female narrator's greatest thrill was watching her lover come and not utter a single sigh. Silence wasn't optional, patriarchy required it. The only sanctioned relief for men's emotional turmoil was violence. Violence in sports and in domestic relationships. You couldn't cry, but you could crush anyone who challenged your authority.

Cal was getting used to Kai's body, its simplicity, its lack of soft bulges or sculpted limbs. There was an ease in every of her moves, as though she were invisible and didn't want to alert anybody else to her presence by causing loud clatter or by stirring the air, and yet she projected confidence as well. She trusted that her body was up to any task asked of her. It wasn't her body Cal was drawn to, it was how she inhabited it.

"What will you do for Christmas?" he asked. His tree was glowing even though daylight was eating its shine.

"Is this what I think it might be?"

"What?"

"An invitation?"

He shrugged. "No, I haven't made any plans yet. I can't make any plans anymore. I put money down on a house. It's in escrow now, but I'm not sure anymore how good that idea was. It's a bit of a fixer-upper, and I won't have the money to fix it up, and I won't be able to travel."

"Then why do you want to buy it?"

He sat on the brown sofa in his pajamas, the house still smelled of croissants he'd baked an hour ago. Dog hair wafted over every surface not covered by carpet. His hands and feet were icy. "It's complicated."

"Bullshit," she said. "Who is she?"

"My wife."

"I might be visiting my grandparents over the holidays," she said. "Are you still in love with her?"

"I don't know," he said. "But I'm not yet separated from her. Not fully. So much of what I did I did with her."

She sat down next to him, put a hand in his hair. "So why are you buying? Does she live close by? Or is it like a trap you're setting, so she might get caught? How does it work?"

He shook his head, pulled her onto his lap. She kept stroking his hair, she pulled at his ears, his cheeks, calmly and methodically like a mother de-lousing her child. "I have second thoughts about being here," he said.

"Nice compliment."

"I don't have second thoughts about you."

"Such a relief." She pulled so hard on his earlobe he yelped.

"Where do your grandparents live?"

"Not too far away. I might be back before New Year's Eve."

"Would you spend that with me? If Covid doesn't kill me?" How would she make sure not to infect her grandparents? As far as he knew, she hadn't even been tested. As far as he knew, they might already carry the virus.

"We'll see. That's way too far ahead. Thinking ahead gets me in a bad mood."

Kai was gone by early afternoon, but he would see her again that night, for one of the final shoots. Weston had rented a space in Kenwood but had not divulged anything more. He would arrange for the needed costumes. Cal still had a few hours until then and he cleaned the downstairs, showered, then went to check on the house on Lancaster. The Audi was parked out front, and the man who he thought was Shorat's companion was sitting on the steps leading up to the porch.

"You bought this place?" Cal asked.

The man looked up, his face creased by the effort to remember the speaker. But Cal could see how within a second, the man gave up on matching his face to a specific place, day, or event. "Just renting. Just for a while. The seller is a friend, and she couldn't get the asking price, not now during the pandemic, so she let us move in for a few months."

"Us?"

"My wife should be back any second. You live around here?"

"On Auburn," Cal lied, his hand fluttering in the direction of the fixer-upper that might soon be his. Do you own dogs?"

"Dogs? Why? What kind of question is that?"

Cal sensed the annoyance of this man, whose brown wool coat was unbuttoned. He was wearing Budapester shoes and looked as though his skin couldn't sweat. His arm pits would never be damp, his crotch would remain powder-dry. Cal admired men like him, whose skin smelled of cabernet and tobacco, and whose teeth were high-white and regular, small without being ratty, and whose stubble fit like a perfect piece of clothing. "I have two dogs, and they might enjoy company."

The man would not, could not recall their conversation from the day before. Albright Knox, the Meadow, none of that he had retained. This recognition so discouraged Cal that he was ready to make a complete fool of himself. "My father is dying. What is a man who has rejected his father? What does his father's death mean?"

"I'm sorry to hear that."

"I'm more afraid of cancer than of my father dying. Is that terrible?"

The man shrugged. "Family ties are overrated, to be frank. It's a sentimental tale we tell ourselves to hang on to the status quo and fulfill our religious duties. If family works, it can be great, sure. But how often does it really work? There's Uncle Frank who's molesting his daughters, Aunt Betty who beats her daughters for saying their father molested them. There's Uncle Rudy who never repaid the loan you gave him, the sisters and brothers squabbling over who inherits the lake house. Garrett who voted for the president and won't wear a mask even though Aunt Susie died of Covid."

"But what about genetics?" Cal asked.

"What about them?"

"Aren't our parents in our blood?"

"It always grossed me out to think that. Sure, we share some traits with them, and yes, we can't help but share some ticks and idiosyncrasies. That's unfortunate, but it's not the most important part of our life, and there's no need to get all worked up over it. They brought us into the world for purely selfish reasons, and we don't owe them a debt. We are free to live our lives, our own lives. It's brutally simple."

"Do you really believe that?" Cal asked.

"On good days, yes. Doesn't mean I don't wish I'd had better parents, parents I could ask for advice and who cared about who I am. But it didn't happen that way, so I have to do without."

"I heard you went to Paris," Cal said. "Did Shorat enjoy the stay?"

The man got up slowly, as though he needed to ascertain that his legs and back were indeed still working. "Who are you again? Have you told me your name?"

"I lived twenty years with the woman you call your wife. I never took her to Paris, though I should have. She asked me to move back east to be closer to her parents, and I didn't do that either. What is your name? Where did you meet Shorat? How did you lure her away from me?"

The man stood erect now, very erect and very tall. His hands were stuffed into the pockets of his coat. He looked wide-eyed at Cal, and maybe, just maybe, his left knee was trembling. "We're in love," he said, his voice quavering now. "Leave us alone."

"Where is she? Where is Shorat?" Cal waited for an answer even after the man had disappeared inside the house. He went as far as sitting on the stairs in the exact same spot the man had just vacated. He would wait for Shorat, he would put an end to this — though he couldn't quite explain what 'this' really was or what an end might look or feel like.

Yet nobody came. No lights came on inside the house, no police cruiser pulled up to investigate why Cal was sitting on the stairs of a home he didn't own. No Shorat appeared. And once darkness came rushing down the street, it was time to go home, feed Yuuki and Vanya, and drive to Kenmore.

CHAPTER 37

THE ADDRESS WESTON HAD GIVEN HIM belonged to a church. "The bishop issued a formal decree that removed the consecration of the building," Weston explained. "Now they rent it out for weddings and dance parties." He pointed at the ceiling where three large disco balls glittered in the faint light coming from the stage.

Kai had already disappeared into one of the bathrooms to change into her dress. Cal's Tuxedo was still wrapped in plastic. "I'm allergic to dry-cleaning," he said.

Weston's eyes squinted, he looked irritated. "Never heard that one before."

"Took me a long time to figure out. Couldn't explain why my whole body was itching once I started to teach at a college back in Michigan. Some weird food guru and healer told me. He was an ass, but he showed me what it was. If I told you how, it'd sound like hocus-pocus, but I stopped wearing dry-cleaned shirts and coats, and the itching went away."

"It's just one night."

"If you were allergic to peanuts, would you eat them for 'just one night'?"

A long silence followed. Cal could almost hear Weston's thoughts rattling around his brain, testing out threats, promises, and all the possible ways to get what he desired.

But tonight, Cal wouldn't budge, and he knew he wouldn't, no matter how hard Kai or Weston tried to sway him. Cal was certain that Weston could feel it too.

"Okay. Okay. We'll do it without the tux. Fuck it." The words sounded vicious, though Weston's voice remained level.

"You know, I think I'm done," Cal said. "I've had it. I'm done playing your dad, I'm done obeying your cryptic orders. It seemed like a good idea, but I don't want to work with some two-bit asshole following me around with his Leica and jerking off at night to the photos of his fake mom and dad. I'm done." He felt like shouting, like running from this building that smelled like a high-school gym and where his steps and his voice echoed in the cheap way that only mid-century architecture could produce. Then Kai's arms threaded through his, her hands clasped over his belly. "Weston's dad bolted the afternoon of the wedding. They were about to call it off."

"What happened?"

"He got scared. All the people in their stuffy clothes; all the new restrictions that would be put on his life, his love; the responsibility of never having sex with any other woman." Kai's voice was dry, matter-of-fact, as crisp as parchment. Maybe she sensed that any hint of sentimentality would drive Cal off. "His dad was already on the highway driving to see an old girlfriend, one he knew would acquiesce to his needs, but he turned around. He crossed the median and sped up. He'd stuffed the tuxedo into a trashcan at the gas station near the on-ramp. It was gone when he stopped there for the second time, and he arrived at the church late, without his tux. But by some fucking miracle nobody had left yet, and the priest was willing to talk to Weston's dad for ten minutes and then decided to go ahead with the wedding."

"And the tux?"

"He wore street clothes, he didn't wear a tux, and it was his penance. He would never have the perfect pictures that told everyone about what a perfect day it had been. Everyone looking at the photos would know about his betrayal. He got the bride, but he didn't get to be the husband he'd wanted to be. Every picture taken at the wedding reminded him of his failure. All the memories were tainted and would stay tainted. He never showed the wedding pictures to anyone, he needed to keep them a secret."

"So what are you saying?" Cal asked.

"That you can still save this. Weston's pictures will always tell you what a prick you were for not wearing a tux and refusing to give Weston the happy pictures he was looking for. Instead of making it perfect, you'll see Weston's real dad, the guy who ruined the wedding and felt ashamed about his betrayal for the rest of his life. You, you can still be perfect. This shoot can still be perfect. Look, I'm wearing open-toed sandals, you old pervert."

And while Cal was looking down at Kai's one foot appearing to his right, her arms holding onto him with the effort of balancing on her left, Weston raised his camera. "You can have me later," Kai whispered, "dress and all. I'll make it worth your while. You just have to fucking marry me."

Afterwards, he sat in his car in the church parking lot, rain streaming down the windows, blurring and washing away the world. He was trembling, his face contorting as though it wanted to tear off its skin. His feet turned icy, his hands blue and red, but he kept staring at nothing in particular. Minutes turned into an hour, turned into two. Yet no matter how hard he waited, he couldn't make Shorat appear.

Nightmares came later, dreams he connected to his dying father when he woke up around four in the morning and stumbled into the bathroom to relieve himself. He sat on the toilet rubbing his forehead, afraid of the undead in his dream, odd creatures the walls couldn't keep out. They were able to know everything you thought and fed on your memories until nothing was left. Guilt attracted them like blood attracts sharks. It was December 13th.

Kai arrived thirty minutes later wearing the wedding dress and a gift-wrapped package in her arms. "This is for Christmas, put it under your sad black tree." He pulled a bottle of champagne from the refrigerator, and they had each other on the couch without undressing, then moved to his bedroom to drink more champagne.

"I've been thinking," he said.

"Uh oh," she said. "Do you know the four most dangerous words in the English language?"

He shook his head.

"We Need to Talk. I've Been Thinking comes in a close second. Let me guess, you want to own me a bit more, see more of me, know who my friends are, share your mornings with me even though we both could use some toothpaste and mouthwash after waking up and groping in the half-dark of your semi-filthy sheets. You want to know where I am, you want to be able to call me anytime, text me whenever. You want to flirt with my best friend and you want me to tell you that you're a better fuck than any of my previous men. You want to buy dresses and shirts and shoes for me, shoes that I only wear to fuck you, and you want to make beef ravioli for me, with a salad from a bag — but you created the dressing yourself by emptying all the rests of various bottles left in your cabinets and fridge. You'll get me drunk with shitty red wine because you can't afford the good stuff. No, you are too cheap to buy the good stuff, because you don't like wine that much anyway, and you don't want to spend big bucks on something only your guest will enjoy. You want to regulate me, channel me, make me docile and enjoy me in small and regular doses." She sat down on his erection, bent backwards and sodomized him with four long fingers. "You want me to travel only with you, visit my parents only with you, go shopping only with you. You want to be everywhere, and you'll leave the bathroom door open, so I can talk to you when you piss and shit. And you want to see me shit and piss. You want to taste my piss just so you know everything about me and can claim that nobody else ever knew me inside and out."

He said, "Sorta yeah. I will say I don't want any of that, I just want to see you when you want to spend time with me. I will say I wait for the moments when you remember me and come to my door. I will say I'm not possessive, I will say other men are fine with me, but none of my professions will be true, because I want all of you, whenever I want to, every day."

"Oh shit, you're serious, aren't you?" She was drinking from the bottle now, not much was left. Daylight showed him her smeared make-up. It had to be six-thirty, maybe seven.

"I am."

She started to cry, and when his shirt was full of snot and tears, she went to the bathroom, and he made coffee and served it in bed. Her face was stark naked, unpleasant in the sluggish morning light, too lovely to describe with words that everybody else had been using for centuries. Cal remembered, with great shame, a girl he'd made love to in Berlin, who had cried while he was inside her, and he'd taken it — in vast and vain inexperience — as a sign of devotion to the very moment, if not quite love. But the girl had been pining for another man and had told him so as soon as he had finished.

"That's a No, right?" he said.

They had sex again, but this time was different, this time it wasn't sex, this time it was like crying together, this time they wouldn't let each other escape, this time they locked eyes for as long as his erection lasted, this time they didn't say a word, this time their mouths stood open, breathing the other, this time her nails savaged him, this very time their skin made obscene sucking noises and they didn't laugh, this time there was no laughter, instead he kept his fingers inside her ass, and she shoved hers into his mouth.

"I'm Weston's wife," she said downstairs, sitting on the coffee table with her mug, opposite from Cal who had sunk into the couch. "We've been married for two years. The photo shoot was his idea, of course. He always wanted me to play his mom in the pictures, and I said no every time he asked. I wasn't going to be his mom."

"What changed?"

"I wanted to hurt him. And I knew I could if I agreed to pose for him. There'd be another man, and he would have to look at me, through the lens, and keep his mouth shut. It was perfect."

"Why?"

"What I told you about his father's wedding — the story was true, but it's our story, not his parents'. I waited for him while all the guests were getting nervous and gazing at me with pity in their eyes. It was him who stuffed his tux in the garbage bin and went to see his girlfriend. And they did have sex, but afterwards he regretted his move and drove to the church. The tux was gone, and we got married with him wearing jeans and a button-down and his dick still reeking of his ex-girlfriend. I burned all the wedding photos people gave us, I burned them, all of them, because everybody said, "What a wonderful couple you make," but what they meant was, "He so embarrassed you." And he did, and I still love him, and I will continue to be his wife. I only wanted someone who I didn't mind fooling around with. Only that. You know? Make believe — real touching, no feelings. But it has driven Weston crazy, even though he'll never admit it."

"The dress." He looked around, but it had to be upstairs still, somewhere on the floor near the bed, maybe under the sheets.

"Was my wedding dress. I got married in it, and he had to take pictures of us, had to take pictures of you having your way with me, me having my way with you. This was his penance, but don't pity him for a second. He got his pictures, he got them all, and maybe, maybe, I'm the loser here. Because I'm losing you, I have to, and Weston has his complete set of photos now and doesn't need me anymore. Maybe he doesn't even love me anymore. Maybe he hasn't in a long time. Maybe he only returned for our wedding ceremony, after sleeping with his ex-girlfriend, to have another chance at creating the album of his parents' marriage."

"He said there was one more shoot. One last shoot."

"He didn't want you to seize up, to get overwhelmed, to freeze. The church was the very last one, and he knew it."

"You did too."

"I did too." Her eyes were red now, glassy, puffy.

"He knows you're here."

She nodded.

"The dress."

"It's yours."

After she'd left, he walked into his bedroom, picked up the dress and took it downstairs, draped it over a dining chair. In the kitchen, over the flame of the largest burner, he heated up a knife, a cheap item from the dollar store, and when the tip of the blade started to glow he pressed it into his shoulder. He was almost happy afterwards, giddily he walked the dogs. Inside the grocery store that afternoon, people stumbled about like flies whose one day on earth was nearing its end. Like those flies who, pained by what they know must come, overwhelmed by the knowledge of imminent death, sit down on people's faces and hands and thighs, the very places they know will get them killed all the sooner, these people with their red faces, beanies and masks and drab clothing, reached over others, got in one another's path, stopped in the aisles and talked in close proximity, fumbled with salads and nut mixes and pulled at the pieces of cotton hanging limply beneath their noses. The vaccine had arrived at long last. The vaccine had arrived and tens of thousands more would die before the pandemic was over. Another observer might have thought the people inside the grocery store drunk or dazed, but Cal knew better. The pain of the past few months had finally gotten to them, the pain had finally turned to sheer madness; they could barely breathe.

CHAPTER 38

Shorat at the Movies

She's sitting on the hood of my '85 Ford Escort, which I bought from a friend for $350. The year is 1999, and the car has more rust than metal. I've taped the biggest holes – all of them on the left side of the car, go figure, the side you see in the black and white image. I only ever shot black-and-white in those days, it made me look artsier, it was a habit I hadn't shaken, a habit I'd learned in Berlin. I'd taped the holes with duct tape, and in the photo, the colors of the light blue paint and the silver of the duct tape are the same shade of gray.

Shorat is sitting on the hood. It's the end of August and one of the last days of my time in Buffalo. I'll be leaving for Michigan soon, and we've decided to go to the Regal Cinemas on Elmwood. Shorat sits on the hood, in sneakers, pants, and a thin gray hoodie. Her hair is short, she got rid of her pigtails a month or two ago, and her eyes behind the glasses small. Her back isn't straight, but neither does it look rounded. It's a comfortable position, but she's aware of me trying to get a good shot before I leave for graduate school...

330

"You can't fix me in place," Shorat said. "No matter how hard you try, you won't get that picture back. And in any case, only as long as I was living with you did the photo make any sense. I gave it meaning. Now that I have left you, the meaning has changed completely. It's a new meaning. It's also less meaningful. I've taken the meaning with me, I'm holding it hostage, I know how your mind works. Your memory always jumps to the last time you saw the certain someone you're reminded of. So even if in the picture you're happily kissing a girl, if she called you a jerk a week later and left, the picture will always be calling you a jerk. Cal, even if you still had this picture, even if it hadn't burned with all the others, it wouldn't offer you any solace."

"But I want to know this picture existed. I don't want to forget we were happy at some point."

"You were still crazy, your ex was still in your blood."

"I loved you already."

"I know, but you were still poisoned, you were still acting like a junkie. I was your methadone."

"You were much more than that."

"That's nice of you to say. But you have always had the tendency to kill what you loved. You always wanted to dry me between the pages of a book, impale me with a needle, drown me in formaldehyde."

> *...A few days later I drove the three-hundred miles to Ann Arbor and she stayed in Buffalo to finish her degree in computer engineering. After I had the film developed, I taped this photo to the closet in my dorm room — I had taken a dorm room because I couldn't look for an apartment ahead of time, and it seemed cheap and convenient. What I love about the*

picture is that Shorat looks at me with confidence yet without knowing who I really am. We've only known each other since June, but we're planning our wedding. I don't know this girl, this woman who sits on my car. I would never allow anyone else to sit on the hood – I'm afraid something or other will break and stay broken, and the car is my flying suitcase; I don't own the funds to repair it. I don't know Shorat but I have attached my future to her, and we stare at each other in wonder. How can we act so foolishly? She smiles, there really is a hint of a smile. We don't know each other at all – and it's the joke we share.

"You loved that photo more than you loved me. You love dead things. You love to have control."

"I know. I kill everything because I want to determine its meaning. I wanted to control your meaning."

"But now I'm gone."

"Yes, now you're gone. Now I only have these lines about a photo of you."

"You're a fool."

On December 14, the Electoral College confirmed that the President-Elect had indeed won the election, and a day later, a Tuesday, the Senate Majority Leader finally congratulated the President-Elect on his victory. He also congratulated the Vice-President Elect on her historic victory. The first woman elected to this office, the first African-American woman, the first Asian-American woman. The lame-duck President shrouded himself in silence, only tweeting that "tremendous evidence" of widespread voter fraud was "pouring in." He did not provide any evidence.

The year was coming to an end, the pandemic was perhaps slowly coming to an end as well. Conservative and right-wing groups would never accept the election results, of that Cal was certain, but lying on his couch with the light slowly being sucked out of his living room, he felt, for this very moment, at peace. Nothing was accomplished, neither on the national stage nor on his small private one, the one with dirty curtains and loose floor planks. Still, he was alive, the virus hadn't claimed him yet, and that, in and of itself, felt like an achievement. When his phone rang and Marlena, his mortgage broker, asked him to sign the final papers the next day, he agreed meekly, then turned off his phone altogether.

He had forgotten about Kai's Christmas gift, retrieved and unwrapped it after the next drink. No signature graced the finished photo album, and it didn't reveal the names of the actors either. A whole life was there, it was all in place, complete and completed. The history of a marriage was right in front of him, intimate, obscenely so, and always credible. Some of the pictures appeared washed out and badly faded, like the early color photos he'd known from his childhood. A few shots were kept in black and white. The choices seemed haphazard, the way photo albums operated, only put together by chronology, this poor relative who fails to deliver any insight; an accountant he was, and not a good one. Chronology had poor taste, and in the end, his attempts at narrating events always unraveled.

Weston, of course, did not appear in these pages. Neither did Kai or Cal. Yes, if you looked closely, they had lent their bodies to the completion of Weston's obsession. In the end, though, their personalities had disappeared. These were the photos that had been destroyed by carelessness, ill will, and fire. These were the originals, and no matter how hard he tried, no matter how often he traced the contours with his finger, Cal could not detect the woman he'd made love to, could not find a shred of himself in this book. The album was no art project anymore but a book of real memories. It was perfect.

Chapter 39

The next night, he sat with Yuuki and Vanya and Shorat in the attic of his new house, a space heater providing ambience. They were warm; Cal had discarded his army coat and was learning against the dusty and faded wallpaper. "Make me another Red Queen," she demanded, and he mixed the fragrant liquids and added more ice. She had smoked her pre-roll by the open window minutes earlier, she was in the mood to talk. "What are you going to do?"

"I want to install a rope leading from this window to yours, so I can visit you at night, so that you can come to visit me."

"A rope?" she asked "Why can't I come to the front entrance?"

"A rope is so much more romantic."

"I'm not very romantic."

"That's true."

"Don't be mean." She laughed at him in her loud weed-voice. He wasn't fond of that voice, and he already knew he would dream of his first girlfriend tonight, Sophie, for whom he had moved to Berlin. Liquor had given her that tonality.

"What are *you* going to do?" he asked. Yuuki sat by her mistress, soaking up the attention, the cooing, the familiar smells. From time to time she turned to lick Shorat's face and hear her giggle.

"I'm getting my Ph.D.," she said. "In Islamic Art. I'm moving to London, but I will try to study in Egypt, maybe Tehran, if I can get a visa."

"Will he come with you?" Cal asked.

"Who?"

"Your lover? Boyfriend? Partner?"

"You met him?"

"A few times. He seems...I don't know. Hard to say."

She laughed again. "He's my husband of twenty-one years."

"I was your husband for twenty years," Cal said.

"But I don't know you. You're a neighbor, somebody I just met."

"Tell me about your husband, then."

"His name is Cal, though it was Karl when he came to America. He's a few years older than me, and...I don't know, I think we have made it work. We love each other. It's not that I like everything he does — he's a control freak and can be demanding, and he is moody and he's super negative when he thinks about the world, but we've had fun together. He quit his job, and now we're going to see where we'll go next."

"But don't you recognize me? I'm Cal. I'm your husband."

Her laughter answered him, the laughter of his first girlfriend. "I don't think I should stay much longer," she said. "You seem familiar, I give you that, but I'm pretty sure I don't know you, and if I remembered you, I think I wouldn't like that memory."

"Our house in California burned to the ground and we lost everything, all our photo albums, your little Japanese coffeemaker, your mom's quilts, your grandmother's wedding quilt, all your artwork."

"Don't be silly. My house never burned down. My husband and I recently sold it. I have all my photo albums, every picture we ever took. We have boxes full of them."

"But you remember my dogs?"

"They're my dogs, not yours."

"You're in my house. These are my dogs, Yuuki and Vanya."

"Whoever you are, you're such a hoot." She didn't appear offended in the least. "These are my dogs, Shibuya and Diesel. I think I should go now."

"They won't follow you, I'm certain of that. We've been through a lot. You left me in August, and we've been on the move ever since. They like you, they remember you, but me and them, we're family."

"You're convincing. If I weren't so stoned, I'm sure I would come up with a snappy argument."

"Do you remember when you used to feed the dogs a carrot in the evening, and how excited they were? Every night, they were excited again for the very same thing. You must remember that."

"I do, but it's not your memory. It's mine. Cal laughed at the dogs, he might have thought them ridiculous for getting worked up over a carrot. But I am like them, I just want my nightly carrot." She got up, and the very next moment, not even leaving enough time for Cal to gasp, she was gone, and the only sound he could hear was Vanya's labored breathing on the stairs, in the hall, on the street, until he heard nothing more at all.

Chapter 40

The wind had picked up overnight and drove the snow sideways, transferring mounds from there to here and creating valleys in random places. Cal's neighborhood grew soft bellies and ridged spines, white legs and backs slung together. Traffic stopped. New drifts were reaching covered porches and rendering windows useless.

On December 20, his father died. The email from his sister had come while he slept dreaming of open mouths, wide smiles, sneezes, and caroling children going from door to door spreading the virus.

Something like joy spread through him while he made coffee and moved a chair to the living-room window so he could gaze out at the shifting landscapes. He didn't feel ashamed because his grief would find ways to disturb and upset him in his dreams for weeks and months to come. For now, he was happy to escape the feeling of loss and bask in the view of his world disappearing in layers of white.

Cal had finally been forgotten by the man who'd claimed blood ties, the man who had been a compromiser, who had been afraid of harboring dreams bigger than what his neighbors tolerated. Who, in 1959, had served in the German army. The summer had been brutally hot, and he and his fellow soldiers dreamed of life outside their barracks, of drinking beer, cold beer, lots of cold beer.

They'd dreamed of women who wouldn't say no. The next year, when they had finally left behind those barracks, the summer brought nothing but rain. Maybe this story that his father had told Karl was too neat to be a passable metaphor for a whole life.

His father was dreaming now, dreaming in all black, where meaning and view and thoughts were black and no shapes would emerge. Death, the end of all sight and hearing, death who robbed you of everything that could vouch for you. Death was the end of meaning, death wouldn't let you come to your senses.

Cal missed the dogs in the coming days, the routine of feeding and walking them and cleaning up after them. He longed for Vanya's relentlessness, his restlessness, his smelly breath, his insistence, his wet jowls. As soon as the plows reached Auburn Avenue, on the third day of the storm, Cal moved his belongings from the rental into the new house. It took several trips, and he strapped the biggest items to the roof of his old Lexus. The quiet inside the new house didn't know him. The rooms didn't remember him. Only the attic still smelled of Shorat's weed, and dog hair wafted across the floorboards. In the evening, after making his final trip, he sat in front of the attic window and watched the house across from him. Later, he moved his mattress to the third floor and peed into an empty gallon jug whenever he needed to relieve himself during the night.

In the morning, new snow was covering the old. He cranked up the heat and made breakfast. He showered, waited until his hair had dried, then put in his hearing aids, and went for a stroll. Shorat, in a winter coat and furry house shoes, sat on the stairs of the house she and her companion were sharing. She'd lit a pre-roll; the snow had been cleared away, a narrow ice-free lane led up to the porch. When he came closer, she called out to him. "Here," she said. "I told you I have all my albums, all my pictures."

"You do?"

She patted the space next to her. "Sit down. I'll show you."

"My father died last night," he said.

"I'm so sorry to hear that. Were you close?"

She still didn't recognize him, still refused to acknowledge that they had shared everything for over twenty years. "No," he said. "He invaded me like an illness, he knew no borders. I've been trying to separate for most of my life."

"I wouldn't understand that," she said. "I can't imagine life without my family."

"I know," he said. "Why don't you show me your pictures?"

She had been right, they were all there. Shorat getting a haircut, Shorat in front of the Pyramids, Shorat in Toronto. And here they were together, a selfie on Catalina Island. "See," he said and pointed, "see, here we are together."

"Silly," she said. "That's me and my husband Cal. You're not in the picture."

"You really don't remember me?" he said.

"You talk as though you were a ghost, but I can see you quite well. And I can touch you." She put a cold hand on top of his. "But you need to stop imagining things. Let's just look at the pictures together." And she showed him the one at the baseball park in Detroit, at the auto show in Los Angeles, the photos from their trip to Hawai'i, from their trip to Barcelona. All the pictures he'd been describing were there, and many more that he'd forgotten. On the final page, she'd squeezed a black-and-white shot into the photo corners, just that one picture.

Shorat and Cal Before the Wedding

My friend Elliott took the picture at Shorat's parents' house, after the rehearsal and hours before the wedding. I am sitting across from Elliott wearing a dark turtleneck, looking to the left at something I don't remember. Behind me, on the armrest of the sofa, sits Shorat, her chin resting on her hand. She's listening to what Elliott is saying, or maybe I'm responding to something Elliott has asked about the upcoming ceremony. Shorat listens intently. She vomited earlier in the morning, before the rehearsal, but she's feeling better now. Looking at the photo, you don't see any of the before or after, but the two people in the picture are serious and they seem devoted to each other in an easy way. There's nothing showy, nothing clingy, they merely know that they belong together, and the future looks like a project they will work on together, a task they are well-suited for. They are astronauts before the launch.

"I always liked to listen to my husband. He's smart and he can talk for hours if you let him. He loves to give examples, tons and tons of examples." Shorat laughed.

"You guys look happy," Cal said, accepting his role as visitor in someone's else photo album. "Like you're counting on each other."

"Yes, yes we always have. Counted on each other. Even when I call him a douche, or he calls me a nag, when he tells me to fuck the hell off and I say I'll shove the coffeemaker up his ass, we know we'll be together, we know we'll be quiet soon, in each other's arms soon, bruised but happy to feel the other."

I don't look like myself in the picture. My face looks larger and I'm moving, and the contours are just a tad blurry. I look louder than I remember myself, but not in an obnoxious way. I look happy.

"He looks so happy," Shorat said.

"He's going to marry you."

"Yes. Yes, I guess. It's rare that he looks so happy. He can be a sourpuss."

"Yes."

"I need to go soon. But see, I knew I had all the pictures. Nothing burned. You were wrong."

"I was wrong."

I'm anxious and nervous, but none of that shows in the photograph. I can feel the pressure of committing to a life with Shorat, and will I be good enough? Will I be strong enough for the stretches that look straight and endless without shade or solace? Will I be successful enough? Will she love me? Will she remember me after our pictures are gone and after she has left? Will there be anything left of me? Will I find Shorat if I stumble across the right memory, the right question?

He'd been so stricken by that last picture, he'd failed to notice that Shorat had up and left. He was by himself now, and only the smell of her pre-roll lingered. When he'd arrived, Cal hadn't noticed the For Sale sign on the white wooden post in the planter strip, but he did see it now and inspected it as though it were about to share some gossip with him. He wanted to ask Shorat about this sign, wished to ask her when she was leaving and where she was headed, but no matter how many times he rang the bell, she refused to come to the door. No matter how often he knocked and called her name, the door stayed closed.

Also by Stefan Kiesbye

Next Door Lived A Girl
Your House Is on Fire, Your Children All Gone
The Staked Plains
Fluchtpunkt Los Angeles
Knives, Forks, Scissors, Flames
Berlingeles
No Sound to Break, No Moment Clear

About Stefan Kiesbye

Stefan Kiesbye was born on the Baltic Coast and later lived in Berlin, Germany. An award-winning novelist, he has been acclaimed as "the inventor of the modern German Gothic novel" (*Die Welt*), and his work has been called "absorbing and disconcerting" (*Más Cultura*) and "sublime" (*BookPage*).

He lives in the San Francisco Bay Area.